The Spirit Traveler

THE NORTHWEST INDIAN WAR IN THE OHIO COUNTRY

Kirby Whitacre

First Edition Design Publishing
Sarasota, Florida USA

The Spirit Traveler: The Northwest Indian Wars in the Ohio Country
Copyright ©2019 Kirby Whitacre

ISBN 978-1506-908-85-4 PBK
ISBN 978-1506-908-86-1 EBK

LCCN 2020901640

January 2020

Published and Distributed by
First Edition Design Publishing, Inc.
P.O. Box 17646, Sarasota, FL 34276-3217
www.firsteditiondesignpublishing.com

This is for my son Bryce, who through his work at historic Fort Recovery and our many conversations, reawakened my passion for the history of the Native American people of the Northwest Territory. It is also for these same people, who fought so hard to preserve their way of life, that this book is dedicated.

Chapter One

My Wife

Autumn Leaf

As we embraced, our bodies met in deepest desire, the kind of desire that will not wait, but that must be satisfied. She moved like a forest cat, sleek, agile, supple, and dangerous. The light from the fire exposed her small breasts and made her eyes shine like stars on a clear summer's night. As our bodies merged, she wrapped her long legs around mine, and I became completely lost in her passion. Our bodies moved together in rhythm as perfect as the pleasure that we gave each other. The Good Book says that it is meant that husband and wife should become as one. Certainly, I will never believe two people were more suited to be one than we.

She was the most beautiful woman I had ever seen and the years since have produced none more so. She was tall and shapely-thin. Her long black hair came nearly to her waist. Her skin was lighter than that of many of her people, and her features

1

were delicate in a way that belied her great strength of body and character. Those beautiful, soft, brown, eyes seemed to be the gateway to her soul and all her emotions had to come through them to reach full expression.

Her name translated into English from the language of her people the Miamis, was Autumn Leaf. Her father, Makwate-makwa, or Black Bear, had thus named her after viewing his just born first child and noticing the bright blotchy red colors of the baby's face. Upon leaving the birthing wigwam, he was hit lightly in the face with the most beautifully colored leaf blown at him by the cool breeze of the autumn wilderness. Both events came together in his mind to produce a name for his new daughter. Such were the ways of her people, who were so in tune with all of nature that names were obvious, delivered directly to them by the manitous[1] and seldom if ever requiring parental debate such as might occur among the white race.

Autumn Leaf had never been with a man before me and my experience with women was limited to a furtive kiss, or two as a teenager back in Virginia. To be sure, Autumn had not experienced a shortage of suitors; her beauty and intelligence were common knowledge far beyond the confines of her village and actually even beyond the lands of the Miami. She had been pursued by warriors of not only her tribe, but also of the Wea, Shawnee, Sauk, and Potowatomie, as well as French and Englishmen.

As was the Indian custom, her father had negotiated with several of the suitors sometimes in good faith, and sometimes just honoring custom. However, in each case the suitor was rejected out of hand by Autumn. Her father feigned exasperation with her, but it was well known that his pride in her caused him to exceed what was normal for her people in terms of giving females the opportunity to control their own destiny, as far as matrimony was concerned. He understood that she was a person of uncommon intuition and sense. In that regard, he afforded her the right of choice such as was valued among the males of her people, in for instance, deciding to go on the warpath, or not. Such matters were left to individual discernment.

Nevertheless, Autumn Leaf's unmarried status was somewhat of an aberration by the time she reached sixteen years old. Her mother and her female relatives feared that she might become an old maid. Her father on the other hand, had a connection with her and understood that she would never marry any man whom she did not love, trust, and respect. And frankly, he doubted any man existed that was worthy of the daughter that he loved so much and whom he felt was an exceptional being in every aspect.

Though many of her suitors had come from the nobility of her people, including the sons of chiefs and sachems, great warriors in their own right, she was also pursued by young men of lesser character as well.

It was an incident with one of the latter that sealed her reputation among the people once and for all. It caused them to say no more about her marrying. It seems that at the time of harvest celebrations during her 15th year, a visiting ne'er-do well from the Wea tribe had made her father an offer that would make Autumn his wife. Autumn refused, as her father had hoped that she would. She let the visitor know, in no uncertain terms, that she would never consent to marry him. She also let him know that she considered him a contemptible human being for a variety of reasons.

Late one evening as Autumn walked in the moonlight, just outside the village, the Wea followed her thinking to take his revenge for her rejection of him in a carnal fashion. When he thought that she was far enough from the village, he attacked her. This was a huge mistake on his part, actually the final mistake of his life. No sooner had he sprung his trap and grabbed her, than she produced a knife from her waistband and buried it into his heart. There had been no particular struggle, no chance of her actually being overcome. She had simply, with cat-like reflexes and without fear, but with the most deliberate determination slain the young man.

The people had long marveled at Autumn's focus on life which reflected in her flashing eyes and her singular pursuit of her own mind. She had strength of body and of character. She would marry when ready, or perhaps marry never.

In the incident with the hapless Wea, Autumn faced no sanction from her people. His reputation was known as lazy and boastful. He had done nothing to distinguish himself to the people either in war, or in generosity, both areas being held in the highest regard among Indians. Further, he was a bit of a freeloader, and was known to have taken liberties with young females in other villages. Therefore, his death only solidified an aura surrounding Autumn. In that sense she had become the most coveted of prizes among her people and her cousin tribes, but also the least likely prize to be won.

Another time, she was apparently giving real consideration to a handsome young French fur trapper. The Miami allowed him to set traps locally and as an early part of the courtship, Autumn went with him one evening to run his traps. Whether to impress her, or whether a true measure of his character, he demonstrated no respect for the animals that he caught. Often animals in traps are not dead when discovered. Generally, the trapper dispatches them with a blow to the head. The young Frenchman, however, liked to torture the animals first, cutting off a tail, or a foot, or in other more disgusting fashion. This enraged Autumn who knew that animals often have to die to accommodate the survival of people, but also that animals have a soul, as is a common belief among her people. Like most Indians, she took no joy in the death of an animal. She often said a prayer of thanks, for the sacrifice made by the animal, so that the people might live and prosper.

In her tirade upon the young suitor, she slapped him and said many harsh words. He was a tall youth and very strong for his age. Becoming angry, he began to beat her. About that time, Autumn's younger brother, Gray Fox came along. Gray Fox had already distinguished himself in a fight with the Kentucky militia. He came up behind the big Frenchman and shoved him into the stream that he was trapping. In doing so he probably saved the Frenchman's life, for Autumn had already drawn her knife. She had to be restrained by Gray Fox from entering the water after the trapper and dispatching him to the hereafter. Thereafter, the tribe declared the Frenchman to be persona non grata and he was banished from the lands of the Miami.

How I luckiest of men, came to be Autumn's husband when she was 17 1/2 years old, is a story born of the most improbable of circumstances and one that I shall relate later in my account.

Outside the snow was falling silently, but so thickly as to make seeing more than a few feet nearly impossible. The pines a short distance away, had limbs already heavily clad in white. Inside our cabin was snug and warm, or at least we were snug and warm under bearskin and buffalo hide coverings. The fire of our hearth provided the only light, except for two oil lamps. If one could ever relax in a wilderness full of wild beasts, we certainly could on a night such as this. The snow was already over three feet deep and continuing without abatement.

Not that we were defenseless by any means. Around the cabin, at strategic locations were our two Kentucky long-rifles, our trade gun[2], two tomahawks, a Seneca war club, a spear, the two pistols hanging over our bed, and numerous knives. I was a cautious man and in constructing our cabin, I determined that we would never have our home unexpectedly invaded, but what we could give a serious account of our own protection, even if that meant fighting to the death. I even supposed the poker on the hearth would serve as a lethal weapon if need be.

Because we hoped to live in this place for a long time, we had constructed the cabin with great care and no small amount of tedious labor. We had actually almost doubled the log thickness of the walls by starting the cabin with smaller logs as the interior walls, then the more conventional larger tree trunks making up the exterior walls. We filled the space between with clay, mud, gravel, and sand, not only for insulation, but also to render the home more resistant to fire. My thought was that if the outside were fired, as in an attack, it might be gotten under control, or at least leave a possibility of the interior walls still standing. If fire broke out inside, as from the fireplace, perhaps the outside log wall could be spared. In those scenarios we would essentially still have a cabin, or at least a solid shell of one. In other words, we would still have a place to live. I do not know of another cabin ever built with this painstaking care, except the one in which I grew up.

There were only three small windows and these were not typical, but were at a height of well over five feet off the floor. They had shutters inside and out, but no glass. but. The shutters provided some defense against cold in the winter and when open in the summer, allowed for some fresh air to enter. Each was only about ten inches high and 15 inches wide. This was enough to let in some light when both shutters were open, but more importantly to not allow entry by any human being. They were constructed to serve as much as gun ports as windows. On the inside of the cabin I had installed platforms under each window. Upon these platforms we could stand and look outside, or shoot if the necessity arose. In really cold weather we hung furs inside, completely covering the shutters to keep out cold air, but easy to slide out of the way in order to see outside.

The cabin door was double planked oak that required such strong hinges as ever I have seen on any door. I used two huge iron hinges and two thick leather hinges that I had fashioned. A thick oak plank weighing one stone [3] was used to fit across and block off the door on the inside of the cabin. It was supported by slotted holders at about three and a half feet off the floor.

We had built the cabin on a small hill directly over a shallow depression that by some might have been called a cave, but for us was going to serve quite nicely as a root cellar. By use of a trap door in our corduroy floor, packed with clay between the half logs, we were able to use the area for food and powder storage, and also as a last-resort hiding place. The hill sloped very gently to the south, in front of the cabin, toward the creek which emptied into the river to the southwest. About seven rods behind our home the ground fell off precipitously with a drop of 12 to 15 feet, or so, followed by a fairly steep slope into the woods.

I had installed a 50-gallon wooden barrel in the back corner of the cabin where we kept water for cooking, drinking, and washing.

Such was the construction of our home that I dare say some, in fact most forts, in the Ohio frontier country were not so well-conceived or fortified.

There on that cold winter night early in 1792, in the wilds of what would later become northern Indiana, we passed our hours in a passionate embrace as the snow piled ever higher outside.

We awoke before daylight the next morning, lying on two bearskins in front of the hearth. I am frankly not completely certain how we came to be sleeping at that spot. I never did ask Autumn as she seemed not at all surprised by our location. When it came to making love, I considered her somewhat of an acrobat, or maybe a magician.

I immediately threw two fresh logs onto the fire, as Autumn sought the platform at the back of the room to open the shudders and peek outside. As I stood there, I glanced back and stole a proud look at Autumn's exquisite naked form as she jumped up on the platform. Then I went to the south-facing window platform closest to the fireplace in the front of the cabin.

Outside the snow had continued; all was white and the wind had sometime during the night, begun to blow fiercely, piling snow almost halfway up to the windows. Some drifts were over six feet tall. I knew the snow would likely not be blocking the front door. I had built an extra few feet of wood planking onto the sides of an overhang that extended out beyond the door. The roof proper was mud and sod over logs from young birch trees. Only the drifting snow would have a chance to pen us in. However, when I opened the door that was not the case. There was about two feet of clear space between door entrance and the first snowdrift, which was about four feet high. The wind had helped the overhang to keep an area free of snow in front of the door.

We had some big snows in the Virginia mountains, but this storm was like nothing I had ever experienced, except once when I was coming down the Ohio River on my trip west. Even Autumn said that she could only remember one, or two others even close to this one in-depth while growing up.

Normally of a morning, we might go outside to take care of private toiletries. However, this not being a normal day we resulted to using what the wealthy back east, called chamber pots, which for us were wooden buckets.

Autumn Leaf poured some warm water, from the buffalo stomach pouch hung near the fire, into a small basin. From this, she washed herself in front of the fire using a piece of soft deerskin, while I alternated between getting dressed and watching her. She chastised me playfully when she caught me watching, but became embarrassed when I told her how pretty she was.

We had been married in the spring at Kekionga[4] with Autumn's uncle, the great Michikinikwa, officiating, at least in as much as anyone officiates at an Indian wedding. Such are considerably less formal than those of white folks and more about general intent, as in "we intend to be married." They do, however, create a cause for a great celebration among the people. Our wedding was no less than any other in that regard. In late June, we had come to this spot deep in the forest on a hill. The creek ran less than 15 rods[5] from the cabin and emptied into the river several rods more southwest of the cabin. It was on this site that we built our home so that the end result, after much painstaking labor throughout the summer, was as I have described. The creek provided us with catfish and bluegills in abundance. In the river, we could catch larger species which we smoked, or salted according to our needs and our supply of salt. The creek and adjacent land provided excellent trapping. We caught mink, beaver, fishers, muskrat, ermine, badger, wolverine, coon, and otter. Though I have to admit that in regard to the latter, I never did like trapping them. They just seemed such intelligent and playful animals. I always hoped to not find any in my traps.

Occasionally, we might catch fox, lynx, skunk, or possum, though those were seldom our specific intent. We cured the furs and traded them at Kekionga and elsewhere, to supply our needs in other areas, such as for cloth, cooking utensils, planting implements, powder, and shot.The area provided an abundance of waterfowl, deer, bear, turkey, rabbit, and squirrel, as well as other critters not normally eaten, such as wildcats and painters[6]. Roughly two days' travel to the west we could access a large buffalo herd and we occasionally found elk there, or on trips farther north.

This year we had arrived too late for planting, but in the coming spring we would plant the white corn, for which the Miami people were famous, along with some vegetables, melons, and some herbs that I had learned to cultivate for medical usage from old Doc Johnson.

We could obtain honey in the forest, but it was always an adventure to secure it. It required a technique using smoke to keep the bees at bay. Over the course of our married life, I had more than one misadventure with bees in our quest for honey. It was a joke between us, one of the little personal intimacies shared between husband and wife. Except that in this case, I must confess that my ineptitude in the pursuit of the sweet substance went beyond being a secret between us, to serve as the topic that provided laughter on more than one occasion, at Kekionga and elsewhere.

Our forest was a land of abundance, not a place where one would necessarily become rich in money, but one in which the needs of any family could easily be met. As far as we knew, our closest neighbors were the better part of a day's hard walk away at the Eel River Village.

As the snow piled ever deeper, we passed the day in mending clothing, cleaning weapons, and finishing the construction of snowshoes, a chore that we had been engaged in for several days and one that if we neglected any longer, might provide a nasty lesson in wilderness mobility and survival. We used white ash, along with deer sinew, and carefully selected bits of hide, that provided a webbing that held all together. I must confess that Autumn was far better at fashioning the snowshoes than was I. The hard part is in the heating and forming of the wood to the desired frame shape. Various tribes had their own unique shapes and the Miami were no exception in this regard.

For our midday meal, I cleaned some pan fish that I had frozen in the snow outside the front door. Autumn fried these with wild rice. Some Indian corn cakes added a final touch. Shortly after putting her plate down, Autumn stood up, untied the string holding her deerskin dress together and stood naked before me. My protests of, "Oh no, I'm tired," fell upon deaf ears and she sprang on top of me, undressing me and giggling wildly, soon bringing my desire for her to a boil.

Whether all women are so skilled in the ways of love, I cannot say. I can only say that my Indian wife was a creature, not only of great beauty and intelligence, of unexpected surprises, but also one who, having found the man she loved, intended to love him as often and completely as energy would allow. My complaints were largely hollow and we engaged in another two hours of lovemaking on bearskins in front of our hearth. Our cabin being so well constructed and now further insulated by the snow; our great exertion soon had us covered in sweat.

Being the most stubborn of beings about cleanliness, Autumn again washed herself with the warm water from the buffalo stomach near the fire. I often teased her by calling her, "Little Raccoon," a reference to critters so tidy that they wash their food before they eat it.

Personally, I took a more extreme approach on this occasion and ran out the door and dove into a snowbank. I then ran back into the cabin falling on the bear skins near the hearth, thus allowing the snow to melt into water and run off my body. Autumn made fun of me in her language, telling me how silly a white man looked running naked through the snow. Upon reflection, she was forced to admit that any man running naked through the snow would likely prove to be a reason for laughter. However, she added that no Indian male would ever even contemplate such action.

As evening came, the snow began to abate, and finally the moon came out, and the storm clouds vanished. The moonlight beautifully illuminated the brilliant whiteness of the wilderness. We agreed that we should take a short walk into the woods, in order to test our new snowshoes in the deep snow that had all but buried our home. Aside from the proposed test, we just needed to get outside the cabin, having mostly been cooped indoors for days.

We had built our home far off the beaten trails and paths that marked the passage of warriors and hunters about their business. We had done this because times were uncertain and so were potential enemies. The British, though expressly forbidden by the Treaty of 1783 to be in this territory, were nonetheless, virtually omnipresent, hoping to stir the native peoples toward a constant war with the Americans. Of course, the British stood to benefit greatly from such hostility and still held hope; nay, actually made the unofficial policy of inciting the red man, plying him with gifts and supplying his weapons, all toward the goal of regaining control of this rich land.

The presence of an American among the Indians would not have made the British happy. In fact, only the summer before, my presence in Kekionga, the Miami capital, had caused a visiting British officer no end of concern. Aside from such political ramifications, the Miami people had many native enemies. And though it had been some time since the last fight with these, owing largely to Indian alliances against the Americans in the recent Great War, a lasting peace with surrounding tribes was never to be counted upon.

In addition to our near knee-length beaver skin boots, along with our newly made snowshoes, we also had coats of beaver and wolf. Had we been planning a long trip in this weather; we might have worn our buffalo overcoats. But frankly, the sheer weight of a buffalo coat reduces mobility and makes it undesirable, except under the coldest of conditions. Each of us had a martin pelt hat. I am quite certain that no hat in the world is as warm. We both grabbed a long-rifle and a tomahawk then set off toward the river. I knew that in this deep snow that only a very few of the forest's fearsome beasts might be stirring about hungry, after days of being hunkered down in the snowstorm.

We stepped out into the breathtakingly white northern wilderness, and admired the silent beauty of it all.

As we walked toward the river, we could catch a gleam of moonlight off its surface which was yet to freeze, though it did appear very slow and very dark like molasses. The moonlight reflected off the snow and visibility was good. The walking however, was slow owing largely to huge drifts in our intended path of travel. Our snowshoes performed well and a quick hug and kiss to my wife, let her know how pleased I was with her construction of these valuable instruments of wilderness travel.

We got down to the river and it was as smooth as glass, dark, and slow, as I mentioned. There was no wind, but ice had begun to form along the banks in the shallow areas. We stood for some time staring mesmerized at the water. I had long noted that water often had that effect upon many people. We had seen a few tracks of small critters on our way, but not many animals appeared to yet be stirring after the snowstorm.

I moved along the bank to check a few traps that I had set, but found them empty. I expected tomorrow would bring a different result if the weather now stayed clear.

After a while, we decided to take a slightly different route back to the cabin. Had we far to go, breaking more new trail would not have been our choice, but as we did not we wanted to test our snowshoes in an area of small trees and bushes. Most of the latter were buried in snow. I started to mount a large drift under a tall sycamore tree when a hideous and unmistakable scream, caused my spine to tingle with that sickening fright that attends one falling into a dangerous situation, or encountering an enemy. This, with the enemy gaining first sight and thereby the advantage.

I started to raise my gun while staring into the bright yellow-green eyes the forest's most fearsome predator perched on a lower level limb, as it shrieked that earsplitting screech that was the trademark of its kind. It was a screech that bore into a human's soul, and which is singular in all of nature in the effect that it produces.

I was literally looking into the eyes of potential death as my second step on the drift broke through, sending my gun flying through the air, and sending me down into the drift. This was not so much a drift as a huge amount of snow covering a ground bush that was unable to support my weight. I had no more than hit the snow when the huge painter, having hurled itself through the air and landed on my chest, knocked the wind out of me and sent sharp shooting pains through my body, the result of apparently breaking some ribs.

Instinctively, before the painter could prosecute her advantage and despite the weight of the great beast, I rolled over knowing that I had to protect my face from the huge razor-sharp claws and teeth. No doubt, I was driven by the fear of being surprised into a life and death struggle, thrust upon me when only moments earlier, I was aware only of the beauty of the snowy wilderness. I buried my face in the snow with my gloved hands and arms around my head. This movement stimulated the beast to greater ferocity. The painter now raked her huge, disproportionately large feet and the aforementioned claws, across the back of my coat ripping it to shreds and sending a sharp pain into my body.

Autumn had until this point been ignored by the beast, who now shrieked again that hideous noise that was both deafening and otherworldly. Standing some 15 to 20 feet away, Autumn decided upon a scare tactic against the beast. Stepping forward, she fired her rifle high, being afraid of shooting me by taking direct aim. By firing her gun, Autumn had rendered herself considerably defenseless, or so I thought.

Upon the discharge of her rifle, the startled cat rather than retreating, seemed to sense that Autumn had expended her defense when the gun discharged. She sprang in Autumn's direction with a quickness and agility that could be matched by no other creature of the forest. Her murderous intent was obvious. Neither I, nor the cat could have been ready for the adept swing of her rifle, for which Autumn, like a snake was already coiled, and which she executed, connecting with the big head of the beast. The monster was rendered momentarily senseless and Autumn followed the first blow with a second well-placed blow, again to the head, then again. The cat attempted to wobble to her feet but was felled under the force of yet another blow. By then I had recovered and stumbling forward, dove onto my assailant, clubbing the beast repeatedly with my tomahawk, causing an eye to come out of its socket, dislocating her jaw, and ultimately dealing a death blow by sinking the blade into the big cat's brain.

I could not but help admiring the beauty of the tawny brown cat as she lay dead in the snow; the winter coat, the long tail, the fierce eyes, the sleek, supple, and muscular form of her body. Painters are both uncommonly beautiful and at the same time, uncommonly dangerous. Dealing with bears is a serious matter, but dealing with painters is a whole other experience, starting with that shriek that I mentioned. There is nothing like it, nothing to compare and it is as if a demon has come from hell itself. It sends shivers down the spine of anyone that hears. Bears are of course, heavier and I will grant you that they are deceptively quick. Their sheer power is unmatched. But for muscular body structure, speed, agility, and a quickness that is unequaled, not to mention the ability to jump great distances, there is nothing that compares to the painter. The forest is dominated by the bear and the painter and I will tell you, I would rather deal with the largest bear than the smallest adult painter. Bears are fast and powerful while painters in comparison, move like lightning and are also deceptively powerful.

After a quick embrace to assure each other that we were alright, we fell down in the snow breathing heavily and shaking from this experience. I was drenched in sweat and the tatters of the back of my coat were leaching blood at a fair rate.

I gathered my unfired rifle, which had actually landed butt down and barrel straight up in the snow. It was unlikely that the cat had a mate nearby as such beasts are notoriously solitary creatures. However, we determined that banking on that fact as absolute was not wise. We began dragging the carcass back to our cabin. It was not the biggest forest cat I was ever to see, but she was easily the largest that I ever encountered up to that point. We left the cat outside and covered her with snow in order to discourage the assault of other varmints.

By now, I had blood not only coming out my back, but also oozing out of the glove on my right hand. Taking off the glove, I discovered that the great cat had managed a bite that left a deep puncture in my hand, that even as I looked at it, was bleeding less due to the swelling that was closing the wound.

Gingerly removing my coat, Autumn gasped at the extent of blood covering the tatters of the coat and what had been my shirt. Upon removing the latter garment, several deep gashes were visible. Such was the ferocity of the attack, that had I not been wearing my winter coat, my fate might have been far grimmer. That I had to this point, not experienced a great deal of pain, I attribute to the human body's ability to block out all things in the quest for survival. And also, to reach deep down into untold reserves of strength and energy, in the process. Old Doc Johnson had taught me as much and had told me spectacular stories of folks overcoming pain in order to survive, not that my current situation was such as that.

Making me a hot tea of painkilling dried willow leaves, Autumn then rubbed the lesser wounds on my back with an ointment that she had retrieved from a box under our bed where we keep our medicines and such. What exactly was in the ointment, I do not know. I only know that it had long been a favorite of the Miamis in treating wounds.

Autumn determined that only three of the gashes would require stitches and so with the smallest needle and sinew that she had on hand, she put some 20 stitches in the larger gash and just a few in the smallest. The other mid-sized gash, had two channels and required more thought from her. She eventually took her knife, heated it in the fire and cut out a small section of skin in the middle between the two channels. She then pulled the wound together in a fashion that would hold the stitches. She told me that this took about 12 stitches.

If I told you that I was still not in pain, I would be a terrible liar because the sting was now an intense burning. However, just having such a loving and competent wife, inspired within me a confidence and coolness to endure the procedures. I was being tended by a woman who loved me more than life itself and that alone, is a powerful anesthetic. But I was also thankful for willow leaf tea.

Later, we revisited the attack as we sipped Kentucky whiskey that I had on hand for a good purpose. Actually, I suppose if truth be told, I did more than sip, such was my pain.

It was important in wilderness living to always assess the

handling of a crisis and to see if anything was to be learned from the experience. We determined that, given the circumstances, we had handled the attack about as correctly as possible. There is also no room for disallowing, or forgetting good fortune as well. Autumn had likely saved my life with her gamble to fire her gun, to startle the beast. Such gambles are rarely random when chosen by one who has lived her life in the wilderness and whose prolonged existence is based upon sound thinking and sound decision-making under the most extreme stresses.

The next morning, I was mighty sore not just from my wounds, but also in my muscles which must have tensed immensely and borne a good bit of the big cat's weight during the attack. My ribs caused me to wince with each breath that I took. Restricting movement was key to surviving tho pain for the next several days. We continued with the willow leaf tea augmented by some powdered hemp flowers. However, I was not seriously debilitated and, in a few weeks, with Autumn's excellent care, I was once again of sound body.

Of all the experiences that I have had in my life, what some folks refer to as close calls, I can at this moment think of only a few others as nearly completely terror-producing, as my encounter on that winter night long ago with the female painter.

As for the cat's carcass, after a careful curing, it fetched a high price in trade at Kekionga. We made the teeth and claws into a necklace for Autumn's brother, Gray Fox, who prized it along with his similar collection of bear claws and teeth. His uncle by marriage was a great war chief of the Miami, and Gray Fox frequently wore a necklace of claws. In this regard, I think he was like youth everywhere emulating his hero.

Chapter Two

My Family of Origin

Mountains of Virginia

As I write this, I am an old man, far older than I ever expected to be. Some men yearn to live forever, but that has never been one of my particular fantasies. But like all men, I need some part of me to live on in memory, which is I suppose is a sort of desire for immortality. The frontier and the life that I lived and loved, has gone west of the great Mississippi River, and so have most of the Indian people, at least most of those who are not dead. Those that remain do so on small reservations, or as people who live on the fringes of American society, eeking out a living on small plots of land. I suppose I tell my story for these reasons, and lest it be lost to history, or gone for naught. Whether my story has any worth I leave to others to determine. But as someone who lived those turbulent years of early America in the Ohio Country, I will tell my story before all is forgotten.

I have already taken my story out of sequence by telling about my wife and our home in the wilderness. That was just such a happy time that I wanted to start with it, jarring my menory and as a point of reference, for what came before and after. Now, I will relay those events, beginning briefly with my childhood

I do not know a great deal about my father's family beyond a couple of generations back. My grandfather, Demas Jamison, had originally been a seafaring man. After surviving a shipwreck off the Canary Islands, he returned to Baltimore, and became a blacksmith-gunsmith. Later, he settled in Virginia with my grandmother, Esther. He served in the Virginia Militia, and had been with General Braddock at his crushing defeat in the wilderness. [1]During the retreat from that debacle, my grandfather answered to George Washington, who he saw as an extremely brave man, but not one particularly skilled in war. My grandfather reckoned that such skill was the product of wisdom, age, and experience, and in all these assets, he concluded, Washington was lacking. When he went with Braddock, Washington was a very young man in his early 20's. Grandpa never lived to the see the triumphs of General Washington, in the Great War for Independence years later. I think part of his opinion of Washington came about as the result of his losing a cousin, who was killed under Washington's command, at Fort Necessity. Fort Necessity was not Washington's finest hour and it had repercussions for him and for the world, as it contributed mightily as catalyst for the beginning of the French and Indian War. [2]

My father, Dawson Francis Jamison, had been a young seventeen-year-old teamster at the end of the war in 1763, but saw no action. The war was effectively over in the colonies well before the peace was concluded in Europe.

During my childhood, father served with Dan Morgan in the Great War for Independence. He saw action in several skirmishes and in a few major battles. He was wounded at Saratoga and again at Cowpens. In fact, his left hand was rendered only marginally useful for the rest of his life, by a musket ball from a "Brown Bess" at Cowpens. [3] Afterward, he retired from the war at the same time as his good friend, Dan Morgan, both coming back to Virginia to watch the war's conclusion from their homesteads with each knowing that his contribution had clearly helped to set the course for victory. There were not a great many American battle victories in the war, but Saratoga and Cowpens were two of the biggest American victories.

My father numbered Thomas Jefferson among his friends. As a youth I was at Monticello on several occasions and though it was impressive to me, it was still a work in progress and only a shad-

17

ow of what it would become. Often, my father and I would stop, as we returned from father's business in more populated parts of Virginia. Mr. Jefferson always offered to put us up in his home overnight. My father, however, without waiver, always refused, even once during a ferocious snowstorm, the hospitality of the man who would become the third President of the United States. Mr. Jefferson always knew why. As my father told me, "I'll stay in no house where human beings are kept in bondage." My father told this to Mr. Jefferson more than once.

When, on one occasion I asked my father how he could call Mr. Jefferson a friend, but refuse his hospitality, he replied, "Mr. Jefferson is a good man, and I'll drink brandy with him, but there remains the fact that he keeps slaves. And even though he treats them much better than most, and he states he is opposed to slavery, the fact is that the slaves are still there.

My father's views on slavery did not endear him to many of his fellow Virginians, or indeed to many people that I knew, but that was all countered by the fact that he was regarded as a man of integrity and principles, whose honesty was beyond question. He was also known to be fearless and generous to a fault. In fact, it could never be said that Dawson Jamison did not help any man, woman, or child, whom he discovered to be in need, sometimes even taking from his own family to help the less fortunate. This was a lesson on a grand scale for his children, and I reckon that we absorbed that and many such others into the conduct of our own lives.

My father did some planting; a bit of tobacco, a bit of corn, some vegetables, not much really. He raised a few hogs, goats, a few chickens, geese, some rabbits, but mostly he made his living as a hunter and trapper. In later years we always had at least two horses to assist with his travel. He had the wanderlust of the wilderness, and could never be home more than a few days without looking wantonly off the mountain on which we lived, toward wilder lands; not that we exactly lived in the heart of civilization.

My father was supremely at home in the wilderness, and there his soul took its greatest comfort. I learned much from him about tracking animals and men, about trapping and shooting, and about surviving in the wilderness. Most fascinating to me was what I learned from him about the red men. With him, I had visited a few Indian villages, and I knew more than several Indians personally.

Father was a tall, dark-haired man who stood over 6'4". He was literally the biggest man I'd ever seen. He was called by the Indians who knew him, something like, "Big Man Who is Cousin to the Wind." This was owing to his size, as well as his great speed and endurance afoot. He was one of the few men that I never bested in a foot race. He was not just fast, but also possessed of incredible endurance, once running some 160 miles through the Virginia back country, to deliver word about a large force of Indians to the colonial government officials in Williamsburg. He covered the distance in a remarkable three days, crossing rivers, climbing mountains, and navigating through dense forests, a feat still spoken of when I was a first-year student at William and Mary College.

My mother was a Randolph, a member of one of Virginia's oldest and most influential families. That she gave up her place in society, to live on the fringe of the wilderness, bespeaks of her love for my father. They met at a ball in Williamsburg when she was 18 and he was 23. It was love at first sight, and they were married within five months, despite the protestations of her family that the courtship had been much too short.

My mother was extremely intelligent, more independent, feistier, knowledgeable, opinionated about politics, and world affairs, or for that matter almost any topic of discussion, than most women of the time. My handsome father literally swept her off her feet.

Mother was named Kathryn Marie, and she was a beauty with long flowing blond hair. Her features were, as my father said, "of a goddess." She was big-boned, shapely and robust, but not excessively busty, or heavy. She certainly was not a frail society blossom. Until I met Autumn Leaf, my mother was the most mentally and physically strong woman that I had known. Certainly, she was one of the most beautiful.

My father often said that he admired my mother's intelligence almost as much as her beauty. She would chide him by saying, "Almost? Why not as much or more?"

To which he was forced to reply, "I am only a man, and human men can scarcely think of intelligence when looking upon such beauty."

That usually melted my mother. I have heard other men say similar things about other women, sometimes in crude terms, but my father was not a crude sort of man, although he could enjoy a ribald joke, and certainly hold his own with ruffians in a tavern. To that end he had a reputation, not for picking fights, but for being the last man standing if one broke out.

Actually, when mother was not immediately present, he sometimes told what seemed to us to be some pretty tall tales of his exploits in taverns with Dan Morgan, a well-known brawler. According to father, he and Dan once whipped eight men in a fight in a Richmond tavern. I cannot testify to the truth of the story, but I never did catch my father in a lie, and I never heard of any man who had.

While my mother's religion came from the Bible, with a decidedly feminine interpretation, my father's came from the mountains, forests, rivers, and much of the wilderness. In that regard, he was not dissimilar from the Indians. He was in many ways an extremely spiritual person, but most people did not see it. He was extremely tolerant of others, imbued with great compassion, and unusually introspective in comparison with his peers.

My mother's family, like Autumn Leaf's years later, feared that she might end up an old maid. As she turned 18 years, still unmarried and without being engaged, people began to talk. Oh, she was not without prospects, but like Autumn much later, none suited her. Not that is, until my father showed up at the previously mentioned ball. After that romantic first meeting and those first exciting, but scary dances, they were married within five months. It was an almost scandalously short courtship period for proper Virginians. I am continually amazed at society for judging a woman, for not being married, and then for judging her again for marrying too quickly when true love finally appears.

Society was never much to my liking. Oh, I was an educated and a bright young man; my mother saw to that. But rules of polite behavior such as were encountered in Williamsburg and sometimes even in Charlottesville, never appealed to me. I was far more impressed with the rules of the Cumberland Gap, or the Ohio wilderness. Which I suppose is to say no rules at all.

After the marriage ceremony in Williamsburg, my father purchased a tiny farm near Charlottesville. I think it was his way of slowly introducing my mother to more isolated living. It was at this time and place that I was born. It was the tenth month of a fourteen-month residence. I came into the world in the year, 1770.

As a newborn, I was long and thin, with black hair that became blond in early childhood, and ultimately settled on me as a sort of dark sandy blond color that I carried into my adult years.

After a time, we packed up, and moved into the Allegheny wilderness several leagues west of Charlottesville. Father built a cabin on the side of a mountain, where a level clearing afforded a natural homestead site, and had a tremendous view of the surrounding countryside.

The cabin became, over the years, four rooms and a loft, quite spacious for a frontier family. In addition to the outhouse, there were six other small buildings on the property. We had a very small one for the hogs, one for the chickens, geese, and rabbits, with another for grain, hay, and horses. We had a small one for tobacco. We had a fairly large workshop for the storage of tools, skinning, and curing furs, and for the repair of necessaries. Finally, we had a smokehouse for curing meat and fish. We had small underground root cellar near the house but that, of course, was not a building as such. The goats sort of roamed free, except in the most extreme weather, and at those times, we put them in with the horses.

The tool storage shed also served as a shelter for the dogs, of which my father usually kept three, or four, finding them excellent companions and allies on his trips. Father's favorite dog, Jack, lived in the cabin with us for the most part, despite mother's objections. Over the years she came to love this dog whose life spanned 15 happy summers. His presence as a watchdog, children's companion, and family member, richly rewarded the love that was lavished upon him by all of us. The number of times that his diligence prevented mishap, or disaster involving one or more of us children, is almost worthy of legend. I am not sure anyone ever got within a quarter league of our cabin without father's dogs signaling the alarm, with such baying and growling, as would have frightened a continental regiment.

The same as other frontier families, we suffered the cuts, bruises, splinters, accidents and close calls with knives, axes, implements, briar bushes, poison ivy, and unusual situations. Unlike other families, we were never surprised by bears, wolf packs, or marauding Indians on account of our dogs.

My father even once raised an orphan wolf pup to adulthood. KeeKee saved my father from ambush by five Cherokee warriors on one of his far-flung trips into the Tennessee country. She was, however, killed in the incident. Jack was her grandson. I think that owing to his being one-fourth wolf, the family seemed to him to be his pack, and he embraced his role within the group.

During the years on the mountain, Rebeka, Luke, and Sally Ann were born in succession, all about a year and a half apart. Mother apparently began reading to her children when we were about a week old. By five years old, we were all able to read the Bible, and by nine we had been exposed to the classics, to Shakespeare, and to Latin. Soon after we began to learn French. No one could say that we were illiterate bumpkins from the backwoods, as so many of our contemporaries were characterized. However, few of our city counterparts had wilderness skills to compare to ours, and frankly we probably took what we knew for granted because it came to us as a natural part of our daily living.

The Christmas season was always spent as three, or four weeks, among the various Randolphs in more populous parts of Virginia. It was always a hard time on my father, being off the frontier, but he made the most of it hunting rabbits and water-fowl. Here we had access to extensive family libraries, to visitors from all over the colonies, and even occasional guests from England, or France. Of particular interest were various almanacs and political treatises circulating through the colonies. Father had railed against the King from my earliest memory, and reading documents by various colonial authors reinforced within me my father's opinions, even when I was as young as ten years.

My mother refused to allow her children to learn the language of the frontier with its terms such as ain't, t'ain't, 'spose, and such phrases as, "You'ins et, yet?" (Have you eaten?). These were not part of our vernacular. As she often said, "You'll speak the king's English like proper people."

Saying the word king generally brought a mumbled comment about the "blanking king" from my father. Such was either ignored by mother, or served as a cause for reprimand, depending upon her mood. She would tolerate no swearing out of her children, or her husband, and all of us father included, learned not to engage in the use of such words around mother. I would readily admit that all we all, the girls included, had no deficiencies in the knowledge of such words when mother was not present.

If mother had one prejudice, it seemed to be that she didn't particularly care for her children learning the language of the red man. She felt that English, Latin, and a little French were quite sufficient, but she had no interest in her children learning the "tongues of savages." However, father took a more functional view, and knew full well that anyone living in the wilderness had better understand everything about it, including as many Indian dialects as possible.

The above point was driven home for mother when she accompanied father on a trip into the wilds of southwestern Virginia, and father was barely able to talk his way out of a misunderstanding with some Choctaws. The confusion might have gotten quite ugly, and father admitted that his Choctaw was a bit rusty.

It seems that a Choctaw sachem thought he was bargaining a trade for my mother. She failed to see the humor in father's laughter once he explained the situation to her, long after they were out of harm's way. Father was in fact, trading some calico fabric that happened to be similar to that of the dress that my mother was wearing. This is the exact reason he had pointed to mother, not intending to indicate a desire to trade her, as the sachem mistakenly thought, but to demonstrate what could be accomplished with such fine calico.

Considering her narrow escape from life as an Indian, mother did a complete turnabout, and advocated that her children learn as many languages as humanly possible, including Indian dialects. For the rest of their lives together father often teased mother about trading her to whatever Indian would give him the best deal. Mother refused to even so much as crack a smile on such occasions.

Our childhoods were not only about book learning, but also chores, learning survival skills, cooking, and sewing, boys and girls alike. There was always plenty of family fun. My parents were never at a loss for affording time, for their children to have fun swimming, fishing, or playing cards, and board games. We learned checkers by the age of two, and chess by the age of five. My mother was a far better chess player than father, and his frustration over constant defeats to her led eventually to his disavowing the game altogether. He simply could not understand how a man who could find a trail in the densest forest could lose a chess game, nearly every time, to a woman, albeit a very bright one. He never lost at anything else he competed in. How could he lose at chess?

In 1777, and again in 1780, and 1781, we spent considerable time in Charlottesville, and then with the Randolphs further east. This was on account of father's being off fighting in the war. Morgan's Riflemen fought like Indians, only they were much better shots, making devastating use of their long rifles in many key battles. This was father's company throughout his time in the war, and they were to gain fame as one of the most effective fighting units that the Americans had.

It had been in 1777, that my father and his friend, Daniel Morgan, distinguished themselves at the American victory over the British General Johnny Burgoyne, at Saratoga. After this legendary victory father was home for a time, but was gone again periodically. By 1780, the British had brought the war to the southern colonies seeking to capitalize on strong Tory support. Again, Morgan was called to command and again, my father accompanied him. They were often pitted against the dastardly, Colonel Banastre Tarleton. I am very proud of my father's role in defeating that butcher, and other British at Cowpens, in South Carolina. After that, owing to his wounded left hand and owing to Morgan's bad back, both men returned to Virginia seeing no further action in the war.

Morgan's back problems began when as a young man in the French and Indian War, he had received 500 lashes as a result of his knocking cold, a British officer who was flaunting his authority over young Dan. It is amazing that Morgan was able to contribute so mightily to the American cause in the War for Independence, considering the magnitude and the residual effects, of that earlier injury. Perhaps his hatred of the British spurred him to overcome unimaginable pain.

I have little doubt that my own father's lack of affection for the British came in part from the early tutelage of his great friend. His opinions in this regard were formed long before the war. Of course, having fought against the likes of Tarleton, who waged unconditional war on women and children, and having been done permanent injury by a British musket ball, only served to firmly seal the man's total hatred of the British. I think his attitudes influenced mine; in fact, of that, I have no doubt.

At age 13, I accompanied a post-war surveying expedition on an eight-week trip into the northwestern territories, still claimed by Virginia. My father had arranged this with some friends of his who were surveyors, charged by the Virginia governor with assessing the area. I believe my father hoped that this trip would introduce me to the useful skills and potential occupation of surveyor. In actuality, even at such a young age, I was of considerable help on this trip, but not with surveying. My hunting and guiding skills proved to be what won me the adulation of the party's leaders.

It was also at this time that I resolved that I would never be a surveyor. Oh, my math skills were already up to the task, but I had no intention of becoming an agent of reducing my beloved wilderness to farmland. At the end of the trip, I was paid what was for me a king's ransom for my services. Father allowed me to use some of the money on a new long-rifle, having to that point been content with old hand-me-downs. Mother had the balance of my earnings sent to her family bankers, for the purpose of setting up a college fund for me.

On the subject of college, I was conflicted. Going off to meet other young men had some allure, though probably not as much as the knowledge that Williamsburg had a fair number of young maidens. And I was not totally opposed to the concept of unlimited books and ideas. I suppose I also imagined what would be near complete personal freedom, and limited if any chores to perform. However, such an endeavor would have to be purchased at the price of taking me further from my beloved frontier, forcing me to dress in a more gentlemanly fashion, and compelling me to utilize the genteel manners that I had learned at the hands of the Randolphs, since my earliest memory. In other words, I could fit neatly into civilized society, but it held only limited appeal for me.

In the late summer of 1784, I accompanied my father on a trip into the Kentucky country to deliver some supplies to some settlers, and to take delivery of some furs. By this time, my father was refashioning himself into a sort of frontier merchant, a kind of middleman in the fur trade, and deliverer of supplies to the frontier. It was my hope that I would on this trip meet the frontiersman that I had heard so much about, Daniel Boone. However, that hope did not materialize as we never got into Kentucky as far as Boonesborough.

It was on the return trip that I was forced to kill my first human being. I am neither proud, nor ashamed. It just was a situation where I had no choice. However, at the time it unsettled my young mind.

It seems that a Shawnee raiding party thought to ambush us and steal our furs, but owing to the wilderness sagacity of my father and the instincts of his dogs, we turned the tables on them in setting the very trap that they had intended for us.

As we had proceeded up the trail, the dogs alerted father to signs that he quickly and correctly interpreted as those of the raiding party. It happened that on account of our halting, that the Indians came backtracking the very trail upon which they sought to execute their murderous larceny upon us. Because we didn't arrive at their ambuscade within what they thought was a reasonable time frame, they threw their normal caution to the wind and let their greed fog their judgment. They hurried back up the trail toward our location to see what had become of us.

I would like to tell you that I saved someone's life in heroic fashion that day, or that I fought a Shawnee warrior in mortal hand to hand combat, with the outcome being determined by who was the better man with knife and tomahawk. The plain truth is, however, much different, and much less heroic. Hiding in a bush behind a large oak tree, I simply took aim and felled a young brave with a shot through the chest. He never saw me, and he never knew from whence came the shot that ended his life. As my round struck home, my target jumped and fell back much as a deer does when shot. He was dead on the forest floor. He had been about my age.

My father and the rest of our party let loose a lethal barrage from their long-rifles, with two of the eight potential brigands escaping by darting headlong into the dense underbrush, and the others being decimated. Father sent the dogs, who had been patiently and quietly laying low, after the two Indians. Out they went baying and raising a ferocious din. After a few moments, he recalled the dogs with his wooden whistle, quite certain in the knowledge that those Shawnee would not bother us again. We preceded back to Virginia without further incident.

The affair left me with a hollow feeling in the pit of my stomach. I did not have the sense of great triumph that I had imagined in my younger daydreams. In those I had taken aim with my rifle, and saved a settlement from the onslaught of a savage horde. No, I took no joy in taking the life of another human being. My only solace was my father's understanding, and his words the first time that we made camp after the event.

"Son," he said, "it was going to be you or him at some point. You don't need to celebrate the killing, but you do need to be thankful that the Shawnee ambush was avoided, lest we be among the dead, as was their intention. You are only 14 years old, and ought not to have intimacy with killing a man. But remember, it was not you who chose today's events."

Father knew that I was deeply troubled by the killing. We continued our discussion, on and off, all the way back to Virginia. He shared with me his feelings upon his first such occasion. They were not different than mine. My father had a knack for knowing what people were feeling, and for knowing what to say to them. He was a man of remarkable intuition, and his words helped me a great deal in understanding my difficult feelings about the event.

Subsequent sojourns in the wilderness of Kentucky and Tennessee over the next two years, allowed me to finish my wilderness education if such is possible, and to even gain a small reputation among my father's friends. This related to my path-finding skills, my marksmanship, and like my father, my speed afoot. Even among certain Indians, I became known as the English equivalent of, "He Who Shoots Straight and Runs Like a Deer." By this time, I had already won several shooting contests in Virginia. During this time, I took pride in my marksmanship, but considered myself fortunate to not have occasion to once again have to shoot another human being.

Chapter Three

Off To College

William and Mary College

In the fall of 1786, at the age of 16 and some months, after what I considered the most idyllic childhood in the graces of the most loving family, I was packed up and sent off to William and Mary, for my first year of college. No other institution of higher learning was ever considered, and indeed, the choices were more limited in those days. Admission was never a question, never in doubt. My mother's education of her children saw to that but also being blunt, I was of the Randolph family. A pedigree carried weight and its advantages in Virginia, be it in society, business, government, or even education.

Such was the kind of entitlement against which my father often railed. However, both he and mother knew, that none of their children would ever be admitted to any privilege to which they might be displacing someone more capable. They had seen to our manners, our education, our total upbringing, and they had been both thorough and creative. The result was a group of extremely well-rounded individuals. It didn't hurt that we were an exceptionally bright group if I do say so. It would have been impossible to have convinced my parents that their children were not prepared for life's endeavors and that we would not be among the very best at all we attempted. Quite frankly, owing to them I would not be boasting to assert that they were correct in their assumptions.

I arrived in Williamsburg by coach, having completed the final stage of a journey that began on foot, in the early evening hours of September 15, 1786. I made my way to the boarding house run by the widow, Sarah Parkman, a motherly family friend of years long gone. Sarah hugged me so tight as to almost cause pain, even though she seemed to be little taller than waist high in comparison to me. She then preceded to feed me a meal that was fit for a king.

Upon showing me to my room, she informed me that she had few rules, but those that she did have were to be held sacrosanct. Firstly, never was I to entertain young ladies in my room. The parlor would do for such activities.

As she said, "I'm not running a French boarding house (Americans have always imagined the French people as perpetually occupied with sexual liaisons), and I'll not have my reputation, or yours, sullied by such behavior."

I assured her that I had no prospect, nor intention of such behavior. Her only other concern was that she asked that I always keep my rifle unloaded in the home. To this I agreed, though keeping a gun unloaded was most unusual for me.

Sarah was so kind that I could not help but like her. I had not seen her since I was little, but she and my mother were friends of long-standing. Her cooking was truly a daily highlight, and there is precious little that gives a 16-year-old young man more pleasure than good food.

In my first semester I studied a variety of preliminary and required subjects, and began taking many science and related courses, that I hoped would ultimately propel me toward a goal of working toward a medical degree. The frontier had a shortage of doctors, and I felt that would be useful knowledge as long as I was going to be forced to go to college. On a more practical level, I had looked up an old friend of father's, Doctor Bushrod Johnson. He preferred to be called Doc, and completely eschewed any use of the name, Bushrod.

As he said laughingly, "What parent in their right mind would saddle a child with a moniker like Bushrod?"

I explained my interest in medicine, and Doc agreed to allow me to shadow him in his practice. This led to my eventually being a sort of assistant to him. Though I ended up enjoying college life, I learned more from Doc Johnson than from any class. He was a grandfatherly figure to me, and he was most definitely a mentor.

Some of my general course instructors claimed that I had a talent for persuasive writing and debate. Certainly, I engaged in enough tavern conversations, mostly about politics and public affairs, as to make my friends think that I had adopted taverns as a field of study. I cannot state that I was averse to an occasional sip of spirits, but what I found most fascinating was the free flow of ideas about our new country. Ideas about how the government should be put together, and what would be best for the people.

As to my late hours in those taverns, Mrs. Parkman would comment each such morning, "My, my, you were out late last night. Are you keeping up with your studies?"

I knew better than to tell her that I was off studying with friends till the wee hours. She had people who kept her informed of the activities of her boarders. She probably knew our schedules, and our comings and our goings as well as we did.

Our morning lectures usually ended with her saying, "Well, there are some things that a young man just has to learn by experience."

I think she ended this way because she could not bear the thought that we might be angry with her for her nagging, or excessive mothering of us. And besides, she knew full well that we were not up to serious mischief. That information would never have escaped her network of spies.

There was one occasion when one of my housemates was keeping late hours with a young lady. Before this became a scandal, Mrs. Parkman found a way to bring it under control by involving the father of the maiden. At any rate, it became clear to all of us in her home just what our exact boundaries were in regards to her expectations as our guardian. She took the job seriously, and I do believe she loved each of us like a son, though some of her sons were better behaved than others.

Many great Americans attended William and Mary, including three Presidents: Jefferson, Monroe, and Tyler. Also, the famous senator John Breckenridge and famous U. S. Chief Justice, John Marshall, were William and Mary alums. Several Randolphs attended as well. Among these were Edmond, Peyton, Beverley, and Thomas Randolph. During my brief time at William and Mary, I suppose the most notable of my acquaintances, who went on to some degree of success, was Hugh Nelson, who later became United States Ambassador to Spain. Hugh and I raised more than one glass together. He was an interesting companion, though I'm not sure what it says about the crop of students present while I was there, that we produced no Presidents, or Chief Justices of the Supreme Court, nor many others of extreme note, while other generations of attendees before and after, far exceeded our fame.

My second semester was even better, and my first-year ended well. Despite my late nights, my grades were outstanding. Doc Johnson praised me for my inquiring mind and the help that I gave him. And to a very great degree, Mrs. Parkman was my mother away from home.

I went back to my frontier for a summer break of hunting, and enjoying the wilds with my family. I was amazed at how my siblings had grown. Rebeka was a stunning 15-year-old beauty, Luke was nearly 14, and already six feet tall, and Sally Ann had her 12th birthday that summer. She had become quite a markswoman with a rifle. It was with her and the dogs that I hunted all summer. Between chores and hunting, we swam, fished, and discussed the new federal government of the United States, among other topics.

Mother and father were very glad to have me home and the family back together. That summer, they seemed so very happy and were enjoying some considerable prosperity after years of hard work on the frontier. Despite the difficulties, mother was still a fine-looking woman, and father had lost none of his wilderness skills. He had recently returned after leading a group of settlers into Kentucky to establish homesteads. The love between the two was never more apparent than that summer. After all their years together, they remained completely devoted to one another.

All too soon, I was back at Williamsburg for my second year of college. Mrs. Parkman commented at how much I'd grown. I was just over 6'2" now. She then said, "I'll put some weight on those bones this year with some of my special apple pies." Of course, that sounded just fine to me.

The term began with me spending far less time in taverns, and far more time with Doc Johnson. Some nights and weekends, I was with him so late that I slept in his spare room. I think he enjoyed my company and our late-night discussions. He had been a widower for many years, and though he knew everyone for miles around, he had few close friends. As long as she knew I was with Doc, Mrs. Parkman never worried.

Doc found me to be an incurable questioner about the human body and its functions. In reality, I think that he enjoyed having an apprentice. He was always careful to discuss each patient with me after we had left their presence. I learned how to treat fevers and stomach ailments, how to sew up gashes, and what to do about rashes. On one occasion, I even assisted Doc in an operation to remove a musket ball from the leg of a gentleman who had been shot under mysterious circumstances.

Doc later told me that the man's story of his musket discharging while being cleaned was, "as pure a fabrication as ever was conceived." There had been no gun powder residue on, nor hole in the man's stocking. This meant that the gun could not have been discharged anywhere near his leg. Therefore, knowing the man as Doc did, he assumed that the man had been shot while fleeing some irate husband, or father, perhaps over around Jamestown, or some other small settlement.

When I supposed that the man could have changed stockings, Doc's only reply was, "There was no fabric in the wound. I don't think he had his socks or anything else on when he was shot."

On this and other occasions, I considered Doc a most remarkable man in his ability to get at the truth. Whether in the case of a gunshot, or the case of a patient hiding symptoms for some other reason, he treated each case, each illness, as a mystery to be solved, and he approached the solution unrelentingly.

I like to think that I taught him a thing, or two because although he had a very large herb garden, and the woods behind his house was worn with trails where he sought plants to manufacture many of his medicines, I was able to show him some plants that father and the Indians had shown me to be useful. Such were effective in treating sunburn, stomach ailments, and reducing inflammation almost anywhere on the body.

I was so proud one day in October when Doc said to me, "My boy, you will be the finest physician in all of Virginia someday!"

Since Doc was not one to be effusive in his praise, nor to overly estimate a situation or a person, I considered this high praise. It had the effect of my redoubling my efforts and my study.

We had even gotten to the place in our relationship where, whenever stitches were needed for a patient, I got to sew. The exception was when such stitches were needed on the more delicate, or private areas of female patients, or other situations where modesty prevented my being privy to the treatment. But even in those cases, Doc told me all about it afterward and drew pictures that I might learn all the better.

In my third term at William and Mary all was going well and I felt that "I had the world by the tail." Though I missed the wilderness, I had adapted quite well to higher education and to living in Williamsburg. My possibilities now seemed endless, and my two passions, the frontier and medicine, were not at all incompatible in my mind.

And then in December, my world came crashing down around me, and events occurred which even now bring a tear to my eye, all these years later. I received a note from home, carried by a frontiersman, that was more of a plea. It read simply:

> J. R.,
> *Come home quick. Mama, Papa, and Sally Ann*
> *have the fever. They are very sick.*
> *Hurry!*
> Rebeka

By coach, horse, and foot, I made my way back to the mountain of my youth with a haste that may have equaled my father's great feat of many years earlier. I slept not a wink but kept moving toward home from the very moment that I received Rebeka's note.

A light snow fell as I climbed through the forest up to the familiar clearing. I thrust open the door only to learn that father had died several hours earlier, and that mother had just expired moments before I entered the cabin. I railed at the cruel fate of not being able to say good-bye but knew deep in my heart that I could not have gotten home one minute sooner.

With Rebeka and Luke sobbing, almost by instinct I moved to Sally's bedside. I gave her the best examination that I could, trying to replicate what I thought Doc Johnson would have done. I asked Rebeka and Luke questions about the symptoms and tried to ascertain the source of the illness.

Failing in the latter, I reached for the medicine bag that Doc had presented me with just three days before I left. In it was some medicine that Doc had used successfully on various fevers. I had Rebeka brew the herbs into a tea, and I gave it to Sally, who poor thing, could barely lift her head to drink. She did not have the strength to talk.

We all sat up that night with Sally. I was dog-tired from my trip but was determined to do whatever I could to keep her alive. In reality, there was little else that I could do, beyond giving Doc Johnson's cure and applying cold rags to her face and forehead. After a fitful night, the fever broke, and she began to show improvement. After a week, she had made a full recovery. Our great joy was tempered only by our great grief.

It is events such as this, wherein the oldest and youngest members of a family are stricken, but not those in-between, that caused me to wonder about life in the religious sense. How is it that when the ague or any plague hits a populace, that there seems no rhyme, no reason as to who is taken and who is left still living? This I pondered, but sadly, I did not conclude anything soul-settling.

As for mother and father, on the day of Sally's beginning to recover, we built a huge bonfire on the bluff overlooking the western wilderness to warm the soil. Rebeka dressed mother in her favorite dress. Even after her bout with fever, I could not help but notice her beauty, as Rebeka fussed with her hair. For his final journey, Luke and I dressed father in his favorite hunting shirt and his buckskin pants, the ones mother had made for him. He would not have wanted to be buried in his best clothes. His best clothes were not his favorite clothes.

Rebeka had the idea that they would have wanted to be buried together, not just side by side. So it was that Luke and I dug a double grave below where the bonfire had been. We wrapped each of our parents in a blanket, and then wrapped them together in their bed quilt, laying them in their grave on the bluff, overlooking the wilderness.

We did this all with great care and love, as it was the last thing that we could do for the two people who had given us so much throughout our time on earth. Rebeka read Psalm 23 from the Bible, and each of us offered briefly what came into our hearts to say. We cried and sobbed uncontrollably. And thus, it was that we sent our parents into eternity together in death, as they had been in life.

A week or so after Sally Ann's recovery, we held a family meeting, just as we used to do when mother and father were alive. The difference now was that I was the chairman of the meeting. There was no consideration of going back to college on my part. I was now the head of the family, and the person responsible for my brother and sisters. I would have it no other way. I was determined to do my parents proud.

After a brief discussion, we determined to wait out the winter together, and make our future decisions slowly and deliberately, as our options manifested themselves in the coming months.

In a short time, we were visited by my father's brother, Edward, who had come up from South Carolina. Also, many Randolph's who expected that we would immediately pack up to come live with them. However, this was not our inclination, and as glad as we were to see kin, we would not accept anyone making decisions on our futures that we did not plan. In time our visitors left, reluctantly leaving us alone on the edge of the frontier, and making us promise to visit them in the summer, or our being unable to do so they would return to visit us.

We settled father's affairs in Charlottesville and discovered to our surprise, that mother and father had left us each a small inheritance to be received when we turned 18 years old. The shares would serve as modest, but reasonable dowries for the girls at such time as they married, and would give Luke and I some funds with which to start our lives.

While in Charlottesville, I had a note passed to me from a friend of Mr. Jefferson expressing the latter's profound condolences. Mr. Jefferson was a cousin of the Randolph's, but we never knew the particulars of his relationship. He was then in New York with the new government but had instructed his household to put Monticello at our disposal. This was indeed a generous offer from such a famous man, but like my father, and perhaps to honor his memory, I could not accept for us. I was above all, my father's son.

And so, we passed the winter sharing our grief, sharing our stories about our parents, and sharing our love for one another. In February, we received a visitor, a slightly bent but very large old man, who I instantly guessed was Dan Morgan. He looked much older than his years, but still rough and strong.

Dan had come to pay his respects, and beg us to come live with him and his family. He stayed with us for five or six days. They were wonderful days, hearing his accounts of he and father in the Great War, as well as some common brawling. During the time he was with us, he broke into tears more than once, and at times was barely consolable about the loss of my parents. We were grateful for his offer to take us in and for his visit, but we declined. When he left, I had the sense of watching an American legend depart. That he had come to us at all bespoke of his great love for my father.

In April, we received another, but more unusual proposition. It seemed that mother's older sister's eldest sons, our favorite cousins, were marrying sisters in June. Of course, we were invited and expected at the wedding, but that was not the proposition.

The proposal was that the young couples would come and take over our place while we went back to civilization, and continued our upbringing in the loving care of the Randolphs. When we attained adulthood, we could decide what to do with the homestead and with our lives in general. This would allow me to go back to William and Mary. Though I did not mention it to my sisters and my brother, I had already mentally closed the door on that chapter of my life. As far as I was concerned, I had already reached adulthood, and no one could tell me differently.

We spoke the proposal aloud, over, and over. After much discussion it became clear that most of it made good sense, especially for the girls. Indeed, they began to embrace the idea of going east for a while, of living a more genteel life and of meeting young men. Each would miss our mountain home and lifestyle, but each had a yearning for the experiences that they could not

receive if they stayed. To be fair, Sally Ann was not quite as en-
thused about this as Rebeka. However, eventually, she was convinced.

But as to Luke, well he was of a different opinion, clearly of
the same ilk as his father and older brother, he wanted no part of
further upbringing, of education, or of going east. Oh, to be sure,
he had no objections to the young newlyweds coming to our
place, he simply had no personal intention of leaving. Finally, and
with great difficulty, I persuaded him with a compromise. He
would spend his winters at William and Mary, engaged in higher
education, and his summers would be spent on our beloved
homestead with him in charge.

In June we attended the wedding in Richmond. It was a lavish
affair, not only accounting for the Randolph influence but also
because the brides were members of the prestigious Lee family.
After three days of celebrations, we accompanied the newlyweds
back to our home, where we had agreed to spend the summer
introducing them to frontier living. This was a concept more than
a little embraced by Sally Ann and Luke, who more than Rebeka
and I, each had a bit of "show off " about their personalities.

The summer passed uneventfully, and our proteges were eager learners. Sometimes Luke and Sally Ann were a bit overbearing and even condescending, but the cousins and their
brides endured it all with good humor. The former Lee sisters
endeared themselves to us as much as our favorite cousins, their
husbands always had. The cabin was abuzz with life, particularly
at night, when the commotion from the newlyweds was certainly
of a nature of which none of we remaining Jamisons had any direct personal experience.

In the fall, my sisters and I parted with Luke and the cousins.
Luke agreed to follow as soon as our few crops were all safely in.
I intended to leave the girls with my mother's sister, who now
having just lost two sons to marriage, embraced the idea of gaining two daughters to finish raising. My aunt and her husband
were hard ones to convince that I would not also be joining their
family. But I was not one with whom to argue, and eventually, I
convinced them that I would begin my adult life at this time.

My parting with my sisters was much harder than I had imagined that it would be, and we all hugged and cried, until we
veritably shook. I had a most unusual feeling that I might never

see them again, but why I felt that way I had no idea.

I headed off to South Carolina to fulfill my promise to visit Uncle Edward, stopping for two days in Williamsburg to see Mrs. Parkman and old Doc Johnson along the way. Again, I was entreated to change my plans, but such invitations only hardened my heart to my intent. I had changed, and though I wasn't quite sure what life would throw my way, I had no self-doubts as I took my leave of my Williamsburg friends.

Uncle Edward having married into South Carolina aristocracy lived on a medium-sized plantation. I stayed but a few days because, as I have made clear before, like my father I could hold no truck with keeping slaves. It would have done no good to express my displeasure with his lifestyle. Still, I wondered at the difference between his thinking and that of my father. How had two brothers come to such different lifestyles? However, he was kin, and his life was his business. It was not my business, but it was a business that I did not like. As I took my leave, he offered me a handsome sum of cash for my trip, but I refused just as I had refused his offer of a job on the plantation.

After leaving Uncle Edward, I wandered the backwoods of South Carolina, North Carolina, Georgia, and the Tennessee mountains, for several months, encountering Chickasaws, Choctaws, Shawnees, Cherokees, Creeks, and Indians of many other nations, not always friendly in disposition toward me. I suppose I had some more of what I've called close calls, and certainly some adventures that would be worth the telling. On those mountains and in those forests, the sights were often marvels to behold, and only strengthened my love of the wilderness. But those are stories for another time. Mostly, I roamed the wild reaches seeking solace in my beloved wilderness and trying to find a meaning to life. In the latter, I had little luck.

Some considerable time after turning 18, I made a brief trip to Charlottesville to claim my inheritance, and then further east to reacquaint with my sisters, who now I did see again for a few days. Then I spent a few weeks in Williamsburg, staying at Sarah Parkman's with Luke. I had brought Doc Johnson some new herbs out of the southern wilderness, and we had a great time talking medicine and "doctoring." Luke and I had ourselves a considerable time in the local taverns. One night we acquitted ourselves quite well in resolving a fight with three men. They were slightly drunk, and thought they would push us around, first verbally and then in a physical manner. Their evening ended in a horse trough outside the tavern, while Luke and I finished our ale and our discussion.

Finally, I headed north, a direction I had never gone far toward. I was not sure what lay in store, but I was determined to proceed.

Chapter Four

Applying for Adventure and Finding Troubles

Henry Knox

Early January 1790, found me in New York City, the tempo-rary capital of the new nation. Previously, I had visited Baltimore and Philadelphia, after coming out of my soul-searching exile in the wilderness of the South. Big cities held some fascination for me, but only particularly the libraries and the taverns. I always found these seemingly antithetical institutions to be the greatest source of public education, and I think this was especially true in a budding democracy.

On an appointed day, I entered the old Federal Hall and was directed to the drafty first-floor office of, Secretary of War, Henry

Knox. After waiting briefly in the outer room, I was summoned to see the old Revolutionary War artillery general. Knox was a portly man. I judged him to be slightly taller than average, but it was difficult to tell due to the spatial impression created by his girth. He was dressed in an elegant blue military uniform, as befitted the former top American Army General and now Secretary of War. Knox served as Secretary of War under the Articles of Confederation, and presently under the new Constitutional Government.

He had risen to become the top artillery officer of the late war and one of General Washington's favorites. A former book store owner, he had become an expert on artillery strategy by voracious reading and a sort of on-the-job training. Earlier, he had been a member of the Sons of Liberty and was present at the Boston Massacre. Later, he had been an instrumental participant in several major battles of the war.

Knox had risen rapidly in rank throughout the war based upon his achievements. For instance, it was he who had brought the captured guns of Forts Ticonderoga and Crown Point, to defend Boston's Dorchester Heights. He who had set up training sites in several colonies, for improving the readiness of continental soldiers; something he accomplished mostly in the winters, or off-campaign seasons. He had been responsible for the logistics of Washington's crossing of the Delaware, in route to the surprise Christmas victory over the Hessians, at Trenton, New Jersey. He had been commandant of West Point, and he had been present at Yorktown for the decisive battle of the Great War.

"Come in young man, come in. Your reputation has proceeded you," he said.

I immediately took that to mean that he had read the letters of reference that I had dropped off a few days earlier; personal references from Attorney General Edmond Randolph (my cousin), Secretary of State, Jefferson, and from my father's old friend, Dan Morgan. I judged that the latter would carry the greatest weight as a sort of soldier to soldier communication. He shook my hand vigorously and showed me to a large chair near his very tidy desk.

"So, I take it that you want to join us in the expedition into the Ohio Country?" he said.

"Yes, Sir, I would like that very much," I replied. "I thought perhaps I might lend a hand as a scout."

The purpose of my visit was to attempt to acquire an appointment from Secretary Knox, to serve with the army group being sent against the Indian confederacy along the Maumee River, north of Fort Washington in the Ohio Country. This would be an expedition to quell problems on the Northwest frontier. Secretary Knox had a reputation for fair dealing with various Indian tribes, and for encouraging only treaties that were entered into in good faith, with the full intent of honoring them. Meanwhile, the British had failed to live up to the terms of the treaty that ended the Great War and were making a nuisance of themselves in encouraging the tribes north of the Ohio River to war. President Washington, having had enough of the British and the Indians, had ordered Secretary Knox to assemble a punitive expedition to deal with the situation.

From my perspective, I had encountered good Indians and bad, the same as with any race of people. My interest in this expedition had mainly to do with my outrage over the savage acts recently committed by the tribes north of the Ohio, under the guidance and encouragement of the British agitators. Though I suppose if I searched my soul for truth, that truth would be nearer my desire to see the Ohio Country and to be part of an adventure.

"Well, son," Knox began, "despite your youth, I can see that you are already a man of considerable wilderness acumen. If Dan Morgan recommends you then I have no doubt whatsoever that you will serve us well. We cannot pay much, but you will be doing a great service for your country. God willing, perhaps you can have a favorable hand in helping rid our territory of those dastardly British interlopers."

Now he was speaking my language. Here was a man who hated the British, and why not, he'd fought them for years.

"I'll do my best, Sir," I replied. "Goodness knows I have no truck with the British."

Laughing, Secretary Knox said, "Well in that regard my boy, you agree with both Dan Morgan and myself. I'm very glad we'll have a generation of men such as you to carry on what we have begun with the creation of this country. May God grant us success and future greatness as a nation."

"Yes, Sir," I beamed, doing my darnedest not to show how happy that I was.

He continued, "I want you to report to Fort Washington as soon as possible. Your commanding officer will be General Josiah Harmar, a great soldier, and a great patriot. You are to report directly to him. Come back tomorrow, and my secretary will have a letter of introduction for you, along with your commission as a scout. Good luck, young man. I wish I was going along myself."

"Thank you, Sir, I appreciate the opportunity," was my reply. And with that, I turned and left his office.

It is difficult in a few short minutes to take the full measure of a man. My experience had generally shown me that portly individuals are frequently affable and that men of importance often overrate their importance, reflected by a pompous attitude. Sometimes men of both qualities seemed insufferable. Secretary Knox being of both qualities, portly and important, was a hard read. As he had been a famous general, and as he was now a "higher up" in the new government, I reckoned he must be a man of some considerable goodness and ability. He had not tried to impress me with his position, had not treated me brusquely, or with condescension, and had seemed to be an affable sort. Still, I thought I detected just a bit of pompous self-righteousness in the man. But no matter, I had no real basis for that feeling, and I determined that I liked him. After all, he had just given me a great opportunity for adventure and free passage to the Ohio Country.

I returned the next morning, retrieved the aforementioned documents, and set off to the west for Pittsburgh, disembarking point for soldiers, settlers, peddlers and others heading down the Ohio, pursuing their destinies in search of their futures, their fortunes, and not to be melodramatic, but in some cases their deaths.

Getting from New York to Pittsburgh in 1790, particularly in the winter, was a bit more difficult than it is at the time of this telling of my story. Still, despite a few minor hardships I arrived at that point where the Allegheny and Monongahela Rivers meet to form the mighty Ohio River. It was late February, and I had trekked in all depths of snow over mountains, through forests and across rivers, mostly frozen. I had been on a few roads and many old Indian trails. I shall not here recount the trip, leaving it for a later time, or perhaps for not at all.

Pittsburgh was in those days, little more than a small village, grown from the early fort settlements, Duquesne and Pitt. For a small village in actual population, it was at the time of my arrival swollen with activity, and with some people whose sole intention was to leave for the west as quickly as possible, and with other folks whose sole intent seemed to be to get as much of the money of the first group as possible.

I camped a short distance outside the settlement, having arrived at dusk. The weather had gotten much warmer during the last five days of my trip and the river which had been frozen, was roaring with the sound of the breakup when I arrived in the vicinity.

The next morning, I found the old cabin that served as the company headquarters for *Le Beau and Sons, Traffickers on the Ohio*. Probably descended from the early French inhabitants, the Le Beaus had stayed in Western Pennsylvania, through the political upheaval resulting from three different countries controlling the area, within a short span of roughly 30 years. The Le Beaus owned flatboats and a couple of the new keel-boats, each of which carried people and cargo west to Fort Washington and beyond.

Just before I entered the cabin, I witnessed an old woman brooming a somewhat emaciated young dog next door. The poor beast had been in her garbage looking for a meal. At any rate the dog yelped and ran down the street. Had he been human I would have sworn I saw a smile on his face, like he was enjoying this game of survival.

Inside the cabin, I discovered a line of people waiting to arrange passage or the transportation of their goods down the Ohio.

When it came my turn, a short and very old man, looked up and said, "Yes, sonny, what er your needs? Aire ye goin West?"

"Fort Washington," I replied. "I'll be scouting for General Harmar," I added with no small hint of pride.

The intended expedition against the Indian tribes of the Ohio Country was certainly no secret. Soldiers and supplies were everywhere in Pittsburgh, and even the newspapers in New York had featured speculative articles about how the Indians would be tamed. In the coming months I would conclude that a little more secrecy might have been prudent.

"Bit young for a scout, ain't' ya sonny?" he said, with no hint of a French accent. "Course, you're a big' un."

Maybe the Le Beaus had been here so long that their French accents had vanished, or maybe he was just hired help.

"Maybe so," I said. "But years and wisdom are not always the same thing."

I was trying to rebuff his reference to my youth with a philosophical statement but immediately realized that I was coming off like a braggart.

I produced my government papers, and he added my name to an invoice that would, no doubt, someday find its way to Henry Knox's desk.

"Your boat is leaving at noon if'n the ice floes allow. The pier is just down along the river."

"Thanks, mister," I said as I left the cabin.

This ride was on the government's tab. Ah, young, going west, not having to walk, and not having to pay for the trip. I was liking this work already.

I decided to have a meal before heading for my boat. Up the street, I could see folks eating outside what appeared to be a tavern. As I got closer, I could see that it was the Reed Brothers Tavern. The Reed brothers were doing an enviable business. The building was full, and the outside areas were likewise teeming with hungry travelers. Ordering deer meat pie, I went outside to await its delivery. As I stepped off the porch, I heard a commotion in the back of the building, and pretty soon the previously mentioned mongrel came tearing around, with a muscular, stick-wielding, fellow chasing him and shouting obscenities. The wiley canine easily outdistanced the man, running down the street, and looking back to reveal some sort of pie all over his mouth. I swear that dog was grinning from ear to ear.

Finishing my meal, washed down with some bitter frontier beer, I left the stump on which I had been sitting, and headed back up the street toward the pier. It had started to rain. As it was not yet noon, I ducked into a cabin indicating it was the establishment of the local gunsmith. Here I ordered more shot and powder, for the trip downriver, and asked the proprietor if he would give my rifle a looking over. I usually maintained the gun myself, but as I was heading into a fight, I figured letting a professional inspect my weapon would be prudent.

"Fine gun, young man, exceptional craftsmanship and mighty well-maintained. Where'd you get her?" he asked.

"My grandfather was a gunsmith in Baltimore and later Virginia. He made it several years ago. It was my father's. He used it in the Great War," I responded.

"Well she's a beauty son, take care of her. Course it looks like you already do that very well," he smiled.

"Yes," I said. "My pa stressed that in my upbringing. A badly kept gun is not going to help anyone."

"Sound wisdom!" he came back. "A man without a good gun out here is as naked as a jaybird," he cackled. Then he said, "My name's Hoagy Hoffer, what's y'orn?"

"Jariah Jamison," I replied. "How much do I owe you?"

He said, "Two bits for the shot and a dollar for the powder. Good powder is mighty scarce, and this is good powder, not like that what I see being sent downriver with the army."

The prices were certainly high, but like the food that I had just eaten, every necessity of life is sold dear here on the edge of nowhere.

I probably had enough shot and powder for the trip to Fort Washington, and once there I would have access to the fort's supply, however, something that my father once said suddenly appeared in my head, "Never trust army powder." During the Great War he and his comrades had suffered more than once, with inferior powder supplied to the continental quartermaster corps by unscrupulous merchants.

"What about for checking her out?" I asked.

"No charge young man," he grinned, "I just love to see a handsome weapon such as that. My pleasure, yessiree, my pleasure," he cackled again.

I paid and left, waiting a few minutes under cover of the sloping roof because a steady rain had begun to fall, and I noticed the street already turning to mud. I stood there a while and when the rain lifted a bit, I moved up the street toward the pier where I would disembark. Once again, I saw the dog. This time he was being chased by an irate and frightened mother, who was no doubt in fear that the pup might have rabies and might bite her toddler.

This time the dog ran toward me as the woman screamed, "That your dog, young man?"

"No, ma'am!" I replied quickly, to be certain that her anger did not get directed toward me. She had business in her eyes.

I turned off to the right, and onto a little path between buildings that led down to the pier. The canine ran past, outstripping me and heading toward the river. I was often confused by women, and I wanted no dealings with an angry one. I needn't have worried as she broke off the chase.

This dog seemed to sense that I was a kindred spirit, and before I had gone another ten paces, he wheeled about and came running toward me, tail in full wag. I petted the young troublemaker, and he responded enthusiastically by attempting to jump on me. I used a hand gesture that my father had taught me, and he immediately came to heel.

"Wow, you're a smart fella, aren't you?" I said.

Suddenly, I realized it was already too late. I had been adopted. I wasn't looking to be adopted, but it happened within the blink of an eye. Make no mistake, if a dog wants to adopt you, you are adopted.

"Ah, what the heck," I muttered. "A dog would be good company, and besides this one needs to get outta Pittsburgh."

And so, "Troubles" and I became companions. I don't think that I ever had any choice in the matter.

Troubles was a mutt, a youngster probably about a year-old give or take a few months. I was guessing that he had just recently grown into those large paws and gangly legs that often mark a good-sized dog when they are between puppy and adult. He was not gigantic like some of the mastiffs that I had heard tell of in New England where once upon a time they were used to hunt Indians. But he was not little either. I would say he was on the smaller side of being a large dog. I could tell he was smart and could see that he wanted to please made me. I was certain that he would be easily trained. It seemed that he must have had some training, but what had happened to separate him from his master was anyone's guess.

We finished our walk down to the river which was not completely choked with ice floes, but certainly not lacking them, as they floated quickly southwesterly. Two flatboats and a new keelboat, all marked as belonging to Le Beau, were being loaded for the trip west. The Le Beau Company it turns out, normally shipped people, and goods west in three boats at a time. The lead boat was the keelboat, and the other two were flatboats. The keelboat was easier to maneuver, which was done by poling and sometimes even sail. They were relatively new to the river traffic and were all the rage. A keelboat could more easily be brought back to Pittsburgh than flatboats. The latter were almost always disassembled at the trip's end and sold for the wood, which fetched a very high price.

"J. R. Jamison," I told the man welding the book with the passenger manifest.

"Ah," he replied, as he noted my name on his sheet. "Ere you takin' that dog?"

"Planned on it," I said.

His reply was, "Never minded havin' a dog along. Been alerted to injuns and critters mor'n once, while camped, because of a good dog. He's a good dog ain't he? Don't bite, does he?"

"Young, but good, not a biter," I lied, not knowing whether he was a biter, or not. I sensed Troubles was smart, but his behavior was an unknown quality to me.

"Kin ya handle that rifle?" he quizzed me.

"Better'n average, I suppose," I boasted.

"We got guns for the crewmen, but most don't shoot good at all. Truth is, most of the soldiers we take up river ain't too good with a gun. We could use you some for lookout, and maybe you wouldn't mind shootin us up some fresh meat along the way?" he said.

"Glad to help out," I replied. "How soon will we be in hostile country?"

"Don't take long, maybe 20 miles downriver, maybe less," he said seriously. "Name's Lester Lindley, but they call me 'Captain.' I'm in charge of this trip and all the boats."

"Pleased to meet you," I responded.

As I was about to board one of the boats, a messenger came running to Captain. In a few moments he told me the bad news that this military cargo, supplies, and men, had been ordered to wait three more days before leaving. Not all the passengers had arrived in Pittsburgh, and the ice floes were deemed too dangerous. While that didn't please me it turned out just fine. Troubles and I went off into the woods. There, outside the village, we proceeded to have three days of the most intense training and bonding possible.

In the coming weeks this delay and the subsequent training of my new companion would prove a godsend. I secured some fish for Troubles. He looked as if he needed some good nutrition and there is nothing better than fish for doing that. After three days in the woods, I was certain I had never worked with a smarter animal, including any of the ones that we so valued in my growing up years. After those three days, he and I were best of friends.

Finally, after the delay, we went to the dock, and departed for our trip down the mighty Ohio. Most of the ice was now gone, except for along the shore in a very few places, and for some small floes coming out of tributaries

The keelboat that I was on, we called the #1 boat. It was carrying mostly supplies for Fort Washington. Besides myself, we had eight crewmen and the man called Captain. He was more accurately a river pilot. We also had a military courier and two recruits with us. On the #2 boat and the #3 boat, aside from the crews, each had six recruits destined for the Fort Washington garrison. Many were young, some even younger than me, but also some were a bit old for Indian fighting if you asked me. They probably figured their prospects were better out west, but I wondered how many knew what awaited them. Maybe some shared my wanderlust, maybe some hoped-for glory. I had learned long ago that fighting Indians was not a particularly glorious endeavor. But to be fair, I must say that in my youthful ignorance, it still held a sense of excitement for me.

Chapter Five

To the Ohio Country

Flat Boats

As we shoved off it began to rain in earnest, and all passengers went below. We sat in the hold, sleeping, smoking, or talking quietly. I lay down on one of several sacks of cornmeal. I climbed up to lay down on the sacks that were piled near to the top of the hold. Troubles came right along showing amazing agility. He lay down beside me. I had learned from my father about training dogs, and I figured to have enough time on this trip to further bring Troubles into line before we reached Fort Washington. He lay sleeping. I suppose he had not been so relaxed in a long time. Having been on his own trying to survive, he had to be alert constantly. Some dogs who have been on their own, don't take to having a master. However, the nature of the beast is such that these are rare. I think it can be generally said, that dogs want to please humans when they are treated well. Now, Troubles had a master and protector, and he settled in for a long nap.

Up on deck, only Captain, and a minimal crew necessary to man the rudder and assure our steady, safe forward travel, labored in the rain. The day proved uneventful except that the rain

50

became a driving torrent, and I was mighty glad to be dry down below. Toward evening, we put in for the night into a small sort of inlet on the south shore of the river. It was our custom to camp on the south shore of the Ohio. The north shore was much more dangerous. Most Indian attacks occurred on the north shore, but there were exceptions.

Starting a fire that night proved fruitless because of the rain. So, our evening meal consisted of jerky and hard biscuits, along with a couple of sweet potato pies that Captain had secreted from the other boats, having been provided him by his wife back in Pittsburgh. I can attest that Mrs. Lindley was a seriously fine baker of sweet potato pies.

I volunteered for the midnight watch along with one of the pole men from boat #2. I thought to use the time off the boat for some training with Troubles. Throughout our trip, I would largely use deer jerky and some smoked fish for training treats, along with liberal praise. Luckily for me, Troubles responded well to both rewards. Some folks trained dogs by beating them for their transgressions. Father always said that kind of training led dogs to obey only out of fear, not out of love, or loyalty. A dog holding no true loyalty to his master might run off or might skulk away in a crisis. On the other hand, a good well-trained dog, owing loyalty to his master could usually be counted on, and might even be an ally against many dangers. Such a dog might even be willing to give his life if necessary.

Our watch passed uneventfully, and then we got a few hours of sleep.

The second day we traveled in intermittent rain and falling temperatures. We put in on the south shore before nightfall, where a large creek emptied into the Ohio. Again, a fire proved impossible, and I volunteered for the midnight watch.

As we began our watch, the rain turned to sleet. Troubles was keen to track critters, the scent of which he had picked up along the shore. We were working on getting him to disengage from that occupation upon my command. To be certain, he was extremely motivated by jerky or any food that he did not have to secure by his wits, as he had done back in Pittsburgh. But he also had an uncommon desire to please me and to not let me down. I was convinced that my earlier assessment of his potential was correct, or maybe a little incorrect, in that daily he was proving to be smarter and better than I had imagined. And that is saying a great deal since I was already mightily impressed with him. I again wondered about his early months and possible owner, but that speculation led to no real conclusions, except that he had not always been a stray.

After our two hour shift, we were relieved by two of the Fort Washington recruits. It was now snowing heavily. We went into the hold of #1 boat and curled up under some blankets as the temperature plummeted. The snow thickened and fell in big wet flakes. For the moment, the weather was our immediate enemy more so than Indians.

We awoke in the morning to more than a half-foot of snow on the ground and still coming down at a ferocious pace. The river was swollen from the rain. Ice floes absent on our trip this far, were now present, having entered the Ohio from tributaries up-river above Pittsburgh.

Captain explained, "Come down from the breakup way a'past Pittsburgh, on the Mongahela and Allie-ginny." He always seemed to shorten Monongahela, and to put particular emphasis on his version of the word "Allegheny." He enjoyed the way he said it the way some men enjoy a good pipe.

"T'ain't ideal to travel the river with floes present, but I spect we'll be alright."

"Specting" we'd be alright was not exactly comforting to me. I was not particularly used to river travel, and this was the biggest river I had ever seen. The fact that I was a strong swimmer offered some sense of comfort, but then again, who wanted to have to swim in an icy, high-speed current.

What Captain was saying was that the increased volume of water and the current speed would hurry us down the river, though not without the danger of unexposed snags as well as the ice floes. These, combined with the difficulty of steering our heavily laden boats at such speeds, did pose a considerable hazard. However, the Le Beau company existed for-profit and the faster a trip was made, the sooner the crew could return to assist with future trips. Captain saw the opportunity, dangerous though it was, for increased speed. Since one never knew what delays might lie ahead, any opportunity to gain some time was taken. We pushed off and moved rapidly downriver.

It was snowing hard, hard enough that visibility was an issue. We did our best to maintain our position in the middle of the river. We had traveled two or three hours covering a great distance when we came to a sharp bend where a stream emptied into the river from the north shore, and also one on the south shore. These were nearly directly opposite each other. It was at this point that some considerable trouble began.

It seemed that all the water coming down river so fast, combined with what was emptying in from each stream, created a large eddy, or whirlpool opposite the bend. With either luck or skill, our boat negotiated the turn without being swept northward toward the whirlpool. At this point, Captain brought our boat sharply about and to shore on the south bank of the river. There we anchored, to observe the fate of the other boats, there being virtually no chance of our assisting them.

The #2 boat was not so fortunate and was swept right across the river sideways into the whirlpool. It came out backward with such a lurch that two crewmen went overboard into the icy Ohio, and were swept ahead of the boat, which was now traveling out of control toward a huge ice jam. The jam appeared to be hung up on a giant fallen tree. The fallen tree may have itself been snagged on rocks, or other unknown impediments beneath the water.

The two unfortunate men were swept toward the ice jam, with the #2 boat trailing a short distance behind, but coming on rapidly, hellbent on slamming into the ice. One man seeing that what was about to happen was lethal, and being a confident swimmer, ducked under the water no doubt in hopes of going below the snag, perhaps under the tree and on. That bit of clever thinking saved him from the flatboat, and we saw him bob up on the other side of the jam.

Unfortunately, he being nearest the opposite shore to our position, was swept on downstream with no hope of assistance from us, the current being so swift as to put even the very best of swimmers into the immediate danger of life and limb. He rapidly disappeared from our view as we watched helplessly. His only hope would be to somehow get to shore, or to at least get snagged up close to shore by another downed tree or other debris. Beyond that, he'd have to get out of the water quickly or die of exposure.

Helplessly, we watched as the other man, who was snagged up on the ice jam, was about to be hit by the #2 boat, crushing his head between the ice that was supported by the tree trunk and the boat. Three boatmen tried gallantly to limit the impact with their poles, with two poles snapping in half, such was the force. After the impact, others were able to drag the man aboard #2, as the boat was now nearly still and completely snagged. We saw the unmistakable flow of blood pouring forth from a huge gash in his face. His lack of movement inclined us to the view that the hapless boatman was dead.

This was not the end of our horror, however, as now the #3 boat, lagging back a ways, came round the bend, missing the whirlpool, but being driven by the current straight toward the #2 boat. There was nothing that could prevent the inevitable crash of #3 into the # 2 boat. There was however, enough time for both crews to brace themselves, and that coupled with the skill of the #3 pilot, avoided a direct hit from his bow to the side of #2. Nevertheless, even the glancing blow did some considerable damage to both boats, though thankfully no one was thrown into the torrent.

From our vantage point we could see, though the snow was some considerable impediment, what was happening. However, we heard none of the sounds, the screams, the yells, the collisions, nothing. The wind blew ferociously, and the swollen river roared while the snow pelted us to near distraction. No doubt there was much sound occurring at the point of the catastrophe, but we heard none of it.

We now shifted into rescue mode. Captain, knowing full well that we were worthless on the south shore, weighed anchor and pushed off. With he and another man on the rudder, we set a course as best we could for the opposite shore. With the current being so swift, the best we could hope for would be a landing a considerable distance downstream from the accident. The only good thing was that neither the #2 nor the #3 boat were able to move. Of course, the bad part about all this was that it left them susceptible to further damage from ice flows, or other debris coming downstream and crashing into them.

We struggled mightily, but finally made the shore, some 50-75 rods on downstream from the accident. It took us nearly an hour to accomplish this. We landed, dropped anchor, and tied off on a gigantic oak tree. Captain and his crew, along with the courier, raced along the shoreline back upstream to assist our comrades, leaving the two recruits to guard #1 boat. Until they saw them coming toward them, those on the #2 and #3 boats did not know what had become of us, since we had made land out of their sight.

Now the danger became overcoming the accident, the weather, and of course, our being on the north shore. We were now in Indian country. Before parting I encouraged my comrades to remain vigilant, but I informed them that Indians were highly unlikely to be about the river in weather such as this. Troubles and I headed west, along the north shore, with we intended to find out what had become of our man that had been swept away downriver.

We followed the shoreline some 200 rods or so. During this time, we found not a trace of the missing man. With Troubles alternately leading the way, and sometimes at my heels, we ran back upstream to assist in the rescue. By the time that we arrived, we found that the crews of the stranded boats had the wherewithal to tie them together. This had the dual effect of stabilizing them from repeatedly being dashed into one another and also guarded against one possible breaking free and being swept downriver.

A couple of brave crewmen had been able to jump, swim, and wade to shore with ropes attached to them. These, they then tied off on two stout maple trees that stood side by side. With a combination of adding more ropes and strenuous pulling, the trees provided leverage enough to get the boats to the edge of the shoreline. In this matter we were aided by the ice jam, in that it had the effect of creating something like a small artificial harbor. And though the current flowed swiftly through this harbor, nonetheless, it was buffered at the point of the ice flow and downed tree, and was strong enough to hold the boats snagged if they should break their mooring.

The #2 boat was severely damaged and was not river worthy. Since it was not possible to pull the #1 boat upstream against the current, we were forced to have two separate camps. It was now mid-afternoon, and we were grounded until we could make repairs.

Upon arriving at the wreck site, I inquired of the injured crewman and found, to my surprise that he was alive, but seemingly just barely so. He was below in the #3 boat and was unconscious, his breathing very shallow. Informing Captain that I had some medical training, I began to simultaneously exam the man and to bark out orders.

"Bring a bucket of snow," I cried.

"What the hell for?" came the reply from the largest of the crewmen.

"Son of a bitch!" I bellowed. "Just do it! Do you want this man to die?"

This outcome was already a foregone conclusion in my mind, when looking at the man, but words that come out in anger are not always logical.

A bucket of snow was produced by Captain, and with the large crewman muttering about a "wet behind the ears kid" ordering real men around for crazy reasons, I put as much of the wet snow in a thin cloth as I could, squeezed it to form an ice ball, and then applied it to the eight-inch gash that extended from the injured man's chin up the left side of his face, ending well above his left ear. The ear was partly severed and so was a chunk of his scalp. I was attempting to reduce the immediate swelling a bit. His icy plunge in the river had lowered his body temperature and thus limited the bleeding after the original gushing. It probably didn't hurt the swelling either.

"Blankets, I need lots of blankets," I hollered.

The man's icy clothing had been pulled off, and he was already wrapped in two blankets, but shivering uncontrollably. I wrapped him in the additional blankets, as Captain held the snow compress in place. I now began to massage his limbs to help warm him. I needed more light, and was brought two torches held by crewmen who were friends of the injured man. I was hopeful that we had no gunpowder on #3 boat. I asked for the hatchway to be covered to keep out the wind.

At this point, enough swelling had gone down that I could see the man's nose was broken and displaced so that it touched the left side of his face. This no doubt, accounted for his breathing being shallow and through his mouth. Old Doc Johnson had once had me help him set a broken arm. And although an arm and a nose are two very different appendages, the lesson learned afforded me a starting place for resetting the nose.

Since he was still unconscious, I had Captain hold his head with both hands while I placed the heel of my left hand between his nose and right cheek, using my fingers to pull the nose to the right, while at the same time, pushing upward and to the right, with my right hand against the nose, I heard a snap and then a groan. I took the groan as a good sign, but I could tell the position of the nose, while much improved, was not quite right. Securing my left thumb in his right nostril, I pinched the nose just below the bridge, between my right thumb and forefinger. I then pushed to the right in a quick and strenuous motion. Again, some sound came from the nose and the man. It looked much better, not quite normal, but darn close. With that, I decided I had exhausted my luck in re-setting noses.

I could not tell if any bones in his face or head were broken. The right eye was a swollen slit and had he been conscious, there is no way he could have opened it. Now, I decided to stitch the wounds while the man was still unconscious. I got thread from my kit and sewed for two hours, finally reattaching the severed portions of the ear and the scalp, the best that I could. My patient came to twice during this time, and I had Captain administer a stiff shot of whiskey each time. When I had finished, I soaked the gash in whiskey and covered it with the cleanest linen that we could produce. To this we applied ice balls of squeezed snow.

"Nothing to do now, Captain, but keep him warm and wait. I don't know if he'll make it," I said. "I think he may be hurt beyond the help of any man, certainly beyond mine."

"Jariah," Captain said, calling me by my Christian name instead of the usual sonny, or son. "That was some fine work. Where'd you learn how to doctor?"

"Well," I said, "I worked with old Doc Johnson back in Williamsburg."

Captain replied, "Well it looks like he teached you a lot. I never seen any doctoring sich as that a'fore. No sirree, that was something to look on."

My only word was thanks, as I moved out of the boat. Perhaps I needed something to let off steam, and I had something in mind. It was something stuck in my craw.

I went to the campfire, which had been started with some

gunpowder off #2 boat. With the wind and snow ferocious, some crewmen had found a very tiny clearing amid some thick pine trees, and there built the fire with some degree of shelter.

I said, "Just who was it took offense at my asking for a bucket of snow?" I knew damn well who it was.

Having thrown down the gauntlet, I heard, "That would be me boy. Got a problem?"

Well, I did have a problem, and I didn't like my judgment doubted when dealing with a crisis, and now I also didn't like being called boy, by a man who had, by my reckoning, done precious little by way of helping the injured man that I had been working on for hours. Throughout my hours with the injured man, only one thing interrupted my concentration, the comment, "a wet behind the ears kid."

Where I came from a person on the frontier was accorded a certain respect, regardless of age, and in Virginia, I figured I had earned respect. I guess I just hated the type of person who would comment on that in a crisis. Now I had worked myself way past angry, I was mad-dog mad, and I was spoiling for the only thing that was going to shed me of that mindset. I suppose that in reality I needed some quick stress release, after playing the part of a doctor for a critically injured man.

Rather than further talk discussing my problem, as he stepped forward as if to intimidate me by his girth, which was quite considerable, with three quick blows I rendered the man lying semi-conscious in the snow. I suppose in tavern parlance it would have been said that I beat the hell out of him. That was my exact intent. I had a little of my father in me, or maybe a lot. He and Dan Morgan would have been proud. Mother, on the other hand, would have been mortified that her oldest son acted as a common ruffian. But my stress was relieved and as a result, my traveling companions had a new respect for the boy from Virginia, especially since my victim was a very large man. I had struck a blow for equality, something the frontier was supposed to be famous for assuming. But mostly I just did it because I could not stop myself. I realized the character flaw but had no desire to correct it.

The short fight produced another what I considered a fortunate piece of information. As the brutish boatman had begun to posture in regards to me, Troubles had jumped between us snarling and baring his teeth at my antagonist. Only my proficiency with my fists had protected the lout from a dog attack. I was again reinforced in my opinion of my new dog.

As the snow continued, and we gathered about the fire, Captain said, "We'll have to stop here a few days to see if we can fix #2. It t'won't be easy, but one er' my pole men is a carpenter, and two of d'others helped to build deez boats. I think we'll be fine."

The last time he thought we'd be fine was starting off the day traveling in an ice jammed river. I had my doubts.

Jerky and biscuits were the fare again for supper. I told Captain I wanted to return downriver to check on the men left guarding the keelboat, but he said he needed me to stay and keep watch over Hawkins, which was the injured man's name. He sent five recruits, and two boatmen to spend the overnight at the #1 boat. After eating, they left following the shore westward.

During the sleepless hours of the night, I had cause to ask myself what no one else had. Why had I not disclosed my medical training, and gone straight for the injured man when #1 boat was landed and secured? The darkness of the night is, and always has been, a time for a person to ask themselves such difficult, soul-searching, questions. As I thought about it, I told myself that the status of the man swept away in the icy current was an unknown, and as such, those of us raised on the frontier, were predisposed to seek after helping the living, or those who might be alive. I may have figured that there was little to be done for the injured boatman. Also, I had Troubles and figured my dog was likely to alert me to the missing man if he were snagged up in the water, or if he had managed to clamber ashore. Maybe I reacted instinctively searching for the man who had no one else with him, no one looking for him and no possible help.

In the end, my final answer, or what continued as a self-question, was whether I avoided going to the injured man for fear that I would not know what to do, that I would be confronted with injuries I was incapable of handling, or that I might even hasten his demise with my inexperience? To this day, I do not have a definite conclusion about my actions on that day. One thing that I do know is that I did the best I could. I don't know if I was right, or wrong, but it is something now lost in time, though not yet lost to memory.

It was a restless and fitful night of moans and groans, as well as twitches, for Hawkins. His head moved often from side to side even though he was not conscious. He was a critically injured man, and he would be lucky to make it through the night. How he was not killed outright, I did not understand. I was to later discover, in talking to those who had been closest to the accident, that as the ice slashed his face, caused by the boat hitting the left-right side of his head, and driving his left side into the ice, that the ice had broken and given way. Had it been thicker, Hawkins' head would have been crushed between the boat and the ice jam. Of course, at the time of the accident we were far enough away to only see the events distantly, and to presume that is exactly what had happened.

About two hours before daylight, Hawkins seemed to be gaining consciousness and emitting low groans. I slugged some more whiskey down him, a considerable amount, and mixed in some powdered hemp flower from my kit. The combination of the two painkillers put him out for the next several hours.

It was during this time that I discovered that he was having chilblains.[1] I wrapped his hands and feet in rags that had been held near the fire and hoped that would ease some portion of his suffering.

The snowstorm had continued all night, and by morning seemed to have achieved the status of full-blown blizzard. Snow was now over three feet deep along the riverbank, and the trees were thickly covered, with their branches straining under the weight of the snow. Our entire contingent hunkered down in the holds of the two boats that day, except for a small party, that went to relieve the men at the #1 boat. Nothing would get done until the storm abated. My job was to stay with Hawkins. The pilot of #3 boat spelled my vigil, so I could sleep nearby on some sacks of flour.

When I awoke after a few hours, it was to find Hawkins conscious and much improved. I made him some willow leaf soup, mixed with just a bit of crumbled biscuits. I asked Captain to watch him, and give him some more of this mixture in a few hours if the current meal stayed down. In the meantime, I asked that we keep a snowpack on his face to reduce the swelling which was markedly improved.

I told Captain that I was going to take Troubles off into the woods a ways. The snow had now stopped.

He asked, "What fer?"

"We need the exercise, and it won't hurt to look about," I said.

"You'll find neither man ner beast about in this weather," he retorted.

My father had often set off in abominable weather with young dogs, figuring that it was the best way to expose them to adversity. He considered this an excellent training opportunity.

As I had no snowshoes, the going was briefly a bit tough. Once in the forest we were able to poke our way around. The snow not being quite as deep, had been blocked by high trees thickly set together in the forest. I was convinced that few if any dogs alive could track in this weather. I was soon proven wrong. Troubles went off tracking. At first it must have been a faint scent, but as we moved deeper into the woods, I was able to discern some tracks. They appeared to be made by wolves.

"C'mon fella," I said. "We don't need any wolf trouble."

Troubles reluctantly left the scent and followed me off in another direction. While I was glad that he obeyed, I was also amazed at his coming upon the wolf scent in this weather, to begin with, and with his reluctance to give up the chase. We now took a course more closely following the river west.

We passed the #1 boat and stopped to visit for a few minutes, inquiring about the man that had been swept away. His fate had still not been discovered, but he was most assuredly dead. We left and walked the shoreline.

Half a league, or so down the river, only a bit further than we had originally gone when first we had landed the #1 boat, Troubles rushed ahead of me making a grisly discovery. It was the body of the man who had gone overboard and been swept away by the current. The body was frozen stiff and covered with snow. It was not bloated, owing to the cold. Something immediately caught my eye. It was the top of the man's head. His scalp was partly laid bare. Upon closer examination, the unmistakable conclusion was that the man had been scalped.

I looked for signs of Indians, but the snow had covered up any that may have been there, and Troubles was having problems finding any scent. There was very little blood, but some bits of hair were still attached in the scalped area, a most unusual occurrence. I concluded that the man was dead and frozen stiff when he was scalped. If that were the case, some Indian was probably intending to boast of his prowess in war, when in actuality his attaining the scalp was more accident than anything. Even among the redmen, some don't mind a bit of dishonesty or taking advantage of Providence, if it serves their purpose.

I imagine the victim had either made it to shore and then froze to death, or had gotten hung up on a snag near the shore. He had died before he was found. No scuffle, no struggle, just a bit of a rough job to do pulling off a frozen scalp, for whatever Indian had done the deed. It may have been a young teenage brave who took advantage of the situation to possibly secure his first war trophy.

I packed more snow around the dead man and covered him with branches. There was no way to bury him in this weather, had I even the shovel to do so. The fact most disturbing to me was that Indians had been here sometime within the last 24 hours. Indians normally don't go about in winter storms. I made a conjecture that it was a small raiding party, caught off guard by the weather, just as our little expedition had been.

Just then Troubles alerted me to something sticking up from the snow. Going to him, I brushed away the snow to discover a canoe turned upside down. For me that confirmed that it had been a very small party, most likely coming back across the river from the south shore. That meant that it may have been less likely to have been a party intentionally watching the river more closely than usual, because they knew troops, and supplies were regularly coming down on their way to Fort Washington. However, just by their discovering the body of the dead man, our plight may have been uncovered. Indians could be racing for help, thinking that if the dead man floated downriver by the current, upriver there just might be a boat in trouble to be plundered.

Troubles and I made a quick trip back to the #1 boat and told them our story. At this time, with men having gone back and forth, there were nine men total at #1. That fact didn't surprise me, as #1 held most of the whiskey bound for Fort Washington.

I told the men around #1 to keep their guns handy and to stay alert. I encouraged the cessation of drinking. I doubted a small

group of Indians would attack, but if they had gone for rein-
forcements, they might by now be on their way back toward us. I
was counting on the weather rendering this nearly impossible,
even while doubt raced through my mind.

I hurried on to boats, #2 and #3, and after I explained the situation, Captain ordered a two-man guard at all times. He passed
out arms for all the men to keep at hand. The carpenters had
rigged a sort of hoist and pulled the boats out of the water, aided
by snow as a lubricant on the bottoms, avoiding dragging them
directly across rocks. They were proceeding with repairs, and I
was impressed at their progress thus far. These were men who
knew what they were doing.

It was good to see Hawkins having some salt pork and biscuits. He would survive.

"I understand that I owe you my life young man," he said, with
the gratitude in his soft, gravelly, voice evident.

"No," I said, "I think you owe your life to those that pulled you
from the river. I mostly just patched and sewed, and tried to ease
the pain."

"At any rate, I'm mighty grateful," he replied. "Are you a doctor?"

"No," I was forced to admit, "I wanted to be one, and I had a
mighty fine teacher for a while, but I guess those days are gone."

After that Hawkins inquired about my home, my family, my
reasons for going west, and so forth, before falling back to the
sleep that those who are severely injured seem to so desperately
require for recovery. I had just made a friend. I, was more than a
little bit excited about his progress, especially given those
self-recriminations that I previously explained. I also gave a silent thanks to old Doc Johnson for how well he had taught me,
and to the good Lord for his assistance in the matter. Regarding
Doc Johnson, no one knows how well they've learned what they
have been taught, and how they will respond, until they've been
put to the test. I imagined he would have been proud of his pupil.

As we ate supper around a fire, in the course of the conversation, I learned that the man whom I'd had my brief fight with the
day before, was named John McGilvey. It turns out that he was
the one most responsible for some of the decisions that had
lessened the impact when the #2 and #3 boats collided. He was
also the one who pulled Hawkins from the water. This gave me a

little remorse for having misjudged him.

During the evening he commented to me, "Mighty fine punch you pack, son."

"Yeah, sorry about that," I said.

"Not too many men ever bested me in a fight," he said. "Course that fight was over before I knew we wuz fightin. No one ever got a lick in on me so sudden like. You're a quick one."

I wasn't sure whether he was indicating he thought he'd been sucker-punched or caught off guard, but it soon became evident that was not the case.

"Let's put it behind us," I said. "My ma taught me not to fight."

Given my youth, the fact that I had nearly knocked John out, and the fact that I was now mentioning my mother, the entire company fell into a hearty laugh.

"T'aint no hard feelings from me," he said.

That was a bit of a relief to me, as we still had a long way to Fort Washington, and I thought for certain I had made an enemy. It turns out that I had made another friend. Some things just turn out a great deal differently than one expects.

We passed the night changing watches every two hours, while the carpenters worked by the light of campfire and torches. The night was clear, cold, and starlit. My mind wondered about Indians, despite the cold and extremely deep snow. Troubles and I used four, or five hours to scour the surrounding woods, and work on our training. Having mastered so much already, I was beginning to wonder if I might run out of things to teach him.

Morning dawned crisp and cold, but with sunny blue skies. Hawkins was moving about. Captain sent Troubles and I in search of fresh meat, but we all knew it was a fool's errand. It would take a warmup, and some melt off before game began to stir.

The Le Beau Company had chosen their crewmen well. The carpenter and two men who had helped build these boats affected repairs that I would have guessed impossible, and they finished the work before nightfall. Between their skill, and the grunt labor of the other crewmen, the speed and quality of repairs were a marvel to me.

The next morning dawned with the skies again clear and the temperature warmer. Attached to ropes, several men waded into the icy water, and after a short time of hard work, with axes and other tools, broke away the tree, along with other debris, sending it on its way downstream. As I said, it had provided a sort of natural harbor for us. This was only fair since it had also caused our woes the past couple of days. We were now clear to resume our journey, and by noon we were on our way.

About an hour before noon we had "hallooed" two flatboats, of a rival company, passing by on the river. The current was still swift, and, so there was no opportunity for them to land, or to exchange news. We signaled that we were fine, and they continued down the river where the current carried them swiftly out of sight. The flatboats set out and Troubles and I, along with a few others, ran along the shore to board the #1 boat. The path, now well-worn from so much transit back and forth between the two camps. We boarded and pushed off, the flatboats being ahead, but still visible on the river.

Our progress was quick, too quick, too quick to be safely controlled. We had entered a flood plain area, and the Ohio had left its banks well above the flood stage. Our speed, combined with the danger of hidden obstacles and the rising water level, put us in many types of danger, including ending up well out into the flood plain, on what would normally be dry land. In this event we could easily lose the channel and current, and maybe even be grounded. The temperature now began to warm a good bit. This would mean more snow melt off and more rising water. This was all potentially lethal, and so Captain signaled all boats to put into an inlet on the south shore. This was done with considerable effort. We tied off to trees that were normally onshore but now were half underwater. There was no dry land in view, and leaving the boats was impossible. We would be stranded here for some undetermined time.

We ate a cold meal on the boats and broke out some of the whiskey, with Captain carefully rationing each man's share, lest trouble develop in the form of intoxication. Moderation is a value not practiced well by undisciplined men, especially when in the wilderness, there is little else to while away the time.

We did our normal watches except that these were done on the boat and frankly, fear of surprise attack was virtually nil. As such, that endeavor by the Indians was a near impossibility, just in terms of getting within musket range.

During the night the water rose another two feet and so did our boats.

"Nothing to do but wait for calmer waters," Captain said.

And so, we passed that day and the next, playing cards, smoking, and sleeping. We discussed the scalped man, Ogden, but there was not a lot to be said, except how unfortunate the whole affair was. I knew Captain was holding himself accountable, and a few of the men were thinking in the same manner. My experience and thoughts were that, what was, just was and it was now past. Focusing on the moment was the only thing that we could control.

The weather continued to warm and was now quite spring-like. We saw the last ice floes go by at mid-morning of the second day. We could tell the river was slowly trying to return to normal.

Hawkins was doing just fine and had returned to light duty. His face didn't look great, but he was in good spirits. As the swelling receded, he had full use of both eyes, and I felt certain that he had no broken skull bones, but was uncertain about those in his face. He complained some of headaches, and his nose was clearly bothering him, but overall, he was doing quite well. By now we had lost well over six days of travel time.

Eventually, Captain determined the river to be safe to resume our trip. The Ohio was sinking below flood stage now, and we set out by mid-morning.

There was some comment among the crews as to whether we might once again see the two boats that had previously passed us.

We traveled two days without incident, sometimes camping near a bluff of dry land, and sometimes tying up to trees, and always staying aboard the boats. Each day the weather grew warmer, and the river continued to return to its normal rhythms.

One morning we had gone about an hour downstream, when we could see a disturbing scene on the river's north shore. There, were the smoking remnants of the two flatboats that had passed us days before. Onshore were several bodies, bloody and mutilated beyond recognition, had we known them.

"Injuns, Injuns, Injuns," the call went from one boat to the other, and back again.

Men scrambled for muskets and rifles as we steered past the site. There was no sign of life on the shore. Even had there been, stopping would have been foolhardy, and placed us in grave jeopardy. The Indians were known to employ tricks such as setting wounded individuals in prominent positions where they could cry out for help from those on the river or often using a white captive to lure unsuspecting boats to shore, only to be attacked. Often these white captives had become Indians and were willing participants in the trap.

The scene haunted our thoughts the rest of that day and into the evening, as we steered to a creek to put in for the night on the south shore. Being some bit of daylight left, Troubles and I immediately set off scouting the area and looking for game. Traveling some 150 rods on open ground and then into the woods, Troubles came upon deer scent, and a bit further his pursuit surprised the beast who nearly jumped upon us. One quick shot and the deer was down and dead. It was a young doe, and I slung it over my shoulders and headed back for camp, self-impressed with how quickly I had secured the evening meal.

I was happy that Troubles had tracked well, but a bit annoyed, that he allowed the deer to surprise us, about as much as we surprised her. Still, discipline on the trail was a work in progress, and we had not been together that long. Maybe I was expecting too much out of a dog that was essentially little more than a pup. But it was his exceptional nature to date that had put my expectations so high. Then I realized no one is perfect, and that includes the perfect dog.

My sense of importance was not lessened any, as praise was heaped upon me from all around when I appeared with the deer. Sitting around the campfire after eating, the conversation turned to the scene that we had viewed that morning.

Some of the greener men out from the east wondered aloud if we shouldn't have gone ashore and buried the dead, then looked for possible survivors. Captain quickly put an end to that talk by explaining some of the things he had seen along the river last summer.

"We cud all be dead. Those red devils just waiting for us to come ashore," he relayed.

I doubted it in this case because there was no bait to lure us. I supposed the raiding party had done their dastardly deed and moved on. However, Captain was right, there was no use in risking it. Just when you think you know Indian behavior you find out that you are wrong.

The images of the morning caused us to triple the guard that night as we went to sleep pondering the fates of our traveling brethren, and of the enemy into whose country we had come. I supposed everyone tossed and turned some as I did.

Camp came to life while all was still dark. Captain liked to be on the river by first light if at all possible. Pork was sizzling on the fire when Troubles began to bark ferociously. Suddenly a shot rang out, and a crewman fell motionless to the ground some distance from me. War whoops followed more shots, and one sentry was dead where he stood against a tree, a musket ball through the side of his head. Still trying to rouse ourselves to arms, and to overcome the initial shock, we were rocked by more musket fire and a few arrows.

Then came a full-scale attack as the heathens descended from the woods, shrieking their hideous cries with war clubs, tomahawks, and knives at the ready. As we had yet to discharge our guns, we now did so with the effect of killing four, or five of our attackers in one barrage.

The outward most sentries fell amid the onslaught while Captain, firing his pistol, dispatched one attacker who was closing rapidly on him. Shooting now came from the few crewmen still in the boats. This brought down a few more of the savages, and I dropped one black-faced demon with a shot from my knees upward through the bridge of his nose, just short of the well-known, right between the eyes shot.

As the remainder fell upon us, hand to hand fighting ensued with axes, tools off the boat, knives and even a few more muskets. This close-in fighting was akin to the brawling that river crews are famous for. Throw in a few hatchets, sledges, and poles from the boat, along with the instruments mentioned above, and we had some serious hand-to-hand fighters on our side.

As I looked to my right after my last shot, I caught sight of Troubles in midair, sailing high off the ground toward the face of a very surprised savage. He had not seen Troubles coming, and the dog took him to the ground in fear and surprise. His first thought may well have been that we had a pet wolf. Troubles was relentless, and I ran to his assistance, where my tomahawk finished what he had started.

In hand to hand combat, no one proved more fierce than John McGilvey. Just before I engaged an attacker with knives, I saw John take a tomahawk blow to this left shoulder, withstand the blow, and deck two Indians with a log that I doubted I could have lifted. He then fell upon the two with vengeance, and they were dispatched without ever having regained their feet. He then grabbed another onrushing brave and tossed him, in one motion, into the campfire.

After that I was occupied with my issues, but owing to my size, and the fact that my immediate opponent was a teenager, I easily overcame him. As I did so, I turned to see McGilvey grab from behind me a fearsome-looking fellow with a black face with white stripes. The Indian had his war club raised, intent on bashing in my brains. John held him by the throat and off the ground, with his feet running in midair. John then planted his boatman's knife in the man's gut, finishing him off. As he did so, he was shot from behind by an Indian wielding a pistol. Troubles ran the shooter over and was clubbed by the handle of the pistol. This irritated him, and he ripped the man's throat wide open. He then tore his off part of his face. I moved over to put my knife through the man's heart, but I doubted it was necessary.

At this point the attack ended as quickly as it had begun, with the biggest of the Indians giving a howl, sounding the retreat. They had underestimated our fighting ability. At the howl, the remaining dozen, or so warriors withdrew into the woods from whence they had come, like ghosts leaving just before the dawn.

I ran to where McGilvey had fallen, but he was dead. He had saved my life, and he was now beyond my help or repayment. Hawkins was down nearby having been shot in the stomach.

As I came to him, he muttered, "Sorry, not this time, Doc," and then he expired. In all we lost seven men, but counted 15 dead attackers.

Now the faint glow of the sun shone in the east, and we pulled our dead onto the boats, gathered our gear and made haste in departing. We had acquitted ourselves well in recovering from the initial shock and surprise of the attack, but we had paid a dear price as well.

Once in mid-channel, we assessed our damages. In addition to the seven dead men, we had another four wounded, all of whom had been put in the keelboat for my care. Only one was seriously wounded, and he passed away within an hour after we joined the river. He had sustained an arrow through his left lung. His last hour was pure hell, gasping for breath and moaning in pain. I had given him some pain-killing herbs, but they never had time to work.

Whether our attackers would have mounted a second attempt, we could not know, but I doubt it; they had sustained too many losses. Being attacked on the Kentucky side of the river was unusual in itself. This was likely to have been a raiding party come back from an incursion into Kentucky, and not the same group who had created the grizzly scene on the north shore the day before. They had likely come upon our camp during the night and sought to pick up some additional booty and perhaps some scalps.

John McGilvey's death increased my guilt over the fight we had, but it also saddened me like none before, except that of my parents. I had such a welling up of emotion, tears streaming down my face, greater than even what I felt when I first heard of the death of my grandparents. Big John was a brave man indeed, and he had died a brave death while saving my life. Physically I was fine and Troubles likewise. He too, like John McGilvey, was a true hero.

That day we made great distance downriver, putting ashore early that night to bury our dead on a bluff overlooking the river. We slept on the boats, with double sentries being changed on the hour, instead of every two hours. This meant that most of us took two shifts that night. The next morning, we left Big John, Hawkins, and the others of our companions, in the dark rich earth of the Kentucky countryside.

The rest of the trip was uneventful. We had no other Indian trouble or sign. We lost a couple more days for more repairs of the #2 and #3 boats, which were taking on some water. When we camped, Troubles and I almost always were able to provide fresh meat for the evening meal. Every day I put that dog through a regimen of training off the boat and a good bit in the water. He had a knack for swimming and took to it as if having been bred for it. My father had some great dogs, but this was the single finest dog I had ever known. And, he was a great friend to me. I was mighty proud of that dog.

We landed at Fort Washington on April 5, 1790, our trip had taken much longer than expected and had cost us the lives of many good men.

Chapter Six

Fort Washington

Fort Washington

I lept from the #1 boat, finally reaching my destination, and despite the downpour and the gloominess of the day, my gaze was immediately drawn about 175 rods up the flood plain to the magnificent structure that was Fort Washington. The edifice dominated the landscape. I could see immediately how the Indians would take umbrage at this outpost being located on their side of the river. It was a fort to best all forts. It had a stone foundation and reinforced walls. Its four-square sides were formed by the walls of two-story buildings on each side of the square. The gates of the fort faced the Licking River, a tributary of the Ohio. On the north and west side of the fort were ravelins[1] that only added to the defensive capabilities of the structure, already provided by five, two-story blockhouses. All these with canons on the top floors.

As I later learned my way about the fort, I ascertained that there was, in addition to headquarters: an officers' quarters, enlisted quarters, commissary quarters, clothiers store, galley port, hospital, blacksmith, carpenter, armorer, wheelwright and turn-ers' areas. It was essentially a self-contained town.

Inquiring as I jogged toward the fort, I followed the directions that I received and soon found myself in the headquarters of General Josiah Harmar. The General was the senior officer of the entire United States Army, having followed George Washington and Henry Knox respectively, into that position. After waiting in a large ante-room, with a roughly hewn wooden floor, two chairs, and a bench, I was called into the general's office.

Josiah Harmar was a thin man of roughly average height. He had a broad forehead made all the more so for the fact that his hairline didn't begin until about a third of the way back on his head. His mouth was small and pursed. He had a long nose, turned slightly downward, not completely unlike the beak of a bird of prey. His most striking features were his eyes. They were dark and piercing, giving the impression of someone extremely alert to his environment, again not unlike a bird of prey.

During the late Great War for Independence, Josiah Harmar had started as a captain and finished as a colonel, serving along the way under Generals Washington and Henry Lee, both Virginians. Harmar himself was from Philadelphia where he had received a Quaker education.

Following the war, he had the honor of being named courier for delivering the Congressionally ratified Treaty of Paris back to France, to Benjamin Franklin, head of the American peace delegation. Later, he was to serve seven years as the senior-most officer in the U. S. Army. Part of that time his rank was brevet General.

In 1789, having been sent into the Ohio Country to establish a United States presence in the Northwest Territories, General Harmar constructed Fort Washington on orders from Territorial Governor, Arthur St. Clair, himself a distinguished soldier in our country's fight for independence from Britain and former member of Congress. Despite the rain, the place was as alive as a bee-hive in early autumn.

Standing before General Harmar had little resemblance to my earlier visit to Secretary of War, Henry Knox. Harmar was all business, a man shouldering the great burden of preparing to fight an Indian war, as I was to learn, with guns that were broken, bad powder, poorly trained and incredibly ill-disciplined troops.

The general peered over my papers at me as he said, "Well, I suppose Henry wouldn't send me a scout who was not experienced enough to do the job." I took this as a reference to my youthful appearance.

"No, Sir," I said, half confidently, and about half-annoyed at once again dealing with the issue of my age.

"Of course," he continued, "he keeps sending me muskets that are broken, the powder that won't ignite, and men who scarcely resemble soldiers."

His irritation with Henry Knox becoming apparent, and the possible insult to me becoming obvious, my irritation with him was rising to a quick boil.

"I doubt you'll find me defective, Sir," I said, with enough edge in my voice to make my feelings clear.

"Oh, no, no, I'm sure," he said, momentarily causing me to think that he had realized his offense.

But then he mumbled, "Time will most certainly answer many questions." I couldn't tell if he was continuing to offend me, or if he was referring to something else.

My father had taught me to respect my elders, especially those who had successfully served in the Great War. Those lessons may have been the only thing that kept me from delivering a square shot to the jaw of America's highest-ranking officer at that moment. I suppose I shouldn't get irritated so easily, but arrogance and stupidity just seem to get under my skin. His attitude I considered to be a form of arrogance, or all-knowing, that no one could possess. His seeming condescension was just bad manners to me. Bad manners no matter what his rank.

Perhaps sensing my anger, he told me, "See Sergeant Hanks for your billeting. After that, acquaint yourself with the fort and immediate surrounding vicinity, as well as with the other scouts. Dismissed."

And with that I was out the door in search of Sergeant Hanks. My search got me only about three steps out of headquarters before I was approached by a gruff old curmudgeon, who introduced himself as Lowell Hanks, a regular soldier, and veteran of the recent Great War. He had been notified new troops had arrived, and he had come to headquarters expecting to show the men to their bunks. It was at this point that it became clear to me that no information was particularly secret at Fort Washington. He had already heard about the young scout who had doctor skills, the courier, and the other recruits that had accompanied me down the Ohio from Pittsburgh. News traveled around these parts much too fast for my liking.

Lowell Hanks, for all of his crust was a kindly soul. Before long, he adopted a fatherly attitude toward me. I can't say that he treated all the other men as well, but then I can attest that their endeavors were not always as earnest as mine, nor was their respect for him as genuine as mine. Men size each other up and relate not so much on a level of equality, as on a level of fairness that is based upon the mutual interaction one with the other.

To be sure, Hanks teased me about my age, but he often said things like, "Years of experience don't always make idiots soldiers and young men ain't always idiots."

Whenever he said things like that, I just smiled knowingly, whether I did, or did not know what he was talking about. This time I think he got it right in his way, though hardly a ringing endorsement of the talents of youth.

That evening, I had my first taste of army food, and I was not impressed. I was so disgusted that I resolved to provide some fresh meat for the cooks at the fort, hoping the problem was the quality of their supplies, not their skills in cooking those supplies.

Later around a campfire, I became acquainted with several of the soldiers. Some were army regulars, but few like the men who had accompanied me down the Ohio were recruits and others who had been Indian fighters, or woodsmen like myself. The vast majority were men from the east without the means of making a living and hoping that the army would stake them to a start on the frontier. There were farmers, sons of preachers, men who had been indentured servants, apprentices from various trades, even a former banker, some teachers, teamsters, lots of debtors, and many others of various, or previously no occupations. But there were also some former convicts, thieves, drunkards, and lazy, no good, dregs of society. The latter group, I was sure would run at the first site of hostile Indians. For the former group I held some hope that with proper training, some might make decent soldiers. Of course, my main hope for success lay with the regulars, most of whom were veterans of the late war. These veterans were already present at Fort Washington, unlike the various militia troops who had yet to arrive.

That same evening, I was introduced to the other scouts assigned to the expedition by the War Department. There were four others besides myself. The lone white man was a Kentucky backwoodsman named, Jim Tucker. Technically, I guess you could say we were federal, or regular army scouts. Various militias such as the Kentucky militia would bring their scouts.

Tucker said, "I'm from Kaintuckee and if der's anyone don't like it, dey can either run or stand ta take der beating like a man."

He laughed heartily at his boastfulness, and I immediately took a liking to him. He was not an educated man but was just as a man who understood the woods, wild animals, and Indians. Such a man was a comfort to have around when going to war in the dense forests of the Ohio Country. In the following weeks, I was to come to know him as a great shot with a Kentucky long-rifle. To this day, I've seen only a few men who might compare.

The other three scouts were Indians. One was a Choctaw, and two brothers were Chickasaws, up from the Tennessee country.

Black Duck was the Choctaw, probably in his early 30's, he spoke reasonably good English and several Indian dialects. He was Jim Tucker's closest friend on earth, each having saved the other's life upon in various fights, most often as scouts for the Kentucky Militia. As regards that employment, I had been told by Jim that he would never scout for those ass-hole officers of the militia again.

He did not elaborate except to say, "Those dumb-asses cud git a man kilt."

But as for Black Duck, I would come to view him as a quiet man of integrity and dignity. While he spoke little, he was also a fine companion to have in the woods, very smart and always alert.

Gray Otter was the older of the two Chickasaw brothers. Of him I can only say that he was a fat, slovenly, drunkard. He appeared to have come north for no other reason than to drink Kentucky whiskey, for any other spirits that he could obtain. He was as worthless a man as I ever met. Just as many white men are not a credit to their race and do not especially recommend themselves to others, so it was with Gray Otter. He was a despicable Indian. He would have been equally despicable had he been a white man, a black man, a Spaniard, or a Frenchman.

Blue Dogs Run Him was the younger of the Chickasaw brothers. He was of medium height, which made him a good bit shorter than me, but lean and muscular. He was roughly my age. He was a handsome Indian; indeed, he was a handsome man regardless of race. He seemed to realize his good looks and to keep himself clean and well-attired. Never did a man on the frontier present a better appearance. As a youth he had been known as Sleepy Owl. However, like many Indians in their adolescent years, he earned a name more fitting. I was a bit curious about his name. Relying on a bit of French and Black Duck's Chickasaw, I got the gist of his story.

He and his brother had a French mother, who had been captured by a raiding party when she was about 14 years old. She was given as a bride to Blue Dogs' father, who was then a young man of seventeen, or eighteen. She raised her sons to speak French and their native tongue. Indians are often good about language. It seems that they know the power of words and figure that the more languages someone can speak, the better off they will be in life. When they capture a person of another race and turn them into a member of the tribe, they often benefit by having the new language spoken, but only after the captive has learned the Indian language. However, that is not always the case and sometimes in a few short years, captives lose command of their native language.

It seems that as a lad of only 12 or 13 years, Blue Dogs had accompanied a raiding party into a French-occupied area of the Louisiana Territory. As the youngest member of the group, he had been denied a key role in the stealing of French property, and the minimal exchange of gunfire between the French and Chickasaw raiding party. Being a resourceful brave, he ascertained that he would steal some glory for himself using his quick wits. As the Frenchies began the pursuit of the raiding party, they were using their legendary and ancient breed of hunting dogs, the Bleu Gascogne, for trailing the Chickasaws. Indians don't like being trailed by dogs, and while the rest of the group took to the creeks to throw the dogs off the scent, Sleepy Owl absented himself from the group, circled a wide area, then climbed a bluff to take off in another direction through the woods. He dropped pemmican every few feet to ensure that the dogs would continue tracking him. The Frenchies, not knowing that the rest of the party had taken a different route, assumed their dogs were on the trail of the main group.

After safely diverting his pursuers from the main group for several hours, and just as the hounds were within earshot, Sleepy Owl spread some ground up Indian peppers dusted liberally at the end of his trail, along with some nettles that he secured from a nearby bush, just before he crossed a stream. Making a clean get-away, he heard the dogs howling from a distance to indicate that the peppers were indeed burning their nostrils and that the nettles were into the pads of their feet and possibly their noses as well. He had left clear signs at the river, with his moccasin prints, that he was the only Indian crossing the river. This was his way of letting the Frenchies know that they and their famous hounds had been taken in.

When he caught up to the raiding party and relayed the story, he was viewed as a hero. The Bleu Gascogne are pack-hunting dogs. To have outrun and outwitted such a pack was indeed a remarkable achievement. Upon returning to his village, Sleepy Owl immediately achieved the full status of a warrior with the name, Blue Dogs Run Him. Such a name may seem demeaning, or dismissive to the sensibilities of white folks, but to the Chickasaw it was just the opposite. It was a name of extreme veneration and honor.

I could speak a bit of French, Blue Dogs could speak it well, but not so much English. Nevertheless, for whatever reason, we became friends despite our language differences. Maybe it was owing to the similarity in our ages that we were drawn together, a sort of bond against those who discriminated against youth, or maybe it was the common love of the wilderness that we shared. Whatever it was, he was to become a good and trusted companion almost from the first day we met.

Blue Dogs did have the one-character trait that, while I have occasionally noticed it in white men, black men, and even other Indians, was not an innocent trait, and one that could most assuredly have lethal consequences to him. Owing to his good looks and fine body, Blue Dogs was, shall I say, a bit of a ladies' man. And to him, and apparently to the ladies, it made little difference whether the ladies were white, red, or black. Further it seemed to make no difference whether they were single, engaged, married, widowed, slaves, indentured servants, or ladies of noble, or even low birth. He was sometimes forced to be absent for days, or weeks at a time while waiting for some offended husband, or father to go down the river with his family, continuing his plans to be a trader, or settler. In other cases, his absence was to give them time to cool down until convinced by their wives, or daughters that nothing had happened.

I was worried a bit about Black Duck and the Chickasaw brothers getting along. The Choctaw and Chickasaw are cousins, but they were frequently at war with one another. I picked up that information and had some experience of it, in my backwoods travels down south. I needn't have worried. There never occurred any problems between them.

During the week after that first evening, Blue Dogs, Troubles and I provided several deer, twelve wild turkeys, numerous waterfowl, and some two dozen rabbits and squirrels, along with one very large black bear for the cook's larder. We quickly became popular with the soldiers and with the cooks, who had tired of the abuse heaped on them when they served up army food.

During this time Blue Dogs and I became close, and learned to navigate the wilderness as a team, a team that included Troubles as a trusted member. All of this had the effect of a good-natured rivalry with Jim and Black Duck, who seeing our popularity, determined to duplicate our efforts. To that end they were highly successful, and the entire fort ate like kings. Of course, Gray Otter, was a nonparticipant in the hunting portion of the endeavor, but the same could not be said for the eating component.

One night after a particularly successful hunt, a great feast was held. It was here that I first met Arthur St. Clair, recently ensconced at Fort Washington as the Governor of the territory. The fort was built on his orders as I said earlier. He was a Scotsman who had been with Washington when he crossed the Delaware and again at Yorktown. In the middle times, he had surrendered Fort Ticonderoga to British General Burgoyne's overwhelming force. Later he served as President of the Constitutional Convention in Philadelphia. Some historians have suggested that this made him the first President of the United States.

St. Clair was a man of considerable experience and accomplishment, but a man always haunted by the surrender at Ticonderoga. In reality there was nothing else he could have done, except to defend the fort and be slaughtered by a British force over ten times the size of his. Nevertheless, I am told that he always considered it a stain on his military record. No doubt such feelings were encouraged by critics who had never even remotely faced a similar situation. His later appointments and services to his country, point to the fact that he was a man in whom people did put their faith, and against whom only a few ridiculous critics held the Ticonderoga surrender.

St. Clair had heard about my medical assistance on the way out and after inquiring of the men where he might find me, introduced himself after supper that evening. He told me that he had attended medical school at the University of Edinburgh. He then commented on my family friend, Dan Morgan, as a great soldier and patriot. Of course, he knew many of the Randolphs as well. Our talk was cordial, but brief, and then he moved around to speak with as many of the soldiers as he could. I supposed he was attempting to ascertain the general level of morale among the men, and perhaps to take stock of those about to engage in the coming expedition.

Even General Harmar summoned us and told us to keep up the good hunting. He had noticed a steady increase in morale as a result of our endeavors. However, he could not help but conclude our audience with remarks about not neglecting our scouting.

Concerning our scouting, at those times when we had no direct orders from General Harmar, we made Jim the nominal head of scouts, since the army hadn't made any such designations. He wasn't entirely comfortable in that role and rather than actually command, he'd render his opinion on something that needed to be done and then take a vote. We never deviated from his opinion, just reinforcing what mutual respect can accomplish among men.

As scouts the only training in which we were required to participate was shooting practice. After our first five shots on the first day of those drills, we were all excused from further such nonsense. No one could match our shooting. Even Gray Otter was excused, though not because he was ever sober enough to shoot well, but because the drill instructors did not wish to deal with a drunken Indian in front of the recruits.

One day during my second week at the fort, Troubles and I went out unattended by Blue Dogs, who was on one of his unexplained absences. We were northwest of the fort each of us on opposite sides of the same stream, heading northward. By this time Troubles knew innumerable verbal commands and a half dozen, or more hand gestures.

After going some distance, a rainstorm blew up with thunder and plenty of lightning. I could have called Troubles over, but he was busy tracking, and by now I knew he would never stay out of my sight for more than a few minutes without checking on me. Also, the storm being so loud, he would not have heard me. So, I found a stand of pine trees and settled down under them, out of the wind and rain. It was not completely rain-proof, but certainly the density of the branches on such trees afforded some shelter, and reduced the amount of rain hitting me. The fallen pine needles made a nice little ground covering upon which to rest. In front of me was the stream and some short distance behind was me a stand of canebrake. I wasn't too afraid of lightning striking the pine trees above me, because they were immediately adjacent to some towering old oaks. Likely, the oaks would be hit first if lightning were to strike.

The storm was deafening as I looked across the stream for signs of Troubles. Suddenly, he came lickety-split, indicating that something was wrong. He did not have his usual happy countenance but was proceeding, practically running on the water with teeth bared and likely growling, though I could not hear. I stood up. As he neared me, I thought he had gone mad and was coming after me. As he bounded into the air, just to my left, I ducked and dodged to my right.

That move on my part, saved my life, thanks to Troubles. Unknown to me a gigantic male black bear had come out of the canebrake, and was taking a swat at my head with his huge right paw. It would likely have been a death blow for me. However, it never landed, as Troubles sailed overhead and straight into the bear, knocking him down. As he fell, Troubles was securely attached to his neck. He stood and wildly swung both paws at the dog's body with Troubles hanging in mid-air. from the beast's throat. Finally, the bear succeeded in knocking him off. However, instead of being discouraged by the bear's strength and size, Troubles again launched his attack. By this time, I had recovered my sense, as well as my rifle.

It was impossible to shoot without being in danger of hitting Troubles. The bear was whirling this way and then that, trying to shuck Troubles, this time off of his shoulder. When the bear again slammed Troubles away with one of his huge paws, I fired a round into his heart. He fell, rose again, then came after me. I pulled my pistol and shot him through the brain, near-simultaneously falling upon him with my tomahawk. However, he was finished and breathed only a few more labored breaths, expiring with Troubles on his back, tearing into the side of his neck.

I cleaned Troubles' wounds in the stream and the rain did the rest. He licked his wounds and crossed over the stream again, back on the trail that had been interrupted by the bear. He had no thought of rest after his recent exertion. After the rain lessened, I constructed a crude travois to carry the bear meat. I skinned and butchered the bear, keeping aside a huge chunk of meat for Troubles who soon returned. Reflecting on my dog's tenacity, it was clear that the concept of losing the fight to a beast some six to ten times his size was never a concern of Troubles. He fully expected to win his battle with the bear with or without my help. He had saved my life, and my love for him could scarcely be expressed. He was daily reinforcing the wisdom of my father, who had often said that a good frontier dog was worth his weight in gold. That, and the fact that he was my very best friend in the whole world, human or animal, made me smile just thinking about him. For Troubles, it was nothing remarkable, just all a part of our day together.

I should say that bear meat is not much to my liking. First of all, the hide is full of parasites, and the meat has to be boiled nearly all day to gain any semblance of tenderness. Even cutting it in strips and cooking it over an open fire takes considerable time. Nevertheless, the novelty of bear meat was just fine for the soldiers at the fort, and word of our adventure only enhanced our standing among the men. Troubles was now receiving attention from everyone and had become a sort of unofficial part of the fort's contingent. Some soldiers referred to him as, Private Troubles, others had the good sense to call him, Corporal Troubles.

Two days after our incident with the bear, General Harmar summoned me, via Sergeant Hanks, to his headquarters. The general told me that a patrol of regulars had come across Indian signs to the northwest of the fort the afternoon before. He directed that Blue Dogs and I reconnoiter the area and beyond. He suggested we stay out several days, and watch the trails to see who came and went. He said that he had already sent Jim and Black Duck due north before this latest intelligence had arrived at the fort.

The general planned to send Gray Otter to scout for a small patrol of regulars going northeast of the fort. Gray Otter had been in the stockade drying out for a week, and under Lowell Hank's supervision was to be released for patrol. The general's final orders were that, under no circumstances, was anyone to get more than two days' journey distant from the fort.

Asking about for Blue Dogs, I found that he had not returned to the fort following his most recent amorous adventure. However, before dawn the next morning, we discovered that he had returned during the night. After inquiring about a certain French trader with a 16-year-old daughter, he was relieved to find that they were on their way to St. Louis. In French I explained to him our mission and we were off.

We were about a day out when we discovered a campsite abandoned for only a few hours. Upon examining the area, the moccasin tracks, the construction of the fire pit and other more subtle clues, Blue Dogs concluded that some Miami and possibly some Delaware had been there. After using the camp, they appeared to have headed in a straight line toward the Ohio River, which was to say, not in the direction of the fort. As there was evidence of less than ten warriors, we concluded that it was likely a raiding party, either going to see what they could profit along the river or maybe they were headed across to Kentucky.

With Troubles touring the campsite, soaking in the various smells, I decided to see if he could track the raiders. To that end he headed south toward the river. The river several leagues away, we expected that the group would be long gone by the time we arrived.

The trail was not hard for Blue Dogs, or Troubles to follow. However, after traveling about a league, we saw a clear sign that four of the party had headed southeast in the direction of Fort Washington. We might have missed this clue since the small group had climbed atop some rocks on a small hill at the point of the split, while the rest of the group had proceeded to leave a careless amount of tracks. However, Blue Dogs picked up on the tracks ruse, and Troubles caught the scent up and over the rocks, and down the other side. We had no choice but to track the group headed toward the fort. This may have been the group whose signs were discovered by the regulars on patrol two days earlier. They may have been mucking about the area and not on a raiding party. If that were the case, we may have passed just north of them, or perhaps they were even nearby in wait watching us.

We moved rapidly until we approached a heavily wooded ravine that we had to cross. Troubles began to sound the alarm. With difficulty I convinced him to heel, and we lay in the brush attempting to decide what to do. We finally decided to send Troubles straight forward, while Blue Dogs took a more circuitous route to the right and I the same to the left. Moving deliberately, it took several minutes before we reached the bottom of the ravine. Troubles had already been at the bottom for some time, barking in one place. This could only mean he had discovered something, and it was not something fighting back at him, at least not something able to kill him. Upon converging on his position from our separate directions, we discovered he was standing over a dead Indian.

"Miami," said Blue Dogs.

Neither of us knew what to make of this development. Quickly looking over the man's clothing, we could discover no visible wounds, or probable causes of death. This was something that made no sense for several reasons. One of which was that had the man been previously wounded, or sick, the party would not likely have been headed toward the fort and potentially more trouble. Secondly, it was unlikely that they had come into contact with anyone with whom they would have had a shoot-out in this location. Finally, why would the group leave a dead comrade uncovered in the brush?

And then, Blue Dogs took a more considered look at the man's face and hair, and in French said, "L'homme n'est pas a Miami. Lest vestements sont Miami. L'homme est Choctaw."

His words were confusing. He had said that the dead man's clothes were those of a Miami, but the man was a Choctaw.

At that, he cut off the man's shirt to disclose a deep knife wound in his chest in which the puncture was clotted over. The man had been knifed to death and then dressed in Miami clothing. He had been a prisoner. This we ascertained when looking at his wrists, where the now-gone rawhide had cut bloody groves into his skin.

In all likelihood, we were walking into a trap. That we had not been shot at thus far could only mean that the three braves in wait did not have a position and an angle from which to ambush us, or more likely, they had moved on up the trail. We rose slowly from the corpse and took several steps. At that point, our answer came. A bullet tore through my buckskin coat sleeve, narrowly missing my left wrist. A near-simultaneous shot buzzed past Blue Dogs right ear like an angry hornet, missing him by maybe a finger width he later figured. As we flattened out on the ground, the facts struck me that either our assailants were not very good shots, or we were slightly out of accurate range and that they were probably using, not long-rifles, but less accurate muskets, probably British muskets. They may have underestimated their distance when they set their trap.

Nevertheless, we were pinned down in a crossfire, which meant no more than two of them could be on either side with the other one opposite, or perhaps elsewhere.

Troubles was nowhere to be seen.

Suddenly, Troubles was heard in full attack mode on our right, some short distance up the slope. Blue Dogs knowing that I was a good shot signaled me that he would go toward Troubles. As he popped up to run, I hesitated just one second and popped up looking to my left. Sure enough, a brave had stood up to aim Blue Dogs. My long-rifle shot was quicker than his and true to my target. I felled the would-be assassin with a shot through the throat. I then ran to follow Blue Dogs, screaming as I went, to attract attention.

Upon hearing my gunshot and then my scream, Blue Dogs

wheeled round to his right in time to aim and get off a shot at the second Indian, who had risen just above the brush where he was hiding, in an attempt to shoot me. The Indian fell, apparently indicating that Blue Dogs' shot found home. Our ploy for flushing out our opponents had worked perfectly, more evidence of our complete synchronicity in dealing with danger, as well as considerable good luck.

By our count, the only one left was the one that Troubles had. As we ran, Troubles let out a yelp. He had been cut by the knife of the brave he was attacking. Before Troubles could resume his assault, Blue Dogs dove at the brave and buried his tomahawk downward from the spot on the man's left side, where his shoulder met his neck. It was a death blow.

I ran quickly across the ravine to the opposite slope, where the Indian that Blue Dogs had shot, lay dazed and not dead. The shot from Blue Dogs had grazed his skull and he was bleeding profusely, but the wound itself was not anywhere near mortal. I considered dispatching him with my knife but decided that a prisoner made more sense. I raised my tomahawk until Blue Dogs could come. We bound him with the very rawhide that he had used on his Choctaw prisoner, which was still hanging from his waistband.

Blue Dogs took the scalp of the man he had killed that had been cornered by Troubles. He identified the man as a Miami. He indicated for me to take the scalp of the man that I had shot. I was hesitant, having never done such. However, the primal feeling of this small battle overcame my squeamishness, and I took the scalp feigning great relish in doing it, to make the prisoner convinced that I was a great warrior.

Reloading our guns and gathering our prisoner, we went over to where Troubles lay licking his wound. I still cannot fathom how that dog let me sew up his wound. So complete was his trust that he allowed me the eight stitches with barely a whimper. The gash was on the outside and slightly under his left front leg. I deemed it not likely to be life-threatening unless infection set in. To that end, I had some of Old Doc Johnson's salve which I liberally applied, and which he immediately began licking off in earnest. Even the smartest animals don't always know what's good for them.

With that, we rested, and then set off for the fort with our prisoner. We traveled rapidly the rest of the afternoon and through the night not knowing where the friends of our attackers were. We arrived well before dawn. Turning our prisoner over to the sergeant of the guard, we went straight to headquarters where we awakened General Harmar's adjutant, who then awakened the general.

"What's happened?" the general snapped as he came out of his private quarters in his nightclothes.

"We were attacked, General," I said. "We killed two and took one prisoner. There were signs earlier of another five, or so, who had gone off toward the river. They were not part of the attack on us."

"Where did this happen?" the General questioned.

"Less than a day to the northwest," I answered.

"Good work, gentlemen! Have the prisoner brought in," he said to his adjutant.

While we were waiting, the general seemed to notice the scalp hanging from my belt. First a look of horror and then one of disgust is what I imagined I saw on his face. However, he said nothing.

Sergeant Hanks and three guards brought forth the prisoner, still bound, before the general.

Trying to get him to talk was an exercise in futility. The general didn't speak Miami and neither did Blue Dogs, or I. My opinion was that the prisoner would not talk anyway.

The general sent for Black Duck and Jim Tucker. As it turned out, they had returned to the fort a few hours earlier having encountered a large party of Shawnee moving southeasterly, well away from the fort.

Our captive was wearing the dead Choctaw's clothing, Black Duck was baffled, knowing full well a Miami when he saw one. Blue Dogs, filled Black Duck in on the events of the day. Upon hearing of the execution of his tribesman, Black Duck drew a hand around his knife and moved menacingly toward the Miami, but was retrained by Tucker who knew immediately what his inclination was about to lead him to do.

After a calming few moments, the general relayed questions to Tucker and Black Duck, to translate to the prisoner in Miami. They were able to make themselves understood, and in turn understood that the prisoner would not talk.

It was at this point, that I received an education in interrogating a captured Indian from Jim Tucker, who knew the one thing that would most likely make a captive talk. Tucker grabbed the poker from the fire. I thought at first that he intended to torture the prisoner. I was mistaken but puzzled as Tucker made use of the carbon on the poker end to create a drawing on the wooden floor. He produced a crude likeness of a gallows and noose. There is perhaps no greater death that an Indian fears than the ignominious end produced by hanging.

Thereafter, the prisoner chattered like a blue jay answering whatever questions were proffered. However, the only real useful intelligence that the prisoner provided was that the tribal confederation knew well of the plans to move against them soon. We also learned, as we had suspected, that the dead Choctaw had been a prisoner, and he was sacrificed to lead us into an ambush.

"So much for the surprise," said the general."Take him away."

"Good work, men, dismissed," he said. And then, as an afterthought added, "Anyone hurt, anything you need?"

"No, Sir," was my reply. "We are fine."

At that Blue Dogs and I left the headquarters. With his limited English Blue Dogs had not attempted to talk. This seemed to be his natural tendency in the presence of white men, particularly officers.

We spent a few minutes with Black Duck and Jim, filling them in on our trip and listening to their findings as well. With that, Jim, Lowell Hanks, and I went outside. We had a few cups of some frontier whiskey that the good sergeant had secreted under his bed. Blue Dogs and Black Duck went off together.

We finished the darkness hours with some talk and some tall tales. At first light, Jim and I retired to some well-earned sleep while Sergeant Hanks went on duty.

Chapter Seven

Preparing for War

Josiah Harmar

The spring turned to summer, and the months wore on hot and humid. July at Fort Washington was the most miserable heat and humidity imaginable. The cicadas came out at night, sounding a loud cacophony as if they were protesting the unrelenting heat. The only relief was our frequent treks into the woods. But even there, mosquitoes were unrelenting.

A campaign that should have begun in June was still no closer to moving in August. The troops continued to drill, new troops continued to arrive with more broken muskets, defective gun powder and poor provisions. Had it not been for our hunting and thus providing fresh meat, the morale of the troops would have been even lower than it was. Some men claimed that their enlistment would be up before they fired their first shots at Indians. Others simply slipped away from the fort and were never seen again.

Through it all, General Harmar and his staff attended to every detail and did what they could to prepare. Still, even with the officers the impatience was growing, tempers were short, and blame was hurled back and forth throughout the fort and as far east as New York, straight to the desk of Henry Knox. The militias which were to make up the bulk of our force were slow to arrive and by early August, were not yet present.

A great many people came from and went to Fort Washington that summer, settlers, traders, various Indians, and even a couple of French priests. I suppose I took note of them in general, but none of our visitors particularly stood out, save for one. Sometimes there are just certain things a person notices and can't get out of his head. Why this was the case with one young man, I don't know.

I saw him one night in late June. He came to the fort to trade a few select pelts. He was a tall, handsome, well-built, meticulously dressed young Indian, who claimed to be a peace-loving Shawnee, named, Daniel Red Stick. His English was impeccable and a short conversation with him proved him to be a man of great intelligence. As I said, he was young, roughly my age I guessed.

He was with us that one night at our usual campfire. He mainly listened and had little to say. The campfire was outside the fort on this night, and some of the men drank Kentucky whiskey or Fort Washington beer. Daniel Red Stick did not drink.

He sat with us a while until we were joined by a French fur trader, named Louis Bourbon, who had been at the fort a few days trying to catch a ride downriver to St. Louis. As Bourbon joined us around the fires, Daniel Red Stick left quietly, but quickly. Bourbon noticed this, and although he already had some serious amount of alcohol before he joined us, he began to speak excitedly.

"What eez ee doing here?" he said.

"Who, Daniel Red Stick?" someone offered.

"Who?"Bourbon said. "I am talking about zhee Indian who gest left."

"Yeah, Daniel Red Stick," came the reply.

"My friend," Bourbon slobbered, "zhat man's name eez Panther Zhat crosses zee Sky, not Daniel Baton Rouge."

"Ah, what does it matter?" someone said.

"Eeet matters, my friend," Bourbon continued, "because, zhat is zhee brother of zee Shawnee, Chesseekau, who has been leeving with zee Chickamauga Cherokees in Tennessee and fighting against zee Americans. Zee two brothers were living with Dragging Canoe and hees people zee past few years. I was trading with zhem only a few months ago."[1]

Now as I said before, Indian names were often unusual, but as in the case of Blue Dogs Run Him, this Panther that Crosses The Sky really stood out to me. Certainly, not cut of the same cloth as the common English names like Smith, Jones, or Johnson. Even among people known to have unusual names this one was an attention-getter. The name by itself had a connotation of importance, power, or bravery. Panther that Crosses The Sky had a sort of mythic quality as if this fellow was someone special. Among the Indians certain names just emitted great importance, or "big medicine." I guess you could say they had a portend of future greatness.

Now, no one among us had heard that name before, so Redstick, or Panther, or whoever he was, had not already become a famous warrior or leader. Nevertheless, I resolved to speak with General Harmar about this incident. That conversation never took place. The General became too busy to see anyone but his most immediate subordinates. However, I did pass the information on to Major Ebenezer Denny, a very competent officer, whom I trusted. Years later, Denny would publish his journals of the final years of the Great War and the turbulent years of the 1790s in the Northwest Territories. I do not doubt that historians have greatly benefited from his work.

As regards the young warrior, that was the only night that we saw him that summer. Perhaps he sensed suspicion among us, or more likely, he recognized the Frenchman and feared his true identity becoming known. I never saw him again until a year later, at a place and time which I shall relate further along in my story.

Many years later, I would hear his name often with nightmarish dread among the whites and generally with reverence and respect among the Indians, although he had some enemies among them as well. In these latter years, I had time to reflect upon the young Panther that Crosses The Sky that I had seen at Fort Washington. He was destined to become a great Shawnee war chief. White Americans would come to know and fear him as Tecumseh.

At several of our campfires that summer we had discussed such of our upcoming adversaries as were known by name. The two most oft-mentioned names were Tarhe, The Crane, a Wyandot chief generally acknowledged to be a leader of the allied tribe, and Black Hoof, a Shawnee chief who was said to have been present at the defeat of Braddock, way back in 1755, and who would ultimately live to be about 90 years old.

Many of the old woodsmen who had signed up to be soldiers knew well of a Delaware war chief named Buckongehelas. It was not known for certain that he would fight with the Indian confederation, but if he did, he could likely bring several warriors to the fray. A few men with knowledge of the Shawnees were aware of a firebrand named, Blue Jacket, so-called for the attire he wore into battle.

The only Miami name that came to us was that of Michikinikwa, or "Little Turtle." Few among us had heard of him. Jim Tucker was an exception and filled us in. Summarizing, he told us that during the Great War for Independence the Miamis had allied with the British. A Frenchman fighting for the Americans, Augustin LaBalme, who Jim had known briefly, led a force against the Miami capital, Kekionga when most of the braves were gone. He did considerable damage to the village and the crops.

Within a few days, the warriors returned and under the leadership of Little Turtle, wiped out the 20 men LaBalme had left at Kekionga. They then proceeded to track down LaBalme on the Eel River and kill him and all of his men. Despite Little Turtle's relative youth his leadership in this affair established him as the tactical leader of the Miamis. The story made an impression on me because Jim always seemed to relay information without exaggeration. Jim seemed to be the one man around the fire that night who knew this fellow, Little Turtle, and he seemed to want him to get his due in the conversation.

And so, there was every indication that we were up against a well-led confederation of Indians who were veterans of frontier warfare. The tribes that we would fight against would likely include Miamis, Weas, Shawnees, Wyandots, Potaowatomies, Delawares, Ottawas, Chippewas, and possibly some Iroquois. Beyond this, we expected that there would be Sauk, Fox, and Illinois, all close cousins of the Miami.

Of all the great chiefs and all the warriors that we would eventually encounter, none would exceed the valor and strategic genius of Little Turtle, or the perseverance and ferocity of Blue Jacket. And years later, after the Indian Wars of the 1790s had ended, none would be more famous than Tecumseh.

In early September, several companies of militia had arrived from the east and Kentucky. Their late appearance meant that there would be no time to drill or train. This army would venture forth without the ability to act as a cohesive force. Word around the campfire did little to inspire my confidence in the Kentucky Militia in particular. Up to this time, they had conducted several excursions north of the Ohio and had solidified a certain reputation, by either running in the face of the enemy, or capturing villages defended only by old men, boys, and women; sometimes villages that had been friendly to whites. The thought of this kind of men constituting a bulk of our force was discomforting, to say the least.

One celebrity of sorts did arrive with the Kentucky group. He was Joseph Boone, nephew of the legendary Daniel Boone. His arrival spurred rumors that we would be joined by his famous uncle, but that did not occur. Joseph held the rank of corporal. His father had been killed by Shawnees some nine years before, so his motivation to fight in the upcoming conflict was understood. My few conversations with him convinced me that he would be an asset to the campaign. Some of us had many questions about his famous uncle. He complied politely and with patience, clearly used to such interrogations.

Finally, in very late September 1790, we scouts were sent forth and told to go no further than a day or so ahead of the main column. The main column would leave Fort Washington between September 26th and 30th, militia first, followed by the regulars under General Harmar. In all, about 1,100 militia and 300 regulars began our foray to the north. The body took only some very small and limited artillery, as we would be following old Indian trails through dense woods and brush. The lateness of the season necessitated moving as fast as the group could and not being burdened by excessive baggage, nor attempting to build roads as we went.

Jim Tucker and Black Duck were sent to the northeast, the route the column would take for a very short distance before swinging back to a more northward path and later one to the northwest.

Blue Dogs and I would scout off the main route and go northwest, to ensure that the column not be surprised by an ambush from that direction during the early part of the march.

Gray Otter was sent with some militia scouts directly north. I suppose it was figured that was the least likely direction of contact with the enemy, and he was less likely to be a liability going that way. Various scouts for the Kentucky Militia scouted directly ahead of that body throughout the entire campaign.

I had to give General Harmar credit for how he kept Jim and Black Duck on one flank and Blue Dogs and me on the other. This was his best assurance of avoiding a large-scale attack from either direction. By doing that, it virtually assured that if he were going to be attacked it would come from straight ahead. Here I am not trying to denigrate the militia scouts, but I knew darn well the army's flanks were secure.

Fording streams and climbing the rolling hills of what would become southern Ohio in a short few years, Blue Dogs and I made good time going northwest crossing often back and forth over the future state line between Ohio and Indiana. After one hard-paced day out we had found no sign. We guessed as to the approximate location of the main column, and after going one-half day to the northwest, we began to cut back eastward to a predetermined rendezvous with the main column near the Great Miami River. There we would report our findings and secure further orders.

We arrived at the rendezvous about a half-day before the main column and spent our time swimming, resting, and patching our moccasins. The militia scouts and Gray Otter had been there already since the day before. He had polished off most of the spirits that he had secreted for the trip. Tucker and Black Duck arrived several hours after the main column.

Blue Dogs asked Gray Otter if he had seen any sign. Gray Otter described coming upon the camp, a day or two old, of a very small party of Indians, going north. All indications were that they were Delaware and therefore the enemy. We assumed that they had been watching the fort for the time of the troops moving out so that they could move north and sound the alarm to the Indian confederation.

We reported to General Harmar once Black Duck and Jim arrived. He asked us to share all that we had seen.

Having done so, he replied, "It is for certain that they know we are coming, and they know the strength of our force. I think we can expect that they will attempt some sort of ambush, or delaying skirmish long before we reach the villages on the Maumee River."

"Yes, that' ad makes sense," said Jim. "Sure'n there's likely to be some sort of ree'ception committee to welcome us and it t'won't be a pleasant welcome."

"I plan to track north by northwest from here," the general said, as he rolled a map of the territory on a short table in front of us. "We are here at the Great Miami River. Do any of you men guess as to where might be our first contact with the enemy?"

Tucker replied by saying, "It cud be soon, or not'a'tall. These-uns will do that what we'uns least spect 'em ta do."

At this point, Black Duck informed the General that, "Men should not wander from camp. Indians will be with us from now on. Men who wander will not come back."

"Agreed," said Harmar. He then sent his adjutant to issue orders to that effect to his officers.

"So, what you are telling me is that we can expect contact of sorts, maybe small, maybe large, from here on?"

"Yeah, General, that'ad be the case. We're being watched now. Further north the numbers of those-uns watching us u'll be mor'n more," said Jim.

Harmar then stated, "Our overwhelming superiority in numbers should suffice to scare these rascals enough to avoid a full set battle. I think we'll have little trouble delivering a punishing blow."

To this Tucker replied, "T'wud't be good to take these here fellas light. Our'n numbers t'won't equal their grit."

And from Black Duck, "These warriors defend the land of their fathers. They will fight like soldiers have never seen; killing will be great."

At this the general eyed Black Duck and even Jim, with a look of annoyance. Perhaps he was thinking they were being defeatists, or cowardly in their talk. Black Duck was neither. Jim was neither. They were veterans of frontier warfare and they were telling the complete truth.

"Anyone else wish to say anything?" the General more or less snapped.

I replied, "No, Sir," and the others assented by silence.

"Very good then," Harmar concluded.

Then he said, "Blue Dogs and Jariah will continue working the northwest just off our route. Tucker and Black Duck scout straight north ahead of our force. Gray Otter will now take the Northeast with the scouts from the Kentucky militia."

The General knew Gray Otter. Sending him Northeast was smart, as there was the least likelihood of major trouble from that direction.

Gray Otter had no gripe with being exiled out of harm's way. He may not have liked having companions who could report on his diligence to duty, or lack thereof to the General, but that was balanced by not having to be in the woods alone.

"Leave after supper. Dismissed," said Harmar.

"Real talker that' un," Tucker said as we were out of earshot of the General.

"Yep." I responded, "He does things his way. But just one thing bothers me?"

"Wha 'sat?" Jim asked.

"How many Indians has he fought?" I said.

"Yup, redcoats ain't Injuns," said Jim, and with that we moved on.

We grabbed such fare as was served that evening and disappeared into the woods in our assigned directions. Going into the woods would henceforth mean a very good likelihood that we might encounter Indians. I was arrogant enough to suppose that Blue Dogs, Troubles, and I would likely handle ourselves well. But I knew full-well that any inexperienced soldier venturing away from the main force would not come back alive. Desertions became a problem for the force as we got further and further into Indian county. In the middle of the night, men would simply head south retracing the column's route and disappearing. Most never made it back to the company of white people.

Blue Dogs and I traveled about an hour before it became dark. At that point we were atop a small hill overlooking a stream and with a clear view in three directions, the fourth being obscured by forest. We would take turns sleeping and watching, with watching consisting of moving about the hill searching for movement in all directions. There would be no campfire. We would cold camp from here on.

I think even Blue Dogs' respect for Troubles allowed him a peace of mind that we were unlikely to be surprised in the night by any intruders. Passing an uneventful night, we headed off in the predawn with each agreeing to take a slightly different trail through the woods, to more accurately determine if anyone else were there with us.

We crossed a stream about 20 rods apart and reentered the woods at divergent points. Shortly after regaining the trees, Troubles begin whining and drifting off toward the direction that we knew Blue Dogs had taken though we had no sight of him. Now Troubles began to growl.

Sensing that Blue Dogs might be in danger, I told Troubles, "Go, boy, go get Blue Dogs."

He needed no further prompting and he tore through the thick underbrush at top speed, now barking loud and clear. I was in pursuit but was not keeping pace.

Blue Dogs, upon hearing the commotion caused by Troubles, turned about just in time to see a black bear crashing at him out of a thicket that he had just passed. It was a young sow. Despite the danger of rousing any nearby enemy, Blue Dogs had to fire at the bear. His shot struck the bear in the left shoulder but did not stop her. Now, Troubles coming up from behind attacked the bear and distracted her enough to allow Blue Dogs to reload.

About this time, I came up. I attempted to call Troubles off, but he would have none of that. Finally, the bear broke off the attack, sensing my presence and retreated to the thicket with Troubles in pursuit. Now, I produced a wooden whistle which I had carved and with which I had been training Troubles as the ultimate, come to my command. Reluctantly, he broke off the attack to come to me and we ran to Blue Dogs. We continued quickly north together.

"No doubt, a mother with a cub or two in the thicket and you surprised her. With any luck she'll survive to raise the cubs," I said in English, then realizing Blue Dogs may not have gotten all that.

As we ran off, Blue Dogs replied, "Fichu, qui etait un grand ours! Troubles mont sauve'll est un grand guerrier. Il a sauve ma vie." That is, "Damn, that was a big bear. Troubles is a great warrior. He saved my life."

"Vous avez raison, ami. Je suis d' accord," I agreed. I didn't want to ruin Troubles reputation with Blue Dogs by telling him that the bear wasn't all that big. I think that the close call had distorted his perspective.

He reached down on the run and patted the wily canine, who seemed to be smiling ear to ear. He had taken on a bear and saved my friend. A pat on the head was a perfect reward as far as he was concerned.

The three of us traveled swiftly ahead on the trot now, leaving the wounded sow bear and her presumed cubs well behind us and putting distance between us, and any Indians who might have come to investigate the commotion.

Over the next several days we traveled steadily and as stealthily as scouts can. The column was moving more slowly and Blue Dogs and I checked in with them every day, or day and a half, sometimes more often, as the distance from them west to east, decreased owing to their slow swing toward a northwesterly direction.

During these times we saw Jim Tucker and Black Duck but once. They reported considerable hostile movement. It was also during these meetings that we discovered that several militiamen had disappeared, or been found in a grizzly state of death because, despite orders, they had wandered too far from camp. Others had deserted individually, or more commonly, in small groups slinking off in a directly southern direction.

During our visits to camp, we often saw Gray Otter. I suspected that the closer we got to Kekionga the less inclined he was to stray from the safety of the main army. He was mostly assigned to scout with the Kentucky militia, but I think they were on to him and often left him behind which was fine with him.

Blue Dogs and I became ever more vigilant and on more than one occasion, had to hide to avoid detection by small scouting parties of Indians from the alliance. Troubles was a trooper in those situations. Controlling his natural inclination to bark, he hid silently with us in ravines and thick underbrush and once in a very large hollow oak tree.

Around October 17, we had arrived very close to Kekionga and the other Miami villages along the Maumee River. When we scouts all reported the proximity of the villages, a council of war was held with General Harmar, Colonel Denny, and Colonel Hardin along with other senior officers present.

"In the first light we shall sweep through the outer villages, overcoming any resistance. We will destroy the food stores and burn the villages," said Harmar. "After that we'll regroup and attack, destroying Kekionga."

It was unsettling to me that we, as representatives of a so-called civilized society, would wage war on women and children. Destroying food stores of recently harvested crops and burning villages, with the onset of winter only a few weeks away, was waging such war. I realized that the Indian alliance would fight the same way, but it still bothered me.

The General went on to describe which sub-commander would be attacking which village, with which troops. Blue Dogs and I were assigned to Colonel John Hardin of Kentucky. We would guide him to the villages just south of the St. Mary's River.

A few more details were exchanged between the General and his officers. Then we all went our separate ways, the scouts to our private pow-wow and the officers to prepare their subordinates for tomorrow and to get the men down for the night.

At first, silence prevailed, as we scouts gathered together some distance from the nearest campfire to eat our supper and chat. I should say that the main army never kept cold-camp at night, figuring that there were not enough Indians that would dare attack a massive force such as ours.

"Wha'dya think?" said Jim Tucker to the group.

Black Duck spoke first saying, "Big killing tomorrow, very bad."

Tucker said, "Yep, these fellas ain't just gonna let us dance around y'ere das-troying their homes."

"Why haven't they stopped us yet? Why did they let us get this close without any resistance?" I asked.

"Because these Indians hav'a plan and they'll act 'cordingly," Jim said. "We ain't catchin' them off-guard, and we ain't catchin' them shorthanded."

Here, he was referring to the fact that, although contact had thus far been limited to the few men stupid enough to wander from camp, all of we scouts had seen enough signs to know that there was a large force of warriors awaiting us at a location of their choice. How large a force was the question with which we wrestled.

Gray Otter waxed loquacious, telling us what he'd do to the enemy on the morrow. This bravado was the result of his making love to a bottle of whiskey that he had somehow managed to obtain. Being about two-thirds through with the bottle, he was feeling no pain. As such we ignored him though he babbled on.

We all looked to Blue Dogs, as there was a mutual respect for the opinions of the others among the four of us.

Blue Dogs responded in French probably because he didn't want to be overheard, "Nous sommes men'es par les imbeciles qui croient que nous avons un advantage."

"Wha' tad' he say?" said Jim looking at me.

"He said," I explained, "We are led by idiots who think that we have the advantage."

With this, Jim and Black Duck did not argue.

I took Blue Dogs to be giving a direct reference to Colonel Hardin whose reputation as an Indian fighter was not a positive one among friends or foes. Though he had a good service record in the late Great War for Independence, he was the possessor of a dark reputation when fighting Indians. A few years earlier, he had led an attack upon a Piankeshaw village killing the inhabitants in a massacre. The problem was that the village that he attacked was friendly toward the Americans. His act lost the Americans several allies among those Indian leaders who had yet to embrace the British in the conflict. And among those was Pacanne, a Miami chief. Later Hardin took twelve scalps back to Kentucky following a raid on a friendly Shawnee village. This got him promoted from Captain to Colonel in the Kentucky Militia.

I think it fair to say that we regarded Hardin as an overconfident leader whose abilities and judgment were highly questionable. His tactics had no respect among us. He had brought several scouts of his own from Kentucky and we knew that he was unlikely to defer to Blue Dogs and myself.

Knowing this, Black Duck and Jim, quite fairly considered as the senior American scouts, were not at all displeased to have their assignment be with Colonel Denny and a company of regular United States soldiers.

We, scouts, slept nowhere near any campfires not wishing to become silhouetted targets of the night. We slept the restless sleep of men whose future on earth could not be established beyond the moment at hand.

Chapter Eight

War

Little Turtle

Before first light, Blue Dogs, and I reported to Colonel Hardin. He informed us that we were to work with his scouts in leading his troops to the villages. With that, we set off with his scouts all Kentucky woodsmen or Chickasaws. We showed them the direction of the first village, and the bulk of them went ahead to reconnoiter while one went back to fetch Hardin and his troops.

There was nothing about the morning that bespoke of the glories of battle. We went to one village after another, each deserted by its entire population. The troops laid waste to Indian dwellings and food supplies by fire. Soon, smoke was seen billowing for miles around. Inexplicably, our entire expedition met with no resistance and village after village was burned. The Indians had carried what stores and supplies they could in evacuating ahead of our assault. It was felt that the British and French traders may have packed and headed toward Fort Detroit with their goods.

Later, on October 19, emboldened by the success of our endeavors and encountering no foe, a group was ordered to the Northwest. Blue Dogs and I were excluded from service with this group for reasons unknown, but perhaps having to do with Harden insisting on using his scouts.

Colonel Harden and 180 Kentucky militia along with a cavalry troop led by Major James Fontain, were accompanied by 30 American Army regulars under Captain John Armstrong. This group led the attack. A lone Indian decoy lured Colonel Hardin into a chase leading directly to an ambush and an attack from three sides by the Indians. I later learned that Little Turtle had skillfully arranged this ambush.

The Kentucky boys quickly fled, but lost 40 men killed. Only eight of the thirty regulars survived after gallantly standing and fighting. Captain Armstrong and the survivors were forced to retreat and hide in a nearby marsh.

It was here that a near-miraculous event involving Corporal Boone occurred. Being wounded in the leg, he could not travel quickly and there was danger of that being the cause of his demise should the Indians catch him. And probably also, the deaths of his companions. So, his friends promised to come back and get him if he could hide temporarily. He found a hollow log and crawled in. There he lay for hours, Indians walking all around, but never bothering the log. That night his companions were good to their word. They went back into the dark swamp and managed to find him. They were able to get him safely back to camp. A great roar went up as he and his friends appeared. It was truly good to see him. Word of his having originally been left behind had gone throughout the camp. It was the best event we had experienced since the expedition began. Whether any officer permitted his friends to go back and find him, or whether they just fulfilled their promise without permission, I don't know. I thought that finding him in a dark swamp, in a fallen log, was mighty impressive.

Boone's rescue was about the only good fortune we experienced. The next day on October 20, Ensign Phillip Hartshorn's force was ambushed just eight miles above Kekionga with a loss of 19, including Hartshorn. Rather than sending help, Harmar fell back and refused to allow even a burial party. Morale dropped to a level akin to nonexistent. Rumors began to spread about Harmar being often drunk and afraid, as these events began to unfold. I personally never saw the General take a drink or act drunk, but I cannot prove that he wasn't drinking. However, my personal opinion of his performance as a commander was something else. His actions were ill-conceived, and he seemed to be indecisive when it was time to act. It was this type of leadership that lead to men getting killed unnecessarily. Also, there was his unflinching tendency to send Hardin on the most important attacks. That confused the hell out of me. We held vastly different assessments of Hardin's leadership. And certainly, Harmar himself was not leading attacks, nor was he even leaving the main camp.

By this time, Blue Dogs, Troubles, and I had missed being involved in any of the big action, each time being detailed in directions some miles from the ambushes, or kept in camp. Although Tucker and Black Duck had not been with Hartshorn, they had disobeyed orders and gone to his aid along with eight or ten regulars. This act saved the few men who escaped with their lives.

For the next two days, the army stayed within its fortified camp, as General Harmar pondered his next move, or perhaps, was paralyzed by fear. He was rattled and so were some of the other officers and men.

On the 22nd, the militia under Hardin and the First American Regiment, under Major John P. Wyllys, was ordered by Harmar to attack Kekionga where it was supposed the Indians had regathered. Colonel Hardin was ranking senior officer was in charge of this detachment.

Said Harmar, "Surely the devils will defend their capital. But whether they do, or do not, this is the village we were sent to destroy, and destroy it we will, establishing control over this area."

After a brief council with Wyllys and Colonel Hardin, Blue Dogs and I were informed by Hardin that his scouts would lead him to the ford crossing the Maumee River. At that time his troops would advance sharply to their left, moving toward the confluence of the Maumee, the St. Mary's, and the St. Joseph Rivers. They would then attack Kekionga. Blue Dogs and I were then ordered by Wyllys to scout west of the St. Joseph River on his left flank. A few dwellings from the village spilled over to the west side of the river. The strategy had some military acumen because we could make certain that no Indians overtook our main column unaware after it crossed the ford. We might also be able to ascertain the strength of any group of Indians that might be lurking on his left flank. We were accompanied by five American regulars.

The plan might have worked had Hardin followed it. However, seeking glory, he nearly outstripped his scouts in fording the Maumee River and plunged, on horseback, toward the village. He ignored the warnings of Wyllys, who was unfortunately subordinate to Hardin. In doing so, he did not give Blue Dogs and me an opportunity to fulfill our mission which would have likely resulted in us discovering the trap laid for Hardin's and Wyllys. A trap set by about 1,000 warriors led by Little Turtle as I much later found out. Hardin, upon getting resistance at the ford, did send a rider back to Harmar asking for support. However, the General stayed tight at his fortified camp. I learned this fact in months to come from some of the Indians present at that battle.

Much later, I also learned that Wyllys had been killed along with many of his men. This may have been caused when the undisciplined militia went off to chase small groups of decoys sent by Little Turtle for that purpose. This left the regulars alone and they were attacked from three sides. Major Fontaine, who was a last-minute addition to the force, was led with his cavalry into an ambush and he also died. Hardin, it was said, put up a valiant three-hour fight, despite making some bad decisions. Eventually figuring that Hamar would not come to his aid, he retreated. But I am again getting ahead of my story.

By the time Blue Dogs and I and our small entourage had reached a point near the confluence of the St. Joseph and the Maumee Rivers, it was clear that a battle was joined on the other side. Hardin had been ambushed. Though we couldn't see anything because of the trees on the far side, we knew the action was heavy and very close to the river. We waded and floated the relatively shallow St. Joseph using a log conveniently in the river, accompanied by our five regulars. Troubles, that excellent swimmer, led the way and we were undetected by the enemy. We came up behind an Indian force that was occupied pouring lead and arrows into Wyllys' and Hardin's troops and not expecting the river behind them to be crossed at that point.

Assessing the situation, once we were in among the trees and able to somewhat accurately ascertain the Indians' position, we quickly concluded that our comrades were about to be massacred. At that point, we determined to re-cross the river and attempt to go and find Harmar's troops. Before departing, we decided upon a very risky stratagem that might afford some relief to the Americans under such stress. Blue Dogs and I would fire our long-rifles from hidden vantage points behind the enemy off to the left, while our comrades went to the right, thereby attempting to convince the Indians that they were being attacked and perhaps flanked from the rear by a significantly large force.

It seemed like a good idea, but it was about the only idea that we had to attempt to take some pressure off of Wyllys. Ultimately, it proved a bit foolhardy. We each fired, moved to a new position, and fired again. Owing to the din of the battle each of our first two rounds would have gone undetected except for the four warriors they felled, noticed by the warriors beside those now dead. Several braves whirled round and took cover, attempting to see from whence the shots were coming. We continued our fire, loading and falling back toward the river. This took some pressure off Wyllys. However, after a few minutes, our ruse was discovered and it became clear we had stirred up a hornet's nest of wild savages.

We must have had forty or more warriors coming our way with that insane sort of anger that spurs a man onward when defending his home. Running was not an option because we would quickly come to the river and while re-crossing we would be easy targets.

The regulars that we had sent further off to our right, or east-southeast, were fighting as a group. However, by now we could only hear their gunfire and not see them in the dense woods with smoke everywhere from guns.

Blue Dogs and I each felled one more warrior. Then we were compelled to draw tomahawk and knife and to begin a desperate hand to hand fight for life. We were about 30 paces apart.

By this time, Troubles was fiercely speeding toward the nearest oncoming Indian to begin his signature leaping attack. A warrior fired a shot at him and missed. He sailed through the air at the throat of our closest opponent. His force drove the brave to the ground, and Troubles immediately went for the throat as the brave howled for help. Troubles was easily winning his battle when he was struck from above, by the war club of the second warrior, the one who had fired the shot that missed him, now coming up to the fight. As he struggled to get to his feet, all wobbly and groggy, he was dealt another blow from the club and he fell lifeless to the ground.

I tripped an attacker running at me by a quick sidestep, dropping low and sticking my leg out as his momentum carried him past. I followed this with a tomahawk blow to his head before he could rise and turn to face me. I looked up in the direction of my friend Blue Dogs, just as he was hit simultaneously, by not less than four musket balls. His body recoiled first to the left and then just backward, his arms outstretched upward. As he went down and did not move, I was lit upon by three braves, who got close enough to make attempts at stabbing and clubbing me.

However, by now, my consuming rage at the apparent deaths of my two friends had me in a state such as I had never been before. I became possessed. I felt almost superhuman strength and hatred such as I never had.

I remember thinking, "I'll kill every one of these sonofabitches!"

Dying did not enter my thoughts, not once, as I set about the process of the killing that I wanted to accomplish, systematically one Indian at a time. At that moment I can truly say that I had no fear. I only wanted to deal death from my burning hatred. My purpose was singular, my resolution absolute.

Two of those three braves died by my slitting their throats. I clearly remember the fear in their eyes and I am convinced that they thought they were facing the devil himself. I have never seen Indians, who normally look so cruel and unrelenting in battle, have facial expressions like these warriors. Their fear was palpable and only served to fuel my fury. The third died when my tomahawk crushed his right temple.

The killing was done swiftly and with the absolute most savagery one might ever imagine, in any man, no matter what his color. I found a strength that I did not know I possessed and I overcame these men in a fashion that seemed to me not difficult at all. However, by the time I had accomplished this, I was set upon by another six or more coming at me like wolves to a kill. I swung tomahawk and knife but was clubbed unconscious with a blow to the back of my head, by a warrior I never saw. His blow ended the prosecution of my intent.

When I came to, which was some very long time later, I was only marginally coherent. My head felt as if it would explode. Throughout what I believe were several minutes or longer, I became aware that I was no longer near the battle, that it was night, that I was in an Indian village, and that I was tied securely to a stake in the ground next to another man, an Indian. Slowly, I became aware that I was being pelted with stones, hit with sticks and clubs, and being spat upon.

My assailants were five adolescent and pre-adolescent boys who had taken it upon themselves to get an early start on the torture that most surely awaited me. My entire body ached and was swollen from the battle as well as the abuse thus far heaped upon me. My head throbbed and my vision was blurry.

Eventually, I became just aware enough to recognize the man that I was tied with, was Gray Otter. However, any attempt to communicate with him, or to find out how he was captured was useless. He howled like a dog and cried like a baby. He well knew what was in store for us and he was not a brave man. He was so scared as to only barely be able to sing his death song and that in low whispers, inter-meshed with sobs and gasps for air. He had completely lost the rhythm of normal breathing.

After a long time of listening to drums and screaming, several braves approached us. They were led by a red-headed Indian whose skin was whiter than mine. This group untied Gray Otter and dragged him away, whooping and yelling with a blood lust that might have scared me had I not been still groggy, sort of coming and going in consciousness. As he was dragged away, kicking and screaming, the red-headed Indian bent down to look me straight in the eyes.

In perfect English he said, "You are a great warrior. Die like a man, it will bring you honor and honor to the people."

His claim that I was a great warrior had to do with the events just before my capture.

My response to him, I think, was something akin to, "Eat horse shit, you son of a jackass!" I could only mumble, so great was my pain and so foggy my awareness.

He replied, "Your hate may serve you well, at least until the fire begins to burn away your flesh. Then maybe you will scream like a woman or cry like a baby."

For the briefest of moments, I wondered about Wyllys and Hardin. Were they massacred? Had they escaped? However, I was just too damned groggy to keep a thought long and in too much pain to care.

It was at this point that I realized I had been stripped to the waist. My small medicine pouch around my neck was left untouched, but the red-haired Indian now reached for it and ripped it from my body. For some Indians touching a man's "spirit medicine bag" was very bad luck, but this warrior seemed immune to such thoughts. Looking inside he saw only dried plant material. It was four doses of dried opium and five dried hemp flowers. I always kept these pain killers having learned of their power from old Doc Johnson.

The warrior started to cast the contents to the ground, but sensing this, I muttered, "Let me eat the herbs." Then, whether out of kindness or as a sadistic act, he stuffed all the contents into my mouth and gave the deerskin bag to the oldest of my guards. He had no doubt, seen dried hemp before yet he gave it to me, perhaps intentionally to lessen my pain, or perhaps without thinking. Maybe, he just wanted to see me choke on the dry plants. He then said something to the boys in the Indian language and walked off to attend the festivities surrounding the murdering of Gray Otter.

As I choked, the oldest of my adolescent tormenters raised his breechcloth baring his private parts, while the others grabbed me and held my mouth open by jamming their fingers into my face at various pressure points. Thus eliminating any chance of me pursing my lips closed with a clenched jaw. The older youth preceded to urinate in my mouth.

As I attempted to struggle against those holding my head and with a hatred caused by such humiliation that I thought would give me success, I found that I had no strength. They then held my mouth shut once the urine had been deposited. I could not gag, cough, or expel the urine, so I swallowed hoping it might speed my demise.

Much later I would come to realize that this humiliation had turned the tables on my tormentors and allowed me to swallow the herbs which set off the digestion of the plant material.

Now I became aware of the hideous screams of Gray Otter and the joyfully malevolent jeers and cheers of the red devils, delighting in his fear, as they set about ending his existence in the most gruesome fashion. I knew that Gray Otter would soon be dead and that as the white captive, I would be the star attraction of the evening's festivities. I knew enough from my time with the southern tribes, that my end would be slow and painful. I also realized that the Indians valued a brave death and if I could but keep from crying out, or at least from doing so too much, they might be duly enough impressed with my bravery to dispatch me quickly to end my suffering.

This was my hope, but before they came for me it became clear that I was dealing with masters of torture. Whatever I had learned from the southern tribes may well have little application here. These were experts, not just adept at the killing, but obsessed by the most minute detail of the torture that it might bring more pain to the hapless victim and more joy to the onlooking crowd. I could tell all this by just hearing Gray Otter's cries, howls, and screams. By now, I was less groggy and I could feel my body once again attempting to put strength at my disposal. But I was just simply too tightly bound. I found myself having a moment of pity for Gray Otter, a man for whom I had no actual respect.

After perhaps 30 to 40 minutes, it is hard to know just how much time, no more sounds came from Gray Otter. I had only the slightest view of his execution, but I knew he was tortured in various fashions long before the fire was introduced to his skin. The savages liked a slow death, one they could savor. I sensed my turn coming quickly. However, time drug on. I expected them upon me, but they did not come. Perhaps another 30 minutes passed. During this time I heard yelling and whooping, but could not see what my future executioners were doing.

My guards had left me so that they could join the main group, all except the youngest, who might have been ten. He seemed reluctant to torment me, but just stared at me in silence as if taking in my every breath, the smallest movement of my body, or twitch of my muscles. And then they came, . . . several adult braves, painted, howling, and laughing, all in an attempt to make me beg for my life.

As they cut the hide bonds that bound my body, they left my hands securely tied behind me. They drug me away toward my stake, bound me to it, and piled firewood around me. I hoped that the herbs I had taken would spare me as much pain as possible and maybe even kill me. I had taken enough opium and hemp to kill two, or three men and was already beginning to have even more blurry vision, thinking that the overdose would cause death to come swiftly.

I was experiencing none of my former pain, but I was again fuzzy in the brain. Well actually to be fair, I was a considerable distance gone beyond being merely fuzzy.

Oddly, I do remember looking up and noticing that it was almost a full moon, something often called, "Hunter's," or "Harvest Moon," at this time of year. It was a beautiful orb lighting the wilderness. With all that was happening and about to happen it is unfathomable to me that I remember the moon.

Maybe I was out of my mind enough from the drugs to be lacking in fear appropriate to my situation. This seemed confusing to the savages, as they were experienced enough to know how most white men begged and pleaded, upon such occasions. This was sorely disappointing them, and they began to hurl insults at me, as well as actual objects, not the least of which were big sticks and large stones.

At my stake next to where Gray Otter had been tortured, I could see his blackened body slumped over and burned to a crisp, with grease from his skin sizzling onto the larger logs below him that still glowed with ashen embers. Even this sight did not clear my brain. I think I laughed when I saw the sight. Nothing I did made sense. I was crazy out of my mind. Smells, such as that of Gray Otter's burnt body, which would normally conjure up strong emotions, had no fear-inducing effect upon me.

I'd like to say that I now vowed to myself that the sonofabitches would not see me cower or cry and I would give the savages precious little satisfaction. But the fact is, that I'm not certain what my thoughts were. I was close to being beyond logical thought and awareness of my plight.

By now, my herbs had numbed my entire body, except that my toes were tingling. I began to have hallucinations. These were probably heightened by the hyped-up yells and dancing around me of the savages. Colors seemed vivid and I laughed a great deal finding the whole hideous scene surreal, but pleasant. This confounded and angered the red men. They had never seen such behavior out of one about to die. They thought I was mocking them and they tried to taunt me evermore with the thought to cause me to be afraid. I had no such fear. The light from the campfires danced before my eyes which were unable to completely focus.

After I was secured at the stake, a warrior came forth and cut off my left ear lobe with his knife. This naturally produced an outpouring of blood that excited the savages to frenzy. The roar of their cheers was as loud as cannon fire. I stared smiling at my assailant. I felt no pain, though I did feel the blood flowing down the side of my neck and onto my shoulders.

Now a woman came at me, she had either a shell, or some sort of stone knife. Whatever it was, it was not very sharp. With this dull instrument she cut off the first digit of my small finger on my left hand. Resisting crying out was not hard. I still felt little pain. Normally I might have sworn at the bitch, but my staring into her eyes made her elicit a gasp of fear as if she'd seen a demon. I later learned that Indians worry a great deal about demons.

A short warrior stepped forward. With his hunting knife he cut a line across my chest from nipple to nipple, again producing blood. For just a moment, I became lucid, more aware that I was being tortured, but still not in any serious pain.

I had the wherewithal to look him in the eye and I told him, "Why do you tickle me, you son of a hairless dog? Free me and fight me like a man, you cur."

And then I laughed hysterically as I stared directly at him. He recoiled, apparently in fear and disbelief.

Of course, he didn't know what I had said, but I noticed the red-haired Indian sharing a translation with him, after which, he had to be restrained from tomahawking me on the spot in order not to lose face. I'd like to believe that I assailed him further with the most foul epithets and insults, wishing only that I spoke the language of my tormentors so that all could hear and understand. Thus understanding, they would kill me instantly in anger and sparing me the fire to come. But that is perhaps what I later convinced myself I did, perhaps heroically. The fact is, I have no recollection that I could say with any great certainty was the truth.

I think I began to laugh again uncontrollably. Within the whole process in which they were so actively engaged I saw strange sites, a strange glow, dancing lights from the campfires, visions otherworldly, but not wholly unpleasant. My vision blurred further, cleared just a bit, and blurred again.

Now came the torchbearer, and waved the fire in my face. My eyes followed it, glazed over and mesmerized. It was to me only a fascinating light show and not the portent of death that my captors intended. I was virtually beyond pain and this confused the hell out of the heathens.

Doc Johnson had used hemp as a pain killer in severe cases and had used the opium when he had to do surgery. These were his most potent medicines, and they kept me from giving the savages any result that they expected, or that they had ever seen in other victims of their hideous abuse.

By now, they had attempted to have their fun with me, perhaps another 30 minutes from the time I was removed from my original stake. But I must admit, that is only a guess. I had no real ability to assess the passing of time.

It must have been at this time that the herbs rendered me nearly unconscious, or completely lost in my visions and thus so far out of reality that even my poor memory of the events that I am describing mostly ended. For the rest of my account, I will rely on what was later relayed to me by many of the Indians present that night.

Several leading warriors had pushed through the crowd intrigued by my resistance to pain and by my laughing at the torture being administered. Among these was Little Turtle himself. I am told that he peered into my eyes and told those close to him that I had gone into a spirit world and that based upon this and the way I had fought before capture, he feared that I might possess much personal medicine and power. He wondered aloud if I could even be killed.

The short fellow who had cut me stepped forward and pointed out the blood to Little Turtle.

As later told to me, Michikinikwa said to him, "Would you like to try to kill him?"

The man answered in the affirmative, again saving face, until Little Turtle said, "Let us cut him down and I will give him my tomahawk. You will battle him alone."

At this, the man became quiet except for urging Little Turtle to administer the fire.

Before lighting the brush and wood beneath me, the torch holder held the flame to my left leg taking off hair and some skin. When I did not react, a general awe came over the assembled savages. To further confound them, it was at this time that I began to vomit as a reaction to the opium and hemp overdose. My first outpouring was a direct shot into the face of the torchbearer. He fell back, unable to see and rattled. As I continued, I was later told that vomit shot several feet into the air from my mouth, projecting out toward the crowded horde in a way that must have seemed almost as if I were attacking them with my intestinal fluids. The crowd backed up in reaction with a degree of fear and with a collective, "Ahhhhh. . ."

My body was fighting a drug overdose, but of course, the Indians didn't know that. I would later wonder if the red-haired warrior knew that he had given me the powerful medicine that was so confusing my tormentors.

Now, some Indians might see a victim vomiting and view it as weakness, as a gutless fear reaction of the body. However, the Indians present on this night saw it as my body rejecting their tortures and spewing evil back at them. The fact that my vomiting was so intense and violent, only helped increase the effect upon the savages. This sealed my fate and saved my life. As Indians dodged my airborne stomach fluids, Little Turtle ordered that I be cut down, telling the gathering that I was a brave man with much personal spiritual power and that I must be spared. The spirits were protecting me from the people's torture. He told them that killing me might have grave consequences on what, heretofore, had been a day of great victory for the people. I am told that some of the people believed that I was indeed a demon and could not be killed, while a few others thought they should try to kill me on the spot.

I was taken to a dwelling, unconscious, but alive. I continued to vomit for a long time. They could not have known how close I was to death, not from them, but an herbal overdose and frankly, perhaps from the blow to my head at the battle. Indeed, by all standards of which I was aware, I should have died that night. As I said, the overdose of opium and hemp was toxic enough to kill three men. Hell, maybe many more than that. Instead, I entered a coma that I am told lasted three days. In later discussions, the savages referred to this time as my "spirit trip" and it was this that earned me the name, "Spirit Traveler," which I was to be called by the Indians from that time forth.

When I awakened after three days, I was still pretty sick and nauseous. I was extremely confused and disoriented. After several hours, I was able to hold down a few dried berries pounded to powder and mixed with a bit of water. The fact that the most beautiful woman I had ever seen was taking care of me, did not register until two days later when I felt much improved. This was my first consciousness of Autumn Leaf. She had been ordered by Little Turtle to care for me and to watch for other signs of spiritual power. Autumn Leaf had such a reputation for bravery that her uncle knew she would observe me well, and would not be afraid of me as other women and even some of the men might have been.

Nevertheless, to her she was performing a duty to her tribe on orders of her uncle, not out of any great compassion for me. She was neither pleasant, nor unpleasant toward me. However, she was extremely observant of me.

I did notice that I was covered with a bearskin and was naked other than that. I surmised that for however long I had been out of my senses, my bodily functions must have been tended to and cleaned up by this woman. I have to confess, I felt more than a little embarrassment. However, I was far more puzzled than embarrassed. Where was I? What had happened at the bonfire in my honor? Why was I still alive? What was going to happen next? Where was the American army? These and many, many, other questions troubled me. I babbled for answers but got none.

On the evening of the fifth day, when I was able to sit up and eat, the red-haired Indian entered the dwelling where I was kept. I had only a fuzzy recollection of having seen him before. Gradually, however, my memory of him became more clear. He was not a tall man, but would certainly stick out in an Indian crowd because of his hair and very fair skin.

He said to me in perfect English, "You are a brave man and

you are to be allowed to live." While that produced some serious relief to me, I assumed that I was still a prisoner.

I said, "What of the soldiers?"

"All gone," he replied. "We killed many and the rest ran like rabbits."

I would later learn that a good many of the Kentucky Militia not only ran but didn't stop until they got to Kentucky. Their hard-earned reputation as Indian fighters remained intact, I thought sarcastically.

"When they come back we will kill them all. But you are not like them, you have power given you by the manitous."[1]

I was not about to disagree or to say anything that might change my status in the minds of the Indians.

"How is it that you speak such good English and have flaming red hair?" I asked.

His response was, "I was captured by the people a few years ago. Now I am one of them. My name is Apekonit." This, I later learned was a reference to his red hair. It meant carrot top.

"What was your white name?" I asked.

"It does not matter," he said. "I am Apekonit." It was at this point that he relayed to me the events of my near-death and the intervening time how long I had been unconscious, and other events of my illness. These included some convulsions, more vomiting, and profuse sweating. I found out that I was at a place the Miamis called, in their language, "the Island."[2] It was near Little Turtle's village on the Eel River. The place was sacred and used as a camp for religious activities as well as the torture and execution of prisoners. He told me that Little Turtle's niece, Autumn Leaf, was my nurse. And then he said something both puzzling and disturbing at the same time.

"Do not try to be a man with her," he said. "She will gut you like a shot deer and leave your bones to be gnawed by the mice and the animals of the forest."

I took this as a warning not to look upon her as a woman. I pondered his words, not that the thought had even occurred to me, though her beauty was by now, self-evident.

"What is your name?" he inquired. "J. R., er, Jariah, Jariah Jamison," I responded.

His final words to me at that time were, "You are brave, not a coward, not a fool, like the whites. You have been saved because you have power. You must think about how you can help the people. If you are wise, you will become one of us." And he added, "Your name is now Spirit Traveler."

I did not tell him that I had little intent to help these bastard savages. But even as I had that thought, I experienced a strange sensation of guilt. After all, I owed these people my life not only for sparing me from death at the battle, then the fire, but also for tending to me during my coma. The payment of a debt is and always has been, a point of honor in my family, as it is with most red men. Still, these were the same people that killed my best friends in the world, Troubles and Blue Dogs Runs Him. It was all so very confusing.

My head hurt from such thoughts as mixed within my mind, perhaps from the fog created from my head injury and also my near death from the plants. At any rate, hate and gratitude do nota settling mixture make and thinking on these things brought no resolution to my mind.

It was difficult to reconcile with the deaths of my two best friends. In my recollection we were just together moments before the current, but now they had been gone for several days, days that would stretch to forever. I never saw their bodies after they fell and they had no burial. This ending haunted me, no goodbyes, no last words. I had been unable to tell them how I felt about them. It occurred to me that this was not dissimilar to the death of my parents.

In the ensuing days I began to heal. I was given the clothing of a brave who had been killed in the recent battle. It didn't fit well. Few Indians could match my height. Apekonit came to speak with me several times each day. Always, he stressed his loyalty to the people, apparently to encourage me to the same vein of thought. He seemed always interested in my thoughts and I surmised, that he was attempting to assess my escape potential. He inquired often about my three days in the spirit world. I think he was frustrated when I gave him little information and frankly, I had little to give from those three days that I had lain comatose. But I don't think he believed that. He thought I was deliberately not telling him about my coma experience.

Months later, I would learn that Apekonit's frequent visits had been ordered by Little Turtle. I would also learn later that Little

Turtle had inquired of the braves who had been present as to the events leading to my capture. They had given him a glowing account of my battle conduct leading up to the time I was clubbed unconscious. This had the effect of further validating his belief that I was a man of great power, spiritually, but also a fierce warrior.

Of course, perhaps the braves embellished their stories to Little Turtle. After all, they would, themselves, look very good if they had captured a great warrior.

I asked Apekonit about the capture of Gray Otter. He said, "Oh, was that the name of that whimpering dog?"

He went on to explain that the evening before the battle in which I was captured, the Miami needed a prisoner who might explain the plans of the Americans. Gray Otter was easily captured on the outskirts of the main camp while answering the call of nature. Apekonit was amused that the Miami didn't even have to torture him to get the coward to talk. However, most of what he knew was of little use, partly because he had not been privy to the final council of war among the American officers and partly because he was so drunk at the time of his capture. The Miami did not expect to benefit greatly from his execution, but it was decided he would likely die begging for mercy and would be a good example to the young Miami boys of how not to act when captured. It would also be excellent entertainment for the people. So Gray Otter was kept until after the battle, at which time he was properly and with due Miami diligence, tortured to death in the fashion that I have previously related.

Each day I began to move about more, though never without a retinue of followers, mostly young boys eager to be near the man whose reputation was growing, and who the people now called Spirit Traveler.

My wounds healed quickly, the burn to my leg had been very slight. I have to say that for some reason, missing a digit on my little finger didn't bother me near as much as my missing that ear lobe. I still cannot tell you why. It was just an odd sort of thing. I'd reach up to touch my ear, and could feel that a piece was missing. So naturally, I kept reaching.

Each day I also mourned the death of my two best friends, Blue Dogs, and Troubles. I missed them terribly and reflecting on them never left me in a good disposition toward the Miami. They were gone from my life forever. The loss was heavily on my mind. I guess I keep harping on this point because it produced within me a great sadness and an emptiness of unfulfilled finality. My mood was melancholy and would last for hours at a time following my thinking of them.

Through it all, Autumn Leaf continued tending my wounds, bringing my food and most usually treating me with a sort of seeming indifference. Perhaps I was her burden and she did her duty by her people by taking care of me.

After several days in her care, I truly began to notice her as a woman, one who moved with a grace that I had never before seen and one that stirred within me feelings which I had never before felt. She did not speak English but did understand a few words. Upon prompting from me she began to teach me some Miami terms, mostly for the food I was eating, or for items around the camp.

After a few weeks, I noticed that her indifference toward me had softened and I imagined that she looked forward to our meetings. At least she seemed happy being around me. She was often bemused and never more so than one day when she stared long and hard at my clothing and burst out laughing. The fit was just so poor, and she had come to a point in our relationship where she felt comfortable being perfectly honest. Up to this time, I had been formulating plans of escape. I now felt strong enough to do so. However, something held me in place.

The very next day, I was presented with new clothing that I was told, had been given by Little Turtle himself. The clothing fit much better, as Little Turtle was an Indian of uncommon height. But still, Indian leggings and a breechcloth were a bit awkward to my sensibilities. White men are used to full trousers and these britches were just a little too airy if you know what I mean.

In time I had no more pain from the missing earlobe, and the top digit of my little finger on my left hand. The burns on my leg had long-since scabbed over and were well-healed. My chest bore a scare from the knife wound, but it was of no consequence to me.

One night after supper, Little Turtle asked me to walk with him along the river. He spoke moderately good English but used Apekonit as an interpreter while he asked many questions posed in the Miami language.

"When would the white army come again? Was I a famous warrior? Did I have a family and would I be missed by my people?" With these and other questions I was tested.

And finally, "Who would be the next white chief to come make war against the people?"

During our lengthy conversation, I was given my final assessment from Little Turtle's view of the battle now some two months in the past. He knew he had won. Still, it had not been a decisive rout and he had not killed so many whites as he had hoped. He knew full well that more war would be coming to Kekionga and that the Americans, not suffering a loser, would have a new commander.

He very directly asked me if I intended to stay with the Miami people. I honestly told him that I had much confusion and did not know what course my future would take. I believe he respected my honesty. He also thought I am sure, that I was holding back, being cautious in answering his questions. Still, he told me through Apekonit that it was good that I was not like other whites who seemed to talk just to hear their own words and whose words carried no truth, but were often created for deceit.

During the time we were together, I could not help my feeling of admiration for this noble man. He was a brave and resourceful war leader, a man who carried himself with dignity and whose words reflected his desire to protect his people and their way of life. He admitted to having no great trust of the British but was pragmatic in knowing that they were an ally of power and convenience under the current circumstances. Still, he had found their promises of military assistance to be lacking on more than one occasion. It was also clear to me that Apekonit and Little Turtle shared a great respect between them.

As our walk concluded, Little Turtle told Apekonit to cease having me watched and guarded. He told him the time had come for trust to be developed, or for me to be allowed to choose to leave. He felt keeping someone of spiritual power against their will could not, but cause harm to his people.

Perhaps Little Turtle knew that which I did not, that I would not leave the Miami. If he did, that information may have come from his niece, Autumn Leaf. Later that same evening I was sit-

ting alone in the wigwam with Autumn Leaf laughing at my pro-
nunciation of Miami words, when she quite unexpectedly leaned
toward me and kissed me. After this, she became momentarily
silent, blushed with embarrassment, paused after looking deep
into my eyes, then she was gone. I was happily dumbfounded.

This was the first confirmation that I had of her feelings and
was her manner of declaring her intention. I was so stunned that
I only stared at her. But I hasten to add, that my eyes told her all
she needed to know. My heart lept within my chest and I was
moved as a man is moved by the attentions of a beautiful woman
about whom he dared not even dream. Slowly, I was grasping
that which Autumn already knew. No, I would not be leaving the
Miami people.

It had been a most memorable day from Autumn's unexpected kiss to my walk with Little Turtle and Apekonit. What
would come next, I could hardly have anticipated. During my
captivity, after sufficient recovery I had as my bunk-mates three
young braves who no doubt were to guard me, but also to observe m, and to learn about the unusual white man to report my
behavior back to Little Turtle. On this night they did not show up
at the usual time and I drifted off to sleep full of wondering about
the many events of the day and about all that had happened to
me. Of course, I also thought about my future.

I could not have been asleep long when I was awakened by a
warm body beside me under the covers. I was extremely shocked
when it turned out to be a naked Indian maiden cuddling next to
me. It was Autumn Leaf and I suppose I need not relay any further facts about that evening, except to say that it was the single
most memorable night of my life.

Chapter Nine

Life at Kekionga

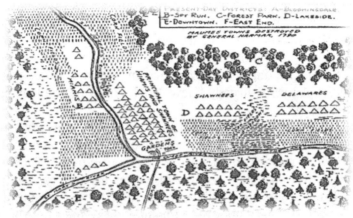

Map of Kekionga

It was now late March of 1791, following my capture in October of 1790. I had been with the Miami for some five months. During that time, I had been moved from the Eel River camp to the capital of the Miamis, Kekionga. It was located at the confluence of three rivers, the St. Joseph, the Maumee, and the St. Mary's. The St. Mary's was on the western edge of the Great Black Swamp that one day in the future William Henry Harrison would lead an army through in relief of a besieged Fort Wayne, in a war yet to come.

The village was an important trading area and crossroads, due to the portage between rivers that essentially connected Lake Erie to the Ouabache (Wabash) River and on to the Mississippi. The area had been important to the French as the shortest route between Canada and the Louisiana country.

Kekionga means something like, "place of the blackberries," in the Miami language, and it was certainly that and much more. All sorts of berries and wild fruits, roots, and plants grew in the area. The three rivers provided abundant fish. Trapping was not as

good as it had been a few years earlier, with beaver bearin.
brunt of the trade and now reduced to very small populatio.
but it was not bad and raccoon, muskrat, and mink, among others, remained easy pickings. A huge herd of buffalo was within a two and a half-days hard trek, much less by horse. Deer and other critters were plentiful. It was a rich land of forests, many waterways, and swamps. There were none of the mountains of my native Virginia frontier, but then no place on earth ever matches one's home.

The Miami were a tribe known for their bravery in war and had long been an enemy of the powerful Iroquois, though not so much in recent years, as the French domination of the area had been replaced by the British influence. The Miami called themselves the Twightwee, an apparent reference to their sacred bird, the crane. I have learned that the name may have first been applied to them by the Delaware people.

Miamitown, as Kekionga was sometimes called, had a few of the more temporary wigwams which are an oval sort of dwelling with walls of woven reeds and roofs of bark. It also had several cabins, probably fifty in all, a long-house for village meetings typical of many woodland tribes, and a somewhat separate French section of six or eight cabins. I suppose there had been a few more French dwellings before the 1760s when the French were allied with the Miamis. Some French continued to live and intermarry with the Miami even though they found the British presence objectionable.

The village extended on both sides of the St. Joseph River, which sort of formed a western flank. The Maumee River was the southern boundary of the village. White folks may be surprised to hear of savages living in cabins. This had been the custom of the Miamis in their permanent settlements for some time and was true of many other woodland tribes as well.

Due to the sheer amount of furs that came through the town each year the British correctly placed great economic importance on the location and upon maintaining a close relationship with the Miami. It was of little consequence to them that they were not supposed to be anywhere south of Canada, by terms of the treaty that ended the war for American independence. Damn interlopers.

The hereditary civil Chief of the Miamis, Pacanne, lived at

Kekionga. He was the son of Aquenackaqua, which means the Turtle. He was older half-brother to Little Turtle. They shared the same father but had different mothers. Pacanne was the civil chief of the Miami, while Little Turtle was a war chief regarded as lesser than a civil chief in the hierarchy of tribal life.

Pacanne, I was to notice, quite oddly bore a facial resemblance to General Harmar. If Harmar had shaved his head and worn a nose ring, they would have looked enough alike to be brothers. Pacanne did have a nose ring and the only hair on his head was a tuft that began in the middle of the crown and continued down to the middle of the very back of his head. His eyes were piercing, and his nose was somewhat turned down resembling the beak of a bird of prey, again like Harmar.

The Chief was a fatherly sort to his people, but he was also a businessman whose family controlled the key portage of some six, or eight miles, that I mentioned earlier between the Maumee and Wabash Rivers. He profited greatly from that control because many fur traders needed its use. In the latter regard, I suppose you could say Pacanne was somewhat like a wealthy and influential white man. Certainly, this type of control of commerce is not unheard of among the tribes, but it is yet another fact that would surprise most white men; that is to see such a flourishing entrepreneurship among the so-called savages. Nevertheless, a good portion of Pacanne's family wealth was used to benefit his people.

Pacanne was a man well-versed in the politics of his race and the intrigue of alliances with more powerful nations. During the War for Independence he was a confidant and traveler with the infamous British officer, Henry Hamilton, known to Americans as, "the hair buyer," for his penchant for paying Indians for American scalps. As far as I know, he was with Hamilton when George Rogers Clark captured Vincennes from Hamilton, after summarily executing some important Indian captives with a tomahawk.

In an odd twist of fate, Pacanne had been pro-American after the late War for Independence and had even been an accomplished scout for Josiah Harmar. However, when a Kentucky militia raid killed many innocent and pro-American Piankeshaws, Miami cousins, Pacanne angrily denounced the Americans and became as ardent an enemy as he had been a friend. As I may have alluded to earlier in my tale, the Kentucky militia certainly never to my knowledge, did the American cause any favors and they never distinguished themselves in battle. Their reputation of cowardly attacks upon women and children and tribes loyal to the United States is truly a testimony of the worst kind.

Another somewhat influential Miami chief lived in one of the outlying villages. His birth name had been Waspikingua, but he was known as LeGris, or more precisely, LePetit Gris, to distinguish him from his father, who had died years earlier in a smallpox epidemic at Kekionga. He had been well-known to be very favorably disposed toward the French. LeGris had come to be a leader just after the French and Indian War when a group of the Miamis from his particular band living on the Tippecanoe River stayed loyal to the French near Fort Ouiatenon. However, LePetit Gris kept his group near the St. Joseph River loyal to the British. All of this became unimportant after the 1760s when the British seized Ouiatenon and ended French influence. Unlike the more reserved Little Turtle, LeGris was talkative and outgoing and had a distinct fondness for liquor. He was to outlive most of his contemporary chiefs. Our dealings with each other were more as related to our involvement in tribal functions, and we had no particular bond. I knew he was somewhat of a "self-preservationist." He had been with Pacanne and Hamilton at Vincennes when George Rogers Clark had taken the fort. Le Gris had kept his men outside the settlement until he saw which way the battle would go.

And of course, there was Michikinikwa or Little Turtle. He was a man of few words, but of regal bearing and about six feet tall. His eyes were dark and bright. They could reflect a soft and compassionate soul at times, while at other times they shown with the full fervor of a warrior in battle. His nose was both broad and long. He had a receding hairline, or he may have cut it that way. It was hard to tell. Miami men were somewhat vain about their hair. They generally shaved the sides and brought the top to a sort of cock's-comb appearance.

Little Turtle sometimes deviated from tribal style and wore his hair down and flat, but this probably happened more in his later life than earlier. Miami warriors dressed their hair daily with bear fat. Among the whites this hairstyle would have seemed outrageous, except maybe with the French who seem to have little in the way of behavior that they consider outrageous. Among the Indian people it was the height of fashion. Additionally, it had the added effect, when combined with facial warpaint, to give braves the most fearsome appearance which some have likened to devils or demons.

Little Turtle frequently wore shells and metal earrings hanging long from his ear lobes. He liked to wear bear claw necklaces and sometime medallions that had been given him, or that he had stolen from foes that he vanquished in battle. He usually wore silver armbands that were broad and ornate. He drank alcohol only moderately and was never drunk. The whiskey trade with his people was something that he worked for years to stop, but with which he was largely unsuccessful. He was a family man and deeply loved his wife and four children.

Despite the ever-growing reputation of Little Turtle as a war chief, he was essentially the American equivalent of a General in rank. He did exercise rule over his own smaller village on the Eel River as I have previously related. He was also a man who at various times had slaves. These he occasionally captured in raids on white settlements and a very few may have been escaped, slaves. My observation was that they were slaves in name only, as he treated them and indeed all people with respect. In time, some of these negroes became integrated into the tribe. In times to come, I never considered Little Turtle as a slaveholder because the normal slave-owner relationship that I had experienced in the South was completely lacking. I believe he captured some on raiding parties to free them from bondage and to infuriate their white masters. Some of these blacks finished their lives with the Miamis, in fact most did. But a few chose to leave and to exercise their new-found freedom.

Little Turtle and I had a relationship of mutual respect. He held me in high regard and I felt the same about him. However, I would be wrong to say that we were close, or that I was anything like a regular adviser to him. But he would from time to time, consult with me on particular matters related to the white race. His closest advisor was Apekonit.

Life at Kekionga was considerably more interesting than that at outlying villages. Little Turtle called it, 'the Gateway of Ideas," going north, and south, east, and west. This was mostly due to the constant commerce, the coming and goings of English and French traders, clergy, and visitors. Weekly mass was held in the village by a French priest. News arrived here first from the four directions and then was relayed to the outlying villages. It was in every respect a hub, or a gateway between east and west, north, and south.

It was during my early time at Kekionga that Apekonit and I became fast friends. We hunted, we walked, we talked, we found we had much in common. I learned that he had been captured as a 12-year-old in Kentucky in 1782. That would make him precisely my age. He had adapted well to Indian life and became a warrior. His mother had died several years before he was captured and his father was killed by Indians, just three years before. At the time of his capture he was living with relatives. His white name was William Wells. Though he had met his older brother, Samuel, who had come looking for him, he had declined to return permanently to Kentucky. This was probably because he was by then married to a Wea woman and had a child. I will relay more of this latter.

Apekonit lived at a village some considerable distance to the southwest, called Kenapakomoko. The chief was Gaviahate, the Porcupine, who was Apekonit's Indian father. Lately Apekonit had been spending more time at Kekionga because of the war, as well as his special relationship to Little Turtle.

The former white man taught me much about the Miami, including continuing my language lessons begun by Autumn Leaf. It was somewhat easier learning from a white man whose original language like mine was English. I had learned a few words from Autumn, but I had not been in any disposition to put earnest effort into learning the language in those early days of my captivity.

As I have relayed earlier, he was a red-haired young man with skin fairer than mine, which would have made him an unlikely Indian, except that Apekonit was so good at being an Indian. He was revered by many of the people because of his generosity, his intelligence, and his embracing of the culture. He was an outstanding woodsman. Before long, he would be accounted one of the greatest Miami warriors.

Living a short way from Kekionga were three white brothers.

They were James, George, and Simon Girty. All had Indian families. They had fought with the British in the late war after initially siding with the Americans. All had been captured as children, along with another brother by the Seneca, who adopted them into the tribe. Though Simon had gained a very bad reputation among the Americans as a ruthless and merciless renegade, the fact was that many an American prisoner was spared from a horrible death at the hands of the savages by his intercession, and sometimes by his use of his resources in buying the freedom of the hapless captive. However, he had not always been able to successfully gain the release of prisoners and on at least one occasion, as he tried to intercede on behalf of a captive, he had been threatened with death if he didn't cease his pleas. Ceasing, the prisoner was burned alive.

I came to know Simon and the other Girtys that summer, to one extent or another. I would not say that I became close friends with them, but I think they enjoyed our conversations in English. They might have been distrustful of me, but for my relationship to, Autumn Leaf and Little Turtle, which seemed to give me a degree of credibility and trust in their eyes. They were accomplished frontiersmen, but not greatly different from the Indians among whom they lived. Still, I think they liked having another white man around and we got on very well. I certainly did not find Simon to be the monster that he had been portrayed as being in American newspapers and railings among the white people.

After a time, I stayed in the cabin of a warrior who had lost his entire family to disease and war, Mihkolenaswa, or "Red Buffalo." He was probably about ten years my senior and an agreeable fellow, known among the people as a brave and generous man. It was through his good graces that my long-rifle was returned to me, or rather purchased by him at a hefty price, from the brave who had it since my capture. It cost him numerous furs to buy back and it took me nearly an entire day to clean it and put it back in good repair. The rascal who had been it's temporary owner did not take the same care as I with such a fine weapon. To Red Buffalo I was truly indebted, and he was to become a lifelong friend and adviser to me.

With my gun back, I spent the spring hunting in the company

of Red Buffalo, and Apekonit. I established a reputation among the people as a great hunter and as a generous man; nothing being so prized among the people as generosity, except maybe powers in war. And frankly, my reputation in the latter was already pretty well-established from the time just before my capture. Oddly, the people also attributed to me that third Indian virtue accorded to so few, but held in such high regard, that of spiritual attainment. I did not share their view of me in this regard, but I also did not discourage it, being a foreigner in a strange culture.

It was during this time that I also accomplished the task of amassing considerable furs and whatever wealth that I could, for a very important purpose that I had in mind.

When I thought I had twice the wealth necessary, I presented myself to Makwatemahkwa, or Black Bear, father of Autumn Leaf. He too was a great warrior and a favorite among the people. His wife's half-sister was the wife of Little Turtle. Formally entering his cabin to ask for his daughter's hand in marriage had me more nervous than I ever remembered being in my entire life. He quite seriously motioned for me to sit down and asked the purpose of my visit, something of a scowl upon his face. I was pretty certain he knew darn well my purpose.

I used Apekonit as my interpreter and within an hour or so of formalities and long, mostly solemn speeches, smoking and eating, all eventually turned to laughter. I left having achieved my goal. I was met outside by Autumn who ran into my arms, nearly knocking me down and squeezing the life out of me She had known what the outcome would be long before I ever entered the dwelling, but not having told me because the ceremony is so important to the Indian people.

After it was over, Apekonit told me with some relish that Black Bear had expected my visit for some time now and that he was not at all adverse to Autumn marrying a warrior of such repute as I had among the people. Quite the contrary; he was said to be very pleased privately, and quite happy that his daughter had finally deemed someone of whom he also approved worthy of her hand in marriage. He well knew of Autumn's love for me and that was all he needed. Of course, we still went through the whole Indian ceremony dickering over the gifts to be given the family and so forth. I guess for some things there are no shortcuts and custom is custom. And maybe like potential fathers-in-law everywhere, Black Bear enjoyed seeing me uncomfortable and squirming is his presence.

I later learned that he had laughed heartily when I had left. He told his wife he had availed himself of much fun with me, but that their daughter was gaining a husband worthy of her. He told her that I was a great warrior and a man of integrity. I was pleased that he thought highly of me.

Five days later we were married, with Little Turtle, Black Bear, and even Pacanne officiating. Representing me in a sort of best man, or best men roles, were: Apekonit, Red Buffalo, and Autumn's brother, Kwaalaantepaapamkamwa, or Gray Fox. Like any wedding it was a grand cause for celebrating and the entire village had swelled to near double the normal population. There were many good wishes and much love for the new couple. Unfortunately, there was also excessive whiskey drinking and rowdiness; the whiskey was a byproduct of exposure to so-called civilization.

That night in our honeymoon wigwam, Autumn presented me with the finest buckskin hunting shirt and white-man-style-pants that I had ever seen. The pants she had made as trousers in the white man's fashion, that is without breeches. She had spent weeks on these presents and the workmanship was exquisite. I presented her with a silver ring that I had purchased from a French trader. She was thrilled; all the more so when I explained the symbolism of the wedding ring among my people.

By late May in 1791, the village had been abuzz for months already, almost since the battle in which I was captured. The subject was the next army likely to visit the Miami towns. It was well-known that General Harmar had been replaced in command at Fort Washington by Arthur St. Clair, the territorial governor, and that General St. Clair was raising an army to attempt to accomplish what General Harmar had not.

I have said that for a time the Miamis had been French allies, but later, out of shifting power consideration, they had become closely allied with the British. Of course, by the articles of the 1783 Treaty of Paris, there were to be no British south of Canada. The British ignored that portion of the treaty and the relationship between the Miami at Kekionga and the British at Fort Detroit was relatively strong. The portage was on an important route of travel and the commercial and strategic significance of Kekionga made British interests understandable, if still detestable in my eyes.

It was early June when three redcoats came calling at Kekionga, accompanied by eight Chippewa warriors. It was a bit unusual to see Chippewas so far south, but they did considerable scouting for the British from Detroit to Fort Mackinaw and beyond into Canada. Whether of British urging or their own volition, the Chippewas were to make their presence known more in the Indian alliance in the coming years. These British were from Detroit and apparently in Kekionga to pledge their support should the Americans come calling again as was anticipated.

The ranking soldier was a young lieutenant, who immediately noticed me. He took umbrage at my presence at Kekionga. He was convinced that I was an American spy. He harangued Pacanne about me but was told by the chief to mind his own business. Later, when he had concluded his meeting for that day with Pacanne, he took it upon himself to search me out and begin questioning me, "Who are you and why are you here? Why do the Miami allow you to live among them?" What an arrogant asshole!

For my part, I detested being taken to task like that and I had no intention of answering. I wasn't about to talk to a damn redcoat, just having such a low tolerance of those fellows. And so I answered his questions with a hard right to the jaw followed by a roundhouse left. Wow! That felt good. I had just struck my first redcoat. My father would have been proud. At any rate, it would have been far more taxing to engage him in conversation and listen to his uppity prattle.

Oh, I neglected to say that there were no further questions. He was on his knees in the dirt, seemingly counting ants on the ground in front of him. Of course, I never heard any counting, so he may have just been admiring the Kekionga soil.

As I finished my response to the officer's questioning, his two redcoat subordinates came running with weapons pointing. However, Gray Fox and Red Buffalo seeing all this happen, were at the ready. They disarmed them rather quickly and certainly very easily, much to the surprise and humiliation of the redcoats.

As for the Chippewas, they took no part. They might assist the British in war, but this was more of a personal thing among men and like most Indians they didn't normally intervene in such affairs, especially among white men. Watching white men fight each other was a good bit of entertainment for Indians. But likely as not, they also knew that if I was living with the Miamis, I must have some sort of good standing and eight of them against all the Miamis would have been a foolish engagement. But then, Chippewas in general are smarter than British soldiers though that may not be saying a lot, as, in my view, the dumbest skunk in the woods was to be considered a better companion than a redcoat.

Of course, my prejudiced actions placed the Miami in a difficult position related to their British allies. The young lieutenant made a quick effort in lodging a vociferous complaint with Pacanne. Pacanne's practical response was that I had done nothing wrong, was considered one of his people, and what right did the young lieutenant have interrogating me as if I was the enemy? Which is exactly what he thought I was. While that was his public stance, privately he had Little Turtle and Black Bear whisk me away back to Little Turtle's village on the Eel River, several miles out of harm's way. There, Autumn Leaf and I spent a few days before deciding upon going out on our own.

In mid-June, Autumn Leaf, Gray Fox, Red Buffalo, two of Autumn's teenage female cousins, Loon's Song and Blue Sky, and I went in search of a place to build our home in the wilderness. We ended settling on the site that I described at the beginning of my tale, after traveling the better part of a day laden with supplies, north by northwest from the Eel River village. There we began to build our home.

Chapter Ten

Nebi Skog

Nebi Skog

As I have previously relayed a detailed description of our home, I shall not here repeat myself. Certainly, it was more of a citadel than a simple home. To that end, the work took considerably longer than a normal cabin building. I felt safer in that house than I would in any other home north of the Ohio River.

In Miami culture, as among most Indian tribes, the women bear the brunt of the physical work while the men hunt, make weapons, and make war. Certainly, Autumn's two cousins, Blue Sky and Loon's Song were absolute worker bees. Red Buffalo was more typical of the male members of the tribe and absented himself on the days of the heaviest labor. Nevertheless, his contribution was felt as he kept us in game for our evening meals, which were much more like daily feasts. For his part, Gray Fox was somewhere in the middle. Typical of Miami males and like many a teenager that I have known, he had an aversion to extreme physical labor. However, Autumn was able to cajole and threaten him, as well as using other means of extracting the maximum work from him. He was, I can truly say, an asset to the process if not always a willing one.

I should say that Red Buffalo having helped build many of the cabins at Kekionga, was quite knowledgeable of such activity and I learned from him a few skills that even my father had not imparted to me. He was particularly adept at joint work, that is where the logs came together at corners of the cabin. He used a technique to strengthen the joints that I had not seen before. It was a sort of pegging the joint together. He used a bore to create a hollow shaft-like space. These he filled with long, thick, wooden rods to fit down into the center of the junction of the logs. This along with a special mortar that he created from clay, tiny pebbles, sand, and water, made the joints stronger. They were also less prone to rotting from exposure to the elements and termites.

It was a fine summer in the wilderness area that would later become northern Indiana and southern Michigan. The sun shone warm, or hot and life seemed to abound all around us, in the forest, the creek, and the river. We worked from daylight to sunset on most days and enjoyed feasts and much story-telling around a campfire in the evenings.

We had good help, pleasant company, plenty of food and we were building our home. Autumn and I were very happy and I think those with us shared our joy. They seemed to thoroughly enjoy our company, just as we enjoyed theirs.

Once a week or so, we would take a day just to fish, roam the woods, look for berries, or just in general, acclimate ourselves to our new surroundings. On one such day, Autumn and her two cousins were across the river in the woods looking for berries while Gray Fox and I had traveled to the north. We wanted to see just how far our home site was removed from traveled trails up that way. Red Buffalo had gone off in a northeasterly direction, claiming that was an area that he had not yet explored for game.

Gray Fox and I had traveled rapidly for the better part of several hours, engaging in more than one-foot race and multiple tests of each of our abilities for long-distance running. This all before we discovered any small trails that showed signs of some usage by area tribes. This confirmed my earlier hope that our cabin would be off the beaten paths used by wilderness inhabitants and therefore afford us some degree of safety related to traffic on main trails. The Miami were not at war with any of the tribes known to be closest to our homestead, albeit, still a very considerable distance. But neither were any of those tribes currently allied with the new United States. My presence in the area might not be viewed well by many inhabitants of other tribes.

After a lunch of some pemmican and wild strawberries, Gray Fox and I headed for home, determined to make even better time than we had on the out-trip. That was going to require a great deal of running. Embracing competition, we arrived in the vicinity of our homestead about four hours before sunset. As we slowed to catch our breaths, we both had an eerie feeling. We didn't hear any sounds from atop the hill. Surely the others would have been back by now.

We proceeded cautiously up the hill and steep drop-off behind the cabin. Instead of breaking out into the clearing, we took a moment to lay low in the foliage, at the edge of that clearing. A shocking sight greeted our eyes. Gagged and tied to a horizontal log, in our pile of logs to be used building the cabin, was Red Buffalo. The carcass of a dead deer lay a few feet away. I guessed that he had killed the deer and then been surprised, not expecting trouble in his own tribe's territory. A few feet away within the unfinished cabin, which was at that time about 4 feet high without a roof, were five of our Chippewa "friends" from several weeks ago in Kekionga. We saw no sign of redcoats.

While the Chippewa curs would not help their British masters in a man to man fight, they had no problem doing the lackey work of the same and looking for me in the wilderness. This was probably on orders of the lieutenant who had questioned me. Their intent was clear; eliminate, or capture the American spy living dangerously close to the Miami people.

It stood to reason that the other three Chippewas, of the original eight at Kekionga, had gone off searching for the women who had left obvious signs as they had gone west across the river that morning. Either that or they were in the woods looking for us in the hope of surprising us.

We had no chance of surprising the five in and around the cabin construction. There was just too much of the clearing we would have to cross. We would be shot dead long before reaching Red Buffalo. If we fired upon them, they would likely kill him.

I motioned for Gray Fox to back out of the area where we lay and we made our way back down the drop-off. I had determined that we would carefully head off to the west in hopes of springing our surprise on the three missing Chippewas. I could only hope that our women had not fallen afoul of them. Not knowing where the Chippewa were, our progress was painfully slow and quiet.

We crossed the river much further north than I normally would have, ignoring the shallow ford further south and going for a late afternoon swim to accomplish our ends. Going into the brush on the west bank, we followed the river south. Reaching the aforementioned ford we stopped and lay low a few minutes. It was at this point we heard sounds coming toward us from the west. After a few tense moments we could see a Chippewa in the lead and the other two bringing our women along, tied hands behind their backs with ropes around their necks being led like dogs. I was furious but able to be deliberate in calculating our actions.

The second warrior pulled Autumn with some difficulty, apparently some considerable difficulty, as her face was bruised and bloodied. She had resisted and had been severely beaten. If I knew only one thing, it was that the warrior leading her was not going to survive the half-hour. Loon's Song and Blue Sky were pulled along by the third brave. He too was soon to be a dead man.

At this point, the first brave had outstripped the other two by some distance and we determined to allow him to enter the river while we attempted to take out the other two. Upon reaching the river, the leader paused, dropped down, scanned the area, and finally let out a bird call meant for his buddies back at the cabin. In a moment, he received his all-clear call from his companions on the hill at the cabin site, whose view was blocked by trees and brush. He let down his guard and started across the river making an arm signal for his partners to follow.

At my signal, Gray Fox sprang upon the last brave and I upon the second one. As Gray Fox jumped out, the two captives pulled back in fear, but when recognizing him, pulled at their ropes until their captor abandoned his hold and attempted to draw his knife. Gray Fox took him to the ground before he could do so and dispatched him quickly by the knife.

In the meantime, I had also caught my opponent off guard. I slashed his throat before he could offer resistance. Autumn yelled and I turned around to see the warrior in the river hurrying toward me, tomahawk raised. I rushed to meet him with my tomahawk. But as he came on, he decided instead to pull his rifle. I attempted to close the distance between us by racing into the water. However, by the time I had taken a few steps he had me in his sights and I little imagined what I could do. I hurled my tomahawk, but he ducked and it sailed past his head. Just before he pulled the trigger a shot rang out, clearly striking him in the back. It had come from the river's east bank and it took him face down into the water. At first, I thought he was hit by one of his comrades come from the cabin site. But then I saw that while it was indeed an Indian, it was not one I had ever seen and was not a Chippewa.

We cut the women free of their bonds and Autumn grabbed me for a hug of grizzly bear proportions. Turning again to the river, there was no sign of our ally, but we knew all too well that the captors of Red Buffalo would soon be racing our way. Gray Fox and I grabbed our guns and right on cue, four warriors came racing toward the river's edge on the east bank, just across from us. The first one to appear was felled with a chest shot from Gray Fox's rifle. At this, the other three fell back into the brush. Picking up the rifle of Autumn's captor, I fired quickly at the brush where I thought I had seen one warrior. I heard a yell but doubted I had made the kill. I threw down the borrowed rifle and secured my own a few yards away. Gray Fox and I slipped behind a downed log, as the girls fled back into the woods upon Autumn's orders.

We exchanged fire for a few minutes when I directed Gray Fox to move to cover to the south, while I went north and up on a small bluff above the river. From here I had a much better view and by following the smoke from his firing, was able to identify the hiding place of one of our opponents. With this knowledge and my father's Kentucky long-rifle, I was able to shoot him in the face and kill him.

The other two were now on the move, like Gray Fox and I had done, in opposite directions securing new cover. Gray Fox seemed to locate one and fired, but missed. He now lay low while reloading. We exchanged fire, maybe four shots each, over a short few minutes, before the entire battle ended abruptly.

The end was prompted when one of our opponents, the one opposite Gray Fox, was shot from behind by an unknown assailant. I assumed this might be our friend from earlier, but as I was making this assumption a ball whizzed by my head from the remaining warrior, just missing dealing me a death blow. Upon discharging his weapon, that warrior, along with another body, came flying from the brush and into the river. He had been tackled by our previous ally and was now engaged in the fight of his life. It was short-lived when our friend used what I would later notice as a very nasty looking warclub. He killed the man with a crushing slam to the left side of his head and a repeat backswing blow to the right side before the man fell into the river.

Who was this friend?

As I looked more closely, my eye was caught by Red Buffalo who was off to my left and emerging from the brush on the river's edge, opposite Gray Fox. It was he who had killed the Chippewa with whom Gray Fox was engaged. But how had he gotten free? And what of the remaining Chippewa?

Red Buffalo signaled us to come out of hiding and I assumed that the unaccounted-for warrior was indeed now accounted among the mounting toll of dead Chippewas. I was to discover this to be true. Our unknown friend had swung round the cabin site undercover of the woods and caught the lone captor left guarding Red Buffalo distracted. As the gunfire on the river was continuing and the captor was gazing in that direction, he was cut down by a lone rifle shot from our friend, who had circled and fired from the east. We had not noticed the shot as we were pretty well engaged ourselves.

I gave a call that Autumn and I often used it as a sort of safety signal. She brought the girls up out of the woods to the river's edge. We all sloshed into the river, washing off mud and blood, as we slowly made our way across. Autumn had me by the arm, assuring me that she had not been violated and regaling me with the fight she and the girls put up, before being subdued.

Red Buffalo ran to join us while our friend, stood in the river, opposite to the point where we were fording. I could see him now. He was a tall man, though not as tall as I. He was very lean, but at the same time muscular. He moved with a dignity that I had rarely seen. Even now I marvel that I am telling a story that includes how a man was moving, just after a life and death battle. But such was the impact upon my memory of that initial encounter with him.

It was impossible to guess his age, though I figured him to be a good bit older than me. But his physical condition was remarkable regardless of his age. Indeed, one might gauge him to be in the prime of life. He was a handsome Indian, with dark, well-combed hair, dark piercing eyes, and a long nose. Yet he struck me as odd. And by odd, I don't know what I exactly mean, other than the aforementioned dignity of his movement and a calm that virtually radiated from him, even after he had just killed men. His clothes and manner of dress, I had never seen. And where had he come from at such a propitious time? He made no move to scalp any of our dead opponents, which was extremely unusual among the red men that I knew. Red Buffalo and Gray Fox would later take charge of that chore, with a certain degree of relish, aided by Autumn and the girls. I declined, though I don't know why. It just seemed not the thing for me to do, maybe because our friend did not do so.

As we all assembled on the farther shore, I turned to our friend and offered my hand along with my heartfelt thanks. For surely, without his assistance, strange as it was, this whole affair might likely not have turned out well.

He appeared to look deep into my eyes as if he were looking into my very soul and said simply, "Kway."

He then shook my hand by grasping my forearm. His grip was strong and almost sent a chill down my spine. I have no idea why. Maybe it wasn't a chill, maybe it was sort of energy. I had no frame of reference for it in experience and it was just yet another unusual thing about this already strange situation.

I had no idea specifically what "Kway" meant, but given his accompanying arm gesture, I took it as a sort of greeting, though it seemed a bit formal to my sensibilities. This especially so, after we had just "gone to war" together.

In English and Miami, I asked, "Who are you and how did you come to be here?"

He merely responded, "Friend," in English and ignored the rest of the question. He was indeed an odd sort. Perhaps, he didn't understand English and was just guessing at my Miami. I concluded that such was a weak argument.

As we gathered, we sort of all checked each other out and determined that no one was seriously injured, though the same could not be said for the eight Chippewas, all of whom were dead.

Our friend, seeing that we were all fine, appeared to bring up the rear as we slowly advanced back to the cabin site, with darkness falling. Autumn and I were in the lead, and after walking several yards, I turned around to check on our party and noticed that our friend was gone, vanished! I had full intention of feeding him and finding out more about him, but he had vanished into the forest, gone without a good-bye, or even a sound. Now, I could clearly state that the tingling in my spine was a cold chill.

I looked at Red Buffalo who had been the closest to him. He had not seen him go, but he also did not appear greatly surprised, only shrugging his shoulders. This was an indication to me that Red Buffalo was not taking this all as quite the spooky event that I was.

Upon reaching our cabin site, as the others began to pull together some food and to butcher the deer carcass while starting a fire, I pulled Red Buffalo said, to find out what he knew that I did not.

"Who was he?" I virtually pleaded in Miami.

"The Indian?" he responded.

"Yes, yes, the Indian," I blurted out, exasperated with his response, which was not matching the intensity of my interrogation of him.

"He is Nebi Skog, the Water Snake," he responded.

Hallelujah! we now had a name. At this rate I was still going to be getting piecemeal information even as the next day struck dawn.

I cut to the chase, "Tell me all that you know about him."

"You do not know about him?" Red Buffalo replied. I sensed he was enjoying this too much and that he was playing upon my impatience.

"If I knew him, I would not be asking all these questions," came my irritated reply.

Red Buffalo said, "He is an Abenaki." Here, I stopped him before he could utter another word.

"An Abenaki?" I said. "An Abenaki in the Ohio Country? Their land is hundreds of miles east of here."

"That is true," said Red Buffalo. "But he is a lone warrior of great spiritual power, who travels the forests, to help those in need. Some of the people say he is a manitou."

"He's a god-spirit?" I interjected.

Non-nonplussed, he continued, "He was raised by the Iroquois, the Oneida people. He still wears some of their clothing, but mostly he dresses like an Abenaki."

Whoa, now we were getting somewhere and Red Buffalo was waxing positively loquacious, compared to his previously painstaking release of information.

"What else do you know about this man and how did he come to be here at this time?" I said. And then, "Have you seen him before?"

Red Buffalo seemed a bit confused as to why I had not by now, been given all the information that I needed.

Nevertheless, he said, "He was here to help us. I do not know him, nor have I ever laid eyes upon him, but the stories of him abound among the people of all tribes. It is said that he moves like the wind, that he is a man who does not sleep, that he might be anywhere at any time. It is said he can walk through walls and that the animals of the forest obey his commands. Until now, I did not know if he even existed. Stories about him seem more to describe a spirit than a man. It is said that he might be from the other world. He is said to possess great powers. There can be no doubt that this man was he whom the stories describe. A man who appears to help those in need. This man was Nebi Skog, the Water Snake."

"A spirit, eh?" I muttered incoherently and then dropped the exhausting conversation completely. I had to help with the removal of the Chippewa who had died at the cabin, shot by Nebi Skog, or Water Snake, or whoever he was. I put no stock in tales of spirits and I kept the rest of my questions to myself for the time being.

Red Buffalo was positively beaming with delight over his story. I could easily imagine that he made the whole thing up, except for the fact that he had not appeared to be thinking about his words while remembering tales he had heard beginning long ago.

Of all the people I had encountered in my life to that point, this Nebi Skog was perhaps the most perplexing. He seemed to grip my imagination and I could not get him out of my mind. His hold on me was inexplicable, even though I dismissed this otherworldly stuff. I felt grateful to him, yet strangely unsettled by his appearing from nowhere and his disappearing in the same fashion. Still, spirits don't shoot and fight, but then there was the handshake that I assumed spirits also cannot do. Nevertheless, there was a creepy component to the man. As I thought once again, a cold chill ran down my spine.

As we gathered around the fire for some venison that evening, it dawned on us that we had a potentially serious problem on our hands. Notably, we had just killed eight Chippewa warriors, albeit ones who had black-hearted designs upon our persons. Nevertheless, the Chippewa were British allies and as such, officially allies of the Miami. While those who knew us in our villages would understand and support us, completely believing us to be the victims in this affair, the outlying tribal allies were not so likely to feel positively disposed toward us.

After much back and forth discussion, we came to a few conclusions. One, if the British did send these curs to find me, they were not going to admit it since I was held in esteem at Kekionga. The British could not afford to damage their relationship with Pacanne and Little Turtle. Two, the Chippewas being hundreds of miles from home, would have no relatives, indeed no one who knew specifically where they were, or what they had been up to if they had done this on their own, which was highly unlikely. They would have simply vanished without a trace. No one would be immediately looking for them. No one would ever find them, or know their fates.

Therefore, our course of action was determined. In the morning, we gathered the bodies and piled them on a large fire, kindled by dry brush and a substantial amount of wood. We used some of their powder as an incendiary. This process took all day but eliminated almost all trace of them. The bits that were left: some bone, charred clothing, and so forth, we put in the river and watched float southwest, or sink away from any place where the British could discover the remnants.

We secreted a few of their weapons in a hidden cache in the forest, in the event we ever needed them. We kept their remaining weapons, powder, and shot, at the cabin. We all took a vow that none of the events of the day before would ever be spoken to other human beings.

I should say that burning a body is not a normal Miami burial practice. Most of their burials are in the ground like white folks, but sometimes on top of the ground carefully covered up, maybe even with a small structure built over the corpse. Finally, upon occasion, they put the body in a wooden coffin suspended high up in a tree.

As regards the Chippewas, we were not so concerned with funerary tradition as with eradicating any evidence of their presence on our land.

Having disposed of the Chippewa bodies, I found my thoughts turning back to this strange man, Nebi Skog, the Water-Snake. He was indeed a dilemma and one that I would ponder daily for some time to come.

Chapter Eleven

The Whisper of War

Arthur St. Clair

In the days following our battle with the Chippewas, things returned to normal and within another three weeks we were nearing completion of the cabin. During all those days, I quietly pondered this strange Abenaki Indian, Nebi Skog. Where had he come from and where did he go? Such were thoughts that occupied my mind many times during each day. I asked Autumn if she knew of him and she essentially repeated what she had previously heard growing up. That was pretty much identical to what Red Buffalo told me. Lots of hokum pocum, manitou-stuff, with supernatural powers.

For the last week of our cabin building, I hired a French carpenter from Kekionga, who was also a fur trapper. I paid him in pelts for his work: nine muskrats, three minks, seven big beavers, two badgers, and a wolverine. In exchange, he brought his two teenage boys with him and they helped finish the cabin. They also did some of the finer woodworking required inside. When done, he pronounced the cabin, "the finest in all the land." I agreed with that assessment.

We had not arrived in time to plant crops, just a small garden, so we made an extra effort at our fishing, smoking a large quantity for winter. We gathered and dried all the berries we could find and, in the fall, we would gather nuts and wild fruits, such as pawpaws.

Sometime in early August, two Miami runners came to the site to deliver some news. Large contingents of troops and supplies were again arriving at Ft. Washington via the Ohio River, in what were obvious preparations for war. That could only mean that the army would move against the Miami and their allies yet this year. It was noted that Territorial Governor, Arthur St. Clair, would be the commanding General. The old soldier had been given one last command by President Washington. His vitality was well-past the task, but good soldiers always answer the call to duty and he was a good soldier.

The Indian confederation had spies all about Ft. Washington and having heard some of the details of their intelligence, it was clear to me that we had been naive the summer before. We had not realized just how close we were being watched. This of course, was disconcerting to me. Blue Dogs, Jim, Black Duck, and I had all been out many times assessing the traffic in the area and not finding much more than I earlier reported in this telling.

Another thing that becomes abundantly clear was that this summer's army, just like last summer, was once again not ready to march in what should have been the prime campaign season, but rather was engaged in waiting for troops and supplies to arrive. Miami, Shawnee, and Delaware spies estimated the earliest leave date for the army to march out of Ft. Washington, as sometime in early September.

The runners who came to relay this information were two teenagers, Little Beaver and Angry Cloud. They requested that Red Buffalo and Gray Fox tarry no longer, but come to Kekionga as soon as possible, preferably within the week. War councils would be held as soon as the allied tribes could be gathered. For my part, I was told to expect a visit from Apekonit any day.

Very little of this was good news to me, save the impending visit of my friend, Apekonit, though I knew the visit would have something to do with the upcoming invasion by the Army.

For some time now, I had been conflicted about staying in this wilderness instead of reporting back to Ft. Washington. But then how could I now fight against the people of the woman that I loved more than life? By the same token, I could not fight with the Miami against my people. I was moody and disturbed much of the time, as I pondered the impending events and tried to reconcile my current and past lives. It was during this time that it finally dawned on me that my name had probably appeared on official army records as among those killed last autumn and that by now these lists had been published in eastern newspapers, letting my relatives, especially my dear sisters, think that I had met a grisly end on the Ohio frontier. Still, I knew no way to get a message to them to ease their anguish.

I figured Luke had received similar news, but with him it was different. He wasn't as apt to be accepting of such news. He was more of a prove it to me personally. So, I kinda figured he might doubt I had been killed. As youths in the wilderness, we often joked about being immortal like the heroes of Greek mythology that mother made us study, and we had made a pact to always look for the other if one came up missing, or was ever reported dead without proof.

In the next two days, we finished the cabin, and Red Buffalo and Gray Fox left for Kekionga, while the cousins tarried to help Autumn finish the interior to her liking and to gather roots, berries, plants for medicine, and whatever else it is that Miami women do. The girls and Autumn had a special bond and the girls practically worshiped the ground she walked on. She was a mentor and so great was her reputation within the tribe and beyond, as previously mentioned, that they considered her just about the greatest person they knew, excepting, of course, Little Turtle. She might as well have been their older sister, so great was their affection for her. Of course, I shared their admiration and more. My love for her only grew each day that we were together.

Due to the recent close call with the Chippewas, I was reluctant to stray far from the cabin, though I doubted any kind of further trouble would immediately be coming our way. We settled on eating a lot of fish during these days, mostly the various catfish and smaller panfish, caught easily each morning, fresh from the small stream.

One day, as I was shooting a few squirrels near our clearing, I saw coming across the clearing toward the cabin, my friend,

Apekonit.

"Aya aya!" he shouted.

I answered, "Aya aya! Teepahki iishiteechinaanki keewiihkawilotawiaanki!" This is a Miami greeting akin to, "Hello, we are glad you have come to visit us."

Unlike their cousins, the Illinois, who share a very similar language, the Miami tend to stretch words out, to enunciate and to make speech sound very formal. The Illinois speak their words more quickly, with less enunciation, and fanfare.

Apekonit spoke to me in English and said, "My friend, your language skills are improving greatly. Autumn is a good teacher."

"She's a good teacher, alright," I muttered. And then lower, "But language isn't her best subject."

He understood and laughed heartily.

We spent an hour, or so catching up; Apekonit telling me news about the various people that I knew from the Eel village and Kekionga. I asked about news from Fort Washington.

"The whites are again gathering an army. They will come in the time of the white corn harvest, or later," he said.

"St. Clair is coming for certain?" I said.

"Yes, he is coming with a great force, this time he will bring cannons," he said.

"Bringing cannons will force him to clear trees and make roads," I said.

"Yes, he will come slowly and thrash about like a clumsy fool through the forest. He will have no chance against us. All the tribes will fight. This time the soldiers will not be allowed to get close to our villages," he said.

He shared this last information as a forgone strategy to be employed in the impending battle. I took it to mean that the confederation of tribes would attack the army farther south and away from the villages.

He went on, "My friend, I wish you would join us in the fight. You are a great warrior, a brave man, with much spiritual power, the people would be proud for you to fight with us. You would inspire many."

At this, I grew silent. My torment becoming obvious to him after a short time.

He said, "Remember, I too was white, but this war is wrong, these white men are greedy for land. They will kill the people.

This is very wrong."

I certainly had come to that conclusion myself, but as for fighting against the army, I could not.

I said, "My friend, I understand you. I think you are right. But I have not been with the people as long as you and I cannot fight the people of my birth."

He replied, "Your people are the Twightwee, not the whites, you are now one of us."

"You may be right," I replied, "But my thinking is not yet clear on this. My head is confused and fuzzy. My heart tugs in two directions. Understand that I hope that the whites would leave the people alone if the British would go away and quit agitating between the two."

"In your heart, you know this is not right, not true," he said. Then he continued, "The British are not to be trusted, this we know. But they can help us against the Americans by giving us guns and powder. In the end, the Americans will come, British or not."

I really could not argue with this point because I knew all too well that he spoke the truth. I knew, from the Americans that I had seen coming west, that they considered getting land as their great opportunity and their land acquisition would come at the expense of the Indian people.

I said, "The British have broken their word which they gave when they lost the last big war. They use the Miami to fight and die for them while they sit back and promise much. Their words are lies and they only want to reclaim what was lost to them in the war. They are dogs that lie and cannot be trusted."

"And how is this different from the Americans?" he asked.

My silence gave him the answer that I knew in my heart was the truth of his words. The Indian people were fighting for their land and the survival of their culture. The British were their best hope of success in the short term. Still, my soul was in turmoil. I was split between the two sides and could not commit to either. For once in my life, my usual self-assured determination was absent.

Choosing had consequences that I could not accept. Failure to choose was a torture just as bad, but without clear results for my future. Maybe, I reasoned, if the British were not involved my choice would be easier. I hated those bastards. But I even doubted that reasoning and my mind was tormented more than it had ever been. Always before, I had seen right and wrong. This time, the two were not clear.

Sensing my torment, Apekonit said, "Pacanne expected that this would be hard for you. He knows that you could be of great help to the people, but he also knows each man must serve his soul in these matters. He sends me a message for you."

"His message is this, do what is best for you at this time. In time, your thoughts may change. Perhaps you will have a spirit vision, perhaps your choice will become clear. The people will respect your decision as they respect you in all things. If your choice is to remain out of this fight, you must stay away from the villages when the British are present. Your presence will only cause problems with them, and in this matter, we cannot have anything that would take us away from our attention to defeating our enemy. Our families are at stake, and we need the British guns and powder."

I told Apekonit, that I understood and further, that I appreciated the understanding of the great chief. I would follow his advice. It amazed me that Pacanne had such a complete understanding of what I was going through and that he would send me such a message.

I wondered what Little Turtle thought about all this; I needn't have.

Apekonit, with intuition and perspicacity uncommon to the educated, let alone a citizen of the wilderness, told me, "The great Michikinikwa has said similar words to me as Pacanne has said. He told me that he feels in time you will help the people, but maybe not in this fight, not at this time, it is too soon for you. He said that for us to try and force you to help would be no good. We must let you wrestle with your thoughts and seek your path. The manitous will guide you. Only then will your spiritual power be freed from the bondage of confusion in your thoughts."

While I appreciated this information, it probably only added to my guilt. Here was a group of people who had taken me in, who seemed to understand what I was going through and who in standard Indian fashion, allowed me the space to chart my course of action. I could not imagine that white folks would have afforded me the same understanding and consideration.

Though I had had only one conversation with Arthur St. Clair, I judged him to be a good and decent man, a patriot. I had had many more conversations with Pacanne and Michikinikwa. I knew beyond any doubt, that they were admirable men.

By now, Autumn and the girls had come out of the cabin and noticed Apekonit's presence. Screaming and hugging followed, as Autumn and her cousins were very fond of the young red-head and ran full speed toward him.

We spent the rest of that day visiting, eating and showing Apekonit around our homestead. He marveled at the place we had chosen, and at the craftsmanship of the cabin. He said we had done well.

That night, we spoke of our intention to go on a buffalo hunt within a few days. There was a large herd maybe 18 to 20 leagues to the west, near another river known also as the St. Joseph, this one much bigger than the St. Joseph River at Kekionga. The Miami had once lived on this larger St. Joseph River, which the French called, "the River of the Miami." But a hundred or more years ago, the Miami had moved to the Kekionga area and the Potowatomie had moved into the area around the river and near the Buffalo herd.

Apekonit and Autumn had both been on hunts before and described the land in the area of the herd as both beautiful and bountiful in game. There was all that anyone could want for food. All the tribes knew of the place and there was buffalo enough for all and indeed many other animals.

We talked late into the night and the next morning Apekonit and I went into the woods, after he expressed an interest in seeing more of the area adjacent to our homestead. After about three hours of just scouting the area we came back to the cabin, and he again pronounced that we had done very well in the choice of the site for our home.

We ate some food that Autumn and the girls fixed and then Apekonit wanted to leave. He was on his way to Kenekomoko, where he had not been for some time. He was eager to see his wife and child, but he was also carrying the message to the outlying tribes of a council of war to take place at Kekionga as soon as all could gather.

And so, we parted.

We would later find out that Apekonit had arrived at Kena-pakomoko to find that it had been raided by the Americans under James Wilkinson, operating out of Vincennes and under the command of a Colonel Jean Hamtramck. Some 40 people from the village were missing. Among them were his wife and child, as well as his Indian mother, Gaviahate's wife. Apekonit blamed himself for not being present, for having tarried too long at Kekionga, for not having had his wife and child with him, indeed, all manner of self-recriminations. The simple fact is, had he been present when Wilkinson came, he probably would have been killed by the superior American force.

Apekonit, with the savage ferocity of a caged animal, impotent to act immediately, vowed vengeance upon the Americans. Within a few months he would have the opportunity to fulfill his vow. He would do so in the most savage and death-defying fashion imaginable. In the process he would become a legendary warrior among the Miami people, and indeed, among all peoples of the Indian confederation.

Chapter Twelve

Parc Aux Vaches

Buffalo Herd

I had questioned Autumn extensively about our buffalo hunt. Since we did not have any pack horses, would we be able to carry the meat out? She told me that four of us could carry a great deal, more so if we created some travois for the purpose. She also told me that the last third or so of the trip could be made by water, as the St. Joseph River came pretty far east before taking a north-westerly direction. Even though the Miami in general, seemed to disdain the use of canoes, the tribe kept hidden two canoes near the river for use by hunting parties. Whether they would still be there, or still be in good condition was anyone's guess. If so, we could pack the meat by canoe at least part of the way back. Either way, she felt that there was no serious problem, as she said, "We aren't feeding an entire village."

To this I replied, "But you know how much Loon's Song eats," giving the youngster a good-natured ribbing. We all laughed.

We secured the cabin and left early in the morning, the young cousins particularly excited about their first buffalo hunt and also about traveling to places about which they had only heard in the stories of others. It was about an 18 to 20 league trip to the place where we would find buffalo, 12 to 13 leagues on foot if we were lucky enough to find canoes for the last part of our journey. The first part of the trip was made through the forest. Then about two, or three leagues from our home, were many well-traveled trails that came and went to the area of the buffalo. We camped in the late afternoon of the first day and the same on day two, when we were just at the St. Joseph River.

Once at the river, Autumn began looking for the canoes. After about twenty minutes she found a spot, very overgrown with bushes, that she thought looked familiar. She dug in and indeed produced two canoes. One was home to some varmints, who went scurrying when she pulled it out of the tangled vegetation. That canoe while lacking any visible holes, was in poor condition. A tree had fallen on one end and pretty well destroyed that portion. The other canoe was in better condition but certainly would not hold four of us.

Further investigation of the dense underbrush yielded four usable paddles. I took the good canoe out into the river and paddled around to make certain that it was of a condition to make the trip. It proved to be just so.

I decided that Autumn and the girls would take the canoe. I'd follow along the river. The meandering of the river would greatly increase the distance I'd have to travel but would allow me to better explore this amazing land.

And so, off we went. While my three ladies were not high-speed paddlers, nevertheless, at certain points I was forced into a run to keep up. At other points I fell behind due to the vegetation along the river being too dense to transit, or in having to cross tributary creeks and streams entering the river from the north, the shore upon which I traveled. In several hours, we arrived at our destination.

The area we sought was called Parc Aux Vaches. That is something akin to cow park, or cow pasture, by the French, but cow pens, by the Indians. This because a very large buffalo herd had calved in the area, longer than anyone could remember, specifically on the east bank of the St. Joseph River. It was a land of abundant wildlife. In addition to the buffalo, there were bear, lynx, wildcats, wolves, several kinds of fox, mink, fishers, river otters, skunks, porcupines, beaver, possums, raccoons, squirrels, rabbits, wolverines, badgers, elk, deer, quail, pheasants, painters, prairie chickens, and so many others.

There were hickory trees, birch, ash, and a few kinds of pine, among others. But mostly there were giant old oak trees. These were the kind called red oaks.

The woods were full of nuts, berries, and edible roots. There were open prairies with grass so tall and rich, as to encourage the buffalo to stay year-round just gorging themselves. In addition to the St. Joseph River, there were wetlands, marshes, and streams. The latter were abundant with fish and waterfowl.

Yet for all the abundance, Autumn told me that the buffalo were much less plentiful than they had been just a few years ago. The herd was shrinking at an alarming rate.

On the higher east bank of the St. Joseph River, amid tall grass, trees, berry bushes, and in the cool shade, it was very much like a park, a park where hunting was easy and food could be obtained without limit. It was a relaxing place, where calm seemed to prevail, and where the fat buffalo lounged lazily about.

Across the river was a much lower, but level flood plain. The girls landed their canoe, and we quickly set up camp. We then went downstream to a point where we had to climb up a very steep bank. The river here was deep and wide, but languid and slow.

Taking the whole, it was in many respects a most incredible combination of the best of the wilderness, except that there were no mountains as I've complained before. Mountains add majesty to the wilderness. Though I will admit that climbing mountains can be a pain in the ass.

And speaking of pains in the ass, there was a danger about this place that I did not like and that Autumn had informed me about before we had left home. Just up the river, perhaps only half a league, was Fort St. Joseph, a fort originally built by the French, but for some time now, garrisoned by the interloping British. If they caught me this close to the fort, there would be trouble of a nature I hoped to avoid.

As we neared the top of the bank, the trees stirred with a cool breeze. From our vantage point we could see buffalo lazing about and grazing in a wide-open area that bordered a wooded area.

This being my first buffalo hunt, I consulted Autumn in detail. Her people frequently used small grass fires to entrap the buffalo herd where they could most easily be harvested. However, since we needed only one buffalo, ours would be a simple hunt with my long-rifle.

It was determined that we would take a yearling if the opportunity presented. The meat would be much more tender and it would be smaller and easier to butcher. We planned that I would descend back down to the river level and move toward the herd by going down along the water to move undetected. Autumn told me to make my way slowly and carefully, being as stealthy as possible. She told me that I needed to leave myself an escape route just in case the herd stampeded in my direction. This was incredibly unlikely, but Autumn had more than one relative who had died on a buffalo hunt.

I did in fact, move stealthily and after what seemed like a half-hour, though I couldn't be sure, I was within rifle range. As I crept slowly up the high embankment at a painfully slow pace, struggling to find my footing and to not make noise, I crested the top and crawled behind a wide bush of some sort. From my vantage point I could see a female with a calf that had been born in the spring, off to my right and almost on the edge of the embankment that led down to the river. Further away, but in a direction more directly in front of me, were young females grazing and moving slowly toward me. Back further, where this clearing caught the edge of a line of trees was most of the rest of the herd, lying in the shade, or quietly grazing.

Off to my left, but not near the riverbank, were two bulls snorting insults at each other, but not committing themselves to serious physical conflict. It was nearly the rutting season and before long, these bulls would likely be fighting instead of posturing. Now, a young male came up into the vicinity of the two female yearlings. His instincts seemed to tell him that there was a reason he was interested in the ladies, but in reality he had no clue what that interest was. He eyed the females, moved closer, then jumped a couple times in an attempt to gain their attention. Having been successful at that, he didn't know what further he was to do and so he lay down and rolled on his back as if scratching an itch. The females at this point looked at him, looked at each other and then began to wander back toward the tree line.

After rolling about for a short while, the young bull stood up and started slowly in my direction.

Aiming through the bushes, I fired a shot to his head. I was shocked when he did not immediately go down. I reloaded quickly and fired a shot to his chest that most certainly hit his heart and finished him. It was at this time that I noticed the mother and calf, along with the rest of the herd, had spooked from the gunfire and ran into the tree line onto a very wide path. It was the way that they had come to this area. The two bulls that I mentioned earlier, one extremely large, trotted behind but seemed not to share the fear of the rest of the herd. They paused three or four times, to turn and look in the direction of their dead young comrade.

By this time the girls and Autumn, having watched from a distance, came running along the bluff over the river to the bush where I was. This attracted the attention of the largest bull who stopped dead in his tracks. He seemed to be considering what to do next, and if he had been human, I would have sworn he was working himself into being very angry. He took a few steps in the direction of the girls and Autumn, who were now nearly to my bush. They were not paying any attention to the bull who was some considerable distance away.

For my part, I now stood up, in full view of the bull, reloading my rifle. My appearance out of the bush seemed to infuriate the giant. He lowered his head and raised it again, repeating this in a sort of bouncing motion. He snorted and began to paw the ground furiously, kicking up a small storm of dust. After this display, he charged in my direction.

"Get down to the river," I shouted at the girls, pushing each in that direction. I didn't care how fast a buffalo could swim in pursuit of a human, the human could swim faster, at least that was my thinking.

Owing to my distance from the bull, I had plenty of time to aim. However, a ton of furious muscle running full speed toward me was more than a little disconcerting. I took a breath, told myself to relax and to aim at his chest. I slowly squeezed the trigger of my rifle. My aim was true but had absolutely no discernible impact upon the beast unless it was to make him more furious if that were possible. There was no time to reload, not time to run, not time to leap down the river bank. The latter was not a viable option anyway, because I had no intention of leading him anywhere near Autumn and the girls. I wasn't about to guess at buffalo behavior. I had never been around them.

My heart was racing as I stood watching the beast hurdle toward me. I now became aware of a sound like thunder, as his hoofs pounded the ground. The very ground was vibrating like an earthquake. I was inclined to run but knew that would be futile in the short term. I would have to somehow escape his first thrust at me and perhaps while he was turning to come again, I might affect an escape.

I stood my ground, staring into the fury that was in his eyes. Our minds seemed to meet. He came on with deadly intent. Now he was just feet away, "wait, wait, . . . , wait, . . . , I told myself. . . ," until at what I thought was the last safe second, I feinted one big step to the left and then dove into the air to my right. He went for the feint, but he was much quicker to adjust than I imagined he could be. As I was in mid-air, he continued past going right over the ground I had just been standing upon, carried by his momentum. However, as he did so he swung his mighty head and struck my left leg a blow with his horns, causing a tremendous pain. He tore a gash perhaps six inches long and deep to the bone between my ankle and my knee.

Fear drove me to disregard anything in my head except escape. I rolled head over heels and was somehow able to stand up. However, my plan to run along the bluff above the river, in the opposite direction from the girls, was thwarted, when by my third step I was down. My leg was telling my body what my mind would not, that is that it would not support my weight. I landed and rolled over to see that the huge beast had come to a screeching stop sliding perhaps twenty feet. He was nearly at the precipice of the embankment over the river. He turned and knowing that he now had me, pawed the ground once, twice, three times; then on he came on to finish me off.

He was maybe thirty feet away and coming hard, head-lowered. I remember thinking to myself, "J. R., you have no plan."

I attempted to crawl and roll toward the river embankment edge, hoping to roll over the side and gain some more time. Suddenly, the improbable happened; a shot rang out from upriver not far from where we had set camp and where the clearing ended.

The shot tore through the left eye of the beast and blew out the right side of his head, just under his right ear. Confused, he stopped and stumbled becoming wobbly on his feet.

At this point, I was aware that Autumn came racing past me. I yelled for her to stop, but to no avail. She was not going to stop. She had been so busy getting the girls to safety, then scrambling up the embankment; now she rushed the great beast with her trade gun and shot him almost point-blank in the face. Her shot took the giant bison down, though I think he was perhaps already dead on his feet.

She blew his face off. Her courage was unquestionable.

With my heart racing, I saw Autumn and the girls, hurrying toward me. I looked toward the direction of the first shot. It was a long way and I could see a figure, but could not believe that a shot from that distance could have been successful, let alone packing the wallop that it did. I remember thinking, "My gosh, was whoever fired using a cannon?"

I could not even make out the person, whether man, or woman, Indian, or white. Autumn hugged me and turned her attention immediately to my leg. I became nauseous and dizzy and lay my head down on the cool grass. I could see the figure who fired the shot moving toward us on the run. Just before I passed out, I uttered recognition with a shallow breath, it was, "Nebi Skog!"

I am told that it was hours later when I regained consciousness. Our camp had been moved to the exact place where I had gone down. This was for the primary reason of not moving me, but secondarily so that the cousins could begin butchering the two dead buffalo.

As I awoke, I noticed that my leg was heavily bandaged and was propped up on top of several blankets that had been filled with grasses, loose bark, any number of things, to create enough substance to support the leg underneath from mid-thigh to ankle.

Greatly swollen, my leg was propped up in the manner described and according to Autumn, this was done at Nebi Skog's insistence, due to extreme bleeding. As he explained to her, we must put the leg higher than the heart to help control the bleeding.

I am guessing that the buffalo had ruptured an artery in my leg and that I was lucky to have not bled out and died. Autumn relayed to me that our friend had applied a tourniquet above my knee for a short time, while he used some plants unknown to her, in a powder form sprinkled deep into the gash. As I previously stated, my flesh was laid bare to the bone. He had then applied some leaves that he had in a medicine pouch and then use hand-held pressure for nearly an hour.

At that point, convinced that his procedures were working, he applied a tight pressure bandage over the wound. Nebi Skog had told the women that someone must be with me at all times and not allow me to move the leg, for an indefinite period. I marveled at the medical savvy of this strange man and wondered if Doc Johnson could have handled this any better, or even as well.

As I became more coherent, Autumn administered some of our usual pain killers in the form of a sort of soup.

Autumn had worried that my leg was also broken. I can tell you that it felt like it was.

However, Nebi Skog assured her, "Leg is not broken, but the wound is very serious."

Although he was not loquacious, they had conversed in Miami, his usage of the language near perfect.

Now, I looked at him as he sat by the fire near me and said in English, "Thank you friend."

He responded by deflecting my gratitude and saying in English, "The buffalo was large, but your wife is skilled with a gun."

Now I remembered that Autumn, too, had fired at the beast.

I looked at her and she was crying. I asked, "Why are you crying?"

She said, "I am sorry, I should have shot sooner."

"Nonsense," I replied. "I think you were a little busy. This is not your fault. Once again, you helped to save me."

As I said this, I took her hand and kissed it causing her to sob all the more. And she was not normally prone to crying.

This gave her some relief, but she was distressed that she had not been able to do more and also, as I later found out, that she was at the point of this discussion, not certain I would live.

Nebi Skog said only, "You are badly hurt and you must do what I tell you."

He was not demanding, not condescending, just matter-of-fact. He also had the good sense not to tell the patient that the injury was life-threatening. What a strange and unusual man he was. He seemed so committed in his humanity and yet so detached from personal feeling, or emotion.

While these conversations were occurring, Blue Sky and Loon's Song were busy butchering buffalo and setting up a make-shift smoke tent, so that we could preserve as much of the meat as possible. Normally, we would have set off for our cabin after the butchering, but with me unable to travel, we were certain to lose some of the meat to spoilage. Nebi Skog took several large chunks of meat to a nearby cold spring of which he was aware, that fed into the St. Joseph River. He intended to preserve these chunks for roasting in the next two, or three days, so that we could enjoy fresh meat without having to eat it smoked while camped. How he knew about the cold spring, I do not know and made a conscious determination not to even ruminate about. This man was an enigma and all my pondering was not going to solve him. And questioning him was not going to produce much more information. However, I did determine to get what information I could from him, in as many conversations as possible.

To that end, I looked at him and said, "Tell me, my friend, how is it that you are always around when we need help."

His reply was to shrug his shoulders and say, "Perhaps you need help when I am just nearby."

I had to try and get my head around that statement. It seemed simple, seemed unassuming and yet I suspected that it was meant to stop my inquisition somehow.

OK, now I tried a different subject, "How is it that an Abenaki is so far west and alone."

"I travel alone and listen to the wind. My life is in the forest," he said.

Well the "listen to the wind" comment seemed to have a religious connotation, sort of a soul-searching type thing, but the rest was non-committal.

I persisted, "But you travel the lands of many people, you must encounter much danger. How is it that you move so freely and no one bothers you?"

He seemed to be thinking, it was now nearly dusk and he

piled more wood on the fire.

Finally, he said, "The forest is my home. I move quietly and with great care, so I leave no footprint upon the land. Good people know that they have nothing to fear from me."

With this comment, I could imagine that he was referring to his ghost-like comings and goings, but I suspected that was just my imagination. He was not going to tell me anything in detail.

I said, "Have you no home, do you not long for the home of your youth?"

His reply was, "Things have changed in the land of the Abenaki, and of the Iroquois, with whom I lived. Times are hard for some people, and their land is taken for farming by whites. My home will always be the land of bear, deer, and wolf."

"How is it that you knew how to take care of my wound?" I was trying to pin him down.

"I am guided by the manitous. My knowledge is the knowledge of all men," he said.

At this point I gave up, deciding that he must indeed be a deeply spiritual man and very privately so. I could only be grateful once again, for his presence.

Seeing Nebi Skog up close, I can only reiterate what I said earlier. He was taller than average for an Indian. His long hair was shiny black, with just a hint of gray and was very well combed and kept. His clothes were neat and fit him well. He wore a dark green long sleeve shirt of cloth, with a necklace of multicolored beads worn close around his neck. His breach-cloths were long and of dark brown cloth. His leggings were of buckskin, done with beautiful craftsmanship. His moccasins, though worn, were of exquisite quality and design that I had never before seen.

He was slender but muscular and I would say he was a handsome man. He had a long nose and piercing dark eyes. He wore a single eagle feather in his hair. He had no tattoos that I could discern, a somewhat uncommon trait for his race. His skin was brown, though not extremely dark. In fact, not so dark and certainly not so wrinkled, as one would expect of someone who spent their entire life traveling in the great outdoors. I continued to feel that he was older than he looked, though I cannot say why I had that impression Perhaps there was a look of wisdom about him.

It was a rough night of pain and I slept only fitfully, as Autumn, Nebi Skog, Blue Sky, and Loon's Song all took turns making sure I did not move the leg and watching for signs of renewed bleeding. They frequently administered the pain-killing soup.

When I awoke in the morning, my leg had been splinted on two sides and tied between two stakes in the ground, on each side to prevent movement. It was of course, still propped up. There was a sort of compression wrap on it that was very tight, but not so tight as to cut off my blood circulation. At this point, I knew this was Nebi Skog's doing and I had no intention to question it.

I slept most of that day after Autumn had administered a large dose of pain medicine. I awoke to see the stars above my head, the fire crisply talking, a gentle cool breeze blowing, and everyone eating buffalo.

I wondered that Nebi Skog was not leaving us. Years later, in relaying this whole event to a doctor friend of mine, he told me that I was lucky to have survived. With that I came to think that Nebi Skog had stayed to nurse a critically injured man, a man who had no idea how critically injured he was. Nebi Skog would not leave until he was convinced of a reasonably positive outcome.

The next morning, Autumn and Nebi Skog, who had been collaborating while I was asleep, administered a foul-tasting soup that immediately left me feeling euphoric. They then removed my bandages and using a variety of plant leaves and powders out of Nebi Skog's medicine bag, treated my wound and then sewed it up. They had previously left the gash open except for the bandages. The procedure took over an hour. Fortunately, whatever they had given me blocked most of the pain, and I was just glad to be there. That is to say, feeling better than any drunk I was ever on.

After sewing my wound, they applied a fresh bandage and the compression wrap. Nebi Skog pronounced that we would stay two more days and then travel back to our cabin. Had I not been so out of it, I would have wondered just how I was going to travel that far, but they had everything worked out.

Loon's Song had built a travois, and Blue Sky was packaging meat in the buffalo hides. The hides had been curing in the summer sun for three days.

Later that afternoon, Nebi Skog disappeared for several hours, taking with him a hefty amount of buffalo meat. I was coming down off the pain killer and was convinced that he had left us. But after a short time, he came into the clearing and much to my surprise was leading a horse.

I had to ask, I just had to, "Where did you get a horse?" I was exasperated at this man's resourcefulness.

His response was, "He was alone in the forest, I needed him and he came to me. I left buffalo meat hanging in a tree in case he had an owner. He will carry you home."

Yeah, sure, a horse alone in the forest. I was supposed to believe that and that he found the lone horse in the vast expansive wilds of the Ohio Country. If it wasn't Nebi Skog, it would have been more plausible to assume that he was a horse thief and stole it, possibly from some nearby Potowatomies, or perhaps from Fort St. Joseph. In that case, we might have some unhappy horse owners after us in a very short time. Oh well, we had a horse and who the hell knew where it came from.

The morning after next, I was hoisted on the horse and the travois that Loon's Song had built was packed with smoked buffalo. It was also set up for the horse to pull. Autumn led the horse as we headed for home. Blue Sky and Loon's Song took the canoe, and the rest of the meat, with Nebi Skog, who had said he would see that we got safely home. We met them again at the place where we had originally found the canoe, though we could see them on the river most of the way.

By this time I had become very tired and it was decided that we would make camp. After resting there until the next morning, Autumn mounted with me so that we could attempt to get home faster. Nebi Skog and the girls would come walking after us. After just about four hours, we were forced to stop and camp in a clearing along a stream. I was simply too tired to go on. Our party joined us and we spent an uneventful evening. The next morning, we set off again.

Normally, forest travel on a horse is not swift. However, the preponderance of clear trails got us to within an hour, or two, of our cabin before we had our speed even slightly compromised. At that we made it to our cabin about two hours ahead of the girls and Nebi Skog. The trip was uneventful and upon arrival, I was immediately put to bed by my loving wife.

When Nebi Skog arrived, he and Autumn, after a brief confab, cut off my bandages. There was some leakage of body fluid and a bit of blood and pus. An infection was developing.

Nebi Skog disappeared into the forest for an hour or so and upon coming back, spoke in low tones with Autumn. He took great pains to show her how to boil some unknown plants, some wild onions, and some bile from the horse's stomach that he had obtained by coaxing the horse to vomit. After the boiling, he added a few tablespoons of whiskey that we had in the cabin. With these ingredients he created a poultice that was applied and then covered with clean bandaging. The effect was amazing. My leg felt warm, but the pain was not there. After a few hours the swelling had gone down further than it had in the previous days since the injury.

Throughout the rest of the day and evening, Autumn and Nebi Skog huddled up periodically, presumably discussing my case in private.

"No secrets," I said, mostly aiming my barb at Autumn.

"Why would you think we have secrets?" she said.

"Oh, I dunno, maybe because you speak about me but in a manner that I cannot hear," I said.

She ignored me. Weeks later, after I recovered, she told me the concern about infection that they had and the very strict detail with which Nebi Skog went to fight it. It was much more serious than I had any concept of at the time.

By the next morning when they made a second application of this secret medicine, the leg was noticeably better.

"Getting better," Nebi Skog said laconically.

"Thanks, it feels much better," I said.

He replied, "Tomorrow you will walk."

"Fine with me, doctor," I kidded. He seemed puzzled at my attempt at humor which was completely lost on him.

Then I said to him, "I've been meaning to ask you about the shot that hit the buffalo in the head. That was amazing! Could I see your gun?"

He handed me his rifle with what I thought was a hint of a smile.

He said, "It is a good gun. It shoots true. For the buffalo I used extra powder in the barrel and so I shot farther."

The gun was a long-rifle, very old, older than my father's, but extremely well maintained and of extraordinary craftsmanship.

It was a bit unusual in that it was probably two inches longer than my rifle, or somewhere around 50 inches. This gun had been custom made to someone's exact specifications. It wasn't that it was as ornate as many later long-rifles were, it was just so well-made. The markings indicated it was made in 1755, in Lancaster, Pennsylvania, a place famous for German gunsmiths and long-rifles.

The craftsmanship was obvious and the simplicity of the gun drew it to the eye. Its barrel indicated a higher caliber ball than the .32 to .48 caliber that was typical of the frontier. I estimated this gun to possibly be a .75 caliber, which would make it extremely unusual, very rare. That would certainly help explain the damage his shot did to the buffalo's head. But what kind of powder charge would he need for firing a .75 caliber ball the distance of his shot, which I guessed at about 38-40 rods?

"Wow, that's a beauty, Nebi Skog," I said calling him by name. It was the first time I had done that. It caused him to pause and look at me for just a split second.

"Where did you get it, I continued?"

He said, "A very long time ago, I got the gun in the French Canadas, near Quebec. A man gave it to me because he thought he owed me a favor. "

"When you say a long time ago, how long?" I inquired.

He seemed reluctant to answer the question for reasons I could not fathom, but finally said, "It was just before the redcoat General, called Braddock, was killed."

This answer stunned me and he most certainly noticed the look on my face. Braddock was killed in 1755 during the French and Indian War. It was now 1791, so he acquired the gun at least 34 years ago. Assuming he was maybe 18 years old when he obtained the gun, that would place his minimum age now around 52 years old. There is no way that he remotely resembled that age. As I have noted before, I had a strange feeling he was older than he looked, but he looked like he was perhaps in his late 30's, or early 40's. I think he knew I was doing the ciphering in my head, but he said nothing and I wisely dropped the subject entirely. I could tell he was uncomfortable.

And so, the next day I did begin walking with a cane, one that

Nebi Skog had fashioned from a hickory limb. I moved gingerly at first but moved a few steps around the cabin several times that day, a few more inside and outside the next, and by the third day I was moving more and with less pain.

Early that morning, we had some salt pork and biscuits for breakfast. Then Nebi Skog stepped outside and without a word to either Autumn or me, was gone. The girls claimed he had said good-bye to them, but I didn't see him do so.

Loon's Song said, "He was a nice man. He was funny and kind."

She said this in Miami, of course, I guess I should have made it clear that I have been translating for the most part, though some conversations were in English, if that is important to the reader. What struck me about Loon's comments was that he was funny. His appearances out of nowhere and the life-saving help that he had provided me left no dissent about his kindness, though I might have used a different word. But funny, really, funny? The man was stone serious for every minute I had ever been near him. I saw nothing funny about him, no whimsical side to his personality, no smiles, no laughter, nothing to indicate funny. Funny-strange maybe, but not funny to make a person laugh. The girls thought he was funny. That struck me as beyond belief. But then I remembered that they had spent several hours alone with him, coming back to the cabin from Parc Aux Vaches.

It was at that point that both girls relayed the details of their trip back to the cabin with him. He spoke more to youngsters. He had joked with them, shown them some plants that they had previously not known were edible and had played games to amuse them on the way. They saw nothing odd about the man, which of course, only made me wonder more about him. With them, it was like he was a favorite uncle. In many ways I now felt like he and I had some odd connection, but in other ways, I felt like I knew nothing about this man, other than his name. Still, I owed him my life twice for certain and maybe three times, as the outcome against the Chippewas had certainly been swayed in our favor by his appearance. There could be no doubt about his shot of the buffalo saving me, and his subsequent care of my wound saving me yet again.

Chapter Thirteen

Doom on the Ouabache (Wabash)

Blue Jacket

As Arthur St. Clair, Governor of the Northwest Territory and newly reappointed General, left Fort Washington on September 17, 1791, he had no idea that his expedition would turn out far differently than he had envisioned. He was not a vain man and not particularly a glory-seeker, lest he would have supplanted Harmar for command during the campaign the year before. I think he was an experienced, pragmatic, old soldier, unexpectedly assuming his last command, doing his duty, all to pacify the confederated tribes along the Maumee River. It was a task that he expected to accomplish in a workman-like manner. The thought of failure probably did not enter his thinking.

He left Fort Washington with a force of nearly 2,000 men. About 600 of his force were United States regulars, basically the entire United States Army in 1791. He also had 800, six-month conscripts, and roughly 600 militia. He also had about 200 wives, children, wash women, prostitutes, and other types of camp followers, hardly a group that would contribute to military success. With his human force, he also brought cannons because Indians hate cannons.

Bringing cannons through the wilderness requires building roads as you go. St. Clair also built forts as he traveled north. Such activities eliminated any strategic maneuverability or opportunity for surprise. They also slowed the army down to a snail's pace. And not starting until mid-September, almost assured that the coming conflict would not be fought in ideal campaigning weather. However, St. Clair felt the cannons would awe the enemy. The forts would be necessary later to maintain a military presence and to monitor the expected peace in the Indian country. I later discovered that the cause of his late start was not dissimilar to that of Harmar. He had waited all summer for troops, supplies, and weapons.

Of course, St. Clair could never have achieved the element of surprise under the best of conditions. Fort Washington had been under constant surveillance since the spring, inside and out, by Indian spies. Nothing about the American expedition was a mystery to the Indian confederation.

Around the beginning of September, Autumn and I had taken Loon's Song and Blue Sky home to see their families. As my leg was better, but still not completely mended, I rode the horse that Nebi Skog had secured after my accident with the buffalo.

The Eel River village and Kekionga, indeed, all the villages, were abuzz with preparations for St. Clair's coming. I felt more comfortable in Little Turtle's village on the Eel River and went alone to Kekionga for one day, to pay my respects to Pacanne, first inquiring to assure no British were present. I also wanted to see some friends. Autumn stayed with her folks. At Turtletown.

It seems that the day before I had arrived, five British officers had been present for a brief war council, but had gone northeast to a British trading post on the Auglaize River, to gather some more muskets to give to the confederation. In that regard, my timing was good, because my presence would have only caused trouble had the British still been in the village.

As I was leaving Pacanne's cabin in the company of Gray Fox and Red Buffalo, I was approached by an Indian who I had seen before, but never met. I did not have any idea that he knew who I was.

His name was Waweyapiersenwa, which means, "Whirlpool." He has become known to history, because of his battle attire, as Blue Jacket.

Blue Jacket was a war chief of great reputation, especially beloved, and venerated among his people, for his unyielding stance against white expansion. He seemed to me to be extremely intelligent. He figured to play a significant role in the coming battle, just as he had against Harmar. The Miamis view of Blue Jacket was one of reverence for a great warrior. Little Turtle himself viewed Blue Jacket as one of the best fighters he had ever seen, as well as an uncommonly loyal ally. He did feel that Blue Jacket could sometimes be impulsive, letting emotions determine his battle strategy. This could cause hasty decisions, instead of the coldly calculated logic, that was employed by Little Turtle himself.

Blue Jacket, who spoke English, addressed me in my language saying, "Hello, Spirit Traveler."

I replied, "Aya, Waweyapiersenwa." I think he appreciated the respect that I accorded him, by speaking his language.

Nevertheless, he continued in English, perhaps to gain favor with me, "Let us talk."

"Yes, Blue Jacket?" I said.

"We have a big fight coming. The people say you have great power, that you are now one of us. We need you to fight with us," he continued, not wasting any time, but going straight to his point.

"As for any great power, I don't think so. While it is true, I have come to know the people and to favor their cause, I am not yet ready to fight against the whites, who are the people of my birth," I replied. "And as you can see, I have been badly injured, and am not yet healed. I would do poorly in a fight, " I continued.

"It matters not if you have powers. It is only important that the people think you do, and that will help us to victory," he implored. "But I have found that those who say they have powers seldom do. Great men who have these connections to the spirits, do not brag about their powers. You do not brag, Spirit Traveler.

Come with us, you do not need to fight. Just be there with us."

"I find your words to be true, Waweyapiersenwa." But I went on, "Saying I have no powers may only be telling the truth. There is one in the forest whose comings and goings I cannot explain. His name is Nebi Skog. And it is said he has many powers. I have met him two times. What do you know of him?"

I was trying to change the subject. But I was probably too abrupt. In any case, I am sure I revealed my obsession with the Water-Snake.

"Yes," Blue Jacket replied, "I have heard of such a one. The Water Snake is brother to the manitous and cousin to the wind. Little Turtle thinks you may have some powers such as I have heard attributed to the one called the Water-Snake. Perhaps, your meetings with him have a purpose to benefit Indian people. That would be of great help to us. But we will speak of Water Snake another time. Please come with us when the whites come to our land. Consider my words, Spirit Traveler."

Blue Jacket was certainly not one to be distracted from his topic of choice. Still, I wondered how much he knew of Nebi Skog. He seemed to be familiar with him, or the myth of him, but he seemed a bit annoyed that I had brought Nebi Skog into the conversation.

"Waweyapiersenwa is a great warrior, and I will consider his words," I said, dreading the thought of continuing to agonize and feel guilt over my mixed feelings. He grasped my forearm in a friendly farewell gesture, and then we parted. I went with Red Buffalo and Gray Fox, to Red Buffalo's cabin.

On the way, I stopped cold in my tracks and did a double-take. There now came running some distance away, a young warrior yelling for Blue Jacket. I searched my brain for a memory of where I had seen him. I was certain he was familiar. It quickly came to me. He was none other than the one called Red Stick, who I had seen at Fort Washington over a year ago. He was the one that the French merchant called, "Panther That Crosses the Sky."

"Who is this?" I said to my companions.

Red Buffalo replied, "It is Tecumseh of the Shawnees. He spies on the whites. He killed his first enemy at 14 years, just as did Gray Fox."

At this statement, Gray Fox lowered his head but smiled with the pride of a warrior.

"I have heard him called, Red Stick, but also, Panther That Crosses the Sky," I said.

"Yes, Tecumseh is Panther That Crosses the Sky," Red Buffalo went on to say, "But Red Stick is not his name."

Gray Fox joined in, "Tecumseh is a friend of Waweyapiersenwa. They are both Shawnee. He brings messages to Waweyapiersenwa, and speaks of what the whites are doing."

By this time, the runner had passed us by and continued until he reached the point where Blue Jacket stood waiting for him. He was a magnificent specimen of a young man, lean and muscular, very handsome, the kind of person who exudes a presence. The two men walked slowly away from everyone, while the younger man spoke rapidly to Blue Jacket, apparently with much information.

"Tomorrow there will be another war council," Red Buffalo predicted.

This statement was based upon what happened when Blue Jacket got information. As if in confirmation of this impending meeting, several hours later, Little Turtle arrived at Kekionga, probably having been alerted by runners to his Eel River village.

I decided it best that I not be present for the war council, and had not intended to stay anyway, to honor the earlier request of Pacanne, through Apekonit, that I should not be in the villages until I could commit to the Indian side in the upcoming war. I had already disobeyed that request, and Pecanne had not reminded me or admonished me when I saw him. I would not linger. The longhouse in the village center was being prepared for a meeting, and it was time for me to take my leave.

I was tormented about my decision and had been having dreams for days, about Kekionga and the Eel River village being overrun and burned to the ground by whites. In my dream, I was a helpless observer. This only added to my confusion. I didn't want to have to answer any more pleas that I fight for the people, and I didn't want to cause trouble, with anyone who might not trust me, such as from the outlying members of the confederation.

I said goodbye to my friends and headed for the Eel River village, intending on traveling during the night, as it was now nearly sunset.

As I followed the well-worn path to Eel River on my horse, I passed several braves coming in the opposite direction, to the meeting at Kekionga. Most of these I knew, and some I knew well. We spoke briefly, and I continued through the night, arriving well before sunrise.

Later that same day, we left for our cabin, taking the cousins back with us at the request of their parents. It was a matter of their safety from the upcoming invasion by St. Clair. They were good girls, good workers, and Autumn and I enjoyed having them with us. Family is family, white or Indian.

The entire trip back, I pondered over and over, the upcoming events. What should be my proper role, if any? I came to no different conclusion than I had already. Once back at the cabin, my soul searching continued until two days later, when Autumn took me by the hand and walked me into the woods.

Once at a favorite spot near the river, she said to me, "Your mind is troubled and this troubles me, my love. Let this go, there will be no problem defeating the whites, and you need not be a part of this. In time perhaps peace will return, but perhaps not. Time will give answers to all your questions, which for now cannot be anything, but demons that bother you."

"You are wise, my love," I responded. "But how can you be certain the people will defeat the whites?"

"The season grows late, Michikinikwa and Waweyapiersenwa will not allow the whites to again burn villages, crops, and food. The whites will not come near our towns, and our warriors will deal a death blow to those who come against us," she said.

My response was, "The strategy is sound, but the whites will be many, and they will be angry, after last year's defeat."

She said, "Yes, they will be many, you know this more than even we, but this is our land, and Michikinikwa will lead us to defeat the whites."

I did not respond, lost deep in thought. I could not fight against the people of the woman that I loved. I could not fight whites, no matter what I thought of their motives. There could be only one choice. This time I would not fight. As for the future, that would have to take care of itself at the appropriate time.

The next day with my decision made, a weight was lifted from me, except that I now worried for the many warriors I knew who would participate against St. Clair. Not the least on my mind were Red Buffalo, Apekonit, Gray Fox, and Black Bear.

We now settled into our hunting and gathering preparations for winter. Our small garden yielded some extra food for our root cellar, under the cabin. It would serve us well in the coming winter.

The days were warm and breezy, and our life would have been idyllic, if not for the cloud over us, of the impending invasion. Nevertheless, for the girls' sakes, we did not dwell upon what-ifs. Instead, we dried and smoked fish, gathered berries, pawpaws, and other wild fruit, and had family fun with games, races, and hide and seek each day. Our days reminded me of my childhood. The forest yielded its bounty, and we were well-stocked, as the weather turned crisp and nights began to frost. By now, my leg was healing nicely.

We had had the word in early October that St. Clair was on the march. He was making slow progress northward. He was building forts as he came. We would later learn that he had hanged three deserters at his newly built Ft. Jefferson. This was a considerable distance to the south of Kekionga. The charges against two of them were "attempting to join the enemy." That struck me as highly unlikely—white men, with no experience in the woods, attempting to join the Indians? Certainly, court-martialing and hanging deserters gave some indication of the seriousness of the American intent regarding this campaign. But it also spoke to the morale that may have been a problem among his men.

One day, as St. Clair was creeping northward, we had our two young runners, Little Beaver and Angry Cloud, come to our cabin from Eel River. Their avowed purpose was to be carrying an important message. I wondered if the real purpose wasn't the collusion of their parents to send them off on an errand of alleged importance, to not offend their warrior pride, but to effectively get them out of harm's way. Autumn seemed to sense this and made great effort to influence the young men to stay a couple of days, by feeding them great feasts. I took them hunting during the day, letting them use some of my weapons.

Their message had been simply to check on me, and to see if I might have changed my mind. I had not, but I feigned to still be pondering, and this helped us to keep them with us some extra time, while I delayed answering their inquiries.

At last, after three days, they began to get edgy, and with an impertinence native to youth, they more or less demanded an answer saying that their mission was most important and that they had to get back for the impending battle. I used one more bit of subterfuge and told them that they were correct in their thinking, and I would give them my answer in the morning. In this manner, we were able to keep them one extra night.

The next morning, Autumn fed them breakfast, as they eagerly awaited my answer. When I told them that I would not fight, they took it in stride and took their leave of us to carry this important news back to the people. We only hoped that we had been able to detain them long enough to avoid them being with the main Indian battle force. We later learned that our stratagem had worked and that by the time they got back to Eel River, the warriors had moved southeast. The two runners were given further orders to stay put to guard the village, protecting women and children, as well as the elderly.

It was now late October and chilly weather had set in. We had seen snow in the air once, or twice already. We had laid in plenty of wood and were ready for the winter.

I knew that by now, the Americans had to be getting close to the Miami homeland and that a battle must surely be imminent if it had not already occurred.

The month turned to November, and I shot a bear who had not yet gone to hibernation, very near the cabin, early one morning. It was about the only distraction I had from my thoughts about what must be occurring to the southeast. The girls skinned the bear, and we stewed, smoked, and dried the meat. After curing it, the girls took the hide to the nearby creek giving it about two hours of cleaning. They wanted it for a blanket with winter coming on, but bear hides are notoriously full of fleas and parasites. It takes considerable work to make them fully usable. But once the girls were done with their Indian cleaning procedure and it had dried, it was ready to serve as a soft and beautiful blanket.

It was around noon on November 6 that the two boys who visited earlier, Little Beaver and Angry Cloud, came racing to our cabin. They had traveled from Eel River most expeditiously, running as much as they could. These two were becoming quite the little messengers and teaching themselves long-distance running in a fashion that was setting them aside from their peers.

Out of breath, they stumbled up to the cabin and signaled for water. After Autumn got them each a good long drink, they began to talk quite excitedly, gesturing with their hands, as they described a great battle. It was one that had been an Indian victory. They demonstrated the scalping that took hours to accomplish as if they had been there.

Each boy had been to the battlefield the day after and had seen the bodies of dead whites strewn about in greater numbers than either had ever imagined could have been with the army. This they relayed to us with great relish. They each showed us knives that they had taken from the dead.

The boys informed us that Autumn's family was asking us to join all the people at Kekionga, where a great celebration was already in progress. Further, with the danger averted, Loon Song and Blue Sky's mother wanted them back for the winter. Autumn's family was anxious to fill us in on the events that had occurred, on what I later learned was November 4. I will remind my reader that the year was 1791. This was a date that would live in American history.

Autumn inquired about Gray Fox, and Black Bear, as well as other family members. One cousin had been wounded, but none of the family had been killed. I asked the boys about Red Buffalo and Apekonit. They did not know Red Buffalo's status but replied that Apekonit was being hailed as one of the great heroes of the battle. He was being celebrated by the people as one of the greatest warriors in tribal legend. It seems he had avenged himself on the whites for his wife and child, just as he said he would. He had done this most gloriously, leading what appeared to be a near-suicidal charge of some 200 warriors against the center of the army camp, destroying the entire artillery corp, and losing only three, or four warriors in the process.

Eager to be with Autumn's family and our friends and to learn the details of the battle, we secured the cabin and left within the hour. We took the horse that Nebi Skog had secured for me some months earlier and let the girls ride double.

As we left, anxious to see our Indian friends, I could not help but wonder how many of my white friends were dead. I was glad the Miamis and their allies would be safe from harm for the winter, but could not help feeling badly that so many whites had died.

We traveled in the light snow, reaching Turtletown well after dark. The village was largely deserted, but we stayed at the cabin of Autumn's parents, as they were already at Kekionga. The next morning, we left early and arrived at Kekionga in the early afternoon. Word of our arrival quickly spread, causing kin and friends to come forth to greet us. To my great relief, my good friend, Red Buffalo, was among them. In addition to the resident Miami, there were many Shawnee, Delaware, Illinois, and numerous others present. Some who didn't know me, cast a suspicious eye in my direction but were usually quickly set straight by one, or more of the residents. I noticed no prisoners, and assumed that they had already been executed at the outlying villages, or perhaps, at "the Island."

Autumn and her cousins went with the members of her family who were present, while I went with Red Buffalo to his cabin. Once there, he began to relay an account of the battle in a positively loquacious fashion for him. The alliance of tribes had agreed early on that this battle would not be fought around their villages, as had happened the previous fall when I had been captured. To that end, General St. Clair was ambushed a fair distance from Kekionga and the surrounding villages.

It seems that St. Clair had arrived at the headwaters of the Ouabache River in the late afternoon, or evening of November 3.[1] The weather was chilly, with a bit of snow in the air. The troops and officers were very tired. He had not put up his usual perimeter defenses although his scouts told his second in command, General Richard Butler, that they saw signs of many Indians (which Butler did not relay to St. Clair), and though his sentries interrupted the camp's sleep with sporadic gunshots during the night, neither he nor Butler took any particular precautions, not even the normal ones, utilized on the entire campaign thus far.

The bulk of the Indians cold-camped about a mile from the American Army. Many speeches were delivered by leaders of many tribes that night, as the strategy of attack was ultimately decided upon. Scouts buzzed around the army camp, observing the finest details, noting locations and concentrations of soldiers and camp followers, the placement of the cannons, and so forth. Throughout the night, nervous sentries fired shots at real and imagined enemies.

"At dawn, the white soldiers stacked guns and gathered for breakfast," Red Buffalo relayed.

He continued, "We attacked first the soldiers from Kaintuckee, who were camped due west of the main units.[2] Many were shot, many clubbed to death, and many ran to the main camp. The Kaintuckee soldiers ran across the Ouabache,[3] and up the banks into the main camp. This caused panic among the other whites, while we began to shoot our muskets from the woods, all around the camp. Many soldiers died with no food in their bellies."

"Who led this attack?" I asked.

"It was from the thoughts of Little Turtle, Blue Jacket, and Buckongahelas," Red Buffalo replied. "Blue Jacket himself led this attack."

"What happened next?" I asked.

"Whites fell, as we probed for weakness, going now here, now there. But it was Apekonit who now ensured that the big guns would not harm us. He led many braves, who first shot from behind fallen trees, killing most of the cannon men. Then they ran into the camp where the cannons were and wiped out the rest who had not been shot," he had continued.

I later learned that the few Americans that had not been killed by the initial withering gunfire into the artillery, spiked the cannons, before falling victim to Apekonit's charge.[4]

Little Turtle had considered Apekonit's attack to be one likely to produce many dead warriors, but he could not argue against its necessity. It was a wild, almost suicidal charge, that ended in anything but suicide for the Indians. This action inspired all the warriors for its bravery, and for the functional fact of removing the American artillery, as a factor in the battle. Seeing the success of Apekonit and his men, all the warriors were buoyed and fought ferociously. The Americans never really had a chance.

"And what of the American General, the man called St. Clair?" I asked.

Red Buffalo replied, "He was foolish in setting no defenses, as he had from Ft. Washington. But he was a brave man. Three horses were killed under him, as he tried to give courage to his men, and tell them where and how to fight. My eyes were upon him many times during the battle. He was old and sick, but he fought like a great warrior. In the end, he was unharmed and fled with those whites that we did not kill. Perhaps he will die the peaceful death of an old man in his bed and not die in battle."

Further he stated, "I do not know why the Americans brought women and children into battle. But all of these died, some fighting, and some shaming soldiers who came to hide in the center of the camp, seeking not to die. But they did die, and we scalped them until we could lift our arms no more. Those who got away ran far to the south, but we did not follow far for they ran fast and were so few as to be of no threat to us. Most of the people were busy finding guns and tools that the whites had left behind. They killed the wounded whites at this time."

At this point in my tale, I pause to relay the white version of an eyewitness account of the battle written by Major Ebenezer Denny. He was an officer who I knew fairly well. He published his Revolutionary War and Indian Wars Journal, in the early 1800's. He was also the officer who formally delivered a report on the battle to Henry Knox, in Philadelphia, where the capital had re-located from New York. What follows is a portion of the account of the battle from his journal:

> *The troops paraded this morning at the usual time, and had been dismissed from the lines but a few minutes, the sun not yet up, when the woods in front rung with the yells and fire of the savages. The poor militia, who were but 300 yards in front, had hardly time to return a shot; they fled into our camp. The troops were under arms in an instant, and a smart fire from the front line met the enemy. It was but a few minutes, however, until the men were engaged in every quarter. The enemy from the front filed off to the right and left, and sur-rounded the camp, killed, and cut off nearly all the guards, and approached close to the lines.*
>
> *They advanced from one tree, log or stump, to another, under cover of the smoke of our fire. The artillery and musketry made a tremendous noise*

but did little execution. The Indians seemed to brave everything, and when fairly fixed around us, they made no noise other than their fire, which they kept up very constant, and which seldom failed to tell, although scarcely heard. Our left flank, probably from the nature of the ground, gave way first; the enemy got possession of that part of the encampment, but it being pretty clear ground, they were too much exposed and were soon repulsed. Was at this time with the General, engaged toward the right; he was on foot and led the party himself that drove the enemy and regained our ground on the left.

The battalions in the rear charged several times and forced the savages from their shelter, but they always turned with the battalions, and fired upon them back; indeed, they seemed, not to fear anything we could do. They could skip out of reach of the bayonet, and return, as they pleased. They were visible only when raised by a charge. The ground was covered with the dead. The wounded were taken to the center, where it was thought most safe, and where a great many which had quit their posts unhurt, had crowded together. The General, with other officers, endeavored to rally these men, and twice they were taken out to the lines.

It appeared as if the officers had been singled out, a very great proportion fell, or were wounded, and obliged to retire from the lines early in the action. General Butler was among the latter, as well as several others of the most experienced officers. The men, being thus left with few officers, became fearful, despaired of success, gave up the fight, and, to save themselves for the moment, abandoned entirely their duty and ground, and crowded in toward the center of the field, and no exertions could put them in any order, even for defense; perfectly ungovernable.

The enemy at length got possession of the artillery, though not until the officers were all killed but *one, and he badly wounded, and the men almost all cut off, and not until the pieces were spiked. As our lines were deserted, the Indians contracted theirs, until their shot centered from all points, and now meeting with little opposition took more deliberate aim, and did great execution. Exposed to a cross-fire, men and officers were seen falling in every direction; the distress too of the wounded made the scene such as can scarcely be conceived; a few minutes longer, and a retreat would have been impracticable. The only hope left was, that perhaps the savages would be so taken up with the camp as not to follow. Delay was death; no preparation could be made; numbers of brave men must be left as a sacrifice; there was no alternative.*

It was past 9 o'clock when repeated orders were given to charge toward the road. The action had continued between two and three hours. Both officers and men seemed confounded, incapable of doing anything; they could not move until it was told that a retreat was intended. A few officers put themselves in front, the men followed, the enemy gave way, and perhaps not being aware of the design, we were for a few minutes left undisturbed. The stoutest and most active now took the lead, and those who were foremost in breaking the enemy's line were soon left behind.

At the moment of the retreat, one of the few horses saved had been procured for the General; he was on foot until then; I kept by him, and he delayed to see the rear. The enemy soon discovered the movement and pursued, though not for more than four or five miles, and but few so far; they turned to share the spoil. Soon after the firing ceased, I was directed to endeavor to gain the front, and, if possible, to cause a short halt that the rear might get up. I had been on horseback from the first alarm, and well- mounted; pushed forward, but met with so many difficulties and inter-

ruptions from the people, that I was two hours at least laboring, to reach the front. With the assistance of two or three officers I caused a short halt, but the men grew impatient and would move on. I got Lieutenants Seam and Morgan, with half a dozen stout men, to fill up the road and move slowly. I halted myself until the General came up. By this time the remains of the army had got somewhat compact, but in the most miserable and defenseless state. The wounded who came off left their arms in the field, and one half the others threw theirs away on the retreat. The road for miles was covered with the firelocks, cartridge boxes and regimentals. How fortunate that the pursuit was discontinued; a single Indian might have followed with safety upon either flank. Such a panic had seized the men, that I believe it would have not been possible to have brought any of them to engage again.

In the afternoon Lieutenant Kearsey, with a detachment of the First Regiment, met us. This regiment, the only complete and best-disciplined portion of the army, had been ordered back upon the road on the 31st of October.[5] They were 30 miles from the battle-ground when they heard distinctly the firing of the cannon, were hastening forward, and marched about nine miles when met by some of the militia, who informed Major Hamtramck, the commanding officer, that the army was destroyed. The Major judged it best to send a subaltern to obtain some knowledge of things, and to return himself with the regiment to Fort Jefferson, eight miles back, and to secure at all events that post. He had made some arrangements, and, as we arrived in the evening, found him preparing to meet us. Stragglers continued to come in for hours after we reached the fort.

As our talk continued, a knock came at Red Buffalo's door. The door burst open and in came Apekonit.

"Hello, my brother," he nearly shouted as he embraced me. "Have you heard of our great victory?"

"I have," I said. "Red Buffalo tells me you were a very brave war leader in destroying the cannon men."

"And did he tell you that he was by my side every step of the way?" Apekonit asked.

"He did not," I replied, looking quizzically at Red Buffalo. I had learned long ago, that while martial bravery is much prized among the people, and therefore bragging expected, that Red Buffalo was a man who seldom spoke of his exploits, though the people knew that he was an exceptional warrior, and a better human being.

As I looked at him, he said, "Apekonit led, I only followed."

"And bravely killed many whites," Apekonit added. "As did the young warrior, your brother, Gray Fox."

"Gray Fox was with you?" I asked.

"He was," Apekonit replied. "His father did not wish it so, but Gray Fox was firm in his desire. His war skills are beyond his years. Black Bear accompanied us to be near Gray Fox. He is so proud of his son."

"Yes," was all I could say.

I had now walked to the small window, and took note of the many scalps on a pole outside the cabin, a sight that for some reason I had missed upon coming near Red Buffalo's home. A cold shiver went down my spine. It caused memories of my fight and subsequent capture. I was able to imagine the din and confusion of battle, the fear of men and women as they lost control of their bodily functions, the musket balls bouncing off trees and wagons, the screams of those shot, the chill of the wind, and the eerie silence, after the rout by the Indians. And I imagined the pleas of the survivors, some who were probably scalped while they were yet alive, and of others who were no doubt led off to the villages, to provide entertainment in being put to tortuous and gruesome deaths. I wondered if any of these scalps belonged to friends of mine.

"The white men got what they deserved. They took my family, and I have revenged myself upon them many times over," Apekonit said.

Red Buffalo said, "We are safe from them now. They will not

come back soon."

"No," I replied, "they will not come back soon. But someday, they will come."

There was a moment of silence, as all of us seemed to consider my words.

Then Apekonit said, "They will die."

As we continued to discuss the battle, and as the two of them answered my many questions, I learned that a friend of mine, Red-Tailed Hawk, had died in the battle. He seemed to have been one of less than 40 Indians who died, versus many hundred whites. Red-Tailed Hawk had a large family of seven children and one on the way. Life would be very tough for them now. The people would help them, but the ability to help would depend upon future harvests and the availability of plenty of game. It was unlikely that another brave would want to take as a wife, a widow with so many mouths to feed.

At this point, I set upon an intention to visit the widow, which I did. I gave her our horse. This would increase her family wealth a very great deal, and she would be able to use the horse to trade for the needs of her children. She cried and thanked me profusely. I told her, in Miami, that Red-Tailed Hawk was a great man, and so for me to help her and the children, was my way to honor my friend, her husband. She cried and cried, and the younger children, who still were not able to understand death, tugged at me to play with them. I obliged them for a while and then spoke what words, however inadequate, came to my mind to say to the older children. I attempted to comfort them. I assured Red-Tailed Hawk's oldest daughter, Dancing Wind, that Autumn would welcome a visit from her in the spring. I said the same to his eldest son, White Corn Man. I would welcome him for a visit to our cabin and a hunting trip in the spring. I pledged that when they had need, or want of anything, they need only find Autumn, or myself, and we would be there for them. I think this gave them some comfort, though, as is understandable, nothing would requite their sorrow. Their father had been a very good man, and it was a close and loving family.

The harvest had been less than past years, and it would be a long and harsh winter for the family of Red-Tailed Hawk. I hoped that my gift would help them get through it.

I have heard in the years since that time, people talk about "the noble savage." I can tell you that there is nothing noble about the way either the red, or the white men, fight wars on the frontier. There is only death and suffering and the breakup of families, whose very existence has always hinged upon the slightest whims of nature, of disease and of the general randomness that is life.

Earlier, as I walked the village, I saw many happy faces. So too did I see the blackened faces of grief, grief for fathers, brothers, uncles, and even grandfathers, who would never again walk among their people. As was custom, the Miamis who lost kin in battle, blackened their faces, and would fast for a time determined by the leader of each family.

It was perhaps, at this point in my young life, that I came to understand the true nature and the hard facts of war. Up to now, I didn't like killing but considered it a necessity, and to some extent I prided myself on my abilities to fight and kill when necessary. And yes, as a young man, I can say that it was often a part of the great and exciting adventure that was life on the frontier.

But perhaps starting then, and certainly in the years since, I have come to view war not as exciting business, not as the great mark of a man's character, not as something necessary, but rather as something ridiculous and abhorrent, born of the inability of men to get along with one another, to share the wealth and bounty of nature, and to help one another. It was and is, a failure to understand our common humanity. Is another man's family so different than my own, just because my people call him enemy? Fear, greed, mistrust, envy, and hatred, all coalesce to create the feeling of the one, that the other must die.

Some of the great warriors that I have known, from both sides, have upon occasion, reflected similar thoughts in my company. They have attained true enlightenment upon this subject, a truth that seems to elude the great majority of mankind.

As I was leaving Red-Tailed Hawk's family, Autumn came to see them. She had heard I was there, and though we had not discussed it, she was very happy and in complete agreement with my gift.

In Miami she said to me, "My husband is a generous man, who makes me very proud."

I grabbed her for an embrace, as I whispered in her ear, "My wife is a beauty beyond compare, and her soul is as beautiful as her face." She smiled broadly and entered the home.

I asked Apekonit and Red Buffalo to take me to the scene of the battle, which was some hours south of Kekionga by hard travel. They assented. We were joined by Gray Fox and two of the Girty brothers. All three Girtys had participated in the battle on the Indian side. We borrowed horses from Pacanne, who expressed delight at seeing me, and approval at learning of my intention to visit the battlefield.

We set a quick pace to the southeast along a well-worn trail and arrived in just over three hours. On route, we passed the cold-camp where the bulk of the Indian force had spent the night before the battle.

I was not prepared for the sight that greeted me upon our arrival at the field battle. It was a macabre picture, grotesque with bodies frozen by cold and rigor mortice, covered in snow, flesh torn and half-eaten by wolves, foxes, and badgers, and nibbled on by mice, rats, birds, and other creatures, some of whom were still at work as we arrived. Had it been another season of the year, I doubt any flesh would have been left on the bones.

The bodies lay haphazardly, scalped, and dismembered, with clothing and shoes removed from them where they had fallen. There were signs that some had been captured alive and tortured on the spot. Some still had arms stiffly reaching for the sky. Most had their eyes gouged out by greedy vultures. There were only bodies, all items that had accompanied them, clothes, weapons, hammers, axes, blankets, pots, pans, cloth, aprons, harness, ropes; all gone, taken to villages to the north, to be used by new owners. Bodies of men, women, and children, who a few days before had been full of life, now lay in death, absolute, irreversible, and in most cases, unrecognizable.

I could not have imagined hell to be a place worse than this. Among the dead, though most were unrecognizable, I saw some whom I had known the year before, officers mostly, though now without any uniform, hat, or insignia of rank.

Years later, I was to read an account sent to St. Clair by a Captain Buntin, who was with Major James Wilkinson's burial and property recovery detail, that went to the site of the massacre in January of 1792, just about two months after my visit. Captain Buntin had this to say:

"In my opinion those unfortunate men who fell into the enemy's hands with life were used with the greatest torture, having their limbs torn off; and the women having been treated with the most indecent cruelty, having stakes as thick as a person's arm driven through their bodies. The first I observed when burying the dead, and the later was discovered by Colonel Sargent and Dr. Brown. We found three whole carriages; the other five were so much damaged that they were rendered useless. By the general's orders, pits were dug in different places, and all the dead bodies that were exposed to view, or could be conveniently found (the snow being very deep), were buried.[7]"

I was not at Kekionga at the time when Major Wilkinson came near with his burial and recovery detail. However, I learned that Miami scouts had reported his presence. Because he had led the raid that took Apekonit's family, Apekonit upon hearing of his presence, gathered warriors, and headed south with murder as his intent. However, the snow being an impediment to travel, with a dreadful cold setting in, the Wilkinson detail was half a day gone by the time of Apekonit's arrival on the scene.

During our visit there was no sign of the cannons that the Indians, under Apekonit's leadership, had hidden so that the army could not find and re-use them in future battles.

Gray Fox took me to a body under a tree. I instantly recognized the hair and the face, most of which was still intact. It was Brigadier General Richard Butler, who had been second in command of the expedition.[8]

Gray Fox asked, "Do you know this man?"

"Yes," I said. "It is General Butler, a famous soldier from the War for Independence, a very brave man, and a fierce warrior. He comes from a family of five brothers, all great warriors. Probably others of them were at this battle. The family has been called, "the fighting Butlers."

"I shot him early in the battle," Gray Fox continued. "But he did not fall, and he wandered away so that I lost track. He must have come to this tree where someone finished him with a war club or tomahawk. His heart has been eaten."

Such was obvious from the gaping hole in his chest cavity.

It is a known fact that Butler and St. Clair did not get along with one another. Survivors of the battle have told of a nasty argument that the two had, just the day before the battle. This probably contributed to Butler, not sharing with St. Clair, the intelligence that he had received on the eve of the battle.

Now Red Buffalo relayed to me an unusual occurrence from the battle that had him and my other companions troubled. It seems that after the few survivors had fled, that the Chippewas ate one of the slain soldiers. I am not talking about eating his heart, as was sometimes done to victims known to have been great warriors, but they ate the whole soldier.

Now, it may strike white sensibilities as odd that Indians who would eat a man's heart to gain his bravery, would shrink from outright cannibalism. But such is just the case. Eating a human is considered just as taboo among most of the red men, as among the white race. It is an abomination, and it carries bad omens with the act. In this case, the show-off Chippewas were roundly admonished, ostracized, and then sent packing, back to their land. My comrades seemed truly disturbed by this act of the Chippewas, and they considered it despicable beyond comprehension.

Perhaps to change to the subject, Gray Fox now interjected, "During the battle, some of the American musket balls bounced off our warriors. At first, we thought this was some great magic on our part. Later as we saw many guns misfire we knew that the American powder was no good."[9]

Years later I would learn of the maleficence of the sellers of the powder, and of other suppliers who cheated the Army. This scandalous treachery put the American soldiers in even worse straights than they might have been with good rifles, sound powder, and a good shot, not to mention, adequate food and fodder.

Simon Girty said, "I have never even heard of a victory such as this. Hundreds of Americans were killed and you know, it was if they could not even protect themselves. Nothing went right for them, and everything went our way. A lot of this was their stupidity, there can be no doubt of that. I have seen it before; why would anyone bring women and children to war?"

He continued, "You can see the Americans lost hundreds, the Indian dead were around forty, with a few more wounded."

I took time to count some of the bodies, the ones whole enough to be certain about. However, I finally lost count, and estimated between 800 and 1,000 whites lay dead. This meant that over one-half of the army of the United States had been wiped out on the very battlefield that I was now surveying. Some of the most respected, most seasoned, indeed most famous United States officers lay dead on the field. Many of them were veterans of the Revolution. Women and children numbered about 200 of the dead. This could not have been well-received news back east. I surmised the public would not only be clamoring for the head of Arthur St. Clair but also an expedition of revenge.

One wonders at St. Clair's actions. He had not followed military protocol in protecting his camp, despite the multiple reported signs of the enemy. Some indication exists that he intended to fortify the camp the next morning, and await the return of the 300 American regulars that he had sent south to protect a supply train and to round up deserters. One can surmise that with the hour of arrival being late on November 3, the weather bad, and the General very tired, and sick, that perhaps he just did not see the need for immediate fortification of his camp. It is known that he felt the Indians could not overcome his army. Likely, he never considered that the enemy would mount an all-out attack.

Red Buffalo, Apekonit, Simon, and Gray Fox replayed the battle from start to finish for me. It was a two-hour affair with about 1,200 Indians attacking. In the end, Arthur St. Clair and the less than 50 unscathed soldiers, had fled southward toward Ft. Jefferson with the wounded; such as could follow and fend for themselves. There were a very few surviving unhurt camp-followers bringing up the rear of this flight. St. Clair later, in his official report, used the term "flight. " He said it was not a retreat.

My thoughts were somber and confused, as we quietly left the grisly scene, and returned to Kekionga.

Chapter Fourteen

The Countess

Ales du Chene

The day after our trip to the battlefield, there sauntered, I cannot think of more apt term, into Kekionga, the female embodiment of absolute trouble, one Alexis Annabelle Antoinette Maria Briand du Chene, Comtesse Duchesse de Champagne Ardenne. That is to say, The Countess and Duchess of the Champagne Ardenne region of France. For all the high falutin' names and titles that she had, she just preferred "Ales."

Ales was dressed as a frontiersman, that is in men's clothing, although there was no mistaking that she was a woman. She smiled at those she passed, who stood and stared. She was tall and shapely even in men's clothing and her long dark hair hung from under her hat, which was of a favorite kind worn by French fur traders in winter. Her beauty was almost equal to only perhaps two other women I had ever seen. Unfortunately, one of those was standing beside me and pierced my ribs through my coat, on the left side of my body with an elbow that left me gasping for air.

I was only damn lucky it was an elbow and not a knife. The blow to my person was followed by a Miami epithet, or two, then Autumn stomped off. I didn't know I had done anything wrong, though my mind sorta knew differently. I must have been standing and staring transfixed, a little too intently at the newcomer.

The Countess had in tow three mean-spirited looking Hurons.[1] To be fair, I thought Huron males always presented a menacing look. They never seemed happy. Years earlier, the Hurons had been sworn enemies of the British. Like so many others, the tribe was most often associated with being allies of the French. However, through the defeat of the French by the British, increased trade, being granted land in Canada, and the American incursion into the Ohio Country, this tribe had become British allies and staunch enemies of the Americans.

The fact that this woman was traveling with these Hurons and that they were taking orders from her, defied all that I knew about them, or for that matter Indians in general. Such were not known to traipse about with a female leader. Many eastern woodland tribes had women in key leadership roles over men, but not generally "in the field," so to speak. This despite the fact, that lineage, political power, and property rights were often matrilineal. Of course, a white woman would have no connection to any of that.

Ales du Chene was the widow of a young British major who had succumbed to a disease in Quebec. Not wishing to return to either England or France, after the death of her husband and yearning for even more adventure, she took the unusual step of opting to put her considerable fortune into the fur business. She then took the very hands-on approach of learning the business from the ground up.

With her husband dead, British officials were not exactly enthralled with having this French noblewoman roaming about their North American domain. Nevertheless, as a British officer's widow she had a certain status about which they could do little. Whether they considered her a spy, I do not know, but it certainly was uncommon for a woman to be doing the type of things that she was doing. Canada is a vast land, as is all of North America. Containing the Countess was not going to be an easy task for the British.

At the time of her arrival in Kekionga no British were present. There had been a couple of officers and others on hand at the time of St. Clair's defeat. Along with some Canadian rangers, they had beat a hasty path to Fort Miamis, a British post northeast up the Maumee River from Kekionga, to inform their commander about the Indian victory.

The Countess made her way to Pacanne's home, where she was received like a visiting dignitary. A short few minutes later, I was summoned to attend the meeting between the two as an interpreter, if needed. The Countess spoke flawless English and of course, French. How many Indian dialects she spoke, I do not know, but I do know she did not speak Miami or Illinois. Pacanne spoke English and French, but he mostly figured the Countess spoke better English than he, so it wouldn't hurt to have me on hand in case he needed a clarification.

The entire conversation took place in English. That is most of it did. The exception was when I entered the room.

Upon looking in my direction, the Countess said to Pacanne in French, "Qui est cet homme 'elegant? Je voudrais le conna'tre." Or, in other words, "Who is this handsome man? I want to know him."

I laughed, responding before Pacanne could speak, "J'ai peu on parle pour lai." This means, "I am spoken for."

I confess that her words had been so seductive as to cause me to wonder if she might be referring, by wanting to "know me," as in the Biblical sense.

She then said, "Oh, et il parle le francais," indicating her surprise that I spoke French.

Pacanne formally introduced me and explained my relationship to the people. She seemed to listen intently, and have to her interest piqued all the more.

I was deeply thankful that Autumn was not present to see the attention that Ales du Chene was focusing on me.

The meeting continued in English, with the gist of it being that the Countess wanted to make some kind of accommodation with Pacanne, to use the portage that his family-controlled and perhaps to establish a storage location to cache her furs at Kekionga.

To all of this Pacanne informed her that a deal could be reached on the portage, but that the British held all commercial rights at Kekionga. Caching her furs in the village would not be allowed without a British license.

At this last news, she turned to me and said, "And how about you Spirit Traveler, what do you think about this matter?"

I was extremely uncomfortable with this questioning. It involved business talk that was none of my concern.

I told her, "Pacanne's family controls the portage, and he will be fair with you. However, the British commercial interests are exclusive here at Kekionga. You will need a British license."

It killed me to have to say this, but after all, I was here at Pacanne's invitation, and my personal opinion was of no consequence in the matter.

Pacanne nodded his head in assent at my statement.

"I see," she replied. "Well, the British are of no concern to me in this matter. I will obtain their permission."

She certainly seemed like a woman determined to get her way and one not used to anything but that.

She continued, "For now, I go to the western side of Michi Gami."[2]

She then looked directly at me and asked if I would be available for hire to guide her to the Lake. I responded that I was not available for that task, but presumed her Hurons could do the job.

"I am certain that they can," she said, "But they are not such fun."

"Perhaps you should pick different companions," I said.

"Ah, then you will come?" she laughed.

"No," I reiterated. "How do you know I would be more fun than the Hurons?"

"I am willing to find out. I shall be here for two days if you change your mind," she said.

I left without further comment.

Behind me she said, "Goodbye, Spirit Traveler, it was nice to meet you."

Nice, my ass, I thought. A woman like that could get a man into a great deal of trouble.

Over the next two days, despite my sincere efforts to the contrary, or at least my intention to have such efforts, I found myself in Countess du Chene's presence on several occasions. She seemed to have an uncanny knack for showing up wherever I was, whether visiting friends, walking outside the village, or playing with the children of Red-Tailed Hawk. She was a coquette if ever I had seen one. She was relentless with her seductive speech toward me.

For my part, I was not at all encouraging of that behavior, and told her more than once that I was married. At this she always just laughed, but I could not tell whether her laugh was intended to convince me that she was only kidding, or that my being married did not bother her. This was all somewhat flattering to me I will admit, however, truly I was not encouraging such behavior. At least, I don't think I was.

One day as the kids and I were playing a rough game of ball in the snow, the Countess came and joined in, just moments before Autumn arrived and also joined in. Well, trouble soon began. With both women going for the ball, Autumn managed to plant the Countess rather roughly on the ground, with a body check. The Countess got up, rushed toward the ball, now going away from her and tripped Autumn from behind, sending her face-first in the snow, so that she arose with a white face and momentarily unable to see.

And that's all it took. Autumn stood up, looked at the Countess, called her a French whore in Miami then shoved her backward. The Countess countered by rushing and tackling Autumn. The two began hair pulling, rolling in the snow in an unbreakable embrace and doing who knows what else to each other. I am certain that wearing winter furs lessened the force of their blows upon one another, but that probably just made them all the angrier. This continued but a few intense moments before Red Buffalo showed up.

As I grabbed Autumn, which was no easy task, I held her as tightly as I could, Red Buffalo grabbed the Countess and held her in the same fashion. Now, they both struggled mightily to get at each other. Both women were hurling epithets back and forth in their native languages. About this time Pacanne came up and inquired as to the meaning of the commotion. Both women answered him loudly, in almost unintelligible tones and then renewed efforts to get free to kill each other.

Pacanne ordered three young men to take the Countess to her guest cabin, while Red Buffalo and I picked up Autumn and took her to his cabin. I don't know about the Countess, but I know it took about a half-hour to get Autumn to settle down. There was no reasoning with her, no easy calming, she was determined to harm the French woman. Pacanne stopped by and gave Autumn a fatherly talking to. But of course, being the leader at Kekionga, Autumn knew that he would tolerate no further trouble with a visitor.

When Autumn was not looking, Pacanne gave me a sly smile. In a few minutes he left. In due course, Autumn's temper abated, and we had a good laugh at her outburst, but she could set herself off again if she thought about the countess for even a few seconds.

The next day I came upon Little Turtle and Apekonit as I was on my way to Red Buffalo's cabin. They were going to see Pacanne. It occurred to me that I was seeing them together even more now than usual. It was a father-son type relationship, but it was even more than that. They were friends and confidants. The respect between them was obvious to anyone who gave it a thought. In a later conversation with me alone, Little Turtle spoke with pride of Apekonit's role in the victory over St. Clair.

He said, "Apekonit led over 200 braves against the American cannons in the center of the soldiers. He wiped them out and set the course for our victory."

"It was a brave thing," I said. "It is amazing that few of his braves were killed."

"Yes," he said, "throughout the battle we lost only one warrior for every twenty whites slain. I had not expected such a victory. Still, the Americans can replace 600, 800, or even 1,000 soldiers. Our people cannot replace even one dead warrior."

"It is true," I said. "The Americans will appoint a new general to come against the people. It may take them some time to recover, but their anger will be great, and within a year they will come back."

"I know that it is true," he said. "The people think we are unbeatable, and I must let them think that for now, but the truth is the Americans will find a leader who is skilled in war and who will bring an army of even greater numbers to our land. There will come a time when we have lost too many men and can fight no more. For now, we are puffed up with pride. Pride is not food for the winter, but it will help us pass the long nights."

"This is true, Michikinikwa," I agreed.

At that moment both of us became aware of a runner off in the distance outside the village. He was coming fast considering the snow on the trail. He ran with the long, smooth strides of someone who was a skilled runner. He seemed somehow familiar, but the distance was too great to get a look at his face.

We watched as the runner entered the village and went to the guest cabin of the Countess. Within no more than a few moments, the Countess and the runner reappeared, and left the village in great haste, the Countess leaving behind her Hurons to gather her gear and follow.

While I was certain that her departure would be good news to Autumn, I was stunned when I finally got a view of her companion the runner, who turned to me upon coming out of the guest cabin, and said, "Kway, Spirit Traveler, Kway."

He then turned and acknowledged Little Turtle. Then he was off with the Countess.

Little Turtle turned to me and said, "Who was that man?"

I said, "A man I have seen before, who is like a ghost in the woods and who has saved my life more than once. His name is Nebi Skog."

Then Little Turtle said, "Yes, I have heard of one by such a name when I was a boy and a few times since. He is a cousin to the wolf. He is said to talk to all creatures of the forest and to travel on the wind. His powers are said to be strong. But until now, I have never laid eyes on him. His comings and his goings, are said to be more like those of a spirit than a man."

"It is so, Michikinikwa, it is just so," I said, surprising myself at my endorsement of the supernatural. I was a little ashamed of myself for my illogical propagation of the myth of Nebi Skog.

"I have had reason to wonder about your powers, Spirit Traveler when remembering the stories of him," said the great chief.

Rather than wasting time denying my powers, I was consumed with the thought that Little Turtle had as a boy heard of Nebi Skog. Little Turtle was at this time nearly 45 years old. Was Nebi Skog older than even I had imagined? And how did Nebi Skog know to go to the guest cabin at Kekionga, a place he had never been? And finally, when he came out of the cabin, he turned to greet me as I described as if he knew I was there. How could that be? The legend of Nebi Skog was growing in my mind, if nowhere else.

That evening a few hours after Nebi Skog had been seen, Red Buffalo, Little Turtle, Black Bear, Apekonit and I engaged in lengthy conversation and smoking at Red Buffalo's cabin. During the evening I relayed to this group of friends all that I knew about Nebi Skog, including all my experiences with him. Red Buffalo was happy to throw in his endorsement of the man. The topic of the Chippewas came up from Black Bear. Gray Fox had told him about it and Nebi Skog. He had told him how the Chippewas had tried to kill us all. Little Turtle took the whole in stride. The death of the Chippewas was perfectly warranted in his mind. I knew it was in Red Buffalo's mind because he had been there. I imagined all was fine with Autumn's father, Black Bear, since his daughter, son, and son-in-law had all been involved and unhurt, despite the intent of the Chippewas. In a later conversation, Gray Fox apologized for breaking his vow to never speak of the Chippewa incident but said that his father's opinion of me as a warrior and protector of his daughter, was now even higher than before.

There was some speculation about Nebi Skog and his powers. The consensus was that he was more spirit than man. Despite my earlier endorsement of such thinking, I wasn't so sure about this. I just had trouble believing in such things. Nevertheless, I had to admit to myself that much that I had seen from this strange man certainly was unlikely, unexplainable, and downright implausible, when looked at in purely logical terms.

Late in the evening, the group broke up, with Apekonit privately asking me to walk into the woods with him in the morning. He had something on his mind and wanted to speak with me alone.

Chapter Fifteen

Apekonit's Nightmares

Appekonit Dreaming

Early the next morning, the day after the Countess's hurried exit, we were walking in the woods with no one else around. I could tell that Apekonit was troubled. He seemed to want to talk, but the words did not come easily.

"What is it, my friend?" I said. "What is on your mind?"

Finally, he responded, "I am troubled, Spirit Traveler."

"Troubled by what?" I said.

"I can see them," he said.

"See who?" I responded.

Every person that I have killed," he came back. "I can see their faces clearly, every single one; I remember them all."

I said, "My friend, I too see the faces of those that I have killed."

"Ah, yes," he said, "but the faces you see are they white?"

I answered before even thinking, "No, I have only killed Indians."

"Yes," he said, "You have only killed Indians. While I who am white have killed only whites. In another time, I might have killed Indian enemies of the Miami people, but now the whites are the enemies for all tribes, and for now the tribes do not fight each other."

"You are one of the people, my friend, you have white skin but you are Indian," was my response.

"I speak not just of those from the battle against St. Clair, but also of those who I have helped capture and who were then tortured to death," he said.

My silence was uncomfortable, but I truly did not know how to respond.

After a time, he continued, "I have had a dream. I was on the battlefield when we fought St. Clair. I was scalping those who I had killed. Seeing a man lying face down in the earth, I noticed his red hair, hair like mine. And so, I turned him over instead of just scalping him."

Here he hesitated, being very disturbed.

Then he went on, "The face was mine. I had killed myself. And then I awoke in my fear, I wondered, 'Who am I? Am I a white man, or am I an Indian? To be a good Indian must I kill the people of my birth?' This troubles me, Spirit Traveler."

Again, I had no answer. His dream was indeed disturbing. I was feeling his deep concern, a concern that went well beyond that which had caused me such heartache.

After that, we said no more, walking back to Kekionga in silence. We parted, each taking the other's arms at the elbows, but saying few words. Autumn and I left that day to go back to our cabin.

The winter proceeded as I relayed at the beginning of my story. The snow was deep, and we were inside most of the season. We did do some trapping and we had the encounter with the painter that I described at the beginning of my tale. Our life was good, but I had much time to think about my friend and myself, about what the future would hold for us both.

Mid-March brought a warm spell, and spring began in the wilderness. On a trip to the Eel River village and Kekionga, we traded the painter hide and visited friends. When in Turtletown I went in search of Apekonit, and found him at the home of Michikinikwa.

"I now know why you could not fight against the whites," he told me. "But when I was taken by the people my white parents were already dead. My only family was my brothers, so the Miami took me as a captive, but raised me as one of their own. They gave me a family. It was natural that I would fight with them. It was natural until now."

"Yes," I said, "it is all very confusing."

"Why must the whites come to kill Indians, and take the land?" he said. "And why must the Indians kill the whites so savagely. In another dream there is death all around me, Spirit Traveler. I am the only one alive. All others, red and white, are dead on the earth. What does it mean, Spirit Traveler?"

"I do not know my friend, I only know that you are right that there is too much killing. It should not be so," was my reply. "Men should learn to live in peace."

"Four years ago, I met my older brother, and I went with him for a time to Kentucky, the land of my youth. I spent time with him and remembered him as my family, but I came back to the people."

"You met your brother?" I said.

"Yes, and I must tell you this Spirit Traveler, he was on the field with St. Clair. I saw him once during the battle."

As he told me this, I sat down on the fallen trunk of what had been a giant oak tree. I was trying to let sink in all that he had told me."

"Was he killed?" I asked, completely shocked at this news.

"I looked at many bodies and did not see him," he answered. "I think he may have gone back with St. Clair. I must find out if he is alive. The day will come in the future when if he is alive, I must go to see him again." He paused and then added, "Will you go with me?"

"Yes, yes I will go," the words came out without me thinking them.

A profound change was coming over my friend. His conflict with himself was something I could understand. Much of it was also mine. It was something that I did not want to be experiencing again in the future.

We spent the next few days with Autumn's family and I had the opportunity to go to Kekionga and to go ice fishing with Red Buffalo.

After that we returned to our cabin, where several weeks later, Autumn suddenly announced that she had to go see her mother. I had learned not to question her when she had these sudden urges. So we went to Eel River for two days, which was for me a largely uneventful time with family and friends. And then just as suddenly, we were on the way home.

On the way home she gave me the news that we were expecting a child. She had wanted to tell me sooner but felt that she needed to consult her mother in such matters to ascertain that she was correct. Her mother, Le Femme Paapamkamwa, or essentially, "She Fox", confirmed Autumn's suspicions.

Autumn's mother's unusual name conjugation in the form of French and Miami, was due to her grandfather who had been a French fur trapper and his first-born, She-Fox's mother, who was a mixture of French and Miami. She-Fox was a half-sister to Little Turtle's wife and of a chief named Mahkwa, who lived in an outlying village.

I was overjoyed at the news of the baby and upon arriving at the cabin, I immediately built one fine baby crib using the best materials that I had. I know I am bragging, but after all, my first child had been conceived and nothing I could do would be too good for that baby.

After that, I began a more mundane project, that of remodeling our outhouse, which I had built in a hurry the summer before when we were building the cabin. This time I double-planked the walls to be able to withstand gunfire and put in a gun-port on each of the four sides. I secreted two of the Chippewa muskets above the door behind a plank, along with enough shot and powder for ten rounds of fire with each gun. I also placed one of the Chippewa tomahawks with the guns. I had no intention that we should ever be caught off guard or ambushed tending to private matters.

But I am digressing. This part of my story is about Apekonit. I should backtrack just a bit to relay some of the events of Apekonit's life shortly after my capture, to which I had alluded earlier.

After the battle with Harmar, and before the battle with St. Clair Ouiatenon had been attacked by whites in May of 1791. Later that summer, Kenapakomoko was burned. Colonel Jean Francois Hamtramck was in command at Ouiatenon, but both attacks involved a subaltern, Colonel James Wilkinson, who played an especially prominent role commanding at Kenapakomoko. By that time Hamtramck was preparing to accompany St.

Clair north. This was when Apekonit's wife and child were taken, along with his Indian mother and some sisters. After that, Apekonit considered his permanent residence to henceforth be on the upper Eel River at Turtletown, the village that Little Turtle had relocated after an earlier village had been destroyed by the Americans.

Whether Apekonit's constant presence with Little Turtle was completely because of their friendship I doubt. I would suggest the possibility of one other reason. That reason was Wangnapeth, or "Sweet Breeze." She was Little Turtle's daughter. A vivacious and intelligent beauty, she made her feelings for Apekonit abundantly clear, just as her cousin Autumn Leaf had done with me. For Apekonit's part, he had resigned himself that his wife and child were dead. Although this was unsubstantiated, it was the rumor at every turn and whenever he attempted to obtain information. By and by, he fell in love with Sweet Breeze. This development pleased Little Turtle to no end.

Catching back up in time, it was by early 1792, about nine or so months after Autumn and I were married, that Apekonit informed me that a wedding was coming soon. He asked if I would participate, as he married Sweet Breeze. This was good news and I hoped that it would give my friend great happiness. There could be no doubt that it was giving Little Turtle great satisfaction.

Courtships are not long in the Indian culture and this one was already bordering on being considered an abnormal delay. I suspected that the couple may have been in love some time, but the recent fight with St. Clair had precluded matrimony until the situation with the whites was settled, for at least a time. All the people knew how the couple felt. Such was the nature of a society where exist precious few secrets. It is generally thought that if two people want to get married, they ought to do so without delay. Life is short, so why wait? A decision was announced and 20 days after, the ceremony would occur, with me supporting Apekonit and Autumn supporting her cousin, Sweet Breeze. The marriage would have occurred sooner, but with such an important couple, it was necessary to invite dignitaries from some distance away. As such, runners were sent in the four directions.

As the day came, Pacann, and a retinue of important and not-so-important families, came from Kekionga. Pacanne would officiate, assisted by Black Bear. Little Turtle, as father of the bride, was also a key participant

On the evening of the wedding, Apekonit presented himself in splendid buckskin breeches, with red loincloths and a blue cloth shirt. He wore a shell necklace that had been given him by Little Turtle and leather forearm bands. He wore an unusually high style of moccasins that imitated the style of white frontier boots. His hair was groomed in the Miami style, standing up shiny with bear fat and partially shaved, with two long and elegant hawk feathers. He wore a long silver earring in his left ear, a style similar to that of Little Turtle. He presented a picture of a proud and strong Miami warrior, despite the unusual color of his hair and the fairness of his skin.

For her part, Sweet Breeze wore a one-piece doeskin dress in traditional Miami style, as opposed to the cloth clothing more normally worn by Miami women during this time. She had gold and silver bracelets along with a most beautiful necklace of multicolored beads. Her dark hair was combed out long, with a beautiful turtle shell barrette. She wore silver earrings with blue shells that had tiny red feathers attached. Her moccasins were new, creme-colored, beautiful, and of the softest doeskin. Their light color further accentuated the beautiful copper color of her legs. She was a stunning beauty, looking older than her teenage years. It was clear to see that she favored her mother, Little Turtle's wife, who was herself a beauty.

The ceremony was quick, as is the custom. As I have described, it involved very little formality and had more to do with the intent of the couple than any sort of religious doctrine, or prescribed admonitions, speeches, or vows, It was clear the couple was deeply in love and as they left to go to their honeymoon wigwam, heartfelt well-wishes were offered by all. The greatest warrior had married the most available and pedigreed maiden, and it was a cause for a great celebration among the people.

Apekonit's Indian father, Gaviahate, came from rebuilt Kenapakomoko. He was an agreeable sort to whom I immediately took a liking. He was getting on in years but still seemed to be highly energetic and very fit. When younger, he had been a warrior of some considerable renown.

Because of the alliance, it was considered good form to invite Blue Jacket and a few other notables from the tribes that had participated against St. Clair. An invitation for the marriage of a warrior who had so distinguished himself, as Apekonit had, was considered a great honor for any of the Shawnees and other allies. Likewise, it made good political sense as a manner of keeping the alliance in the minds of those invited.

Blue Jacket, away from his Shawnee village at the time of the invitation, later sent a stallion to the newlyweds. This was considered an unusually generous gift and only added to his reputation among the Miami people.

Buckongahelas of the Delawares was on hand and gave the couple some well-crafted Delaware jewelry, a pipe said to have come from the plains Indians through a series of trades, and six beaver pelts of the highest quality.

He said, "May you have six children, a baby for each beaver."

At this reference to babies the young couple blushed and laughed.

Tarhe the Wyandot, like Blue Jacket, was otherwise occupied, but later sent blankets and a rifle of exquisite craftsmanship.

All of these bespoke the esteem in which Apekonit was held by members of the alliance, as well as also honoring Little Turtle by favoring his daughter and new son-in-law. And too, the gifts probably bespoke the importance of the alliance in the minds of the three chiefs. They were certainly gifts of extraordinary extravagance and might not have been given in other circumstances.

Of course, Le Petit Gris and the Girtys attended, as did chiefs from outlying Miami villages. There were Piankashaws, Sauk, Fox, and Illinois present for the nuptials.

Chapter Sixteen

Traveling Southwest

General James Wilkinson

In mid-May we made our way to Turtletown, where Autumn would stay with her parents, and learn the secrets of babies from her mother, La Femme Paapamkamwa. Autumn had paid little attention to babies during her time at home, and now she expressed concern about her abilities as a mother. I assured her that she would be a wonderful mother, but for the first time in all the time that I had known her, I could see her confidence lacking. I kissed and hugged her at her mother's door and left to find Apekonit.

Before we left, we had a brief word with Little Turtle, who to my surprise told us that the trip was important, and that Apekonit would fill me in as we traveled. This was to be more than just a family reunion.

We left and began to walk from the village.

"It will be good for you to see your brother. Perhaps we can find a way to end your torment," I said.

He replied, "Spirit Traveler, you know there is no way we can continue to defeat the white armies sent against us."

"This is true," I said. "The whites can send army after army."

"Little Turtle knows this also," he said. "But none of the others will believe him. Our victories so far have been easy, and the people cannot be convinced that we can be beaten and that not all white commanders will be so stupid in conducting war."

"Has Little Turtle had word of what the whites are doing, or of a new commander?" I asked.

Apekonit replied, "St. Clair is back at Fort Washington. He is still governor but is not the army commander. Little Turtle has heard that the American President Washington, has selected a mad man, or a crazy man, or some such thing, to command the army."

"A mad man?" I asked. "A mad man?"

Then I thought for a moment and I burst out laughing, answering my question.

"Oh, Anthony Wayne," I laughed. "The army will be commanded by General Mad Anthony Wayne?"

"Yes, Wayne, Spirit Traveler," he said.

I continued laughing and explained to him that "Mad Anthony" was just a sobriquet that the general had earned during the late War for Independence. He was not mad. Sometime later I learned that Wayne had been selected from four logical choice candidates. The others were: Dan Morgan, George Rogers Clark, and James Wilkinson. Ultimately Wayne was considered the best choice of the field commander, training officer, and diplomat. Morgan and Clark were well past their primes, each with questionable health and Wilkinson was considered just a bit too ambitious for Washington's liking. He, did, however, have considerable experience in Indian fighting.

I wondered about the difference in strategy between Morgan, Clark, and Wayne because I knew little of Wilkinson. Morgan and also I guessed Clark, would have fought like Indians from behind trees and logs, using ambush tactics. Wayne would likely use cavalry, a strategic device that Indians had seldom had used against them.

"If the President will send General Wayne, he is much to be feared," I said.

"All the more reason to go to Vincennes," Apekonit responded.

"We will carry word from Little Turtle to General (Rufus) Putnam. We will speak of peace but no one must know. Some would kill us if they knew that we are doing this," he said.

Well, this was an interesting turn of events. I fully understood the danger of anyone in the alliance thinking we were making secret deals. Beyond that, I had no further need for clarification. But now my suspicions that our journey was more than just a family reunion were confirmed.

"How are your dreams?" I asked, changing the subject.

"I have them often," he said.

I truly felt for Apekonit, a warrior who had just had many months to soak in the adoration of the people for his exploits against St. Clair but also to be haunted every night by dreams and his fears of losing himself. I was not sure what meeting with his brother would accomplish, but I hoped it would lead to some change, some breakthrough in his conundrum, or give him a new direction.

On that warm early spring morning we left the Eel village, and took a southwesterly course to intersect the Ouabache River. We would follow it first to Kenapakomoko to have Gaviahate join us. As far as I knew he was going with us to gain information about his captive wife.

Having gathered Gaviahate we went to Ouiatenon, and then down to Vincennes. I prevailed upon Apekonit that we should trade for a canoe at the first opportunity and perhaps speed our trip. He agreed with me.

At first, we traveled rapidly afoot and arrived at Ouiatenon in three days after leaving Eel River by taking well-worn trails between villages and pacing ourselves. Here we visited some of Apekonit's wife's relatives from his first marriage, staying one day and night among the Wea people. His fame from the St. Clair battle had preceded him, and he was regarded with great esteem by most of the extended Miami people. And of course, everyone knew Gaviahate.

I was not a particular novelty, partly because I traveled with Apekonit, partly because my marriage to Autumn had achieved a certain celebrity throughout the domain of the Miami and their cousins. Additionally, my clothing, thanks to Autumn, was very

Miami-like with a few white man preferences and my hair had grown long, though I did not style it like a Miami warrior.

Ouiatenon was officially now under the control of the Americans, but they could not spare the men to maintain a presence at this time, especially being in hostile country.

At Ouiatenon, we secured an old canoe in exchange for a deer that we had shot, and a badger pelt that I had brought along for any trading necessity. Where the Ouabache widens out to become a large but slowly moving river, we began to travel by water. Gaviahate was a much better canoe handler than Apekonit, having lived on shallow rivers, and used such a form of travel more than the Miami at Kekionga.

An opportunity to view the rich Ouabache River Valley by canoe suited me just fine, and the trip took us through dense forest and expansive open prairie. We saw a great deal of wildlife including a large buffalo herd. It was an abundant land. I had a moment of sorrow in knowing that someday it would all be reduced to farmland. We arrived in Vincennes after three days on the river, our travel occurring without any unusual events, or circumstances and in general being a pleasant trip.

It was during the last leg of our journey that Apekonit again spoke of peace. He also shared with me what Gaviahate already knew, and as it turns out, why he was traveling with us; it appeared that a prisoner exchange was to be arranged as a good-faith gesture to the Indians, by the United States Government. Gaviahate had word that his wife was among those to be exchanged, and had provided Apekonit with the information that his wife and child were also to be exchanged, as they were alive and held prisoner at Fort Washington.

Apekonit was stunned. He could say nothing for many minutes.

While that news was good, I immediately wondered what it would be like to have two wives, a reality that Apekonit would very soon be facing. Not that it was forbidden among the Miami, but I just knew one wife was all I'd ever be able to handle or to want, and I thought things were going to get very interesting for Apekonit. But this was not the time to speak of it. Silence prevailed as we neared Vincennes.

Our impending arrival was no secret, and we were greeted by a young black slave along the pier. The well-spoken young man inquired as to whether one of us was William Wells. Apekonit affirmed that he was William Wells. With that we were escorted to a modest, but well-built structure, especially by wilderness standards, that was home and headquarters to the Vincennes Commandant, Colonel Jean Francois Hamtramck. There we were greeted by Apekonit's older brother Samuel and by Colonel Hamtramck himself.

Gaviahate had gone off as soon as we had landed, to look up some French friends of his from a time long ago, when the French and the Miami were allies. He knew that Apekonit would fill him in on the details of the prisoners' release. In the meantime, he did not wish to be in a meeting with high ranking white men.

Samuel Wells was a self-made planter, and businessman of some wealth, a soldier of the Revolution, a frontiersman, a future politician, and a well-known Indian fighter. Regarding the latter, he had distinguished himself in numerous fights and would in the future attain an even greater reputation for his bravery. He was some 12 to 15 years older than Apekonit.

Colonel Jean Francois Hamtramck was a French-Canadian who had fought with the Americans in the Revolution and later participated in numerous battles against the red man in the Ohio Country. As I noted earlier, he had just missed St. Clair's Defeat by having been sent south to recover deserters and to protect a supply train that was coming north. He nevertheless proved crucial in preparing Fort Jefferson to receive the survivors. One cannot help but wonder how many American lives would have been spared if Hamtramck and his 300 regulars had been with St. Clair during the battle.

The Colonel was not with us during my time with the Army, when General Harmar went north. He was at the time delivering a somewhat furtive diversionary attack from Vincennes northwesterly, toward the Miami villages in hopes of taking pressure off of Harmar. So I had never met nor been around the man. I was however, aware of his reputation as a fine leader and very brave soldier, who was committed completely to the cause of the United States. He had a bit of a French accent when he spoke English, which seemed to engage mostly on certain words or letters such as, for example, "th", which became functionally a "z" for him. His small "i's" were more like long "e's."

Upon our entering the building, Samuel moved to embrace Apekonit affectionately. I noticed a more reserved reaction from Apekonit. This was a characteristic of the Indian people when meeting someone they did not know well. However, I think Apekonit had genuine happiness. He explained to Samuel and the Colonel that I was a friend who lived near the Miami. I was warmly greeted with a handshake by both men.

We were offered some wine which both men had already been drinking when we arrived. Then we were escorted into a dining room where a sumptuous table of fruit, vegetables, bread, ham, and pheasant greeted us. I think to some extent we may have embarrassed ourselves with our gluttony. However, the Colonel and Samuel merely laughed, being themselves well-familiar with the appetite of men coming in after several days in the wilderness. For my part I could not get enough of the ham. It was a favorite that I had not had for a very long time.

During the meal the Colonel questioned me about being an American living among the Miami. I told him my whole story, feeling that if I were going to be considered as a deserter, we might as well get it out on the table so to speak. It turns out that Apekonit had already told him of me on another occasion. Hamtramck was merely getting my perspective on how I came to the current time.

He told me that my commission as a scout would have expired while I was a captive and that the fact that I subsequently lived among the Miami, was in no way any violation of military law, or protocol as far as he was concerned, or as far as he understood it. He had been on the frontier long enough to know of other cases such as mine and he took these as just the way things sometimes happen. I sensed that he may have also felt, that like Apekonit, I could be very useful, though exactly how I could not tell.

My case was further strengthened by the fact that Hamtramck was assured by Apekonit, and by me, that I had not participated against St. Clair. Though I got the impression that even that would not have mattered to the Colonel. He and Apekonit most definitely had some previous contact, and although technically enemies, both gave every indication of cooperation to achieve peace between the Americans and the tribes of the confedera-tion. They behaved very cordially toward each other. They were much more like friends than enemies.

During our meal we were interrupted twice by couriers. Each time Hamtramck excused himself and met with the messengers in a private room. After speaking with the second he informed us that General Rufus Putnam would arrive from Fort Nelson in two days. In addition to his business agenda he was coming to speak with Apekonit.

Wow! My friend was commanding audiences with United States Generals. Putnam had a dual role as also being the Indian Agent of the Northwest Territory, charged with bringing peace to the region. More was going on here than I would have thought at the beginning of our trip.

As the meal ended, Hamtramck asked if I would join him in another room, while Apekonit and Samuel went off to have their discussion. As we sat in what was Hamtramck's office, a servant appeared with sherry. Hamtramck certainly kept the alcohol flowing. But after all, he was French.

I thought he would start by grilling me on my situation among the Miamis. Instead and to my surprise, he broached a completely different topic to begin the conversation. "Monsieur Jamison, I would assume zhat zee army owes you some money, oui?"

"I hadn't thought about it, but I guess I was never paid past the onset of the expedition with General Harmar," I said.

"We shall correct zhat," he said.

He then produced a government payroll form for me to sign, and said he would request the money be sent from Ft. Washington. I knew it was not a great deal, but having left much of my inheritance in a bank in Williamsburg and a bit in New York, I was happy to have any amount coming to me.

And then he delivered a shocker that near knocked me off my chair, "How would you like to earn some more money and to have a beet of adventure at zhee zhame time?" he asked.

"Well Sir," I said, "I wasn't looking for employment. I have a wife who is with child, and I cannot be gone for any great length of time."

"Zhis leettle project would require about 21 days, or so, geeve or take a few," he responded. "And the United States will pay you much more handsomely zhan zhey deed for your time weeth General Harmar."

Cutting straight to the point, I said, "What is the job, sir?"

"I need one more man to go as a part of a small group, to St. Louis to, shall we say, obtain information about zhee current state of Spanish affairs," he responded.

"Spying?" I again went to the point.

"Yes, precisely," he said laughing. "You are a most direct young man. And, I have noticed zhat you do not speak like someone raised on zhee frontier. You strike me as a most educated man."

"Yes, sir, I have had some college, but I was raised on the frontier." I came back with, "Why me for this trip?"

"You are a woodsman, are you not?" he said. "I need zhis done rapidly, and wizout causing any undue Spanish concern. I must send men who have never been seen anywhere near St. Louis, and who are unknown to the Spanish. I assume you have never been zhere?"

"No, Sir, I haven't, but seeing that part of the country has some appeal, especially the Mississippi River Valley."

"Zhen, we shall consider zhat we have an agreement?" he proffered.

Whoa, I didn't want to be rushed, but upon considering the whole thing, I was going to be several more days from home anyway, so this little project might not be a bad idea.

It now struck me that this was not a random job offer and that Apekonit may well have recommended me to the Colonel for this mission.

"Just one question, before I agree, sir," I said. "Who are the other men who will accompany me?"

"Like you," he replied, "zhey are men of zee wilderness but not so educated. Zhey are here een zee village, I shall send for zhem. You can meet zhem, so zhat you may ascertain eef zhey weell be agreeable company for you. Would zhat meet weeth your approval?"

"Oui monsieur, ce serant juste bien," I laughed. I suddenly had the urge to answer him in French, maybe to further impress him, perhaps as a friendly gesture.

"Oh, you speak God's language?" he said, seemingly intrigued.

I couldn't resist, "No, Sir," I chuckled, " just a little French."

We both laughed heartily.

"Voulez-vous purler espagnol?" he asked.

"Non, desole, pas l'espagnol," I answered.

"Ah, trop mauvais," he said.

He then summoned a servant and sent him on a mission to find the men of whom he spoke. While the search was on, he pardoned himself to go, and to attend to other matters but offered me more sherry, and the freedom to peruse his rather extensive personal library. This was in no way objectionable to me, and the time passed swiftly.

In a bit less than an hour the Colonel returned, and announced that the servant's errand had been successful, and then the two men would be with us momentarily.

A few minutes later, a knock came at the door, and a servant showed the two men into the room. This time, I think it safe to say, that I fell off my chair! Of course, they were as surprised as I. It was Jim Tucker and Black Duck. I couldn't imagine how this job offer could be any better.

Jim and Black Duck had assumed that I had been killed, and so they immediately rushed to hug me like bears, and so forth. They asked about Blue Dogs Runs Him, and even about Troubles, and I had to relive the painful memory of their end. Much talk followed, and the Colonel, surprised that we knew each other, but happy that his plan was coming together, now sent us off, telling us to return tomorrow for instructions and to take our leave.

I found Apekonit, still with Samuel, told him quickly what was afoot, and that he could find me later in whatever passed for a tavern in this small village. Jim, Black Duck, and I then went to find such an establishment. Black Duck drank little, but as for Jim and I, it was an intoxicating reunion. We had much to discuss about the time since we had been together. I will not go into all of that here but will bring it up as needed. However, one point was of major interest. The old scouts confided that they were now working for General Wayne. When I wondered aloud what that had to do with St. Louis, they told me that this trip was not Hamtramck's idea. He was just seeing that the mission was carried out.

This assignment came from General Wayne himself and had the utmost priority, and utmost secrecy associated with it. When I probed further, Jim simply indicated that Hamtramck would fill me in. General Wayne had instructed him to keep the reason for the trip completely secret, and therefore he would allow Hamtramck to tell me what it was he thought that I needed to know. Black Duck, being predisposed to be laconic anyway, was not going to talk about the trip. That much I knew about my old friend.

Late in the evening Samuel and Apekonit came into the tavern. Samuel offered all of us billeting with some friends that he was staying with, but my two friends had been staying at the fort, and I opted to stay with them.

In the morning, after some army breakfast, I joined Apekonit and Samuel at Hamtramck's headquarters. To my surprise General Rufus Putnam had arrived earlier than expected. I was introduced to him as I was ushered into Hamtramck's office. There, with Hamtramck, Putnam, Samuel, and Apekonit a sort of mini-peace conference was held. Putnam indicated to Apekonit that he had expected him a month later and that the prisoner exchange could not be made until then.

Apekonit replied that he had come early to make certain everything was in place for the exchange.

It was determined that Samuel, Gaviahate, and Apekonit would go to Louisville for three weeks with Samuel, and then on to Fort Washington to help facilitate the prisoner exchange. Apekonit, along with Gaviahate, would serve as interpreters, ease the Indian prisoners' fears, and would bring the prisoners back to Vincennes by river. From there they would be disbursed to their proper villages. Already, messengers, mostly Frenchmen, were on their way to the tribes to tell them to bring Americans held prisoner to Vincennes to await the prisoner exchange.

It was hoped by Putnam that this gesture of goodwill would facilitate some peace conferences in the autumn.

A list of prisoners held at Fort Washington was produced, and to his great joy, but a certain level of perplexity, Apekonit's wife, and his young child were on the list. I congratulated him while reminding him that he now had two wives. He seemed a bit overwhelmed and most definitely confused. He managed only a weak smile.

It was clear that Putnam desired peace, and would work tirelessly toward that end. Hamtramck was of the same persuasion, and they eagerly listened to all that Apekonit relayed to them from Little Turtle. This excited them greatly, but Apekonit had to caution them that Little Turtle's opinion was in the minority and that he would likely lose standing among the confederation if advocating peace. The Indians truly thought that they could not be beaten by United States troops.

Still, the optimism of Putnam could not be dampened. He thanked Apekonit profusely for all his information and advised him to send messages to Little Turtle, and all other Indian leaders of note. I truly believe that Putnam wanted to end the war and to be fair to the Indians. He was soon to retire from the military, and hoped to conclude his duties as Indian Commissioner, with a major peace treaty that included all the Northwest tribes. He would then retire to his home in Marietta, on the Ohio River.

As Putnam was laying out, and explaining in detail, the land settlement, yearly tribal allotments, and annuities, and carefully drawing on a huge map of the Northwest territory, a servant came to notify Hamtramck that my two old partners had arrived.

At that news, Putnam excused Samuel and Apekonit, telling them to come back in the afternoon. They left after bidding me farewell, and the two new arrivals came in to discuss our mission to St. Louis.

After introducing General Putnam, Hamtramck laid out the plan.

"Gentlemen, you weell proceed weeth all due haste to St. Louis. Zhere you weell pretend to be fur trappers heading west, and under zhat guise attempt to geet proper permits to enter Spanish territory. Under no circumstances are you to admit to anyone to being United States agents, or members of the army. Eef anyone asks you do not know me, General Wayne, General Putnam, Arthur St. Clair, or anyone een zee government. Eef you are somehow detained, you must never admit, even under torture zeee nature of your mission."

"And just what would be the nature of our mission?" I asked.

Hamtramck replied, "Specifically you will ascertain how many British and other spies are een zee area, get an idea of what nationalities are zhere, survey zee gun emplacements over zee river, and get us a map of any fortifications, particularly zose zhat guard the Mississippi."

"A'da alone be'ya tall task," Jim said, knowing full well that there was more.

"Zhat's not all," Hamtramck continued right on cue. "Zhee main purpose of your mission eez to ascertain any information about zhee connection of Colonel James Wilkinson weeth zhee Spanish. We have reason to believe, and zhis eez highly confidential, zhat he eez een zee pay of the Spanish, zhat he eez a Spanish agent. You do know who Colonel Wilkinson eez, oui?"

I assented by shaking my head in the affirmative.

He continued, "You will proceed immediately here, wizout delay, upon accomplishing your mission, making a full report to me and me only. Eez zhat understood?"

Again, heads shook in the affirmative.

At this point General Putnam said, "Gentlemen, I cannot overly stress the importance of this work for your country. President Washington has appointed Colonel Wilkinson to be General Wayne's second in command. We must be certain of his loyalty to the United States. Needless to say, you cannot speak of this to anyone and I mean not to anyone. You will be well-paid for this service. It is of utmost national concern, but is not without danger."

Hamtramck now concluded, "I have here een my hands, a beet of gold, and some silver zhat you may use for purposes of your expenses, for bribery eef necessary, and so forth. Your pay weell come upon completion of zhee mission. You will go to zhee fort, draw any weapons, supplies, and powder zhat you need, and zhen you weell be on your way. Good luck, my compatriots."

Again, we assented with the shaking of our heads and each signed vouchers for the amounts of gold and silver that he provided.

"Good luck!" he concluded.

With that we shook hands with him and General Putnam, and left to secure our supplies.

Chapter Seventeen

St. Louis

Mississippi River

Within less than 45 minutes we were crossing the Ouabache River by canoe and heading overland for St. Louis. We might have taken the river route, but we surmised that we could accomplish our mission much more quickly afoot. By the river we would have had to go downstream on the Ouabache and then the Ohio, and upstream on the Mississippi. Overland, we cut off over 100 miles of the trip.

Once we made land on the far side of the Ouabache, we set out at a goodly speed, sort of challenging one another good-naturedly, to see who might tire first. We spoke of old times as we traveled and it was truly great to be back in the wilderness with my old friends.

I will save you the details of our trip across prairie, through woods, over rolling hills, through swampy wetlands, and fording many streams. The trip was largely uneventful except the speed with which we traveled. We made it in just over three days, by sleeping only four or five hours per night and traveling nearly constantly, but cautiously, during most other waking moments.

One day we began to see outlying cabins, mostly inhabited by French families. As we drew closer to St. Louis, we saw black men and black women working the fields, and the orchards, but there was also something curious about this. Many seemed to be working small plots of land near cabins in which they lived. Later we would find out, that while there were a few free Negroes, slaves were allowed to own property under Spanish law. They had dogs, and plows, and horses, something never heard of in the United States.

Word of our coming certainly preceded us, and we were met about a half-mile from St. Louis by a dozen smartly-uniformed Spanish soldiers led by an ill-mannered corporal named Sepulveda. Under normal conditions, any of us would have pounded him to a bloody pulp on general principle. Given the nature of our mission we could not do that, and we were forced to take his abuse.

It might seem strange to some that we didn't get off the main trail, and skulk around a bit, sort of sneaking up on St. Louis. We figured that was a bad thing to get caught doing, especially if we wanted to impress the Spanish authorities that we were legitimately interested in going to the Rocky Mountains to trap beaver. We could skulk around after leaving the city if we needed to do so.

Sepulveda started by having our guns seized, and asking us in broken English, from whence we came, and what was our business. I explained to the lout in English, and in French, that we were trappers intent on crossing the great plains, and trapping beaver in the Rocky Mountains beyond. He assured me that would be quite impossible, and that we would be spending time locked up for violating Spanish soil without the proper paperwork. His whole manner was abrupt, and was a definite, and planned attempt to intimidate us. Much to his chagrin he was not succeeding. Jim began to laugh uncontrollably, as he towered over the little corporal. Incensed by this insolence, the corporal ordered his men to tie us up. Unable to pull himself together for the sake of the mission, Jim grabbed the closest man's rifle and held the bayonet to the throat of the corporal.

It turned out the corporal was not a brave man despite all of his banty-rooster flitting about. He ordered his men to stand down. I told him that we would come along quietly with him and his men, but would not consent to being tied up. He considered this a reasonable compromise, and we were marched to town surrounded by his men in step, and giving the impression to on-lookers that the Corporal was in complete control.

St. Louis was surrounded by many private cabins and dwell-ings, and the town itself was essentially a wooden fort, with walls about ten feet high, lower in some places, and with a tall stone tower within the walls which had several canons pointed out of top floor gun-ports, not unlike those of a ship. The tower was surrounded at the base by a small wooden stockade. The tower served two purposes in case of an attack. It was essentially a very large blockhouse from which riflemen could fire, and artillery-men could use the canons. It was also large enough to be a kind of last-resort citadel, to which to fall back to if the town were in danger of being overrun by an enemy force.

Streets of mud were everywhere aflutter with activity: dogs, kids, traders, wagons, people milling about. It was a civilization amid the wilderness, and along the biggest river I had ever seen. The site of the Mississippi itself was worth the trip. What a mag-nificent and awe-inspiring waterway, with canoes, small boats, and some larger river-travel boats, tied to numerous piers and small and large wharves, while others were plying the waves of this immense highway.

We took mental note of four, or maybe five redoubts with cannon, on bluffs overlooking the river. We made as good a count as possible of the Spanish soldiers that we saw. We estimated less than 300, which was still a sizable force for a frontier out-post. And it was a clear indicator of the importance which the Spanish attached to the city-fort.

There were certainly as many, and probably far more Frenchmen, and maybe 50 or so Indians of various tribes: Sauk, Ojibwe, Winnebago, Illinois, Chickasaw, and Fox, by Black Duck's reckoning. As the Spanish were not currently on great terms with the English, we did not see any recognizable Englishmen, but to say there were no English spies there, might be an irresponsible, and certainly not proven assumption. If nothing else, I imagined some of the Indians were in British employ for that very purpose, notably the Ojibwe, which is just another name for Chippewa. I expect I've made my opinion of those jackals abundantly clear by this time.

All in all, a very defensible fort, and one that had been unsuccessfully attacked by a large force of British and mostly Indian allies in 1780. With less than 200 Spanish soldiers, Frenchmen, and slaves defending the town, it held against the superior British force, but not without considerable loss of life.

Despite all this, the entire area as a whole was not particularly militarily daunting, and it would be difficult to say that the river was defended beyond any chance of success, by an attacking army. Nevertheless, getting an attacking army to this point would be a feat in itself, and the British could not have done it in 1780, without most of their force being Indians.

We were escorted to an official-looking building within the walls, and presented to a short fat sergeant, with a thin mustache and very greasy hair, named Cespedes. Like Corporal Sepulveda, Cespedes was a bit taken with himself and certainly possessed of an overbearing self-importance. I knew Jim would like to disabuse him of these feelings.

He stood as we were brought in. He was very short, his head a little higher than the middle of my chest. He began speaking to Sepulveda in Spanish. He was asking about us. He barked some orders to Sepulveda, who went hurriedly out of the building. He then proceeded to stare at us, just stare.

"T'ain't a real friendly sort," Jim said. Cespedes cast him the "skunk eye" at this comment.

Within a minute or so, a French merchant came in who spoke perfect English. He was the interpreter.

The Frenchie said, "What are you doing in Spanish territory?"

"We are trappers, we want to purchase a permit to travel to the Rocky Mountains where we will trap beaver," I said.

"What country are you from? Are you from the United States?" the interpreter said.

"Yes, we are from the United States," I answered.

Cespedes knowing what "yes" meant, wasted no time in relaying a response to his interpreter, "This is impossible. We want no person from the United States on our land. You are trespassing and will be thrown in prison, until we can decide what to do with you. If we can prove that you are spies, you will be shot."

When that was relayed to us, I had to restrain Jim again, as he stepped from the back of the room toward Cespedes, intent on mayhem. Cespedes ordered the guards to point their guns at us, and to fire if we moved—at least that is what the Frenchie, clearly frightened, screamed. I blocked Jim's path with my arm and immediately faced Cespedes.

Guessing that he probably understood French, I said, "Pardon, senor, nous avons obtera sur le mauvais pied. Nous voulons seulement a' obeir aux lois espangnoles."

This translates to asking him to pardon us for getting off to a bad start with him. And also telling him that we wanted only to obey Spanish law.

What impact my little speech would have had on him, I cannot say, because while I was saying this, I extended my hand for an apparent handshake, but with a $50 gold piece visible. He quickly took my hand, and made the coin disappear like a magician. Ah, I thought, now we had achieved a common language.

The Frenchie now relayed the sergeant's next comment, "Well, gentlemen, there is no need for hostilities. However, I must ask you to leave immediately and to return home."

He did further add that Lieutenant. Governor, Manuel Perez, was about to end his term in a month or so and that he would be replaced by a Frenchman, Don Zenon Trudeau. Perhaps the new Leiutenant Governor would bring with him a change in policy toward foreigners. Capitan Perez is expecting couriers any day with more details of his replacement. Saying that, he realized he had told us too much and instantly changed the topic to wishing us a safe trip, and that he had no hard feelings.

I was not real happy with this, but I could tell further negotiation was impossible, and might likely lead us to being locked up. I had to ask if we could see Lieutenant Governor Perez, but this was denied on account of his being indisposed with pressing matters.

I told Cespedes we would comply as we had no intent to break Spanish law or to be where we were not wanted. I thanked him and turned toward the door. Now Cespedes ordered Sepulvada to conduct us out of the city, and to the spot where we had first met. We walked in silence, save for the occasional yip and bark of Sepulveda.

"Let me kill him," Jim said, with Black Duck nodding in the affirmative.

"No, Jim, we have to go home," I said.

"Home, but ah. . . , uh . . . ," and then he caught my wink.

The rest of the walk was quiet, and when we arrived at our original meeting spot with Corporal. Sepulveda and his accompanying soldiers, we learned just what a little bastard the Corporal was. Having noticed my bribing Cespedes, he now ordered us searched at gunpoint. Fortunately, he found only a few small coins and one remaining $20 gold piece. We had stashed some money in the woods, some distance away, on our way in. Smaller coins we had packed into the load in the barrels of our rifles. Should we have ever had to fire the guns, it would have been quite interesting and expensive. Now, the disappointed Sepuluvada ordered our guns returned to us. His men kept careful aim at us as we walked away, under the bombastic speech pouring from the mouth of the insufferable Corporal. He pointed eastward toward our assumed homes.

"Just one blow?" Jim said.

"No, let's make tracks," I said. "Only two hours of daylight left."

We knew full well that we would be followed indefinitely to ascertain if we would attempt to circle back. Laughing, we lit out on the run, and within a very few short minutes were well free of Spanish eyes, leaving our tag-alongs sucking air a mile or so behind us.

Careful to make our trail appear to be leading east, and employing a few Indian tricks to that end, we secured our hidden money, and then carefully began to circle back to the southwest, intent on snooping south of St. Louis.

At this point, Black Duck informed us that he would be willing to lay outside the town in the hopes of speaking privately to a Chickasaw, or other Indian, leaving the city-fort.

We thought about this for a minute, when I had a better idea.

"I think we should go near the trails on this side of the river, and see if we can perhaps waylay a courier. We might get lucky."

Black Duck replied, "A good plan, no trouble, these men are not brave warriors."

"Wortha try," Jim said.

"Well, we know at least one courier is expected. Now, whether he comes by land, or river, is the question. If it is by the river then we have no chance." I said.

With that, we moved near the river, just off the mainland trail. It stood to reason that it might be some time before the courier would come, so Jim spent the first two nights on a bluff over-looking the city from some distance. By the location of fires, he could see in what areas the Spanish had set defenses. He drew crude maps of these on some parchment that I had in my pack.

Black Duck moved on down the trail a few miles so that we would not be caught off-guard by someone on the trail.

The early morning of the third day of our vigil, Black Duck came running up the trail to tell us that an Indian and a French-man were coming. They were walking, and carrying a pouch, which could be dispatches, or could be mail for St. Louis. How-ever, the latter was unlikely, as common sense told us that mail would be sent by the river.

Secreting ourselves on both sides of the trail, near a bend it made through the forest to accommodate the geography of the river, we laid our trap. Jim jumped out in front of the two travel-ers just as Black Duck and I jumped with guns at the ready from behind on either side of the trail.

Both men quickly dropped their weapons, and while the Frenchman attempted to protest, his Indian companion adopted a practical attitude and offered neither resistance nor verbiage.

We directed the two into the woods where we tied them each to their tree, sitting down. We began pouring through the pouch. We had struck gold, so to speak, as the pouch was full of commu-nications of all sorts to Lieutenant Governor Manuel Perez, from His Excellency, Francisco Luis Hector Baron de Carondelet, Gov-ernor of the Louisiana Territory, who was based in New Orleans.

The problem is that most dispatches were in Spanish, though a few were duplicated in French. There were what appeared to be quartermaster reports, inventories to be done, troop rotation lists, as well as a host of other documents. I was able to decipher the ones in French, but not the Spanish.

Our Indian captive was a Chickasaw and was conversing with Black Duck in a native dialect. Black Duck was grilling the man like a true professional, but the Indian who also spoke French admitted to speaking Spanish, but also to not being able to read the language. That is an outstanding technique to ensure that dispatches are kept secret. I only hoped that our Frenchman could help us.

At first, he protested but was gently persuaded when Jim offered to use his hunting knife to gut the man from private parts to the throat. After letting that soak in, I told the courier that we had no desire to harm him and his companion in any manner if we learned what the papers said. We would not take the papers, and if he or his Indian friend told the Spanish in St. Louis what had happened, they might be in trouble for falling into the hands of foreigners. So, essentially, the deal was made, "You help us, and we will release you with all papers, to be on your way." And of course, "you say nothing of this encounter." I sealed the deal with a $50 gold piece to each man. They were amazed at this bit of unexpected generosity, and they suddenly became disposed to cooperate fully.

Now, I presented to our mollified Frenchman the document I most suspected to be of use. He read it to me, translating the Spanish to French, which I will here translate to English:

> To His Excellency Lieutenant Governor of Louisiana, Capitan Manuel Perez,
>
> It is my pleasure to report that your replacement, Don Zenon Trudeau, will arrive in mid to late July. Before returning to New Orleans, you are to spend one to two weeks acquainting him with your post.
>
> Don Trudeau will bring fresh orders for establishing licensed traders, and agents to send among the various tribes. This will keep some tribes from going over to the English, and may perhaps bring others back into our circle of influence.
>
> Concerning the American threat, my predecessor, his Excellency Don Esteban Rodriquez Miro y Sabater, currently serving in the Ministry of War, has fully informed Senor Trudeau that the Americans covet access to the Mississippi River, and undoubtedly other of our territory. In this regard, Senor Trudeau will be authorized to continue communications with our agent, Number 13.
>
> While it is no longer a possibility that Kentucky will declare as a separate republic allied with Spain, Agent 13 will still be of use to the crown. You

are to continue to cultivate his services. His pay for services will, as it has, come through St. Louis.

Be ever vigilant against the English and especially the Americans, and should either threaten, seek to convert the other to our cause, for it is clear that they are implacable enemies.

May God keep you.
Francisco Luis Hector Baron de Carondelet, Governor-General of Louisiana.
New Orleans, 1, May 1792

"Well, well, well, we'd 'ya hit ta eye out of the possum on this un," Jim said. It suddenly occurred to me that his colorful use of language was nice to hear again every day, after having been away from him for so long.

I replied, "We haven't proven anything on Wilkinson, but the circumstantial evidence points to him, and that is likely as close as we get. I think we all know that he is likely Agent 13."

I then addressed the matter of the couriers, "Let us get these gentlemen on their way."

I gave the men their dispatches and for good measure, a $20 silver piece each. They seemed quite pleased with this additional fortune as we let them go, and we made tracks for Vincennes.

"Think them" ll be' a talk' in?" Jim said.

"We can't be sure, but I don't think so," I replied. "They have some newfound wealth and have no reason to make the St. Louis authorities angry. Can you imagine what would happen if those pieces were discovered on them, while they were describing their encounter with us?"

"No, I expect they'll be silent," I finished.

Sometimes it's just better to be lucky than good, and all anyone could claim about our getting the proof of Wilkinson's treason, was that it was just plain lucky and unlikely. Nevertheless, that is just how it happened, and a more favorable act of good fortune could scarcely be imagined, let alone expected.

We took the better part of four days getting back to Vincennes, partly because we took a different more difficult route, in case we were followed, and partly because we were curious about the country. We knew if we were followed it would not be by the Spanish, but rather by their Indian lackeys, who were much better trackers, with considerably more stamina than the average Spanish levee.

It was nearing mid-June when we reported back to Colonel Hamtramck, who was extremely surprised, and concerned to see us back so soon. We quickly eased his fears as we relayed every event of our trip, and produced Jim's maps, behind closed doors, in what was probably a two-hour meeting.

Though we had not proven anything against Wilkinson, we certainly had obtained circumstantially incriminating evidence. There was little doubt given earlier suspicions and the reference to Kentucky.

He told us that we were not to speak of our trip's results to anyone, nor to let anyone know that we had been anywhere near St. Louis. For his part, he would relay our report to Fort Washington, where General Putnam had gone. Putnam would send it on to Henry Knox in the new capital, Philadelphia. Jim and Black Duck would report their findings directly to General Wayne. And that was that.

It would not be long before I was to learn, because of some other events that occurred, that nothing was done with the information that was provided up the chain of command to President Washington. Wilkinson suffered no sanction, at least not one that could be discerned by the public. He maintained his status as second in command of the Legion of the United States, and in just a few short years became its commander, the highest-ranking United States military officer. But those facts relate to politics that I do not profess to understand.

My two friends had orders to go back to General Wayne's camp, in the eastern Ohio Country, by way of Fort Washington. They were told that they could confirm the results of their trip to Wayne, and would deliver to him sealed instructions that would be given to them by Putnam.

Hamtramck told me that Samuel and Apekonit were near Ft. Nelson at Louisville. There they were awaiting the time of the prisoner exchange at Fort Washington. At that time Apekonit would be summoned for interpreter duties, and to accompany the Indian prisoners to Vincennes. Gaviahate would wait for him at Vincennes, staying with some cousin Piankeshaw tribe members. Apekonit had left word for me with Hamtramck to either return to Turtletown or to await him at Vincennes, whichever was my pleasure.

I do not know how that last night before separating, that Jim, Black Duck, and I kept our wits about us, or if we did. We ate well and drank even more at a French tavern in Vincennes. Still, the sad parting once again weighed heavily on our minds. We told tales till the wee hours, and finally the time came to say good-bye.

A man of few words, Black Duck only said to me, "May the manitous look over you, my friend. You are a good man who walks straight and speaks always the truth."

Jim added, "Well young' an, I shore'm gonna miss ya. Ya might jest be the smartest man I ever met, better'n them city dandies or fancy generals."

He was not about to let himself get maudlin, or sentimental, but I could see the pain in his eyes. And I knew what I felt. Still, I had to be positive. We had some time together and I hoped for more in the future.

"I will see you again soon my friends, either I will come to you, or you must come to my home," I said. "Goodbye."

I slept in the tavern inn for what was left of that night and in the morning, had a much-needed bath. I wrote letters to my sisters and Luke, in care of the Randolphs of Richmond.

In the afternoon, I asked Colonel Hamtramck to post the letters for me. He gladly assented. He also presented me with back pay for my service with Harmar and a handsome sum of $200 in gold, for the mission just completed.

I also left a letter for Apekonit, but it occurred to me that I did not know how well he could read. Funny thing, you know a person, but perhaps not as fully as you would think. I asked Hamtramck to read it to him if there were a problem. In the letter I told Apekonit simply I would see him at Turtletown upon his return, but that for now I wanted to get home.

Gaviahate was of great help in the prisoner exchange and brought them back to Vincennes. When they arrived in late July, or early August, he was instrumental in the logistics of getting them turned over to their relatives. Some of them he even delivered home himself. There was great rejoicing up and down the

Ouabache River system. But none was greater than the old man's reunion with his wife and daughters.

The prisoner exchange, and good faith of General Putnam, went a very long way toward keeping most of the Oubache River Valley tribes out of the conflict that would come in the future.

And so home I went, some by canoe, but mostly by land. I arrived after a week of hard travel, much of it at night, lest a lone white man be a target for a few braves looking for mischief. I picked up my beautiful bride in Turtletown and after a most joyful reunion, we headed for our cabin.

The summer was fair with plenty of rain and the garden was good. Fishing was very good but hunting only fair, game being less than abundant for some reason. Concentrating on fish, we laid in plenty of food in anticipation of another winter of deep snow. Autumn spent a great deal of time making baby blankets, little toys, and other such things. By Autumn's best reckoning, the baby would arrive in mid-November.

We debated as to whether we would go to Eel River Turtletown, for the birth, or have Autumn's mother and cousins come to us. Ultimately, we decided that our child would be born in our home, and that we would have the aforementioned guests for an extended stay and to help with the birth. That was more than fine with me as the last thing I wanted was to be alone in delivering the baby. I had helped Doc Johnson with two or three deliveries years before, but I was not comfortable with my ability to handle any unusual developments during the birth.

In late-September, we went to Turtletown for five days to arrange for the relatives to come to our cabin in mid-October. Autumn's mother, She-Fox, and the cousins, Loon's Song and Blue Sky, were almost as excited as we. It was determined that Gray Fox would escort the women to our cabin. He was looking forward to being an uncle, though he was uncertain as to what all that entailed. He made it known that he was hoping for a boy.

Oddly, and to my concern, Apekonit had not yet returned by the time of our arrival in Turtletown, and I had no word of him. I did hear that many hostages had been returned to villages along the river system, in what would much later become central and northern Indiana.

Upon returning to our home, I was occupied in harvesting our garden, and laying in additional food in the form of nuts, roots, and pawpaws. The days became shorter and much brisker. Winter was not far away. Signs were that winter would begin early.

Time went swiftly, and in mid-October, the Eel River Turtletown contingent arrived, though the baby did not.

Finally, on November 8, 1792, baby Jamison entered the world, letting all present know that she had arrived. The day she was born the sun rose brightly, after three days of snow. Therefore, her Miami name was Kiilhswa, or "Sun." It was a name that was to be most often used as "Sunny" by her father. It kind of occurred to me that we might be bordering on sacrilege since the sun was highly regarded in the Miami religion. I thought perhaps calling the baby Sunshine might be better, but Autumn and especially her mother, would not hear of it; this child was "the Sun" to them and they meant to have that known to all. A few years later, Little Turtle's granddaughter was named Kilsoquah, meaning "the Setting Sun." This name was eerily prophetic, when applied to the future of the Indian people.

My daughter's English name would be Kathryn Marie Jamison, after my mother. I thought about calling her Katy, but in truth, I never did get past using Sunny.

If a newborn could be said to be the embodiment of her mother, She-Fox pronounced Sun to be an exact copy of Autumn as a baby, in looks and total disposition. From the first day, she was a strong-willed child, but a beauty as well, destined to become daddy's girl. She made her temper clearly known, but would just as easily slip into someone's arms and snuggle them to her will. She was the most beautiful baby I had ever seen, and I could see my mother and Autumn in her face. It caused me to think of my sisters, and my brother, Luke. I wondered whether they were married yet with families of their own. I determined that I had to find out as soon as I could.

Even Gray Fox's initial disappointment at not getting a nephew disappeared, when after having to be strongly coaxed, he held the baby, and she went to sleep in his arms. At that moment he was sold on his new niece. Loon's Song, along with Blue Sky, fought constantly over who would tend to the baby's every need. This child was just born and already living the life of a European princess.

Before long we were joined by Black Bear who had grown

tired of being a bachelor and desired to see his grandchild. He was the proudest of grandfathers. Our guests stayed through December because they were reluctant to leave the baby. It was good to have them and eased both our worries regarding the care of our newborn.

Chapter Eighteen

Apekonit's Decision

William Wells

In late January, or early February of 1793, Apekonit and Sweet Breeze, having traveled in unseasonably warm weather, came to visit. Apekonit's Wea family was not with them. He explained that they were visiting his wife's relatives. As he came near me, I whispered in his ear and needled him about two wives. He could only manage a confused smile of embarrassment.

Sweet Breeze carried their new baby girl, who was about two weeks older than Sunny. That of course means that Sweet Breeze was pregnant when she and Apekonit were married in the spring. While the women ogled the babies, and the babies starred somewhat blankly at each other, Apekonit and I retreated to a far corner of the cabin to catch up.

He explained that he had gotten the hostages back to Vincennes and from there, they all went home. He then deposited his Wea wife and child with Samuel's family at Louisville while he traveled back to Fort Washington, where he continued his work with General Putnam, as an interpreter. He was being paid quite handsomely, and I detected that he was starting to like this white man's concept of working for money, especially when the work was something so natural to him as interpreting and advising Putnam on the general tenor of feelings among the tribes. While he was hopeful that peace would come, he knew well that the tribal confederation was still feeling invincible.

He told me that while at Fort Washington, he had many opportunities to sit in on discussions of recent Indian raids. Several of these were the attributed work of Little Turtle, who despite his desire for peace, continued to wage war, hoping to garner more favorable terms and fair boundaries, in the event of peace.

And then he told me a jaw-dropper. "My brother, I have met the mad general, Anthony Wayne."

"And what is he like?" I asked, laughing at his reference to Wayne as the mad general, and still having trouble believing Apekonit's popularity among the whites.

"He is, as the people say, the man who never sleeps. He is on the move constantly; now here, now there, always training his soldiers. He is a man who will not be beaten," he replied.

"This I have heard," I said.

"He has asked me to join his scouts," he now confessed.

"What?" I verily shouted incredulously.

"Yes, to scout for his army," he said.

"Will you do it?" I asked.

"I have not said yes, I have not said no, but I have spoken with my father, Michikinikwa. He has told me that I must follow my heart. Perhaps, in the end, it is even a better way to help the people than to fight with them," he said.

"How so?" I replied.

"Perhaps, I can help both sides to understand the other," he responded.

"Perhaps," I said, becoming silent, but pondering all that he had told me.

He concluded by telling me that he had some more work to do for Putnam in the spring, and then he must give Wayne his answer in the early summer.

Later, I relayed to Apekonit the details of my visit to St. Louis, except of course, the reasons and the outcome. He was very interested in how the Spanish treated the Indians in the territories that they claimed. Our talk went deep into the night, long after our lovely brides had gone to sleep, and after a bottle of Kentucky whiskey that he brought with him had disappeared.

We had prepared several bear skins, covered with wolf and beaver, near the hearth for our guest family.

As I lay in bed on my back, with Autumn's arm across my chest, I marveled at all I had been told, and at how far my friend had come with his problem. It seemed to me that he was on the verge of once again becoming William Wells. I doubted that this would sit well with the Miami people. I wondered how his decision would affect me, a white man among the Miami, but not committed to fighting as were the Girty brothers. And too, I thought about Anthony Wayne, who I had little doubt would remove all perception of Indian invincibility, once and for all, just as soon as the war renewed in earnest. As I was later to learn, Wayne was wintering his troops in the relative safety of western Pennsylvania, at a place called Legiontown, drilling, drilling, drilling.

The weather soon regained its strength, but by then our guests had gone home to Turtletown. Winter wore on and with each day, Sunny seemed to grow and to learn something new. I loved that child so. She represented joy and happiness beyond anything I could imagine. Life with Autumn had been bliss. Life now was perfect.

The spring of 1793, came later than usual, and Apekonit had gone to Fort Washington. By the end of May or the beginning of June, he was back in Turtletown. He had not revealed to me his final decision, but he said he had two tasks to perform. He intended to go to the site of St. Clair's Defeat and locate the cannons that had been secreted by the victors after the battle. In other words, hidden by he and his suicide squad of braves.

Secondly, he was going to attend a large pow wow of the confederated tribes on the Maumee River later in the summer. The conference was to be hosted by Alexander McKee, a British agent and known agitator. He had been sent by his government to gift the tribes and stir them back to war with the United States.

While I certainly felt that Apekonit was going over to the American side, the tasks I described could be interpreted either way. For that matter, they could even be interpreted as one for the Americans, and one for the Indians. Despite my questions, he refused me any direct, or even indirect answer. As we parted, I was very confused, but he seemed not to be so at all.

What I shall relay to you next is an accounting of his summer activities, as later told to me by Apekonit, shortly after it became clear as to what his final decision had been.

In May, he had gone back to Fort Washington to help General Putnam with some interpreting, and advising him on the current status of Indian dispositions. He also had a meeting with General Wayne in which the General told him that he intended to establish a fort on the site of St. Clair's defeat. He proposed that Apekonit go and reconnoiter the site and if possible locate the cannons that had been hidden after St. Clair's defeat.

This task Apekonit accomplished in June of 1793, reporting back to Wayne that while some bones yet remained to be buried, the site would lend itself well to a fort. Additionally, he had found and secreted four of the cannons. That left one of the original five unaccounted for.[1] The four would have only to be reconditioned to be put into duty. It was at this point that Wayne was so impressed, that he not only reiterated his earlier offer of a scouting position but offered Apekonit the leadership of the scout corps and future rank of captain in the U. S. Army.

Apekonit accepted and immediately set out to establish an elite corps of scouts, a dozen or so who were white men who had previously lived among the Indians either as captives or by choice. This group would come to be so useful to Wayne because they dressed as Indians, frequently coming and going into the enemy's encampments, and because they all spoke at least one Indian dialect. Combining these facts with Wayne's rigorous training of his legion, it all added up to stacking the odds heavily in favor of the Americans in future battles.

At some point in the summer, Apekonit met with Little Turtle. Their meeting produced within Little Turtle a near certainty that the Indians would have to sue for peace. However, he remained an extremely unpopular point of view among the undefeated confederation.

In late summer, the Indians held a huge conference on the upper Maumee River. British agent McKee presided and promised massive British support. He reinforced the feelings of Indian invincibility, and he provided numerous gifts as examples of British support.

The summer before, the Ouabache River tribes, the Wea, Piankeshaw, Peoria, and Kickapoo, as well as other more westerly tribes, such as the Sauk and Fox, had agreed to a treaty with the U. S. Much of this was the result of good feelings created by Putnam's prisoner exchange in 1792, as well as his unceasing work, and desire to foster what he hoped would be a lasting peace by treaty. This good work had the impact of reducing considerably the number of warriors that the allied tribes could put in the field. However, the treaty won of a great effort by Putnam, much later failed ratification in Congress partly, or perhaps entirely, because Putnam had promised the tribes that certain of their lands would be theirs to keep in perpetuity. Congress wanted no part of such guarantees. Putnam had integrity, but the new U. S. Government was not so fairly inclined.

Apekonit attended the McKee Conference, posing as the great Indian warrior he had been while spying for Wayne. Little Turtle did not give him away. However, Little Turtle did council for peace as did a few others, among them, Tarhe of the Wyandots. Little Turtle did not trust the British and thought that when things got rough that they would not honor their promises.

History has recorded his address to the conference, on August 19, 1793. It was short and to the point, when he rose and said:

> *We have beaten the enemy twice under different commanders. We cannot expect the same good fortune to attend us always. The Americans are now led by a chief who never sleeps. The night and days are alike to him, and during all the time, he has been marching on our villages, notwithstanding the watchfulness of our young men. Think well of it. There is something that whispers to me that it would be prudent to listen to his offers of peace.*

Many of those gathered did not wish to hear these words. Not only had the confederation won two major battles, but they had also won virtually all the skirmishes in the Ohio Country. They were full of pride and hubris on account of never having been beaten by the Americans in a large pitched battle. They felt that the Americans could never defeat them in the forests and on the lands of their forefathers. And further, they cited the Americans as being untrustworthy, using as examples the Americans massacring whole villages of peaceful Indians.

Only Buckongehelas, rising to remind the group of Little Turtle's great accomplishments, caused them to pause in their declaring him a defeatist and in some cases, a coward. Common sense prevailed because Little Turtle was anything but a coward. However, he was now out of favor as the Confederation strategist and as the war leader. Little Turtle's good friend, Blue Jacket, now assumed that role by common assent. Blue Jacket was a formidable enemy of the whites. He had learned much to temper his impulsiveness from fighting alongside Little Turtle, and as the tribes had decided against Little Turtle as the leader, they now made their next best choice.

At one point, when it appeared the confederation might continue to disintegrate, McKee upped his rhetoric and his false promises of support, while greatly increasing the gift-giving. Within 24 hours, the Indians were once again firmly within the British sphere of influence.

Tecumseh, still a young lieutenant, was said to be openly hostile to Little Turtle. In future years, this hostility would turn to a burning enmity. But for now, Tecumseh had little practical influence, as he had not attained the status that would make him famous in American history.

After this conference, Apekonit took Sweet Breeze and his two babies (they now had a new one) to live with his brother, Samuel. His Wea wife declined to go back and went to live with her relatives. It was becoming clear that she and Apekonit were at the end of their marriage.

During this time, the Indians were further convinced of British sincerity by the arrival of a small contingent of green-coated Canadian rangers, who later participated on the side of the confederation in various small skirmishes.

In the autumn of 1793, Wayne built a massive fort less than ten miles from Ft. Jefferson. He called this fort, Greene Ville, naming it after his comrade from the Great War, General Nathaniel Greene. Fort Greene Ville may have been the largest wooden fort ever constructed, in the sheer amount of land encompassed, a massive 55 acres, with walls ten feet high, and which ran some 1,800 feet long and 900 feet wide. It had eight redoubts, each with a huge blockhouse. Each corner had a bastion, and additional blockhouses were built in the central wall of each side. Double rows of cabins lined the outer walls, on the inside of the fort, and each could house ten troopers. This was meant to cow the Indians and to serve as Wayne's headquarters of operations for the oncoming war.

In December of 1793, Apekonit led Wayne and a contingent of the army, to the site of St. Clair' Defeat, less than twenty miles from Greene Ville, where the aforementioned bones were buried, and another fort was built replete with the four cannons that Apekonit had produced.

The fort was named Fort Recovery, signifying an American come-back from St. Clair's Defeat. Wayne, it is said, did this to deliver a clear message to the confederation that he was now the paramount military force in the area, and he would build forts when and where he darned well pleased. The Indians naturally considered the establishment of these forts highly provocative. Wayne's other motive in the establishment of Fort Recovery was to increase American morale and belief in themselves as a fighting force. Wayne garrisoned the fort and moved back to Green Ville, for the winter.

In addition to having acquired the moniker, "the general who never sleeps," from the Miami, he was now being called, *Suk-ach'-gook*, that is, "the Blacksnake," by the Delaware. They considered the Blacksnake to be the most cunning and deliberate of all predators, striking only when it felt the moment right, and seldom losing a fight. In time, he would be called, *Ki Ki Fe*, "The Tornado," by the Shawnees, or sometimes, *Wi-we-yi-fi-te*, "The Whirlwind." The Miami began calling him just, "The Wind," and he was, "The Great Wind," to the Potowatomie. Everywhere that he went, he swept in, took control, and moved on, all with overwhelming force, swiftly, decisively, and always leaving behind evidence of his presence. Wayne's use of cavalry reflected his tactical genius. His mobility contributed to his particular nicknames. The Indians were not used to warfare with horses and Wayne used his dragoons to great advantage.

To counter Wayne's moves, and to show good faith to the

confederation, the British built Fort Miamis on the upper Maumee in the spring of 1794. It was an imposing and highly defensible edifice. Unfortunately, the confederation put too much faith in this move, and it would later cost them dearly.

By this time, Apekonit had fallen out of favor with the confederation, as his moves had become widely known. He was branded a traitor, and more or less put under sentence of death. It was my opinion that this did not bode well for my family. The Girtys were fine, clearly aligned with the confederation, but I was a white man living as a neutral in Indian territory and I was Apekonit's friend.

The Miami themselves did not, except for a few, say a great deal about Apekonit. To do so would have been to incur the wrath of Little Turtle. I was, owing to my marriage, generally not spoken out against by the Miami. However, within the alliance, such was not the case, and I was told that there were many whispers and some outright threats against me at the conference that summer. The British encouraged this line of thought; those asshole, red-coated, sonsabitches!

Little Turtle now assumed leadership only of the Miami, except those youngsters who thought him too timid and who ran off to fight with other leaders. Little Turtle still waged war, but far less often, and with his efforts being much more cautiously planned to have maximum effect on future peace talks, and designed to effectively reduce Indian casualties.

It was rumored that even Blue Jacket sent a unilateral peace delegation to Wayne, but it was rebuffed if it ever really happened.

In January of 1794, Wayne once again sent out messages of peace to the tribes. These were generally received with contempt, even while the group favoring peace continued to grow larger.

By now, Sunny was a year and a half old, walking and talking constantly. To say that she was the apple of daddy's eye would have been a gross understatement. To me, she could do no wrong. We lavished our love and our time on that child. She daily impressed us with her intelligence and with her incredible memory. We could explain something to her once and she had it locked in in her mind for good. She was like a sponge and became more so every day, soaking up life, interested in everything around her.

In mid-June, 1794, I received a message from Apekonit. He told me to come to Fort Recovery, that it was urgent. Not wishing to leave Autumn and Sunny alone, I deposited them with Black Bear and She-Fox in Turtletown. And while attempting to avoid the main trails, I headed for Fort Recovery, reaching it the following afternoon having traveled all night.

The fort was not particularly impressive, other than the four blockhouses. The construction of the walls was not particularly of exemplary workmanship, and there were definite gaps that were apparent between the logs. Still, seeing a fort where I had last viewed a macabre and haunting scene, was of itself remarkable.

The sentry called out, "White man approaching."

I was ushered in, and taken to the sergeant of the guard, who asked my name and business. When I told him I was J. R. Jamison, his response was one of immediate recognition of the name, as he said, "Ah, you're Luke's brother."

My mouth must have gaped open and I replied. "Well, uh, yes, how do you know Luke?"

"Why he's stationed here as a scout," came the reply. "Whaaa, where is he?" I stammered.

"He's out on patrol, been out two days with Captain Wells," he said.

Captain Wells, Captain Wells, that name did not dawn on me as a name I knew, but then, like a blow over the head, it came to me.

"William Wells?" I said.

"That's him," came the reply."They been out, but are due back today."

The sergeant then told me I could help myself to some chow over by the barracks, so I meandered over and had a plate. It was awful. Ah, the army, gotta love it!

I waited around for several hours, exploring outside the fort, and catching a nap in the cool shade of an old elm tree. After a time, a shout from the sentry indicated the patrol was back.

What a reunion followed, as Apekonit, now properly Captain Wells, and my brother, Luke grabbed and hugged me almost senseless. Luke told me that my sisters were fine, and had received my letter from Vincennes two years earlier. The girls were both married to influential men. Sally's husband was a merchant in Baltimore, and Rebeka's a Congressman from Pennsylvania.

Luke himself was now about 6'5", making him maybe two inches taller than me. He immediately lorded this over me, until I took him to the ground with a few swift moves, just to show him who was still the big brother. He was strong, but he was also very thin.

He explained that he was unattached and like I a few years earlier had come west to scout for the army, but also to find me. He continued that the receipt of my letter from Vincennes had greatly heartened my sisters, and caused them to rejoice. This occurred just as Sally was about to have her wedding. She had pronounced it the greatest present ever.

Then Luke said, "As for me, I knew you weren't dead all along. It was just a matter of locating you. By the way, I finished college in three years. Doc and Mrs. Parkman send their love."

Then he said, "It appears you're missing some of your ear."

And I added, "Yep, and part of a finger," showing him my left hand.

He just nodded knowingly, apparently already having seen enough in his time among the Indians to figure accurately what had happened.

"Wow!" what a day this was turning out to be.

Then Apekonit, er uh, Captain Wells, lowered the boom, "I wanted you to see Luke, but I am afraid that I may have gotten you into some trouble."

"What trouble?" I asked.

"A large war party, with British advisers and Canadian militia rangers, is coming this way as we speak. They will be here by late tomorrow afternoon, if not sooner. You may want to light out of here."

"No, stay," Luke said.

After Apekonit explained the danger I would be in getting trapped in a fort under siege and therefore it being presumed that I too had gone over to the Americans, Luke said, "Oh, then, yes, get out of here."

I said, "Maybe I'll leave after dark. But, hey, tell me more about the girls, about college, about joining up."

So, after a few protests that I should move out now, he filled me in while Captain Wells got the commandant, Captain Alexander Gibson, busy preparing to receive the impending attack.

After supper and waiting a few more hours, it was dark. I determined to head north. However, I was not far in the woods when I discovered an advanced scout, a Shawnee. He discovered me on the trail, but the resulting tussle proved fatal to him, though he put a nice slash upon my right arm with his knife.

I beat it back to the fort and I had to tell them that the enemy was now essentially present in the woods, lest they be caught off-guard, expecting them late tomorrow. Now, I could go nowhere. I'd take my chances staying, instead of trying to avoid the onslaught traipsing through the woods. Had I known they would all come at once and by a common route, I might have avoided them. But I had no such knowledge and the risk was less in staying. Indians hate besieging forts and they especially hate cannons, which as I indicated, Ft. Recovery had.

It was a night of busy preparation. The fort's surgeon sewed my wound to the tune of eight stitches. The next morning brought no attack, and we assumed that the main force of Indians was not yet on the scene.

Later that morning, a pack train arrived from Fort Greene Ville, escorted by a large contingent of infantry sharpshooters and dragoons (cavalry). After delivering the supplies entrusted to them, they left to go back to Greene Ville. Less than a mile out, they were ambushed by a very large force. Only the quick thinking of Major McMahon, who ordered his dragoons under Lieutenant Taylor to draw sabers and charge the enemy, saved the day.

The horsemen, followed by the riflemen, ran past the temporarily disconcerted Indians and retreated to Recovery under heavy fire. Lieutenant Samuel Darke led 20 men from the fort to cover the retreat. Nevertheless, the Americans suffered 20 killed, including a gallant Captain Asa Hartshorn, who had been hit in the thigh and was being helped away by Darke. When Darke was also hit in the groin, he was forced to drop the Captain, who was then set upon by a large group of Indians. He was finished off cruelly. There were 30 wounded. Some severely so. The fort was now under full siege.

I later found out that Blue Jacket, Simon Girty, and Little Turtle had led this attack. At first, that seemed hard for me to believe, as I thought Little Turtle's classic strategy would have been to let the supply train get several miles down the road, and then attack in a place where there was no chance of escape. However, he may have been yielding to Blue Jacket on this matter. But then I had another thought. It may well have been that Little Turtle was hoping for the garrison at the fort to come to the aid of the supply train. Once in the open, the entire group would be wiped out by the overwhelming numbers of Indians, reacting to the sound of gunfire and hurrying out of the woods. This would have been a repeat of St. Clair's Defeat, on almost the same spot. As it was, those not involved in attacking the supply train were slow coming through the woods to the fort and missed their opportunity to wipe out Darke's command.

The allies now surrounded the fort and began taking intermittent shots, as the fort's surgeon and his assistant set about the bloody task of trying to save wounded men. I rushed to volunteer my service, telling him that I had some medical training. He was glad for the help, and he managed to have seen every patient within five hours. Some were, as they say, just flesh wounds, or results of having been grazed by a shot. Other men died as the surgeon tried desperately to repair the damage done by Indian guns, or should I say by British guns. My best service was in tending to and bandaging those less severely hurt, but in a couple of cases holding men down on the operating table.

I went to one of the blockhouses after we had done all we could for the wounded. I climbed to the top floor, where I found Luke acting the role of a sniper. We looked out a gun-port to see what we could, which proved to be very little. One frontal attack on the fort had already been launched by the Indians and repulsed while I was tending to the wounded. Evening was coming and sporadic shooting continued.

Putting a little extra charge in his Kentucky long-rifle, Luke awaited a possible opportunity to pick off one of the besiegers at the treeline. After waiting more than half an hour, we saw some bushes move just as dusk was setting in. Then we saw red, a British officer! Luke aimed and fired. A lucky shot, maybe, but I say otherwise. The man fell with a rifle ball through his forehead. He was the last redcoat we saw during the siege. The others stayed well back.

Our men fired the canons periodically into the woods, probably without great effect, but the fear factor cannot be overstated, as cannonballs went tearing through trees and loudly crashing into some unseen barrier.

An attack at dark was repulsed with great effort and considerable loss of life on both sides, but more so on the Indian side. Blue Jacket and Little Turtle held their warriors out of the attack on the fort, considering that too many would die. However, Bear Chief of the Ottawa insisted on attacking. He led a force of mostly Wyandot, and some Ottawa who had come down from the Great Lakes region.

Later in the night, only sporadic shooting occurred, but no one slept. We had become painfully aware that we were greatly outnumbered.

Again, I went to work as a surgeon's assistant, this time staying with those duties all night, tending to the men just injured as well as those we had treated earlier in the day.

The dawn brought a ferocious attack that continued for an hour. For a short time, I feared we'd be overwhelmed, but with Hartshone's riflemen on our side and with us behind wooden walls, many more of our shots found their mark than did those of the indians.

Shortly after noon, the besiegers had left. Indians had no real taste for attacking forts; they had given it their best effort, and cost both sides the lives of many good men, but in the end they dispersed back north.

We had less than 275 men in the fort. I later learned that we had been surrounded by over 2,000 Indians. That was the largest force the confederation had ever put in the field for an actual military operation, and they would never again equal this number.

The fact that Little Turtle, and even Blue Jacket, had kept their men out of the attacks on the fort, showed that they both felt that it was an exercise in futility, and a way to get good young warriors killed.

Wishing Luke the best, and vowing to see him again as soon as possible, I made a hasty trip back to Turtletown, attempting to stay wide to the west of the disappointed attackers. I had only one close call, and that was being nearly surprised by a small group who chased me for an hour. They had spotted me along a stream from some distance away. However, they were no match for me afoot, and I eventually outdistanced them.

Not really knowing what the mood was in Turtletown, and figuring Autumn would inform me, I grabbed some sleep. In the morning we headed to our cabin, arriving in the early evening.

I filled Autumn in on seeing my brother. She was very happy for me. I asked her about the mood in Turtletown, and she said it was mostly favoring peace. A few young men had gone off to the siege, and a few others were out on raiding parties, but most inhabitants had embraced Little Turtle's views.

The rest of the day was uneventful until the evening when a ferocious storm blew up. The wind was bad, and the lightning and thunder scared Sunny. The thunder sounded loud like the cannons had at Fort Recovery. We could occasionally hear large branches or even whole trees come down in the woods nearby. The rain was an absolute deluge.

Late in the night, amid the storm, a most unexpected banging came at our door. We looked at each other, wondering who could be out in this weather, and who would be at our home in the wilderness.

I checked out the gun-port, but could not detect who it was in the dark, other than that it was someone holding a limp body in his arms. I removed the door beam, and with Autumn standing by with the trade gun at the ready, I opened the door.

With my mouth agape, I discovered standing, soaking wet, Nebi Skog. In his arms, nearly lifeless, was the Countess, Ales.

.

Chapter Nineteen

Retribution

Indian Weapons

Autumn was excited to see Nebi Skog but not so much the Countess.

Though time had gone by quickly, it had been two years since I had last seen either of them. While I occasionally thought about her and wondered what had happened to her, I spent far more time pondering my strange, earlier, encounters with Nebi Skog, and how he had often saved my life.

Now he appeared not to have aged at all. If anything, he almost looked younger. However, his hairstyle, clothing, and other of his attire was a just little different, just slight differences from what I remembered of him.

Ales, on the other hand, was gaunt, and painfully thin, looking at least ten years older than when last I saw her. However, even in her sickened condition, she retained a certain beauty. Of course, nothing such as that thought came from my lips.

Nebi Skog told us that Ales had a raging fever, as was obvious as her body shook with chills. We prepared a bearskin bed on the hearth with multiple blankets. Nebi Skog instructed Autumn to get the wet clothes off the Countess. As Autumn modestly did so under the blankets, I could not help but notice that she was taking in every inch of the by now naked body, perhaps mentally comparing it to her own, attempting to understand what had so ravaged the formerly young woman, perhaps a bit of both.

Nebi Skog produced some herbs that Autumn made into a tea and gave the Countess, who only grudgingly came to consciousness, enough to drink a bit. We covered her in blankets. It appeared that she was coming out of the chills through the combination of blankets and her proximity to the fireplace.

I was reluctant to allow Sunny near the Countess for fear this was some horrible contagion, but Nebi Skog expressed no concern in that area.

Outside the storm raged. Autumn gave Nebi Skog some stew that we had leftover from supper. After eating, he tended the Countess. As he did so, we asked him about her condition.

He explained that when last we saw them, they were on their way to a Huron (Wyandot)) village on the far side of Lake Michi Gami. There was a plague of sorts there, and Nebi Skog had previously seen the Countess tend to sick Hurons, of which she seemed particularly attached, just as had been her earlier French countrymen in the fur trade, and the business of religion, the black-robed Franciscans. The latter had established many missions among the Hurons. Sometimes things had gone well, and sometimes the black robes had been martyred. I recalled now that the Countess had with her, two years ago, the three Huron warriors. She held some considerable sway with that tribe, almost like a queen, or guardian of those people. She may well have also had an economic arrangement with them They may have been her employees, or her partners in the fur trade.

After treating the people of that village, she and Nebi Skog had traveled to a series of villages, each one further away, tending to the advancing plague, and finally finding themselves among the Indians of the plains called the Sioux. There she was once accused of being a witch, but her success was so great in healing, that her detractors soon lost credibility. After all, people would rather be cured by a witch acting on their behalf, than to die from plaque, having burned the witch.

As the plague died out, the Countess and Nebi Skog found

themselves in Canada, and spent a winter there as the Countess made fur trade allies, and as Nebi Skog wandered the forests and prairies. They were coming back to check on her fur interests near Kekionga when she fell ill. However, Nebi Skog told us that she had not been well for some time, having so tirelessly taken care of the sick Indian people, and not herself. She had refused his entreaties of care, and more food when it was available, and had been in a weakened state throughout the last year or so. He had noticed her aging, and been concerned, but she was a strong and stubborn woman who had insisted that she was fine.

Nebi Skog seemed to think that the Countess's current condition was more a result of months and months of self-privation and not a part of the earlier plague.

All of this news, of the Countess caring for the Indian people in far off places, clearly softened Autumn's opinion of the woman.

By this time, Sunny had been in Nebi Skog's lap for a while. From a bag that he carried, he produced an exquisite hand-sewn and beautifully beaded doll, that he said he obtained in trade among the Sioux. He said he brought it for our child.

"But, but, . . ." I stammered, "how did you know we had a child?"

"Married long enough to have children," was all that he said.

Ok, so how did he know we had a girl child? Maybe he was a liar. Maybe it was a lucky guess. This man was exasperating. But Sunny favored him, and she was soon asleep in his arms, clutching her new doll. Moving as gently as her mother, he stood up, and took Sunny to her bed, carefully covering her. I pondered at the gentleness of this man, who had taken lives to save ours in the past. He was truly an enigma.

We stayed up a bit longer. I offered some spirits to Nebi Skog, but he would not partake. After a time, he asked Autumn, "When will the baby come?"

She blushed and looked sheepishly at me. I said, "We are having a baby?"

"Yes," she said. "I was not certain until the last few days. I am sorry, my husband."

"No, no, no," I said. "I am happy. But Nebi Skog, how did you know?"

He only shrugged his shoulders as if it was a lucky guess, but after all I had seen from him, I knew better. I knew better but did not know how this man was always so right.

The storm raged on, but despite the thunder, Sunny slept. The rest of us lay down for a fitful night of attempted sleep, with Autumn taking a lead in checking on the Countess, even though Nebi Skog lay near her on the hearth, almost like a loving husband.

The next morning dawned, and the Countess was neither better nor worse.

I went outside to chop some wood. Soon, I was joined by Nebi Skog along with Sunny, who began an earnest game of tag over near the drop-off into the woods.

After some minutes, I was startled by a war shriek from Nebi Skog. I looked up to see him engaged in hand to hand combat with a warrior. But much worse was Sunny running through the mud, taking little toddler strides, and being pursued by another warrior slipping and sliding on the muddy ground. He was closing on my baby, tomahawk raised.

I reached for my rifle and realized it was over by the front door. I had no choice. I ran top speed, or maybe I flew, I certainly was not slipping in the mud, though this fact never occurred to me till days later when I replayed the events in my mind. It appeared that I had no chance of saving Sunny. In a situation such as that, there is no conscious thought, only reaction. I pulled the ax back on my left side with both hands, and on a dead run, hurdled it horizontally as hard as I could waist-high. As I left my feet from the momentum of the ax, I more or less dove into the mud, without choice, in the direction of the attacker.

The ax sailed unnoticed over the laughing Sunny, who still thought she was being pursued by Nebi Skog. The ax was still horizontal to the ground as it cleared Sunny's head by less than a foot. It made a huge thump as it slammed into the man, just below his left nipple and then made the unmistakable and normally sickening sound of bones being broken. In this case, it was his ribs, and I was not at all sick about it.

Hitting the ground after throwing the ax and sliding through mud face down to the now grounded attacker, I slammed into his left side with my head. I recovered, slipped, recovered again, dislodged the ax from his body, and from my knees delivered a blow that cut his skull in two. Almost simultaneously, I got up and ran to the baby, who was still running away laughing. I grabbed her under my left arm and ran into the house, telling Autumn to lock the door, as I grabbed the trade gun and my rifle, then going to Nebi Skog's aid.

As I came back around the cabin, I saw that he had downed his assailant, but was now running toward me with three more in pursuit, perhaps 20 feet behind him. As he saw me get into position, he dove headlong in the mud, allowing for me to discharge the trade gun, just as one of the onrushing braves was aiming with his musket.

My blast blew over the now mud-sliding Nebi Skog, hitting the middle man, the one with the gun, in the gut and leaking his insides all around him on the ground, as he fell on his back. My shot also put the other two men down, seriously wounded. Nebi Skog got up, and we ran toward the house where Autumn stood, having disobeyed my orders to lock the door. As Nebi Skog entered our home, I saw several Indians breaching the top of the drop-off at the back of the property. I fired at the closest, downing him with a shot to the chest. I ran in the house and barred the door. We immediately grabbed my other guns and went to the window gun-ports, while Autumn reloaded the trade gun and the rifle that I had just used.

Our rapid-fire took its toll upon the attackers, but there were too many of them, and several were very quickly on the roof, where they began attempting to chop through with their tomahawks. Here my construction proved disconcerting to them because they had never seen a frontier roof that could not be easily chopped through. Ours was going to take more effort, but they were not about to quit.

The room was filled with smoke from our guns. Autumn had lifted the floorboard and put Sunny down in the root cellar. With all the smoke in the room, it was nearly impossible to see, but we could all hear the Countess choking. Without giving a moment to thought, Autumn ran and wet her deerskin rag. She then found her way to the hearth, putting the wet skin over the Countess' face to block the smoke.

By now, those on the roof were beginning to make progress, and each time we could begin to see light, we fired upward through it. The first few times, we hit Indian flesh. After that, they appeared to stay back from the spot at which they were making their attempt to break through the roof. Shooting upward became only a guess as to where they were positioned. Their hideous war cries were so savage and determined that they, no doubt, were confident of their eventual success.

I will admit that all looked pretty grim, but a man fighting for his family, and with the help of a good friend, is not one to give up the fight, or to even pause momentarily to consider the odds. I was certain that these jackals would soon be dropping into the house from the roof, and that hand to hand fighting would rule the moment.

After a few furious minutes, shots rang from south of the cabin, down near the creek. I looked out to see several Miami approaching the cabin out of the tree line. It was Black Bear, Red Buffalo, Gray Fox, Angry Cloud, Little Beaver, White Corn Man, and three or four others, coming to our aid. They shot several attackers, and the remainder began fleeing into the woods.

Our friends set about the task of dispatching the wounded among our attackers, and the obligatory scalping. Capturing one alive, they questioned him, but he succumbed without talking.

As I had seen before, Nebi Skog did not take any scalps, and likewise I did not take any.

Little Beaver and Angry Cloud were now 15-year-old warriors, and I expressed my gratitude to them first of all. But without all of our friends, I doubt we could have survived the hour.

"Ottawa, Chippewa and Potowatomie, warriors of the Three Fires," said Red Buffalo, referring to the long-standing alliance between those three tribes.

"Yeah, British cur dogs," I said sarcastically.

"What brought you up this way, how did you know?" I said.

Black Bear replied, "Talk that some of the men who had been at the Recovery Fort might come for you. This talk came from two of our young men at Kekionga who were there."

"Did they know, I was at Recovery?" I asked.

"They did not say that," he said. "They just said there was much talk against Apekonit and his friend, one called Spirit Traveler. The talk became more forceful once the attack on the fort failed."

"I am mighty glad you came, Father." It was the first time I had ever called Black Bear father. He blushed.

"I'm mighty glad to see all of you," I finished.

My mind raced, did our attackers know I had been at Fort Recovery? Did they know I had again served the United States by going to St. Louis? Did they know my brother was with the Americans? Did they know of my friends, Black Duck and Jim Tucker? Was it my failure to serve the Indian cause? Or, was it my friendship with Apekonit? All these were possible, and perhaps other things that I could not even imagine. But it was clear that our safety as a family was a serious concern until this conflict resolved.

Earlier Autumn came running out, and left the door open to air out the house. Nebi Skog came carrying the Countess and lay her under a tall old elm tree. She had broken out in a sweat, and we hoped that the fever was leaving her.

Suddenly, I bolted toward the house realizing that we had forgotten Sunny. When I took up the floorboard, she was crying, but only afraid of all the commotion. I grabbed her up, and hugged her, as her mother took her from me. I laughed when Black Bear took her from her mother. Indian men aren't known for displays of affection with babies, or toddlers, but Black Bear just kept hugging his granddaughter, and was not about to give her back to her mother.

Now the Countess sat up. She asked for water and Autumn fetched it. Her fever had broken. She was feeling much better but was very confused about the events of the past hour or so. Nebi Skog filled her in speaking rapidly, but softly, in French.

We didn't figure our attackers would be back, and they were probably far north by now. Nevertheless, just as a precaution, and to make the boys feel important, Red Buffalo sent Gray Fox, Angry Cloud, Little Beaver, White Corn Man, and two youths to reconnoiter the woods all about, for signs that might provide more information about our attackers. He admonished them to be careful of ambush in the thick underbrush, but in truth, Gray Fox was now such an accomplished warrior, that we all knew they would execute the greatest of stealth.

After a couple hours, we all settled down to a meal of smoked fish and garden vegetables, topped off with a mixture of strawberries, blackberries, and some wild grapes. We ate outside, as we continued to let the cabin air of the gun smoke.

Shortly after our meal, Nebi Skog explained to the Countess, who was still very weak, that Autumn had taken care of her for the last many hours. This brought tears to the eyes of the Countess, and soon to the eyes of Autumn as they hugged, and jabbered to each other, each in her native tongue, apparently their past differences forgiven, and pretty much completely forgotten.

From then on Autumn referred to the Countess as "Ales," and the rest of us would do the same.

Ah, women, I had no more understanding of them now than I did when I went off to college.

Later, as our friends poked about the woods with the young men, I had a brief conversation with Ales.

"Nebi Skog told me about your doctoring during the plague, where did you learn?"

She answered, "Long ago when I was 17, I was in the Holy Land when a great sickness broke out. I was very ill, but an Arab doctor saved me. As my family had considerable means, I offered him a great sum of money to teach me. He refused the money, but he did teach me, upon the insistence of a most handsome Arab prince that I knew."

A smile of remembrance had crossed her face when she spoke of this prince. Probably he was an early conquest of hers.

"So, you were in love with an Arab prince?" I boldly ventured.

"Love, what is love, mon cheri? I was young, he was young, and he was most handsome. He was a man of great power. But I learned much from his doctor; the Arab doctors are far beyond those in Europe. Later, in Switzerland, I paid a doctor to teach me all that he knew. He was not a dull man, but his knowledge was far inferior to my Arab tutor, but still, I learned a few things."

"That's quite a story," I said.

"Ah, yes, but all true, mon cheri, all true. And then there is Nebi Skog," she said.

"Have you known him long?" I asked.

"For many years. I met him in Montreal and again after my husband died. He is a dear, dear, friend, and teacher of most remarkable knowledge," she said, clearly with the utmost admiration in her voice. "From him, I have learned the cures provided by the forest."

My reply was, "He is a most unusual man."

I don't know whether Ales heard me or not, as she had drifted off to sleep. I left her to sleep for a while beneath the tree, while Autumn came with a very light blanket to put on her.

Our rescuers stayed the night, some sleeping on the cabin floor, some outside. The Countess continued her improvement, and the former enemies, she and my wife, became inseparable.

And as for Nebi Skog, well, he and Black Bear spent all their time with Sunny, keeping her up playing until she fell asleep in her grandfather's arms. He gently took her and put her to bed. Two grown warriors of great repute melted to butter by a babe.

I was seeing a new side to this man, the Water Snake, and he was far more sociable than I had ever seen him. He was not running off, not disappearing, not avoiding all the activities about the cabin. Oh, he was not exactly a bubbling conversationalist, just more sociable than I'd seen before. He thanked me for saving his life from his three attackers, just before we made it into the house. I thanked him for the alert as the events began to unfold, and told him that my debt to him was far greater than his to me. There seemed now to be a bond between us, one perhaps born of mutual respect, one that seemed to reflect a genuine, but somewhat unusual friendship. I counted myself lucky to know this man. I counted myself lucky to have all these friends and family.

The next morning Black Bear urged us to come to Turtletown. There we would be safe from attacks by warriors in the confederation. But would we be safe from attacks by Anthony Wayne's Legion? My sense of independence was sorely being tested. Should I cast my lot with one side or the other? My neutrality had already been violated by my participation with the Americans at the siege of Ft. Recovery, though I had not taken up arms, except with the Shawnee scout. But he had not taken the time to discuss allegiances with me beforehand.

It occurred to me that perhaps I should take my family back east, see my sisters, and perhaps return to our old home on the mountain in Virginia. But how I loved our life here in the Ohio Country wilderness, our cabin, my family.

So, Autumn and I walked the treeline perimeter of our homestead, while Black Bear and Nebi Skog played with Sunny, and while the rest of the warriors scoured the woods for any sign that our attackers would come back. They had gathered the bodies shortly after yesterday's battle. They were going to throw them in the river and let them float away, but Nebi Skog convinced them to burn the dead warriors. This struck me as somewhat curious. That is that he cared what happened to the bodies of dead men, who had tried to kill him and his friends.

I asked him about this, and he said that the spirits of the dead men deserved a proper disposal of the bodies and that floating them down a river was not such. They were warriors and deserved better.

When I questioned him with, "But they attacked us and we had done them no harm. They put at risk a baby and two women."

His reply was, "This is so Spirit Traveler, and it would seem this was an evil act. But if we do not honor their lives by a proper death ceremony, we are as bad as they."

This seemed a mighty forgiving attitude to me, but I would not question my friend any further on the matter. I now believed with all my being, that he was far wiser than I, and I resolved that I would honor his wishes.

As I had relayed earlier, burning corpses was not the usual Indian method of disposal of bodies. Nebi Skog explained that had the deceased warriors been captured by the Miami, or many other tribes, their fate would have been the fire, albeit while still alive. In this regard, we were disposing of them as they would have expected, had they been captured alive. At any rate, floating a body downriver was disrespectful and not to be practiced by proper people.

Autumn and I walked and talked. She told me that she would go with me wherever I wanted, but she preferred the Turtletown option. There her family would watch over us, and their reputation, her reputation, and even mine would keep us safe, even if a few young firebrands spoke out against me.

I asked her, "And for me, what shall I do? I cannot fight my brother. I cannot fight your people."

She replied, "You must do what you have always done and that follows your heart. You are a brave warrior, but this is a fight that you cannot win if you take sides, even if the side you take wins. You, my love, must stay with your family."

"What you say has much wisdom, my darling, but men who straddle the fence are regarded poorly by those on either side," I said.

"How you are regarded is not who you are. In the end, all will know your true heart," she replied.

Trying to lighten the moment, I grabbed her and kissed her for all I was worth.

And then I said, "How did one so beautiful as you, one so young, become so wise?"

"Because the Spirit Traveler is my husband," she replied, returning my kiss and my embrace, twice over.

Being the Spirit Traveler was being someone I was not truly certain that I was, and not someone I was yet comfortable being. It may have also carried with it a burden that I did not want. I was far more often certain that I was not worthy of such a name. To me, I had never ceased to be Jariah Randolph Jamison, but my wife and many of her people continued to believe that I had some spiritual power beyond the normal. I had no idea what it was. Did they see something that I did not? To be sure, I was flattered by the name, and many times when among the Miamis, I allowed moments of pride to invade my head when I was called by the name. I certainly did nothing to discourage the use of it. But being completely fair, I cannot say that I openly encouraged it, just rather that I enjoyed it. It seemed to carry a sort of celebrity with it.

It was in that moment that it occurred to me that Nebi Skog did not profess any sides in life, he did, upon many occasions help those in need by force of arms, but he was not a warrior who joined, nor took sides in war. It was more that he helped those in need, those whose lives were endangered by no fault, or offense of their own. Perhaps my lot was similar. He was, I was convinced, truly a man of spiritual power, or at the very least, a man of advanced and uncommon wisdom. I could after all, do far worse than to follow his example.

As Ales was now feeling much better, and would soon be able to travel wherever she intended, we told Black Bear that we would all come to Turtletown within a few days. He and the others refused to leave us, and they stayed for several days until we went with them to Turtletown.

In the next few days, Ales grew continually stronger and spent her time communicating with Autumn in English. They walked

together, staying near the cabin and as I said earlier, were inseparable.

It occurred to me now that she treated me like a beloved
brother, and no longer the object of her passion, as she had done
years earlier. I assumed this was out of respect for Autumn, but
hell, I didn't know. Again, this involved women. Whatever the
case, she was no longer the inveterate coquette with me that she
had been a few years before. I was kinda happy about that, but
then again, maybe with the pride of a man, kinda sad.

Sunny helped her mother be a nurse, and a very special doctor to Ales, who seemed to enjoy this busy little person giving her
such serious attention. After a couple of days, I caught Ales sob
hing uncontrollably as she took Sunny into her arms. Without us
even asking what was wrong, she explained that she had never
had children, and now, through the attention of this lovely little
child, she was realizing what she had missed.

For Sunny's part, she was confused but seemed to think this
crying was part of the illness. She tried to lay the countess back
down and feel her for fever. I nearly fell to the floor laughing at
Sunny, but completely understanding what Ales was feeling.
Sunny's actions brought laughter to Ales, and she stopped her
sobbing by giving the child a big kiss.

Ales told us that night that she had intended to go to Kekionga, but now with war again imminent, she would instead go just
across the river in Detroit to Canada, and stay with some French
friends. After further recovery, she might go to her home in
Montreal for the winter. Nebi Skog would take her to Detroit.

Chapter Twenty

Fallen Timbers

General Anthony Wayne

It was now mid-July 1794, and the time was nearing when a great battle must surely occur, a battle between the race of my birth and the race of my wife. A battle about rights and freedom, a battle about land, politics, and to some extent, covetous greed. A battle urged by the British, and sought by the Americans, because peace overtures had failed, but perhaps more accurately because both wanted to be in control of this land. To a great degree, the pride of the new Republic was also at stake. This was especially true because the Indians represented a threat to what the United States considered its soil, and because of the British interlopers. The very presence of the latter seemed to indicate that the new government was impotent to guarantee its national borders. It would be a battle of an ancient culture against the amalgamated culture of a new and developing nation. It was a battle that I believed the Indians had no chance of winning. If so, it was a battle that would change life in the Northwest Territory.

We had been staying at Turtletown for several days, when Little Turtle left with a force of braves from there and Kekionga. However, he had ordered Little Beaver, Angry Cloud, and White Corn Man, among other youth, to stay at their homes in Turtletown and Kekionga, for purposes of protecting the people. Essentially, he had ordered the "flower of his people," his youngest warriors to abstain from battle. This was not a popular decision with them. He feared an overwhelming defeat at the hands of the Americans. A loss might put Kekionga and Turtletown in harm's way, and he wanted the villages to be protected. It was also in his mind that the Americans frequently sent diversionary forces from Vincennes when invading Indian lands. Such a force reaching Kekionga would find it undefended if all the young men were gone.

To lead the protection forces, Michikinikwa picked Gray Fox. After his bravery at St. Clair's defeat, Gray Fox was not happy about being left behind. However, he knew better than to question his uncle on the matter. Besides, the choice was logical, he was the most experienced of all the young men in war, and he had an air about him that commanded attention. In addition to the young men, mostly under 16 years old, Gray Fox would have some 30 or 40 more elderly warriors, and French citizens of Kekionga, Turtletown, and outlying villages, to lead in any necessary defense of the home villages. Little Turtle told him to scout heavily southwest of the village, to not be surprised should a diversionary attack come from Vincennes.

Because of his recent stance for peace, Little Turtle would not lead the confederation troops, only the Miami contingent. Some have said this was his choice. The fact was that many warriors from other tribes were too upset with Little Turtle to follow his leadership. And though his leadership might have affected a different outcome, Little Turtle yielded power to Blue Jacket. Indian hubris and overconfidence were great.

Little Turtle knew that a schism among the Indians was unacceptable, and would limit any slim chance for victory. Despite all of his greatness, he never let his ego interfere with his decisions. With Blue Jacket was his trusted young lieutenant, Tecumseh, who more and more, was taking on a leadership of war parties. Many other Indian leaders would be present, but the most well-known of these would be Buckongahelas of the Delaware.

For all of my soul-searching, I now wondered at all that Little Turtle must have wrestled with as a leader of his people. He was a great warrior, undefeated in war, and yet he knew when the time had come for peace. He felt it and believed it long before his fellows. It must have been a tough pill to swallow for him because he knew that peace would not be fair to the Indians. But he also knew the other choice was death, a complete annihilation of his people and of the Indian way of life. Yes, a bitter pill, for a man never beaten on the field of battle, a man whose tactical brilliance outshone all other Indian commanders who ever lived, and indeed, almost all commanders who ever lived. Yet, when others lacked his vision, he did not turn away from his people. He accepted his demotion from the war chief of the allied Indian confederation but refused to abandon his brothers in their hour of reckoning, even though he could see the outcome well before the events unfolded. He was as remarkable a man, red, white, black, or whatever color, as I ever knew.

Sometime in July, the United States Legion under Anthony Wayne left Fort Greene Ville and began moving north intent on meeting the tribes on the battlefield. The final peace entreaty had failed, and now the extremely well-trained army advanced toward destiny.

The army moved to the confluence of the Auglaize and Maumee Rivers and constructed a fort that they called Defiance. This was the northernmost U.S. post in the Ohio Country.

One day, in late July or early August, about three and a half weeks after the Countess and Nebi Skog left for Canada, Nebi reappeared. He had delivered the Countess safely to her destination and now had returned, looking for me. He must have seen the surprise in my face as he came near our wigwam. He always appeared when least expected.

He said to me, "Kway, Spirit Traveler, my brother."

"Kway," Nebi Skog," I said. That was the first time he had called me brother.

"I go now to the Maumee River Valley, will you come?" he said.

"I cannot be a part of any battle," I said.

"Nor I," he said.

"Why not you?" I asked. "You are an Indian, and you could well fight with the people of your race."

"My help in battle would be of no consequence in what will happen," he replied. "The Indian people would gain nothing from my help, just as the Americans can gain nothing from your help."

"What?" I said. "I do not know what you mean. You could kill many whites. I suppose I might kill many Indians, or I could kill whites if I fight with Michikinikwa."

"It is just so," he said. "But in the killing, what would anyone gain? Will the battle's result be changed? I think not. Men such as you and I do not live to kill. Our fight is only to protect the innocent. What will be between the Americans, and these warriors will be without us. It will change the land, but it will not change the hearts of men. Your heart is not like the others."

"Men like us?" I repeated, "I do not follow your line of thought, my brother."

"You have spiritual power, and. . . ." he started, but I blurted my interruption.

"I have no spiritual power, when will people believe that?" I said.

"You are wrong, brother, and you cannot see that you have the power because you do not seek the power, you do not want the power, you do not know how to use the power," he said.

"You are right," I responded. "I do not know this power, and I do not believe."

"You do not see yourself as you are. You do not see as I see you," he said.

"Huh?" I was not understanding.

He tried again, "You and I are brothers. In many ways, we are the same. We are neither Indian nor white. We are only human beings. We did not ask for power, and we did not seek it. But we have it, and we must use it, not for ourselves, but all people. Your first step is understanding, and accepting that you have this power."

I was amazed at what I was hearing. This man that I had come to revere was insinuating, no not insinuating, he was outright stating that he and I were the same. How could this be? He was mistaken. I was nothing like him. He was a special kind of person. I had seen him do unexplainable things, things that some people would consider miraculous. I could do nothing remotely of the kind.

And then he said, as if reading my mind, "I am not wrong, I have the power to see, I do not boast, I do not deny, it is only as it is."

"What is this power?" I asked, exasperated, and needing more proof.

"It is the power of the Spirit. It is the power of healing, the power of seeing, the power of your body, the power of knowing," he said. "The manitous, or perhaps the white God, or both, are truly with you. Though you do not know this, I do, and I am not wrong."

After a pause, he added, "You must be shown this path so that you will believe, just as long ago, another had to show me. I will show you. You will come with me."

"And will you tell my wife?" I asked.

"I will tell her," he said.

Strangely, he did tell Autumn, and more strangely, she gave her blessing, saying only, "he must go."

The "he" was me, and I was being allowed to go off to a distant battlefield without argument.

I wondered for just a crazy moment if he had cast a spell over Autumn. But I came to my senses and dismissed that insane thought.

She looked at me and said, "You must go with Nebi Skog, my love. You do not know what others do. You do not see the good in yourself, and you cannot know, in the depths of your heart, the power of the Spirit that is within you."

Now I felt as if I had just been overwhelmed by a superior force against which no resistance could prevail.

"I will go," I said.

"Come, we go now," he said.

"Now?" I said.

"We go now!" he repeated.

I went into the wigwam, kissed Sunny, who was sleeping, came out, hugged my wife, and we left. I was very confused.

Our trip would end up taking three days afoot, at a leisurely pace. We slept briefly two nights, but I was never tired, and the trip was one I would never forget. I learned more than I had, perhaps in my whole life, to that time.

In the ensuing days, Nebi Skog showed me plants and herbs that I never imagined had medicinal or nutritional value. Arrogantly I thought I knew the woods. He showed me how to move without making a sound. He taught me to traverse a shallow stream while barely getting wet. He showed me how to cross a deep river, using a hollow reed, going above the surface, to breathe underwater, and therefore unseen, all while not being swept away in its current. The latter was accomplished by walking the river bottom while holding heavy rocks as a sort of ballast. He showed me how to climb the tallest tree without effort, scampering up only slightly slower than a squirrel. I do not mean to imply something supernatural about this. I was a pretty good tree climber before. But he taught me an attitude, or perhaps more appropriately, a technique that had more to do with vertical momentum, and with how to pull upon branches and bounce quickly from spot to spot, grabbing the tree in strategic locations.

But more amazing, more exhilarating, and scarier, he taught me how to jump from a height of higher than 20 feet, and to absorb all the shock of the fall in a full-body roll, landing lightly on my feet.

We even ran great distances, and he showed me a striding technique that led to less fatigue, and breathing techniques with a mental focus that resembled something like going into a trance. He enabled me to run longer, faster, and with less actual effort. He took me from being an exceptional runner to being better than I had ever thought possible. It was palpable. I could feel it.

He taught me how to move quickly through the woods on a pitch-black night by looking nearly straight up for the silhouette of trees, against whatever minimal night light was present, and to quietly use a long, thin, and supple willow branch, like a blind man's cane, but held out horizontally, well in front of me, mimicking a cat's whiskers, to feel obstacles.

It was all so amazing for one such as me who had grown up in the wilderness, and who thought he knew it all. I was a beginner, a mere babe, and I knew nothing in comparison to this man.

While camping the second night, I said to him, "The people say that you travel on the wind, do you travel on the wind?"

"Do you think I do?" he said. "Have you seen me travel on the wind?"

"I do not believe that," I said. "But you have appeared to do so at times and have covered great distances so swiftly that I cannot explain."

"That does not make it magic, does it?" he replied.

"No, it does not," I said. "I don't believe in magic."

"And," he said, "that does not mean it is not magic."

I was caught off guard by this statement. He began to laugh, something I had not seen him do before in my presence. Was he mocking me? I did not think so because that was not his nature. Perhaps he was just much more comfortable with me. Each day, we came to know each other better.

And then he said, "I can do nothing that you cannot do, only I know what I can do, and you do not know."

"Are you saying that I can do magic?" I asked.

"No," he said. "I am not saying that."

"But," he added, "I am not saying that you cannot. Only you can answer such a question, and doing magic is not what is important."

"Tell me what is important," I asked.

"Only knowing your mind," he said, "Thinking not in words, but only in actions without words, finally, not thinking at all."

I had no idea what he meant, and no amount of prodding would produce any further or more clear explanation from him.

"Will you teach me what you mean?" I implored him.

"No man can teach you," he said. "I have taught you some things, but only you can teach yourself what you already know."

This might have all have been so very profound if it wasn't all so very headache-producing. I wasn't used to thinking like this, and while I had some curiosity about it, I didn't know where to go with it.

"As for traveling on the wind," he said, "maybe people think that because of the way I have shown you how to run."

"Perhaps," I said, "but there are times when you have seemingly covered distances greater than for which your running technique could account."

He looked pensive for just a moment.

And then he said, something which I had not expected, "Do you believe in the manitous, or Kiche Manetoa, that which many tribes call the Great Spirit, and which the whites call God?"[1]

I answered, "Well, my mother was religious, she had faith in

God. My father was more a man of the woods, a spirituality different than most, more like the Indian people."

"Yet, you learned from both many things, did you not?" he said.

"Yes, of course," I said.

"It is so for all children, but you had better luck than most. You had two parents who loved each other but were different, had different views. Their difference has made you strong, it has made you stand apart from others," he said.

"What do you mean?" I asked.

"I mean," he said, "that you are the sum of their differences, and you have benefited by knowing both of them and experiencing their beliefs."

"More well-rounded?" I quizzed him. "More open to ideas by being exposed to more ideas?"

"It is just so," he said. "But it is even more than that. You are each of them in a certain fashion, and you are you. Your soul is rich, your mind pure, you are a spiritual man, but you do not acknowledge it. Perhaps you are afraid. Perhaps you are running away from it. Perhaps you do not know how to embrace this aspect of yourself."

"Do you believe in the manitous or Kiche Manitoa?" I asked, reversing the table, so to speak.

"It is good for human beings to believe in something greater than themselves. I believe, and I know," he said.

"How do you know?" I asked.

"It is things seen and unseen. It is a feeling that cannot be ignored. It is a power that at times can be felt, and yet cannot be proved to others," he said. "It is knowing without questioning. And that is very powerful."

"Like faith," I said.

"It is something like faith, but it goes further, it is stronger, it is a truth that is real," he said. "When you have it, you have no doubt, none at all."

Unable to process any more of this talk at that moment, I asked him abruptly, "Can you be killed?"

He seemed startled, perplexed, and confused by the question, but as always, he recovered quickly.

"Do you wish to kill me?" he laughed.

"No," I said, "I do not. But you have a sort of, well, a sort of immortal quality about you."

Now, I think he was the one uncomfortable with this turn of the conversation.

But he responded, "I am a man, I can be killed."

"You," I started, "give the impression of one who cannot be killed, cannot be hurt, who can evade any danger while standing firmly in the middle of it. It's like the legend of you traveling on the wind, speaking to the animals of the forest, appearing from nowhere to help when help is most needed. You have an aura of not being human, of being otherworldly, maybe of being a spirit, or a manitou."

His response was typically exasperating, and very matter of fact, "I do speak to the animals of the forest."

Of all that I had said, he focused on and addressed only that.

"What about the rest of what I said?" I replied.

"You make too much of these things," he said.

"It is not only me," I said, "but many have told the same stories about you. Some have said you are a manitou."

"I am only a man. But I will tell you this one thing, Spirit Traveler," he paused, and then added, "People want to believe such things about me, maybe they even need to believe. Life is hard, and it is short, whatever helps can be a pleasant distraction to some, a comfort to others. Some believe me to be a manitou, just as they believe in your spiritual abilities."

"So, what you are saying," I said, "is that all those things that people say about you are not true."

Nebi Skog did not answer, he only smiled. It was a smile of which only he knew the meaning.

I now changed the subject and asked him about his slightly different hairstyle and attire, since coming back with Ales from the plains.

He explained that his clothing had worn out, and his hair had grown longer, and though he could have traded with the French, and kept his manner of dress the same, he made slight changes because he liked the styles of the plains Indians. He felt that looking like the people of that area was not a bad thing. He felt that his healing of the sick was made easier, because he established trust by not looking different from them. Upon his return, he decided to maintain just a few slight changes to his appearance. In that regard, I assumed he looked a bit like a plains Indian, maybe a Sioux, though I had never seen one. Overall, he was still a combination of Abenaki, Iroquois, and now maybe Sioux. I think it was his slightly different hairstyle that made him look like a plains Indian. But then he had never shaved his head, like his brethren woodland tribes. But I digress.

We had cold-camped, so as not to attract attention from any roving scouts of either side of the impending battle. After a time, we went to sleep. At some time during that sleep, I was awakened and could hear some critters very near. I looked at Nebi Skog, who was already sitting up, having heard the intruders.

Before long, he said something in a low, calm, very soothing voice. He spoke in either Abenaki or Iroquois. Both peoples using Algonquin languages, the similarity of some words with Miami, led me to know that he had issued some sort of welcome to "brothers and sisters." The brothers and sisters in this case being whatever animals were snooping around us.

Soon, I could see faint figures in the moonlight, creeping slowly forward, in a sort of submissive movement, from the woods and underbrush, timidly at first and then more confidently. As they came, he used some sort of hand signal which I could not fully see but knew I had never seen done before.

Soon, we were in the midst of a very submissive pack of wolves, that had come more slowly to me, but eventually surrounded both of us, licking us, and allowing us to pet them as if they were dogs. Nebi Skog was to them, the leader of the pack. I was stunned, and amazed, as he continued speaking to them in that low, calm voice.

After a time, he gave each wolf, I think there were seven, some jerky he had with him, and then he sent them off into the woods, again with words, and a hand signal I did not understand. There was either too much to be said, or nothing to be said, so I went back to sleep, marveling at what had just occurred.

The next day we fished in a stream with our hands. I would have guessed that we would catch nothing, but we caught several good-sized catfish by reaching into holes just below the waterline and pulling them out by their mouths with some biting us. We made a fire in the afternoon, cooked the fish, and had some wild rice, and onions that we had found.

After the meal, Nebi Skog produced a small pouch with

something that was plant material, looking like dried mushrooms.[2] He put these, along with a few other bits of plants that he found nearby the stream and in the woods, in a very small cook pan with boiling water. The concoction boiled for several minutes, turning a very dark black color, and then he took it off the fire and covered it with some leaves. He put the fire out again so that once it was dark, a campfire would not attract any unwanted attention.

He then looked at me and said, "Do you remember your spirit trip that the people talk about?"

"No," I said, "I do not. I think there were some dreams in the end, but I do not remember them. This is why I do not think I am worthy of the name Spirit Traveler. I do not think there was any special spiritual connection to that experience, except that I almost died, and of course, the people believed and so spared me."

He responded, "But you did not die, and your name should not be solely based upon that one experience, though that may be why the people gave you the name. I can only assure you that your name fits you and that one incident after your capture is neither proof, nor not proof, that you own your name. You have had other spiritual experiences, and you will have many more."

"How can," I started, "a spiritual man, have a temper such as I have, one that causes me to fight with my fists?"

"Yes," he said, "temper is something that you own, but it is not you, only something you have not learned to tame."

I said to him, "I have never seen you angry, do you get angry?"

His response was, "Anger is something I had once, but anger is no help to me or others. It is a useless emotion that only clouds the mind. I think I have not been angry for a very long time."

We then remained silent for some time as the day came to a close and night came on. When the moon rose, he took the concoction that he had boiled and told me that we would now take a spiritual journey, but that first, he would prepare me by telling me of what to be aware.

"We will drink this, but take only two or three small sips, no more, under any conditions," he said.

"Or what will happen?" I said.

"You will die," he said, matter-of-factly and without any particular emotion.

"If I might die, why do I want to drink that?" I asked.

"If you do what I tell you, you will not die," he said, "You may learn a great lesson, but I will not tell you that it is without danger. If it were so, perhaps there would be no great thing to gain. Do you trust me?"

"I do trust you, my brother," I said.

Above all, I had come to trust this man in things of which normally I would trust no other. Indeed, I did trust him with my very life which I owed him many times over.

"Very well," he continued. "We will drink, and you may sleep or you may not, but you will have visions. Do not be afraid, no matter how real they may seem, no matter how awful, you cannot be harmed. Remove yourself by thinking, 'I cannot be harmed,' and allow the vision to teach you. Are you ready?"

"Yes," I said, with a certain trepidation.

We then each took the prescribed three small sips, he first, to show, I think, that it was not poison. It was not exactly tasty. It was bitter, so foreign in taste that it was hard to get down. I wouldn't have wanted any more than three sips.

I lay on my back, looking at the moon and stars for a time for which I have no reference. I arose and had the urge to dance. Whether I danced to a rhythm in my head, or whether Nebi Skog might have been playing a drum, or a hollow log, or something. I know I was dancing like the Miami I had seen. It was a primordial feeling, a sort of freedom.

Eventually, the trees in the forest began to move as if they were giant bipeds. The rocks and downed logs shimmered into another worldly sort of state. The stream flowed one way and then the other, and then froze like ice, then flowed again. The symphony of sound created by frogs, cicadas, owls, and others, sounded loud like great music but changed to be as if those creatures were giant monstrous beings, and I the human, a tiny being. I was afraid, very afraid, and my heart was racing. The world was closing in on me. All creatures, all plants and vegetation were coming to get me. Then all went black as if avoiding an inevitable and horrible ending. I must have passed out.

The visions gave way to sleep and dreams. The colors were vivid, the action real, the sounds singular, purer than any sounds I had ever heard. Eventually, I began to awaken, I sensed the period before the dawn, and opening my eyes I saw, though fuzzily, just that; that sometimes almost surreal period when it is not completely dark, but when the horizon has not brought the dawn. Slowly, I regained my senses and became aware that Nebi Skog was beside me, watching my every movement.

He said, "Brother, you are awakening from a spirit dream. Take your time, do not let your thoughts race ahead of you, ease your worries, and know that you are fine."

Now he gave me a drink of cool water from the stream. It was the best water I had ever tasted and had the effect of removing a very bad taste from my mouth, apparently the residual effects of the drink I had taken the night before.

"Brother," he said, "I must ask you now, while it is still fresh, will you share your dream with me?"

"Yes," I began, "there was a large meadow, a clearing in the forest, it was miles across. In the middle of the meadow, was a gigantic tree, an oak, bigger by twenty times in size than any tree in the forest. Suddenly the land was covered by a shadow blocking out the sun. I looked up, and it was a giant eagle, not just a big eagle, but an eagle bigger than thirty bears in size. His wingspan was maybe five rods across. The great bird circled the land far and wide, and then landed on top of the giant oak. From there, the great eagle surveyed the land, and I could see through his eyes."

"In time, a band of Indian warriors appeared on the far side of the meadow. The Eagle shrieked, and there appeared thousands of soldiers, bluecoats, led by a general on a white horse. He wore a uniform with the sign of the eagle. The soldiers advanced, and wiped out the Indian warriors, overwhelming them ferociously by sheer numbers."

"Then, there was the silence of death."

"In time, the great bird shrieked again."

"I could see all the Indian people, the villages; I could also see white forts and trading posts with sellers of whiskey. In a moment, there was great suffering from disease, from the whiskey, from the people being cheated by white traders. The soldiers told the Indian people where they could go and not go. Sometimes they took the Indian weapons. Sometimes they raped the Indian women. The people became lethargic, at least those who did not die, and there was no pride. Then came white missionaries. They took away the Indian religion, and replaced it with their own God. And the eagle shrieked again."

"Then, there was the silence of death."

"Then the Eagle shrieked yet again, and a wall of water appeared, perhaps 50 feet high, it was a great flood, sweeping everything before it, the trees of the forest, the animals, the Indian people, wigwams and cabins, everything. But in a flashing moment, the water was gone. The land had dried, and was now divided into farms and homesteads, all owned by white people. The whites were everywhere, more than the ants of the ground. They built cities and roads. The Indian villages were gone. The animals of the forest were gone. All had changed. The land no longer was that of the Indian people, it was all a land of whites. The Indian people gathered in small groups, huddling together, those who had not yet perished, poor, without clothing, without homes, with nothing to trade, with children crying for food."

"Then there was the silence of death. Then I awoke."

"And were you in the dream, my brother?" he asked.

"No," I replied, "I was only an observer, more like a spirit, seeing things through the eyes of the great bird."

"Brother," he said, "you have been given a great gift, a spiritual vision of the future. Do you understand the meaning?"

"The eagle," I asked, "is it the United States?"

"Just so, Spirit Traveler," he said.

"Then," I replied, "the vision is obvious. It is the future of the Indian people. The whites will win the war and then come and take everything. But how can it be, it is so unjust, so sad?"

"The future, my brother, does not have to be fair, without pain, without suffering. You have seen what will happen," he said. "It does not matter whether the general you saw was he who does not sleep, or the one who comes after him, sooner or later the army will defeat the Indian people. It may be now, it may be later, but it will be."

"Is there no way to change this reality?" I asked.

"Only one way," he said. "You were not active in the dream. If you are active in the future, things may change based upon your actions."

"But one person cannot change all of that suffering," I said.

"No, it is just so, brother. One man cannot change everything. But just as the turtle goes through life the best that he can, the wolf the same, and also the fish, each according to his nature, so too, can you, according to your nature, do the best you can. You cannot change everything, but you can change some things for some people. You must change what you can, but you must not assume the weight of all that you cannot. It will destroy you if you take responsibility for all. You can mourn the injustice, the sadness, but you can only change what you can change. But remember this, you do not know who may help you. One person can do much, two can do more, twenty can do a great deal. People of like minds will draw themselves together, white and Indian."

I was quiet for a few minutes, and then I said, "My brother, Nebi Skog, what about your vision?"

He replied, "In truth, I did not drink, I only pretended to do so, swishing it in my mouth, and spitting it out when you had begun your vision. I needed only to have a bit to help me watch over you, to see that you were safe, and to be able to look into your soul as you were having your vision."

"You looked into my soul?" I said, somewhat incredulously until I realized, yet once again, to whom I was speaking.

"In a way," he said. "It is as I have said, you have a great spiritual gift, that was shown to me, as I knew it would be, and I hope it has now become clear to you. You have tolerance, wisdom, and compassion like few others of any race. You must now learn to be in step with your name, for you are he, the 'Spirit Traveler.' He who understands the spirit can do great things."

Though I was much confused, I also felt a sort of coalescence of the "self" in me, mentally, physically, and spiritually. I emerged with questions, but with a new-found sense of, and a better understanding of myself, a confidence that seemed to contain truths that heretofore, I had avoided. I am certain most people avoid too deep an introspection of themselves, their actions, their motivations, really an honest look into their being. I knew fully that my vision had been induced by drugs, I had no illusions about that. However, the vision was very clear and was an obvious portent of things to come. I was now more willing to consider that I was the "Spirit Traveler."

We spent the rest of that day looking for plants, berries, and so forth to eat. Nebi Skog said we should not eat meat that day, as we, mostly me, needed the drugs to leave my body in a cleansing manner, and meat would not help that process. I followed his instructions without question.

We talked quietly, Nebi Skog answering my questions, more openly, more directly now. Gone were the admonitions, and little riddles that "he could not teach me what I knew within myself." I sensed that we had reached a sort of equality between us. But even in thinking that, I was humble enough to realize and honor the knowledge of this most remarkable man, my teacher.

We spent much of August slipping stealthily up and down the Maumee River and the surrounding area, checking on Indian encampments and likely spots for the battle to occur.

About our tenth day out, late in the evening, as we were camping maybe a quarter-mile from a village, gunfire erupted at the village. Laying low, we soon saw about ten or a dozen Indians come racing down the trail, being chased by a much larger group, who were firing their muskets at those fleeing. The fleeing group occasionally turned to fire, in an apparent attempt to slow their pursuers. However, the fleeing group, having attained a considerable lead, the pursuers soon abandoned the chase and went back past us as we hid along the trail.

This event puzzled me as I could not figure who those being pursued were. It did not puzzle Nebi Skog, and he motioned for me to follow him in the direction of those who had fled. By morning we found ourselves on a small hill overlooking the group as they rested along the river.

I recognized Apekonit in the group. Using a bird call that he and I had long used as a signal, I let him know I was in the area. Nebi Skog and I moved down the hill, and Apekonit had his men hold their fire. These were Apekonit's white Indian scouts.

Arriving where they were, we assured them that they were no longer being pursued.

Apekonit was nursing an extremely nasty musket wound to his left hand and wrist. Nevertheless, he was delighted to see me, asking if I had come to join him. I told him that I had not, and tried to make him understand what Nebi Skog and I were doing, but that was not easy, since I didn't fully know what we were doing, and Nebi was suddenly only marginally communicative.

We removed the ball from Apekonit's wrist, after giving him some painkilling leaves to chew on. He said the ball had slammed into his wrist with a thud, and it felt like getting hit with a sledge, producing the most intense pain that he had ever felt. The ball had not passed completely through his wrist but was protruding out the side opposite the entry. In that regard, it was very easy to remove with my hunting knife, after heating it in the fire that Nebi had quickly made.

Apekonit explained that he and the others had infiltrated an Indian war council, and had been discovered after a time. Then there was shooting, and the American scouts fled.

"Have you seen Luke?" I asked.

"He is with General Wayne. He and two others, Black Duck and Tucker, stay with the twenty or so Chickasaw scouts that are with Wayne, leading the main body of the army north, so that there is no miscommunication between them."

"Black Duck and Jim Tucker?" I asked.

"Yes," he said.

Apekonit now told us that the battle was imminent and that it would likely take place further north. Soon, he and his men would leave us to report to Wayne. I asked him to say "hello" to Luke for me.

His hand was quite a bad injury, and it appeared that one or more bones may have been shattered. I was not sure the hand could be saved, Nebi Skog said it could, and he performed just a bit of additional doctoring that I watched carefully. I could tell that Apekonit was hurting. I frankly doubted that he would ever use that hand again. As it was to turn out, the army surgeon would hold him out of the upcoming battle because of the injury, and he would soon be awarded a government pension for the loss of use of the hand.

Nebi Skog and I now headed back to the north, taking a wide berth around any Indian encampments that we encountered. He said he thought he knew where the battle would occur. Of course, he proved to be right, as always.

We did creep close to Fort Miamis, where we spied a large Indian encampment outside the walls. The British were providing food, and powder to the confederated tribes. The fort was an incredible defensive masterpiece, with walls behind trenches, high earthen redoubts, instead of blockhouses, and the river at the backside.

"Filthy redcoat bastards," I muttered under my breath.

Nebi Skog grasped my arm and gave me a look as if to say, such a comment was beneath me.

Well, I didn't think it was beneath me. Those asshole British interlopers need to go home!

Leaving the fort area, we went to the lake called Erie, after the local Indian people, but called Lake du Chat, or "Lake of the Cat," by early French explorers because of the presence of many large painters in the area. I had expressed my desire to see this magnificent body of water, and Nebi Skog took me there.

By this time, Wayne and his Legion were closing in on the Indians. He was supremely confident in his army. On August 14, he is said to have remarked for posterity:

I have thought proper to offer the enemy a last overture of peace, and as they have everything dear and interesting now at stake, I have reason to expect that they will listen to the proposition mentioned, which may eventually spare the effusion of much human blood. But should war be their choice, that blood be upon their heads. America shall no longer be insulted with impunity. To an all-powerful and just God, therefore I commit myself and gallant army.

Later we headed back to the southwest, and we came upon a portion of a woods where many trees had been felled by a recent tornado.

"Here, here is where the battle will be fought," Nebi Skog said. It was a place called "Fallen Timbers" by both sides.

We crossed the Maumee to a very high bluff on the east side of the river. Here we would camp for the night, and observe what would happen the next day.

Wayne had used a tactic for the past two years for which the Indians had no defense. He would have his scouts let word to the Indians that a battle was imminent. He knew that the Indians would not eat on the day of a battle. So, he would keep them in suspense for two or three days, and often have them in a very weakened state from lack of food, by the time he joined the battle.

August 20, 1794 dawned hot and humid. Early, we could detect Indians from the confederation taking up positions among the fallen trees. There were Shawnees, Delawares, Miamis, Wyandots, Ottawas, Chippewas, Potowatomies, Mingos, a few Iroquois, and others, mostly young warriors from tribes no longer a part of the confederation, but young men eager to prove themselves in battle. In all, somewhere between 1,000 and 1,500 warriors. As I said earlier, the Indians were led by Blue Jacket.

Advancing on the Indian position were the Chickasaw scouts, Luke, Jim, and Black Duck included. Wilkinson's Brigade came first, in the second rank were Todd's Brigade, followed by Scott's, and Barber's, and finally Wayne's. In total, Wayne was commanding over 3,000 men, including the Kentucky militia.

The Indian ambush was quickly uncovered by the scouts, and the advance column, who were now coming under heavy fire, but held their lines until joined by the main part of the army, just as Wayne had ordered. The confederation had thought to gain the advantage, and indeed, had wisely chosen their position. However, Wayne quickly ordered a bayonet attack on the Indian center and a simultaneous attack by his dragoons on the Indian flanks. The result was complete American control of the field in a matter of minutes. The Indians hated hand-to-hand combat against bayonets, and this battle also marked the first major use of mounted cavalry against them. The rest of the fighting continued sporadically, and in isolated areas, as the Indians withdrew in disarray.

The result was a complete rout, with the Indians fleeing to Fort Miamis, where they found the gates closed, and the British denying them admission. The entire battle lasted less than an hour, and fewer than 100 men died on each side. There is little else to report about the battle. It was nothing like the earlier battles involving Harmar and St. Clair. It was a complete victory for the Americans, and a deep psychological blow to the Indian confederation, which was now additionally betrayed by the British, just as Little Turtle had predicted. The Indians had no choice but to flee the area. The death of even one person is regrettable, but given the potential for much greater carnage, the causality totals were relatively small.

For the next several days, Wayne's troops scoured the area, burning deserted villages, and destroying crops in a huge plume of fire. They dared not attack Fort Miamis for fear of enveloping the young United States in another war with Britain. Fort Miamis was a formidable defensive structure with 14 cannon emplacements. While it was garrisoned by just over 200 soldiers, it was deemed virtually impregnable.

Conversely, the redcoats would not come out and fight, for fear of starting a war with the United States. The British commander and his troops were forced to watch the Americans pillage the area, and to parade around the fort, just out of range of the fort's small arms.

There is a story, later told to me by Luke, that he witnessed. It seems that General Wayne ordered the British to surrender on August 22, and they refused. Wayne then circled the fort, alone on his horse, easily within pistol range, as an apparent affront to the British. Some confederation members were watching from the nearby woods and were embittered by the British acceptance of this insult. In their minds, there was no more reason to ever trust the British.

I was later to learn that the British Commander, Major William Campbell, complained bitterly in a written note delivered to Wayne under a white flag, about the presence of Wayne's army and the destroying of Indian crops. Wayne's official response was penned by his aide, future United States President, Lieutenant William Henry Harrison, who in the most formal, and flowery sarcastic language, told Campbell to "go to hell," and chastised him for violating the Treaty of Versailles.

The fort was ultimately to be turned over to the Americans in 1796, under terms of the Jay Treaty between the United States and Great Britain, but that was yet in the future.

After the battle, the Americans collected their wounded and dead, but the Indians had no time for that in their flight. As darkness fell, Nebi Skog and I spent nearly three hours searching for any Indians left for dead, but still actually alive on the field. We found two. One was beyond hope, and Nebi Skog gave him some crushed plants to make him comfortable and start his journey to the Spirit World.

The other man we found behind a rotted log. He was an Ottawa, a very young brave. I doubted he was more than 14 years old. He had a serious leg wound, but we were able to render considerable assistance to him, and to move him to our perch across the river and atop the bluff opposite the battlefield. We learned that the young man's name was Thrashing Badger. He was considerably perplexed by the combination of a white man and an Indian working harmoniously together to heal him. He inquired about the outcome of the battle, and he received the news badly. He seemed to sense the oncoming shift of power in the land of the Indians.

In the end, Nebi Skog escorted the young man back to his village on the Cuyahoga River, far to the east of the American Army, while I left for Turtletown, afraid to enter the American ranks looking for Luke for fear of being mistaken as having assisted the Indians in the battle. I was relatively certain that Luke was unharmed. I had seen him on the battlefield several times.

In October General Wayne marched his army toward Kekionga, wresting the Wabash-Erie Portage corridor from Miami control. Shortly, he would do that which neither Harmar nor St. Clair had done. He would build a large American fort which was to be known as Fort Wayne. Thus began the decline of Kekionga as a major Indian center of influence. Before long, it would be all but deserted. The great crossroads of the Indian culture in the Northwest Territory was now reduced to a footnote in history. It was now that the Miami took to calling Wayne, a name that I may have mentioned, *A-lom-seng*, "The Wind," for how he had swept away the allied tribes at Fallen Timbers.

Chapter Twenty One

Fort Wayne

Fort Wayne

Following the Battle of Fallen Timbers, I made my way tenuously back to Turtletown. I traveled mostly at night to avoid members of the confederation who might like to get their hands on one lone white man, to vent their frustrations over recent events. I had little trouble, save for having a small party picking up my trail. I was able to use what Nebi Skog had taught me about climbing trees; climbing and hiding for several hours in a gigantic maple tree.

I made it back to Turtletown arriving a few days before Little Turtle and his warriors, who had attended some impromptu conferences consisting of the defeated warriors of the various tribes. Little Turtle had come back now more than ever convinced that little could be done to thwart the whites and that some agreeable peace must be found.

Autumn and I decided that despite the dangers, we would return to our cabin with Sunny. With Wayne's army still in the field most warriors would be going home to protect their villages and it would be unlikely that our home would again be bothered by a raiding party.

Our cabin was still secured, and nothing was amiss when we arrived home, though the garden had been overrun by weeds and critters. In the woods, pawpaws, roots and nuts, and wild mushrooms would soon be available as autumn gained momentum.

Kekionga was evacuated and Turtletown, along with the more westerly villages swelled with refugees. Red Buffalo came from Kekionga to stay with us. Black Bear sent Gray Fox and his mother, She-Fox, to stay with us. This had the effect of special care for Sunny. Autumn was now two months further along in her pregnancy than when we had been attacked earlier in the summer. She estimated an early February delivery.

September was for securing food for the winter. We hunted one man at a time, always leaving two at the cabin for protection. Autumn knew now to keep the door barred and all weapons at the ready. Sunny was fussing to be outside more while the houseguests did their best to distract her. How she loved her grandmother and her uncle Gray Fox. Red Buffalo likewise, though not a blood relative, was a favorite of hers. Sunny had been speaking for some time now. She understood English and Miami, though she got much more exposure to the latter.

Gray Fox was particularly fond of fishing and he plied the creek, or the river, several hours each day. Soon we had smoked enough fish for the winter even if all our house guests stayed.

Our frequent search for signs of intruders in the woods turned up nothing and my thoughts about the allied warriors having all gone back to their villages, seemed to be the case.

In mid-October, we were greeted late one afternoon by visitors that I instantly recognized, but which left me momentarily speechless. It was Apekonit, Luke, Black Duck, and Jim Tucker!

"What a sight, what a sight!" was all that I could say at first. Then finally, "What are you all doing here?"

Apekonit said, "We are messengers for General Wayne. He is at Kekionga building a fort. We delivered a message to Little Turtle."

"Building a fort, at Kekionga?" I stammered.

It was like a blow to the gut. It would mean an army presence and the virtual end of the Miami capital. I did not like this incursion, not at all.

"Yes, it is a mighty big fort. Not as big as Greene Ville, but bigger'n all the others, except Fort Washington," said Luke.

"How aire ye Jariah?" Jim Tucker said.

"I'm just fine, Jim. It's really good to see you. You too, Black Duck," I said.

Black Duck produced a smile and nodded his customary assent.

The conversation continued about Wayne, about Apekonit's hand, which was mostly unusable but still attached and about what events would come next. Apekonit informed me that Wayne was sending out runners to the tribes, telling them to cease hostilities. He was asking the people exiled from Kekionga to return home, but thus far very few had done so. He had promised blankets and other provisions for the winter, from the government. He was telling the tribes that he would destroy all who resisted his Legion. His words were ominous to the people, but they rang with truth. Here was a warrior who operated with legendary patience in training his men, but waged battle with a ferocity that the Indians had not seen in the other American commanders.

Apekonit informed me that Hamtramck was at Kekionga and that he would be the first commandant of the fort.

We prepared a feast for supper of smoked fish, venison, dried berries, apples, pawpaws, and potatoes. We asked our scout guests to stay the night, but they said that they had exceeded orders already since they were only to go to as far as Turtletown to deliver an invitation for Michikinikwa to visit Wayne at his new fort. They were due back at the new fort site tomorrow in the late morning, so they would have to travel part of the night.

After our sumptuous supper, they left, having obtained a promise from me to come to the fort before winter. Colonel Hamtramck was wanting to speak with me. They seemed either not to know what it was about, or they wouldn't say.

They left after only a few hours with us. During the short time that they were there, I observed Luke more closely than I had at Fort Recovery. He was a man now, taller than our father had been. He was filling out, but as I said earlier, very much on the lean side. He could speak a few Indian dialects and Apekonit told me privately that he was a very fine scout. I was both proud, worried, and hopeful that the war was now really over.

Before long, the snow would fly. I decided I had better go to Kekionga now, and see what Colonel Hamtramck wanted. I left my family in the good care of Autumn's family and went to Kekionga, by-passing Turtletown, so as not to lose time speaking with friends and relatives.

Arriving at Kekionga, I was greeted by the site of a large fort that seemed to dominate the landscape. Previously, nothing had stood so tall in the area, except the trees of the forest. It was not yet finished but was nearly so. Many soldiers were encamped in the area and only a few Miami people were about.

I was greeted at the gates by none other than my old friend, Sergeant Lowell Hanks. He had aged but was still a fit soldier. We embraced warmly, and quickly caught each other up on the events since last we had seen each other. He told me he had not been with St. Clair because he had the fever and had nearly died. He had, however, been at Fallen Timbers. When I told him my story, he marveled. He had known from Jim, Luke, Black Duck, and Apekonit that I was alive and had heard about my capture, as well as my subsequent stay among the Miami. He knew of my family. Before we could finish my four friends came up. All six of us went to the local sutler's cabin and imbibed a serious amount of rotgut whiskey.

Being too drunk to see Hamtramck, I went off with Lowell Hanks to his quarters where I slept on a spare cot which accommodated about half my length.

The next morning Lowell woke me up as he went on duty. I went to see Colonel Hamtramck after grabbing some biscuits and gravy in the mess area.

Hamtramck seemed genuinely glad to see me and I was likewise. My previous relationship in going to St. Louis for him had gone well, and I regarded him as a good man.

He went straight to the point, "Welcome, I trust zhat you are weell, Jariah. Eet eeze good to see you, and I zhank you for coming. My purpose eezz simple. If peace eez concluded next summer, William Wells weell be assigned here to Ft. Wayne as interpreter and scout. He knows zhis area, and he weell be an asset. Zhat leaves General Wayne wizout a Captain of Scouts. I have recommended you for zee position. Would you entertain such an offer?"

My response was immediate and direct, "Sir, I thank you for the offer, and for thinking of me for the job, but my answer is unequivocally, no. I have a family and a home. I am not looking to be away from them. That, Sir, is my final answer. Nothing will change my mind."

"I understand," he said.

"I zhought zhat would be your answer, but I had to ask, my friend. Ees zhere someone you might recommend?" he continued.

"Well, Jim Tucker would probably be my choice," I replied.

"Yes, Monsieur Tucker has served weell, and he has been considered, but General Wayne would prefer a more educated man for political reasons. Zhis man may een time, be involved een delivering high-level diplomatic messages, and zhat might eenvolve zee British, or zee Spanish. Eet will require a special sort of man. What would you zhink of your brother, Luke, as a candidate for zee job?"

"He would be good," I said. "But I think Tucker is more experienced."

His reply was, "True, Tucker ees more experienced een zee woods and as a fighter of Indians, but your brother ees similar to you, he ees educated and he knows zee woods as well."

"All those things are true," I said. "Does Luke know he might be considered?"

"I do not zhink so, but he has been much discussed. He has done a fine job," Hamtramck said.

"Well, I am certain you will work it out," I said. "I really must get back home now."

He replied, as he opened the door, "Again, my friend, zhank you for coming, perhaps we weell work together een zee future. We weell need interpreters eef we can conclude peace next summer."

"That I would do," I said. "That I would do. Just let me know where and when."

"I shall do so. Adieu, my friend, please come to see me often," he said as I left.

Luke, Black Duck, Apekonit, and Jim were all standing outside as I left Hamtramck's headquarters.

"Don't you fellas have work to do, or do you just stand around collecting the government's paycheck?" I asked.

"We're slackers," chuckled Luke.

"Government paychecks be mighty small, cept'n for Capt'n

Wells, y'ere. He gits beeg money, " Jim said, laughing heartily.

Apekonit replied, "Well, Tuck, you know that Black Duck and I do all the work. We carry you and Luke."

This drew an actual chuckle from Black Duck, who, as usual, said nothing. I liked seeing this good-natured ribbing among the group. I was glad that my brother and my best friends had all come together. I knew that they would look out for one another, and this was a comfort to me.

"What did the Colonel want with you, my brother?" Apekonit said.

"Another secret mission," I deadpanned. "He wants his best man for the job."

Everyone nearly rolled with laughter, and the ribbing continued. I told them that the Colonel would, no doubt, be filling them in on the issues he spoke with me about, but for now I needed to head home.

I told them to come see me and they said they would, but figured at least some of them, if not all, would be sent to Greene Ville for the winter. There they would probably draw duty running messages between the many forts now existing: Wayne, Recovery, Defiance, Greene Ville, Jefferson, Hamilton, and Washington.

"Ok, see you boys when I see you," I said.

"Take care," came Luke's reply as he seemed to speak for all of them.

I returned home to await the snow and the arrival of the new baby Jamison. Snow came in late November, and the baby came on February 12, 1795. It was a boy, and we named him after my father and his father. So it was to be, Dawson Demas Jamison, but his Indian name would be Little Blue Dogs, after my friend.

Sunny was completely enamored of her brother with not a hint of jealousy. She now assumed the role of a two-year-old mother to the boy. She was not the most patient of mothers. She expected the baby to learn things much more quickly than he was capable of doing. For instance, she thought he should answer her many questions. When grandmother explained that babies cannot speak, Sunny was beside herself. How was the boy going to get along in life if he couldn't talk? When told there was a time when she couldn't speak, she was incredulous, simply not believing it. As much as she jabbered I could certainly understand her doubt.

Red Buffalo and Gray Fox had built a tiny cabin, just north of ours along the drop-off into the woods. This gave them and us more privacy. I kidded them that we now had a guest house, but they weren't quite sure why that was a joke. I had to explain that rich white folks had guest houses. They still didn't get that I was suggesting we were putting on airs. The Miami were a hospitable people, and they kept cabins for guests. I guess certain humor cannot translate across cultures.

They still took meals with us, which were usually prepared by She-Fox. Black Bear had come a few days before the baby was born. He and She-Fox build put up a wigwam south of the house for their privacy.

Frankly, I felt a lot better about having the extra people around. When one becomes a husband and father, it is a heavy burden to worry about everyone's safety. And in our case that safety had twice been challenged by war parties.

Black Bear informed us that the fort had been completed many weeks before and that General Wayne was sending invitations to all the nations. They were to come to Greene Ville in the summer for a peace conference. Pacanne had hoped the talks would be at Kekionga, but Wayne had rejected this. Pacanne had determined that he would not attend, but would send his nephew in his place.

I asked if the nations were disposed toward peace, and Black Bear said he thought that was the prevailing opinion among many tribes, though the Miami and the Shawnee were very leery about what the terms would be. At any rate, there was little alternative. To continue the war against someone like Wayne would be almost unthinkable.

Black Bear asked what I thought. I told him peace was the only hope. Otherwise, the whirlwind tactics of Wayne's army would become more widespread and many people would die. Still, I told him, peace will not be easy and not fair. The whites will want much land. White settlers will come and they would take even more. I told him I feared for the Indian people and what would become of them.

These talks tended to be short because frankly, the facts were just too sad to dwell upon.

Our days were spent ice fishing and chopping firewood, while grandpa Black Bear reveled in the grandbabies. Although he was very pleased to now have a grandson, it was clear that Sunny was the apple of his eye, and the two were inseparable. I've said it many times, but never before or since have I seen an Indian man take such an interest in a small child. They are typically good at training boys in the arts of hunting and war but are seldom much use with babies, toddlers, and girl children. I think to a very great extent Sunny reminded Black Bear of Autumn as a baby and the exceptional bond that the two must have had. She-Fox often said that this was the case. In recounting family stories from Autumn's early years, She-Fox often said that the two had been inseparable.

In early March, with cabin fever in full swing, Gray Fox and I went to Kekionga to see if my friends were there and to say hello to Colonel Hamtramck.

Luke and the others were not currently there. I found that the peace conference at Greene Ville would convene as soon as all, or most of the tribes were assembled. The tribes were asked to come in early June. The United States would provide food and other supplies for the participants. The Indians would likely bring their families as was their custom when being away from home for an extended period.

We went to see Colonel Hamtramck, and I introduced Gray Fox as my brother-in-law. He was cordial toward the youth, but Gray Fox said little. I suspected he was still in shock at seeing so large a fort on Indian land. Hamtramck gave me an official invitation to attend the peace conference and serve as an interpreter. I accepted, as I earlier told him I would, and he asked me to arrive in late May, for pre-conference talks with the American negotiators. I told him that I would do so and asked if he could arrange a place for my family. He assured me that he would find accommodations for us.

As we left, I could tell something was troubling Gray Fox. Now, nearly a full-grown man and long an accomplished warrior, it was finally dawning on him that the way of life that he had always expected to live as an adult was vanishing before his eyes. I told him what I thought would happen and how I expected the whites to act. There would be good deeds and evil deeds, but the future was changing for the Miami people. I had no pretensions that life would not be very much different, with large American armies so close to home.

Gray Fox was quiet most of the way home other than for a few thoughtful questions that I answered as honestly as I could.

We went home by way of Turtletown and paid our respects to the great war chief, Michikinikwa. He welcomed us warmly to his home, and congratulated me on the new baby, asking his name. I explained the source of the name and he nodded his approval.

Little Turtle, like Gray Fox and Black Bear before him, had many questions for me. He appreciated my honesty, and I think he valued my opinions when it came to predicting how things might be---things which none knew for certain. Gray Fox mostly listened as Little Turtle and I talked into the night. The great man was heavily inclined for peace. He thought that any other course of action would result in the complete and utter annihilation of the people.

I detected a great melancholy in him as he reflected on what life had been for him as a boy, when only French trappers, trad-ers, and priests were around. They had been no threat to the In-dian land, or way of life. In many cases, the French adopted the Indian life. Later came the British. Their goals were much differ-ent. Little Turtle had never trusted them and the recent betrayal only bore out his fears.

He inquired of Apekonit, and I told him that I had seen him a few times. He missed him, and he missed his daughter, Sweet Breeze. He also commented to me about Luke, who had come to his attention through various sources. He told me Luke would make a fine Miami warrior. I thanked him for that compliment to my family.

After many hours we slept; slept on the floor near the hearth in the cabin of the great chief. He was the greatest military mind I had ever met. I who had often, either with my father or by myself refused to stay at the home of a man who was to be a future President, stayed now without qualms, in the home of one of the most feared so-called savages that ever lived. I could have easily seen myself as one of his warriors had I come to the people in another time and under different circumstances.

In the morning we left early, telling Little Turtle that we would be in Greene Ville in the summer and that he had only to ask if he needed our assistance in any manner.

So, we went back home and got on with the usual spring activities, hunting, putting out a garden, mending the roof, and all the mundane tasks of living in the wilderness.

Chapter Twenty Two

The Treaty of Greene Ville

Fort Greene Ville

In late May, we left for Fort Greene Ville. Autumn's entire family accompanied us along with Red Buffalo. The weather was already warm. Sunny had been looking forward to the trip for weeks, which was for her the first big trip of her life. She chattered nonstop, she chattered about animals, chattered about butterflies, chattered endlessly about whatever came into her head. Sometimes she chattered in English, sometimes in Miami, sometimes in both, mixing words and phrases. We all enjoyed every minute of it, especially her grandfather, Black Bear, who was completely wrapped around her little finger.

In Kekionga, we had rented three horses from Pacanne for the trip: one for packs and two for the women to ride. It was Sunny's first time on a horse, and she thought it was amazing. Sometimes we had her horse on a lead, and her mother walked. At these times, Sunny thought she was something. Riding alone was pure joy for her and she gave the horse instructions asking everyone to watch her and informing her grandfather that he would have to get her a horse of her own. Furthermore, it had to be a white horse, or she might be willing to settle for a black one if it was pretty.

Sunny, now well over 2½ years old was somewhat tall for her age. Her skin was copper, mostly from being in the sun almost endlessly but probably also due to her Indian heritage. Her eyes were brown and her hair was actually a very dark blonde, partly from the sun, but partly from her Randolph heritage. She alternated between wearing the dresses of a little Indian girl and wearing pants like a white boy. When she wore the latter, her grandmother complained, but to no avail. I felt pants were more functional for such an active child. My sisters had often worn pants. To say that Sunny looked more white than Indian would be wrong. To say she looked more Indian than white would also be wrong. She resembled both sides of the family a great deal. The only things that made her a little more Indian were her habits and maybe her speech. She spoke more often in Miami but was very comfortable with English as well. Her convoluted mixing of the two was hysterical.

I will admit to not having an unbiased opinion, but Sunny was the most beautiful toddler I had ever seen and I just supposed she was the most beautiful and smartest child in the world. Both of her grandparents agreed and I think her mother did as well but didn't want the child to know. The little girl was the apple of her father's eye, but everyone she met commented on her intelligence and on her beauty. She was precocious, oh, so very precocious. She had already started to read, had a huge vocabulary in both languages, and had a sparkle in her eye, as each day she soaked up like a sponge, all that life had to offer. In her demeanor, she was closer to being 25 years old, not to nearing three years old, if you know what I mean. She was always in charge and always the center of everyone's attention. She was hugely entertaining. I could just sit and stare, while marveling at her every moment for hours on end.

Gray Fox took the lead on the trail to Fort Greene Ville. We did not expect any trouble, but better safe than sorry. My young brother-in-law was tall, handsome, and very muscular. He moved with the grace of a great warrior. Many Miami maidens were hoping he would pay special attention to them, but as far as I knew, he had not yet given women much attention. He was so intent on becoming an accomplished warrior, that he listened respectfully to any advice and was often tutored by his father and by Red Buffalo. And later, he would receive some tutoring from Nebi Skog, who I think saw what we saw in the young man. Gray Fox was an exceptional warrior and an exceptional human being.

Colonel Hamtramck had arranged a large army tent for us in an area reserved for translators, chaplains, medical personnel, and others, who would be functioning in an adjunct way. She-Fox constructed her family wigwam as near us as she could. It proved to be about 15 rods distant.

We had arrived in late May and I was immediately involved in meetings with interpreters. Apekonit would be the lead interpreter on matters involving the entire council. The rest of us would interpret in small group meetings. Some of us would be engaged in explaining the United States government to the Indians while others would be in charge of seeing to the food and other of their needs.

On a day in early June I found myself in the second, or back row around a large table inside General Wayne's headquarters at Fort Greene Ville. In the front row, aside from Wayne, was his aide, William Henry Harrison, Colonel Jean Francois Hamtramck, Captain Henry De Butts, who would act as the official secretary of the peace conference, Apekonit, and Major John Mills a favorite of Wayne's, who was later to be the Inspector General of the Army. In the back, aside from me, were Issac Zane, an interpreter and former captive (he was the son-in-law of Wyandot Chief, Tarhe), Chaplain David Jones, two officers named Merriweather Lewis and William Clark[1], and my brother, Lieutenant Luke Jamison, newly appointed Head of Scouts.

On the table lay a large map of the Northwest Territory. The map was divided into tribal spheres of influence and marked with the location of all the American forts, as well as some illegal British forts.

After pointing out a few things on the map, General Wayne addressed the gathering by saying:

> *Gentlemen, our task here is first and foremost to secure the peace for which so many have given their lives. In the process, we must assure the Indian people that our intentions are of a lasting peace, that we will*

*be their staunch allies and protectors of their persons
and property. Further, that we will look after their
welfare as befits a government and its protected people. We must give our solemn pledge of these things,
and we must make it very hard to impossible that war
will ever again occur between our peoples. Secondly,
we seek land concessions from the tribes, for which we
will pay a price determined by the Government of the
United States. I will be the one and final voice of the
government in all matters related to this treaty. We
are here with many soldiers and there will be many
Indians, perhaps more than we have ever seen in one
location. Past grievances and the heat of summer, will
make it easy for men to forget our purpose and tempers may flare. We must avoid this at all costs, not lose
track of our goal, and maintain calm. We must treat
these people with goodwill, not as a conquered people,
but as future protectees of the United States.*

After letting his words settle upon us, he went on:

*We must strictly limit the access to alcohol of our
soldiers to amounts that could in no way lead to intoxication. There is to be no alcohol available to the
Indians. Any soldier guilty of providing such to the Indians will be court-martialed. Any sutler or trader
doing so will be imprisoned and subject to fine. We
will enforce this steadfastly and punish any offenders.
We have gifts for the Indians, and supplies for their
needs, while they are gathered here. In all that we do,
we must be firm, honest, and sincere. We must keep
civil tongues, letting no offense anger us and no words
of anger pass our lips. What is about to occur here
may well be the most important thing to happen to
our country since the peace ending the Great War. I
ask you all to do your utmost to bring these proceedings to a just and lasting conclusion. Thank you. Are
there any questions?*

There were then posed a few minor logistical questions that I took little note of since they did not directly involve me. I engaged myself in attempting to take the measure of those men present. In a few minutes, we were all dismissed.

As I started to leave, General Wayne motioned for me to stay. This shocked me. I could not imagine what business he had with me.

As the others filed out, he closed the door behind them.

"Have a seat, Mr. Jamison," he said.

"Please call me Jariah, Sir. Mr. Jamison was my father," I said.

"Luke told me that your father served with Dan Morgan," he said.

"Yes, they were comrades, and they were great friends. My father had many fond memories of General Morgan. When my parents died, General Morgan came way out to our home to pay his respects," I responded.

"Well, Jariah, I didn't know your father, but I knew Dan Morgan very well. Best damn soldier this country ever had. If your father was his friend, I imagine he was cut of the same cloth as Dan. Dan knew how to beat those bastard, British sons-a-bitches," he said.

I had heard that the General could swear as well as any soldier and I was getting a touch of that now. But, as I've made clear, my sentiments about the British were of like thought.

"Luke's a fine scout," the General said.

"Well, I expect he is. I have not been around him much the past few years, but my father taught us all a very great deal," I said.

"Jariah, do you know what Little Turtle's intentions are? I mean, Captain Wells has told me a great deal, but do you know anything that would help deal with him?" he asked, getting quickly at his apparent point for our meeting.

"No, Sir, but I have great respect for him. If in his opinion, the offered peace is not just, he will continue as your greatest enemy," I replied. "I do believe he would prefer peace."

"And what of Pacanne who refused to come here, but sent his nephew. What do you know of this man, Jean Baptiste Richardville?" he asked.

"Peshewa?" I said. "That is his Miami name. In English, it is 'Wildcat.' He will be a hereditary civil chief when Pacanne dies.

His mother is Pacanne's and Little Turtle's sister. His father was a French trapper. He is a very intelligent and well-educated man. He speaks many languages. He will do what Pacanne has told him. Pacanne, too, would prefer peace, but it must be a just peace. He and Little Turtle will be of a similar mind."

He now brought up another point and spoke of my mission to St. Louis by saying, "You know, Jariah, Colonel Hamtramck has given you great praise for your work for us in the Spanish territory. Not only that, but I have spoken at length with Jim Tucker about that matter, and he says you are just about the smartest young man that he has ever encountered. He also told me how you laid the trap to waylay those couriers. That was very fine work."

I was never very comfortable being complimented and I suppose I didn't handle it all that well. I was now staring into the corner of the room where the General's dog was nursing six pups. She was a fine-looking dog. The pups appeared to be about two weeks old.

"You like dogs, son?" the General said.

"Uh, yes, Sir," was my response. "My father always had dogs, and I had a mighty fine one when I was with Harmar. He was killed just before I was captured."

At the mention of Harmar, General Wayne raised his eyebrows seeming to forget about dogs and began to question me about the facts around the defeat. He wanted to know about General Harmar, if I ever saw him drink on duty, about what kinds of orders he issued, about his manner with the men, about his response to subordinates being ambushed, and about the strategies that he employed.

I answered his questions trying to remember all that I could about those issues. Of course, much of the time that I was under Harmar's command, I was actually off scouting. Our discussion of Harmar went on for a time. The General stopped talking and walked to the window, turning his back to me.

"Jariah," he said after a time, "it is my understanding that the Indians call you something unusual. Is it Wind Walker, or Wind Talker, or something like that?"

Now he turned to look back at me.

I chuckled, "Well, Sir, those would be flattering names coming from Indians, but what they call me is Spirit Traveler."

"Ah, that's it," he said. "Why do they call you that?"

"Well, Sir, it's probably because I vomited on them when they were trying to torture me," I laughed.

He gave me a puzzled look.

I then went on to explain the details of my torture and near death as I remembered and as later told to me by Apekonit and others.

General Wayne burst out laughing, trying to picture in his mind those events and my projectile-like vomiting. Then he said, "Well, that is the damnedest story I ever heard, but it would seem that you carry some weight with the Indians. It would seem that they respect you. Is that so?"

"Sir," I said, "I think that was certainly true at first and it helped to save my life. But now I am not certain how much weight I carry with the people. I have refused to fight with them against the American army. I think that has caused some folks to lessen their regard for me, maybe especially some of the younger warriors."

And then he said, "Well, Jariah, I'd like to have you speak to some of the Miami chiefs and warriors about making peace. Could you do that?"

"Sir, I am willing to speak about peace, but I will not tell them anything that I do not know to be the absolute truth."

"Fair enough," he said. "We will speak more of this at a later time." Then he paused and again looked out the window.

He continued, "I wanted to get back to your St. Louis trip," he continued. "You know I owe you a great debt?"

He then paused, turned toward me and said in a most serious tone, "This talk stays in this room, understand?"

"Yes, Sir," I responded.

"Of course, it was officially inconclusive, uh, what you found out in St. Louis. But let's be clear, I think we both know that what you found is a glowing condemnation of Colonel Wilkinson. It has certainly caused me to be on my guard. You may have heard that a tree fell on my tent, and knocked me unconscious on my way to Fallen Timbers. Well, some think that may not have been an accident. But I cannot prove it was Wilkinson's work. Nevertheless, sooner or later, we will have our absolute proof, and we will have caught him at his treason. It is only a matter of time. In the meantime, as I said, it has caused me to keep up my guard, and for that I owe you a very great debt."

"Sir," I said, "I was very well paid for my work in going to St. Louis. To tell you the truth, I enjoyed the mission and being reunited with my friends, Jim Tucker and Black Duck. I might have done it for free."

He chuckled again, moving toward his dog in the corner. "Be that as it may, I want you to have one of these puppies. I am very sorry that the Indians killed your dog. I know that dogs can be a great help on the frontier. I understand that you have a young family to protect. These dogs are the finest. Their mother, Peaches, is a hound from North Carolina. She is from a local breed there. They use them to hunt bears and boars, but some folks use them to hunt raccoons."

"Yes, Sir," I volunteered, "I saw these dogs with a family named Plott in North Carolina a few years ago. Mighty fine dogs, unfailing trackers and ferocious fighters, but gentle as lambs with children."

"Yes, yes," he said, getting excited. "I can see that you know your dogs. A soldier named Plott gave me a pair, and Peaches is the granddaughter of that pair. The locals in North Carolina called them Plott Hounds, after the family that breeds them. Anyway, I want you to have a puppy."

"Oh, Sir, that is far too generous a gift," I protested.

"Well, then, how 'bout if we consider it a damn order?" he laughed heartily. "Now let me tell you about the father."

He then opened the door and told the corporal of the guard to go fetch the father dog.

"The father is a Louisiana Catoula hound, also used to hunt bears, boars, and on occasion also wasted on coon hunting. He was given me by the Spanish Lieutenant Governor in St. Louis, along with a horse, and delivered by a French trapper after our victory at Fallen Timbers. The Spanish seem to want to curry my favor. Would that be a fair assessment from someone who has been to St. Louis?"

"Yes, Sir," I said. "They do seem a bit preoccupied about Americans. They aren't necessarily the friendliest folks. I expect to give you a dog and a horse was some sort of attempt to influence you toward them in a positive fashion."

"Well," he said, "pick out a pup and in four or five weeks, or so, it'll be old enough to leave its mother."

"Yes, Sir, thank you. I've been meaning to get another dog. It was just hard because my last one was so special."

"Well, young man, take your pick," he went on.

"Sir, how about that one there that seems to be so active and alert?" I asked.

"That is your new dog, Jariah. He's a great choice. He's the one I'd have picked for you. I am happy to have one of my dogs going to someone who will appreciate and take good care of it."

"Oh, I will do that, Sir. Again, thank you, I appreciate it," I said.

The corporal reported back that he had not found the father dog.

And then I left. In the outer office, Luke was waiting for me, wondering what the General could have wanted with me for so long a time.

I told him, "He wants me to have a puppy."

No amount of questioning could prod me to give him any more details of my meeting with the General. It was maddening for him and funny for me. It was so nice to have my brother near once again, to tease and to talk with. He was beside himself wondering why General Wayne had spent so much time with me.

After a while, Luke gave up pursuit of an answer to his questions about the General, and I. We both began to speak about what was to come and about our presence at such a great event in the history of our young republic.

Luke spoke highly of General Wayne as a just and principled man, who was an outstanding military leader. He told me that men followed Wayne into battle with great confidence.

I went back to my tent and Luke went back to his duties but promised to come for supper and to bring Black Duck along with Jim Tucker. I was glad to have my brother and two of my very best friends here. I wanted my family to know them better.

That night they came to supper, and Autumn cooked a stew that had them asking for seconds and even for third helpings. She was the perfect hostess, and they were all taken with her beauty as well as her manner.

Luke held the baby some but spent much of the evening playing with Sunny. It was clear he was going to be another one of her favorites and so were Jim and Black Duck. Sunny pestered them and they obligingly played with her. She asked all kinds of embarrassing questions.

With Black Duck, she said, "And what tribe are you a part of, Uncle Black Duck?" He laughed at her directness and told her he was a Choctaw.

She said she hadn't heard of Choctaws before, "Were they friendly to the Miami people?"

Avoiding the current, or most recent political implications of her question, Black Duck said, "I think we will be friends of the Miami people now, and you and I shall always be very good friends."

He then showed her specific markings, clothing, and the cut of hair that would help her identify Choctaws in the future if she were so inclined. No doubt, she would be. She listened intently as she always did and with great seriousness thanked Black Duck for telling her that information.

She then turned to Jim and said, "Uncle Jim, what tribe are you from? Are you a white man? You look kind of messy."

Jim laughed because the child was right. He never put much into his appearance and he was a bit scruffy, with his unkempt hair, his beard, and worn clothes.

"Yes, Sunny, I'm a white man just like your pappy," he said.

"Oh," she said, seemingly trying to reconcile those facts. "Well Uncle Jim, you might need a haircut and maybe a bath, but I'll be your friend. We could make you a Miami if you like, just like my papa."

Jim laughed heartily.

It was a pleasant evening that ended all too soon.

As they left, Luke leaned to my ear and said to me, "Brother, beautiful wife, beautiful children, you are a lucky man!"

"Indeed, I am," I said. "I think I know what mother and father had with our family.

The summer wore on hot and miserably humid. Sunny and I played every morning, and every evening in the nearby spring-fed stream. The cold water was refreshing, and just about our only relief from the heat. Sunny took this all as one great adventure and having her entire family present, along with her new "uncles," was a special treat for her. Autumn bathed the baby regularly to keep him cool, but he still suffered some from the heat.

The Indians begin to arrive in early June and as is their tradition, a council fire was lit. It would burn until the peace conference ended. The massive fort was surrounded by many villages of wigwams and tents, representing the twelve tribes who were there to discuss peace.

Normally, peace negotiations would be handled by the civil chiefs and the war chiefs would play no great part. Wayne had insisted on the presence of the war chiefs as well at Greene Ville. This seemed strange to the Indians, but one can understand Wayne's desire to make certain that the message and terms of peace were well-known to all, especially those who had waged the war. Nevertheless, it was a sort of denial, or continued breakdown, deliberate, or not, of Indian protocol and their political structure. It was the young United States asserting its will over the cultural traditions of the Indian people. And I supposed it was the reason Pacanne was not present. He was strong-minded and not the sort to be given orders about going here, or there.

One thing was obvious. Wayne chose Greene Ville for three reasons. The first was simply security. If there were to be any treachery, a large army was present to deal with it and the fort was the most imposing structure on the frontier. As previously noted, it had multiple blockhouse redoubts. It enclosed over 55 acres, had many cannons, and was essentially an unassailable bastion of United States power in the territory. If violence were to break out, it would quickly be crushed. There were more soldiers present than any of the Indians had ever seen in one spot, and Wayne was careful to have them formally paraded and drilled every day.

His second objective was essentially accomplished by his first; the overwhelming military presence indicated by the fort and garrison was intended to cow the Indians into submission if they had any thoughts of not making peace. It was a very definite statement of the power and might of the United States and of the resources that could be brought to bear.

It was all extremely intimidating, and that was the third reason. In making the Indians come to him, instead of say, holding the conference at Kekionga, he was establishing himself as the supreme person in charge of this event. He was the one who would dictate all the details and the one who would tell everyone when and where to go.

As the days wore on, there were speeches from both sides, with especially eloquent and long oratories by the many chiefs present. In these they recounted the histories of their people up to the present time, including in those histories' their legends and their spiritual stories. They described great battles, times of peace and prosperity, times of famine and disease. They stressed their love of the land, of the animals, and the blessings of the manitous. They all told of the coming of the white man and what it meant to their people and how it changed their ways of life. They recounted past grievances, but they spoke with respect of the great white warrior, Anthony Wayne. This may have been an attempt to curry his favor, but I think it also may have been out of genuine reverence for his military prowess. I do not think anyone present entertained thoughts that this general could be defeated in a pitched battle. Some spoke of peace and some were skeptical, but all spoke for fair treatment.

During such important meetings certain Indian protocol was observed. For instance, as one example, when there was an all-present meeting or discussion, those Indians favoring peace sat together, while those opposed to the treaty sat together.

Oddly, Little Turtle did not sit with the peace delegation. He felt the treaty proposal was unfair. He was representing the Miami people and not himself, or his views alone. The Miami were not predisposed to sign an unfair treaty. To them continued warfare was preferable to injustice. Little Turtle knew that continued warfare would mean their end. Nevertheless, he represented their wishes while he used his considerable political acumen to try everything in his power to obtain better terms.

On more than one occasion he caught either General Wayne, or a member of the peace-favoring group, in a broad exaggeration, a misrepresentation, or an outright lie. He and Wayne traded sharp barbs on several occasions. But while Wayne was prone to exaggerate on behalf of the United States, I never heard Little Turtle utter an untruth or an exaggeration. He skillfully led conversations and asked questions that manipulated the group toward the truth that he was driving at, or in an attempt to illustrate a point. However, he negotiated with the utmost integrity, at the same time exposing other speakers in lies, exaggerations, or purposeful misdirection.

Many times, the proceedings seemed about to fall apart, as old grievances and new acrimony surfaced. Each time, Wayne would adjourn as tempers flared, or as he was caught in speaking something about another treaty, a person, or a tribe, that was quickly debunked as untrue by Little Turtle, or others. Wayne also used this tactic when he was asked a question to which he had no answer.

Despite such intensity and the extremely heightened emotions, somehow the parties stayed with the task, though sometimes taking a break for a day or two to restore calm.

In late June, Leather-lips, of the Wyandot, voiced a loud complaint that the gathered tribes were not getting enough food supplies. He complained that everything was grossly inadequate. Whether that was true, I cannot say. Black Bear and She-Fox never complained. My role as an American interpreter ensured that my family had sufficient food. Nevertheless, Indian custom was that the party who had called the peace conference was obligated to provide the necessities for all present. General Wayne was made to understand this. The American quartermaster was thereafter ordered to provide more food to the Indians than they could need. Each household was given a sheep as a part of their allotment.

Throughout it all, the numbers of Indians present continued to grow. I would estimate that over 1,500 were encamped by mid-July.

Present at Greene Ville was an incredible assemblage of famous and soon-to-be-famous Americans, and in this respect, when I say Americans, I am speaking of native peoples as well as the representatives of the United States. That so many prominent individuals were assembled at a remote frontier outpost was truly amazing, when one stopped to ponder. But then, what was about to occur was as prominent a historical event as had occurred since the Revolution and these events would set the course for the future of the United States.

Representing the Indians, were Little Turtle of the Miamis, Blue Jacket and Black Hoof of the Shawnees, Buckongahelas of the Delawares, Bad Bird of the Chippewas (who came from Mackinaw), White Pigeon and Kesass of the Potowatomies,

Leather-lips, and Tarhe of the Wyandots among others from other tribes. Wyandot war chief, Tarhe, assumed the role of the leading negotiator for the Indians. As I mentioned earlier, Pacanne did not attend and would never sign the treaty, though he was an early supporter of it. Tecumseh was not present for the proceedings and always refused to sign the treaty which he repudiated unconditionally.

I think I already mentioned most of the government contingent present, but it bears remarking upon again who they were. In addition to General Wayne, were future President William Henry Harrison, future explorers Merriweather Lewis and William Clark, all who had fought at Fallen Timbers. Additionally, there was Apekonit (William Wells) who was the interpreter for the proceedings. Also present was Isaac Zane, who helped interpret, and who had been adopted as a captive into Tarhe's tribe. David Jones, who despite being in his late 70's, was present as an army chaplain. Henry De Butts, a captain in the 4th Sub-Legion kept the minutes of the peace negotiations. John Mills, who had served in the Revolution and been promoted to major by Anthony Wayne and later to Adjutant General, then Inspector General of the Army, was also present.

On July 21, I needed to be present for an interview between Little Turtle and General Wayne, in Wayne's conference room. The only other person there was Apekonit.

The great chief told Wayne that it disturbed him to find out that in treaties between the British and the Americans, that the British had ceded land to the Americans, that in Little Turtle's view had belonged to his people, not the British, since time immemorial. This was an argument that he had also posed before the entire group earlier. He went on to describe the borders of Miami land as they had existed without dispute since the time of his forefathers. He described the great history of his people. Little Turtle was a sharp negotiator and he was attempting to lay the baseline for these treaty negotiations.

For weeks, he attempted to negotiate with Wayne somewhat separately from the other tribes, attempting to gain the best result for the Miami people. This was a tactic that Blue Jacket was alleged to have also employed with Wayne before Fallen Timbers. However, it did not work then and it did not work for Little

Turtle.

After July 21, another two weeks of rhetoric and long speeches occurred, some in plain language, but most in oratorical metaphor that the Indian people are so fond of using and which to my mind shows their extreme intelligence.

I had observed Blue Jacket during the conference and was impressed with his presentations.

In late July, around the 22nd or 23rd, Blue Jacket did something that changed the whole tenor of the meetings. He had been sitting with those opposed to the treaty. He now, with a certain flair, dramatically switched seats and began sitting with the peace faction. To the assembled tribes, this was hugely significant. If it was not to Wayne, I am certain someone explained it to him, because he then began to act like a man whose goal was now within reach.

Wayne summoned me to speak to the Miami chiefs such as we had discussed much earlier. There were about twelve of us that met in Wayne's conference room. I rose to speak in Miami, using some of their metaphor. Apekonit interpreted to General Wayne in English:

> *Warriors of the Twightwee people, you know that I came among you years ago to make war. Instead, I was captured but spared through your mercy. Now I have a wife of your people. My children are half-Miami and half-white. Perhaps that is the way it will be in the future. I could not make war against the whites. That would have been like fighting against the mother who bore me. Just so, I could not fight against the people of my wife, the mother of my children. I, Spirit Traveler, cannot and will not tell you what to do. My purpose here is not to do that, but to see that the words of he who is called, The Wind, are given to your ears as they are spoken by his mouth. I cannot promise and do not know if his government will honor his words. I do know that many have died, and many more will die if war continues. Sometime the killing must end. Only you can decide if this is that time. You have fought bravely and long for your people. Your*

decision now is difficult and will determine the future. One thing I can tell you with certainty is that your future does not lie in friendship with the British. They do not care about the Indian people, except to use them to fight their enemies. They do not even fight with you against those enemies. They care only for their interests, and they use the Indian people as fodder for the American cannons. I will now leave you to your decision. May you be guided by the manitous and by Kiche Manitoa.

The Miami that were gathered mostly nodded approval when I was done speaking. Many said that my words rang with truth.

I was pretty well convinced that Wayne had intended for me to be more direct in endorsing peace. However, that was something that I could not honestly do, for fear that the future would bring my words to ruin.

When the meeting was over and everyone filed out, the General told me that my forthrightness was a very good thing and he hoped it would play well with the Miamis. He was especially appreciative of my comments related to the British. He considered that separating the British from the Indians was a key to peace on the frontier.

As it was now about the time that the puppies could leave their mother, Wayne took me to the litter, handing me the active male, now grown much bigger, and even more active than the last time I visited. He was a dog that just sort of stood out. He took to me right away, licking me and giving that response that puppies everywhere use to melt hearts.

He was a sort of brindle with dark tiger stripes. Plott Hounds, his mother's breed, were noted for being many colors. I later found out the same about the father dog's breed, the Catahoula Hounds. Like Plott Hounds, they were hunting dogs.

I was holding the puppy when the father dog came in and started growling at me. General Wayne put a stop to it, but the daddy was not happy that I had one of his pups. Prince was the father's name. He was a large hound, brown with darker brown patches that were irregular in shape, but symmetrically placed on each of his flanks. He had speckled legs with white spots on brown and toward his backside, he had a few tiny spots of black. Very unusual, but interesting markings. I was certain the pup that I was holding, being from such stock, was going to be a fine dog for the frontier and a great protector for my family.

I took the dog back to our tent where Sunny was just waking up from a nap. It took her a moment to realize that I had a puppy. Then her eyes grew large, and her face lit up with an unbridled joy that was almost beyond description. She grabbed the puppy, and he licked her as she giggled uncontrollably.

"Pretty good-looking pup, huh, Sunny," I said.

She replied, "Yeah, pretty good lookin' pup, Papa."

"Well," I said, "I think he likes you. Should we keep him?"

Now her joy and excitement got ratcheted up to a whole new level. It was a level that I would have thought impossible after so strong an initial reaction.

I think her response was, "Oh, yes, Papa, oh, yes. I love him."

However, I'm not certain because I was focusing on the tears of joy that came to her eyes. It was all so intense for her. I knew then that the two of them would form a bond that would serve them well back at our cabin.

What she said next, I heard clearly, "I've wanted one my whole life, Papa, thank you, thank you!"

Well, when a person has wanted something their whole life, they should have it, even if their whole life has not been quite three years.

"What do you think about the name, Tiger?" I said, explaining to her and Autumn exactly what a tiger was and why the name fit our dog.

Both mother and daughter agreed that our new family member was a "Tiger."

Autumn now took Tiger to lick the baby awake and the puppy complied perfectly. Dawson was a bit astonished to see this "beast" looking him in the eyes and slurping his face, but he quickly gathered his wits and began to laugh that kind of laugh that babies have that makes everyone around them happy.

Our new family member was an immediately popular addition.

The next day was far cooler than the others had been and was a welcome relief from the heat. On that cool evening, Autumn and I decided on a walk. We deposited the children with Black

Bear and She-Fox, who were more than willing to have them.

We walked a considerable distance from the fort area, along the stream to a place where it widened a bit. There were cattails and tall lush grass near the water. Walking in that direction, we became aware of a slight commotion in the grass just in time to keep us from stepping on two Indian teenagers, making love in the twilight, at a spot they were probably certain would not be disturbed. We discreetly walked away and headed toward a stand of trees that were not too far distant.

It was growing darker, but we could see a solitary silhouette sitting under a tree, playing with some small animals that appeared to be about the size of possums. As we got closer we saw the unmistakable features of our friend, Nebi Skog.

"Kway, brother," I said instinctively, but probably much too seriously, especially given how happy and surprised I was to see him.

"Kway, my friends," he replied with a big smile.

I could now see that his animal friends were two wolf pups, one very black and one a beautiful shade of gray. They were little furballs of energy. He was feeding them jerky and pemmican, and they were crawling all over him. He told us that he had come upon their mother in the forest engaged in a life and death battle with a painter. It was a struggle that the mother wolf lost. After chasing off the painter, he heard the pups whimpering under a bush. Not finding signs of other pups, or the pack, he felt obliged to bring the pups along with him.

Autumn sat down and began playing with the pups. It was hard to tell that they were not dogs. Their behavior was very much like puppies everywhere.

Nebi Skog told me that he had taken the wounded warrior, Thrashing Badger, back to his people after Fallen Timbers. Then he had wandered the forests for a time, before spending the winter in New York among the Iroquois. In the spring, he heard of the peace conference and decided to come west to survey the proceedings.

After talking about what for him was a long time, but was only minute or two, he asked about Sunny. We told him to come with us and he could see her and could stay with us in our tent. He politely refused but did agree to come to breakfast. It pleased him that we would invite Black Bear's family as well. As usual, he was on the periphery of the encampment and probably very few people had seen him. Those who did probably had no idea who he was.

We began the walk back to our tent in the moonlight with a cool breeze blowing stronger. As we retraced our earlier steps, we came near the spot where we had found the teenage lovers. Autumn grabbed my arm and pulled me to the ground. At that moment I knew we were about to imitate those teenagers. I had long ago learned that she could not be told no. And so, in the coolness of that summer evening, along the beautiful stream under the stars, we made passionate love. It was as if the world around us did not matter, as if things were not about to change forever, as if we had no worries, as if it was only we two in a vast and beautiful wilderness, a place of grass, trees, and stars.

We ended our evening bathing in the cool stream. Upon getting out of the water, we were very cold. It was the only time that the entire summer that we were cold, but it felt good.

The next morning as promised, Nebi Skog showed up for breakfast. We put on a feast for him, Autumn's family, and Red Buffalo. He was very happy to once again see everyone, and they were likewise happy to see him. After breakfast and a bit of chasing the wolf pups and Tiger all around the immediate area, Nebi Skog dropped a surprise on us. He insistently offered us the black female wolf pup.

Recovering from my shock, I told him that it was a very fine gift, but that raising a wolf with small children was probably not a good idea.

He assured me that it was a good idea and that two dogs were better than one. He said that Tiger and the female wolf would likely have some fine offspring later on. We would have dogs for many years to come.

I perseverated, as I said, "I think having a wolf might be dangerous to our children and visitors."

He replied, "Not dangerous, you will train her." And he joked, "Maybe I will train you first."

And then he turned the tables on me saying, "Not having her might be dangerous."

Now, I remembered my father's wolf, Keekee and her grandson Jack. I was starting to be convinced that he might just be right.

Then he cracked yet another joke that made us all laugh, especially Black Bear, "Black wolf puppy looks like a dog, no one will know."

He nearly laughed at his joke, but caught himself and returned to a stoic look that seemed to say to us, "What did I say that was so funny?"

In actuality, I had never seen him joke and nearly laugh so much.

Autumn's mother was not as sold on the idea, but when the black wolf puppy came over and curled up in her lap, she melted.

It was Nebi's idea that he would keep the gray wolf and train him as his companion. I thought that was an outstanding idea, especially since I did not incline to raise two wolves.

Now Nebi Skog produced a tiny drum and stick that he had brought with him for baby Dawson Blue Dogs. My son sat and pounded the thing with glee and squealing with delight. Nebi remarked that he might have a future career as a tribal drummer for important ceremonies.

Nebi Skog said that he had some other friends to find. He asked if we would watch his wolf, saying he would call him, "Niben," meaning, "Summer" in Abenaki.

I built a small pen for the three pups and they got along famously. Tiger was bigger than the wolves, but they held their own in the little tiffs that they all got into.

When I asked Sunny if we could call our wolf, "Mahweewa," meaning, "wolf" in Miami, she said, "Yes, Papa, Weewa." And so, Weewa it was to be.

In late July, the Wyandot, Tarhe, spoke to Wayne with flowing, metaphoric energy. His oratory hinted of burying the hatchet and of creating a lasting peace. General Wayne sensed that this was the moment that he had awaited, the turning point of the peace conference, the point when the Indian's chief negotiator finally indicated a willingness to agree to a treaty.

Wayne had Tarhe's words translated for all present to digest. Seizing the moment, Wayne decided that the time had come to award all the chiefs who were present medals from President Washington, with the President's likeness on one side and the U. S. Eagle on the other. The General considered that these would not only add solemnity to the occasion but also make an impressive token for the chiefs. Giving medals to the Indians was to continue to be a government practice for many years to come under many Presidents. I was not convinced that the Indians viewed these as great gifts in the same manner that the whites expected. Nevertheless, it became practice, a sort of official part of any negotiations with Indians. And to be fair, many chiefs proudly wore the medals as jewelry. So, they must have held them in some regard.

A few days later, almost all the pieces to Wayne's puzzle had come together and the formal treaty signing ceremony was scheduled.

On a sizzling hot August 3, 1795, the official signing of the Treaty of Greene Ville occurred. There was much pomp and circumstance, with a military band, soldiers parading to the beat of drums, a salute of arms, prayers by the army chaplain, and other great and somber arrangements, all of which were designed to impress upon all present, especially the Indians, the solemnity of the occasion.

Nebi Skog stood away from the proceedings but cast a discerning eye on all that was happening. Of course, he had no official role and was but a little-noticed observer. Still, I sensed that his presence was necessary, but I could not explain why I felt that way.

General Wayne was smartly dressed in his dark blue coat, cream pants, spit-polished boots, and tri-cornered hat. Most of his officers were similarly dressed in their very best uniforms.

The Indians were dressed in ornate breech-cloths, silver armbands, new moccasins, quill-work feathers, and hairstyles that looked as if they had required hours of fine detail.

One by one, the chiefs of the various tribes arose to make long speeches, interpreted by Apekonit to the entire group. After their speeches, essentially words of capitulation, and conciliation, each moved forward to sign the treaty, most making their mark as an "X."

After giving a brief statement to the assembled company, and to General Wayne's dismay, Little Turtle refused to sign the treaty and went back to his tent.

To be present to see these great men, war chiefs and civil chiefs, humbled to the peace table by American might and now turning away from wars that they almost always won, was truly a moment causing me to reflect upon many things, but most of all the changes that were coming. An era seemed to be ending, and quite probably a people's way of life with it. The lands of their forefathers would now be forfeit to the oncoming white on-slaught. There would be no way to stop the inexorable force which would characterize the American advance. It was a somber time for the Indian people and I think many had a full realization of what was happening. Little Turtle knew well when he refused to sign the treaty. Tecumseh knew too when he refused to even be present. He would never sign the treaty, attempting to the end of his life to create another great Indian alliance that he hoped would, with the help of the British, drive the Americans back beyond the Ohio River.

The preamble to the peace document was a rather simple statement and read as follows:

> *To put an end to a destructive war, to settle all controversies, and to restore*
> *harmony and friendly intercourse between the said United States and Indian*
> *tribes, Anthony Wayne, major general com-manding the army of the United*
> *States and sole commissioner for the good pur-poses above mentioned, and*
> *the said tribes of Indians, by their sachems, chiefs, and warriors, meeting*
> *together at Greene Ville, the headquarters of the said army, have agreed on*
> *the following articles, which, when ratified by the President, with the advice*
> *of the Senate of the United States, shall be binding on them and the said*
> *Indian tribes.*

The preamble was followed by ten articles and finally, by over 90 signatures. By the terms of the treaty, the Indians would receive $20,000 in goods and supplies immediately, and another $9,500 of the same every year. The Indians were to be the sole decision-makers on the distribution of those payments. In exchange, the tribes relinquished claim to 2/3 of what would become Ohio and to a small corner of what would become Indiana. The payment in total represented less than six cents per acre for the land given up.

What of which many had no vision, was a future day when the treaty would not be honored and when other treaties and forced removal of Indian peoples would supersede the Treaty of Greene Ville.

After the signing ceremony was the prisoner exchange, which had been outlined in Article II of the document. There were many prisoners to be exchanged and some were none too happy, having lived with their adopted families, either white or Indian, for many years; in some cases, the better part of 20 years. Some had lost, or nearly lost, all functional use of their native language.

In the case of one Kentucky man, his sons who had been long with the Indians, stole his horses and fled rather than be reunited with their father and family. Of course, there were also many happy reunions for families on both sides. There were, as well, bittersweet feelings by individuals who had been captured, well treated, and adopted, but now were going back to their families of origin, leaving their beloved adopted families. And I am sure there were some prisoners very happy to be out of captivity and returned to their families of origin.

On August 4, the day after the treaty signing, Apekonit and I were summoned to General Wayne's office, where his satisfaction over the treaty's conclusion was dampened by the fact that Little Turtle had not signed. Of all the chiefs who Wayne could least afford to have not signed, Michikinikwa was the foremost. With his stunning and strategic victories over Harmar and St. Clair, as well as in many lesser battles and with the brutality that was common in frontier warfare, Little Turtle had become the scourge of the Americans. He was too well known, and too greatly feared, to allow him to leave Greene Ville without signing the treaty.

Wayne asked if we had any information about Michikinikwa's refusal to sign, anything that could convince him, any little bit of information that could assist the situation. Apekonit knew the man best, but even I knew that if he didn't sign that he had his reasons, and no coercion would change his mind. We tried to explain this to the General as he poured each of us some wine.

A major treaty without Little Turtle's signature was like a pyrrhic victory, and Wayne knew that the accomplishments of this conference would be forever tarnished if the great chief did not sign. We resolved nothing in the next hour except to eliminate the bottle of wine, and after being joined by Lieutenant Harrison, a bottle of sherry of the finest kind such as generals and men of society can afford.

Finally, the General said we could leave but to keep him informed of the slightest change in Little Turtle's attitude. I think he knew we were the only white men who had any chance of influencing the Miami war chief, but out of respect for him neither of us would even entertain doing that.

Upon our leaving Wayne's headquarters, Red Buffalo and Gray Fox came running to find us saying, "To hurry, come quick," to Little Turtle's tent.

Red Buffalo and I lit out on a dead run, while Gray Fox went to find Autumn and her mother. Upon arriving, we could see the despair in the great chief's eyes as he motioned us inside his wigwam. There, inside, lay his wife, Waapi Sheshangomequa, or "White Swallow," gravely ill. Shortly after we arrived, Apekonit came with the fort's surgeon with General Wayne following within minutes.

Between all of us, it became obvious that White Swallow was dying. According to Little Turtle, she had fallen ill yesterday and worsened overnight. He knew it was serious. To me, it resembled a heat prostration or similar illness that I had once seen in Virginia. Certainly, the temperature yesterday had been scorching.

This noble woman, now looking far older than her forty-some years, was slipping away. She had given the great warrior four children, two boys, and two girls. She had been the friend, confidant, and lover to the greatest Indian war chief who ever lived. She had suffered with worry each time he had gone to war. She expired quietly before noon.

We buried her in a grave on a small hill overlooking the stream, under a sycamore tree, wrapped in her favorite blanket. General Wayne sent the Army Chaplain, David Jones, and a military honor guard to preside. Afterward, Autumn's mother spoke quietly with Little Turtle. She-Fox knew Nebi Skog better than

Little Turtle and was convinced of his great spirituality. Soon, at Little Turtles request, Nebi Skog presided over a very brief, but moving Indian ceremony.

As I recall, his words went something like this:

> *My brothers and sisters we now commit to Kiche Manitoa, the spirit of White Swallow, who walked the honorable Indian way as a little girl, as a maiden, and as a wife to Michikinikwa. She was a loving partner in life, may she be a guiding example in death. May her spirit go swiftly to a place beyond the pain of this life. May many manitous greet her. May she be at home and peace in the spirit land of her people. We offer great gratitude for the life she lived and that she walked among us. May she now look over us with her love.*

Michikinikwa now thanked us profusely for all that we had done. He seemed particularly touched by General Wayne's honor guard. I felt sad that I could not have done more. He asked that we leave him alone with Apekonit, the one person who had any small chance of comforting him. We went back to our camp.

Autumn's family went back to their wigwam. Autumn and the kids went with them. Autumn and her mother deeply mourned the sudden passing of White Swallow, She-Fox's half-sister. Little Turtle spent the next several days alone, or in the company of Apekonit.

In time, as it turned out, Wayne needn't have worried about the Little Turtle signing the treaty. Despite a combination of grief and of holding out to make his point with Wayne, on August 12, he agreed to sign the treaty.

Just before signing, Little Turtle said to Wayne, "I am the last to sign and I shall be the last to break this peace."

A drawing of the Signing of the Treaty of Greene Ville, done by one of Wayne's men, prominently features Little Turtle speaking with Wayne through Apekonit's interpreting. As I have stated, this occurred, but most people who have seen it just naturally assume that Little Turtle signed the treaty on August 3, when the other chiefs did so. History may never know the truth of Wayne's distress right up until the day that he obtained the great war chief's signature.

Little Turtle's signing was above all others, the most significant relief to Wayne. He now had his treaty. In a moment alone with him, I asked, "General, is this a just peace? Did the whites pay a fair price for the land? Might it just be another swindle?"

His response was, "Jariah, all peace is good, all war is bad. We have achieved peace in good faith. I am a soldier, following and executing my orders and I do not know if what we paid for the land was a fair price. It was a price determined by the government. White speculators will surely get much more. However, we could, with our superior army and, granted, with greater loss of life, have conquered the tribes completely and paid nothing for the land. I only know that I have given my word as the government's agent and I hope to see that it is honored. But the future is a winding road and I cannot see the end."

I could not help but notice this last statement by Wayne, about the winding road of the future, and how it sounded very much like something an Indian would say.

I think even then, the General knew that the encroachment of the whites would be a never-ending plague upon the Indian people and the politics of that plague would never allow a treaty to be long-honored. But the General was living in the moment, and in the moment, he had historically accomplished his duty.

I cannot say that everything Wayne did was with the utmost integrity. As a soldier, he was a practical man who saw the achievement of the goal as his duty. To him the outcome justified, to some extent, whatever tactics he had to use to obtain the treaty from the Indian people. He was not without honor in most things, but he was determined to present a peace with the Indians to President Washington. That is exactly what he did. Although I considered him a man of complex personality, I do not think the same applied to the military side of the man. He had his orders, he would do everything to successfully execute those orders, and the morality, or future morality of the situation, was not his main concern. That may well have been because he knew that he had no power to influence that future or to see that the terms of the treaty were honored by the government. The future would be completely out of his control, his mission was in the present. I think he did the best that he could when considering everything with which he had to deal.

Chapter Twenty Three

Sunny Disappears

Bear

The next day, after the death of Little Turtle's wife, August 5, 1795, is a day that is etched in my memory forever. It began to unfold as the type of nightmare that every parent has had in some fashion or other and it only got stranger from there. If I live to be 100 years old, the moments of that day will remain with me as if they happened only yesterday.

Early in the morning, Nebi Skog and I had gone to look in on a sick Indian family. Autumn was preoccupied with the baby when Sunny woke up and announced that she was going to Grandma's for breakfast. As she had gone to Grandma's wigwam alone many times before and as it was not far, Autumn merely hugged her and sent her on her way.

Thirty minutes or so later, Grandma She-Fox showed up at our tent, asking if Sunny could go for a walk with her. Upon finding out that Sunny was not with She-Fox, Autumn went into the full-blown panic of a parent in similar situations. She-Fox ran to retrieve Black Bear, while Autumn began frantically calling Sunny and searching the area near our tent. She ran from tent to tent and asked all that she saw, but no one had seen Sunny.

It was about this time that Nebi Skog and I came back. We received the news from Black Bear, who was now searching the area for signs. I too searched, but in vain.

Nebi Skog now pointed toward the dog pen, all three puppies were gone, and the little gate was open. Black Bear and I had been so upset that we hadn't noticed. Quite apparently, the disappearance of the pups and Sunny had some commonality.

Nebi Skog now indicated for us to follow him to the stream. I swear he could track from a broken blade of grass, which of itself would be almost impossible to notice.

We followed the stream about 20 rods or so until we came upon a grove of mulberry trees and various bushes. Now we could hear the high-pitched barking of the pups indicating they were on the hunt. We pushed past some bushes that obscured our sight and there, about four rods away, were the pups surrounding a bear who was now standing on his hind legs facing Sunny. She was maybe six feet in front of him.

Black Bear and I did not have our guns, but we simultaneously pulled our knives, intent upon mortal combat with the bear. Surprisingly, contrary to our natural inclinations, Nebi Skog grabbed each of us by the arm in a vise-like grip that was unbreakable, no matter how we struggled. He seemed to have noticed something more than we.

I now assumed that the man had lost his mind, and he was going to watch a child being mauled by a bear, like a gawking bystander at some big-city entertainment. I should have known better than to think this of a man who had saved my life many times and who was a teacher and brother to me.

He said to us in a low hush, "No, wait and watch."

To me, the man had gone mad. No other man on earth could have convinced me to restrain from attacking the bear.

Wewaa now nipped at the bear's foot and the big beast seemed amused, but certainly not irritated at this little wolf daring to challenge him. He gave the pup a playful swat sending her head over heels some five feet away. Upon seeing this demonstration by the bear, the other pups being very intelligent, backed off a bit.

Wewaa got to her feet, embarrassed by this indignity, but unable to prosecute a better ending, now kept her distance, though she continued to bark to prove her prowess. It was a bit comical, especially as her bark was quite high-pitched, and ridiculous in lieu of what had just happened to her.

With the bear on his hind legs, standing over six feet tall and growling a low, but oddly non-menacing growl, Sunny was standing facing him not giving any ground and not trying to run away.

Again, through natural inclination, I tried to break free, but Nebi's grip was like iron and he only said, "Wait."

My heart was in my throat, and only a cough short of complete ejection from my body.

Sunny was so over-matched, her little body overshadowed by the giant beast. But she stood her ground. I could not see her face and I thought maybe she was frozen with fear. Instead, she was in fact imitating the bear's every move including his low, deep, growl, his stance, and now the movement of his forelegs and paws. These he was holding out like arms.

Sunny suddenly dropped her imitation and commanded the bear, in a very definite and loud voice, as she pointed emphatically toward the ground, "Down, Mahkwa, down now!"

What I saw defied mother nature herself. Telling the story over the years has gotten me the looks of being a crazy man, or a pitiful liar. I swear upon my grave, the bear sat down on his haunches like a trained sideshow animal.

I glanced over at Sunny's grandpa and his jaw was wide open in utter astonishment. My heart was pounding. I was covered in sweat and my breathing was more coming in gasps and heaves than anything approaching the normal ebb and flow.

Sunny now stepped up to the bear and began upbraiding him, shaking her little finger at him and saying, "Bad, Mahkwa, very bad Mahkwa! Leave puppies alone."

She then stared at the bear, hands on her hips, until he lowered his head as if duly chastised and sufficiently contrite.

In an apparent conciliatory move, she now held out a tiny hand for him to sniff, as she had seen me do many times with strange dogs at Turtletown and Kekionga. The bear sniffed her hand, then licked it. And in a movement that was both quick and surprising to her, but heart-stopping to me, he used his long tongue to lick her face.

Sunny began giggling and said, "Ok, ok, I will be your friend." The bear licked her again, as if in gratitude and again she giggled.

Then, looking at the puppies, who were still surrounding the bear, and barking, she adopted a more serious tone and pointed her little arm and index finger in the direction behind the bear, which was for her, pointing straight ahead

Now, as if she were a queen dismissing a subject, she said, "You may go now, Mahkwa, you may go home."

The bear let out a low moan then slowly turned and began lumbering in the indicated direction.

Now finally, all three of us went running toward Sunny, two of us not believing what we had seen with our own eyes. The bear, who had previously seemingly not noticed us, having been mesmerized by the little one, now looked back over his left shoulder and began to trot away.

"Oh, hi Papa, hi Grandpa, hi Uncle Nebi," the little bear-tamer said. "Did you see that silly Mahkwa?"

I snatched her into my arms as Black Bear and Nebi Skog gathered the puppies. We went back to camp as fast as we could with me hugging and kissing her all the way, trying to tell her that she must leave wild animals alone and that she must never leave camp without telling us. Further, she must not let the puppies out of their pen, and well . . . you know the types of things parents say and that children ignore.

Sunny was non-nonplussed and did not seem to realize the scope of what she had done or the danger in which she might have been. Nothing that had occurred seemed remarkable to her. The size differential between her and the bear did not enter her thinking. She only recognized the interaction of two beings and considered that she was the superior, the one who would be giving the commands.

Nebi Skog made eye contact with me and I said, "How could you possibly know what would happen, that she would be unharmed?"

"She is her father's daughter," was his response.

Hmmm, well, the simple fact is that I don't stare down bears, never have; though years hence I would hear a tall tale of a bear hunter in Tennessee who "grinned bears down." [1] I had always dealt with them at the business end of a gun.

I had trusted my strange friend, my daughter was safe and I had witnessed an event beyond remarkable. It was something I had never heard of before, or since.

When we reached camp, her mother and grandmother came crying. They snatched her from me, hugging her, kissing her and all the while expressing their love. And then they began admonishing her sharply in Miami.

The child was confused. What was the big deal? She and the pups had taken a walk and met a crazy bear. It happens all the time. At least that seemed to be her attitude.

It was then that it occurred to me that if this was the type of thing that I could expect from her as a nearly three-year-old, she'd have me in my grave by the time she was ten. The little bugger had just stared down one of the two most fearsome predators in the forest. I might have been proud of the spunk of my daughter, except that it put her at severe risk of her life. I was still shaking from the whole experience.

We left it to Nebi Skog to tell the story. Black Bear and I both knew he was the only one the women would believe and even then after he had told the story, they looked at him like he had lost his mind, or that he had smoked a large quantity of wild hemp.

In telling this story, I have truly not exaggerated one bit. But I understand that it is all very hard to believe. Still, it happened just as I have stated, but in the end only Nebi Skog and Sunny seemed to understand exactly what had happened.

When I later discussed this incident with Nebi Skog, I asked why the bear had behaved so toward Sunny. He said that Sunny's hand signals were so definite that the bear understood. He also said that her calm resolve, her body language, and her fearless approach to the bear, no doubt had some bearing on the outcome. He completely dismissed any thought that the bear understood language. However, his feeling was that it was the tone of her voice and that there was a rhythm to her speech that, coupled with the hand signals, made the bear respond as it had.

Nebi Skog claimed this was perfectly natural and that the

child did it because she believed completely in the outcome. Adults, he said, have too much-preconceived fear and assumption about such an encounter. And he said that people were likely to get just what they expected in such cases. Beyond his specific explanation, he stressed to me that Sunny had a spiritual presence that was similar to that which he considered was possessed by me. But that with her, it was easier to act upon because she believed her actions to be completely natural and possible, without any doubt and without analyzing potential outcomes. I on the other hand, had too much self-doubt and lacked the belief of my action.

Chapter Twenty Four

To Conclude

Signing of the Treaty of Greene Ville

The Indians began to leave around the end of the second week of August and by September most were gone.

We interpreters and others engaged by the government were kept on into September, checking and rechecking documents, being debriefed, and engaged in a host of other duties related to the recording of the proceedings, the verifying of names, and tribes of those present. Finally, on September 5, we were paid for our services and discharged from our duties. I used a good portion of my money to purchase supplies from those sutlers and merchants still present. Having spent the entire summer away from home, we would need the extra supplies to make up for the food that we had not been able to gather. I anticipated that we would share with Autumn's family and others who might have need.

I was personally thanked by General Wayne. An ugly war that had cost many lives, many of them completely innocent, had been ended. I could not help wondering about the long-term implications of the treaty. I think Wayne followed the dictates of the government. But I believe that he felt that he had been fair. He probably wondered if the U. S. Government would keep the promises he had made, but I suppose, in his mind that outcome was not directly within his control. He had done his work as ordered.

Certainly, in retrospect, one can say that six cents per acre for the Indian land was robbery. But then it is only fair to consider that less than a decade after Green Ville, the United States paid France only three cents an acre for the Louisiana Purchase. Some sellers are willing to sell cheap because of need, while others, such as the Indians, sold cheap because they essentially had a gun pointed at their heads.

Of course, there is one very clear difference between the purchases of the Northwest Territory and the Louisiana Purchase. France got their money, but after a time the Indian payments stopped or were superseded by other treaties. Ultimately, most Indians were removed to the west of the Mississippi. In the end, maybe the Treaty of Greene Ville was completed in good faith, but it failed to be honored by the United States. This was the case with all the other treaties ever made with the Indian people.

As pertains to the Northwest Territory, the onslaught of white civilization eradicated the Indian culture and their free lifestyle. First came the traders and swindlers, the whiskey, the diseases, the missionaries, more soldiers, and then the settlers to finish the process. Whites turned forests into farmland, reduced, or eliminated the population of native animals, and replaced trails with roads. Later came railroads and canals. It was inexorable progress but at a very dear price.

As for those who have figured in my story, I will leave the curious reader some details of their lives in the immediate aftermath of the Treaty of Greene Ville.

Apekonit resigned from active duty as a scout, but retained a sort of advisory role for Colonel Hamtramck. He went to Kentucky and brought Sweet Breeze and his two babies back to Fort Wayne. He never did reconcile with his Wea family. Interrupted, or destroyed relationships, were yet another casualty of war. Apekonit built a home just outside of Fort Wayne. He was granted a government pension for his injury and also received a land grant for his service. He and his friend, Colonel Hamtramck, owned a farm together. Ultimately, at the request of Little Turtle, he became the Indian agent for the area and did much to help the Miami people attempt to adjust to the peace. He established a trading post and other entrepreneurial pursuits. He and Little Turtle continued their bond and were as close as father and son, for the rest of their lives. Apekonit lived the rest of his life as William Wells. In total, Sweet Breeze would bear him four children.

Little Turtle went back to Turtletown, where he ultimately took a young wife, Little Bud, who was the niece of his first wife. Accompanied by Apekonit, he made several trips to the East and met with the first three Presidents of the United States. George Washington presented him with a sword of which he was very proud. He received other gifts from many people, including a brace of pistols from Revolutionary War hero Tadeusz Kosciuszko, who told him, "to shoot any man who comes to subjugate you." He was well-thought-of in white society and described as a gentleman with very good manners. He continued to fight against the whiskey trade that helped to destabilize Miami culture. Like General Wayne, he too developed gout in his later years. Through it all, he kept his word to the United States and never again went to war.

Colonel Hamtramck was commandant at Fort Wayne. Later he would take over at Fort Detroit after the British finally abandoned it by terms of the Jay Treaty. His friendship with Apekonit, which I first noticed at Vincennes in 1792, would continue until he died in 1803.

Luke continued to be stationed at Greene Ville for a time. He was often at Fort Wayne and sometimes came to our home. My children adored him as their young uncle who never stopped playing with them.

Gaviahate had died shortly before Fallen Timbers. He was mourned as a good man by his people and certainly by Apekonit. He had been Apekonit's first Indian father and while the connection was not as great as that between Apekonit and Little Turtle, the two were very close.

Pacanne never did sign the Treaty of Greene Ville, but he honored it for a time. He moved his village far from Kekionga to a place near the headwaters of the Mississinewa River[1]. Later, though he had originally opposed Tecumseh's leadership, he re-allied himself with the British, in yet another war against the United States. This was in response to a massacre perpetrated upon innocent Indians by U. S. soldiers, who themselves were retaliating for the diabolical treachery committed by the Potowatomies, at the Fort Dearborn Massacre.

Jean Baptiste Richardville, Peshewa, became the hereditary chief after the death of Pacanne. He participated in many treaty negotiations. He seemed to have acquired an entrepreneurial spirit. A large part of his wealth was acquired by selling Miami land, much of which he purported to hold privately. He ultimately became the wealthiest man in Indiana. Many years later when the Miami were expelled to Oklahoma, he was already dead. However, many of the people were saved from expulsion, because he had arranged for them to live on his land. Indians settled on private lands were not as readily expelled.

Black Duck and Jim Tucker mustered out of the scout corps. They decided to go west and said they might even go as far as the Rocky Mountains. They had heard of beaver as big as dogs and thought they might try trapping. Having been to St. Louis they did not figure it would be any great trick to elude Spanish authorities. They wanted me to come along and I have to admit it would have been a great adventure, but the needs of my young family came before my desire to yield to my wanderlust.

Black Bear and She-Fox returned to Turtletown, alternating living there and in a small cabin that they eventually built on the south of our homestead hill. They were the most loving of grandparents to my children and the children of Gray-Fox. I cannot say enough about them. They became my family and no man ever had better in-laws.

Gray Fox got married and raised a family of his own. He became the last of the great Miami warriors. Later civilization made it so that warriors were no longer necessary because the Miami fought no more wars.

Red Buffalo did not return to Kekionga, refusing to live in the shadow of the big fort. He came instead to Turtletown, though he spent most of his time with us, living in the small cabin that he and Gray Fox had built on our property. He remained my good and constant friend.

General Wayne died just two years after Greene Ville, a man in his early 50's, on his way many believe, to start court-martial proceedings against **James Wilkinson**, in response to Spanish couriers being intercepted delivering money to Wilkinson (in 1796). Although it was thought that Wayne died of a ruptured stomach ulcer as a result of severe gout, the possibility must be considered that Wilkinson poisoned him. Wilkinson had been trained as a physician and would have known about poisons. Also, he had told the Spanish that he would soon be Commander of the United States Army. Upon Wayne's death, President Washington did in fact, appoint him to Wayne's position as head of the army. Later, when implicated in the infamous Aaron Burr treason plot, Wilkinson turned witness against Burr to save himself. Wilkinson finished his days as United States Minister to Mexico, never having been held accountable for any of his machinations, or for being a paid Spanish agent for over a decade. General Wayne did not live to see his great treaty violated and then abandoned by the United States.

And as for the Water Snake, **Nebi Skog**, there is no question that he had become my mentor. And of course, I owed him my life many times over. We were brothers. I never saw anyone else as close to him in that regard except maybe the Countess. But to be fair, I was not with him in all of his travels and adventures, though in the future we would be together more and more while he continued to be my teacher. In general, he was still a solitary sort of being. He had a strong affinity for my family and he always enjoyed his time with us. Perhaps in some regard, mine substituted for the family that he did not have. After Greene Ville, his legend and myth continued to grow. It was the myth of an unusual man and his wolf, Niben, roaming the forests north of the Ohio River.

The war leader, **Tecumseh**, would attempt to establish a new alliance, traveling all over the Midwest and the South, attempting to rally the tribes. In that regard he would have learned his lessons well from Blue Jacket, Tarhe, and Little Turtle, as far as establishing an Indian confederacy. His great adversary would become **William Henry Harrison,** soon to be appointed Governor of the Northwest Territory. The two would be bitter enemies and on one occasion, almost come to mortal blows at a preliminary peace conference.

The Countess, Ales, spent time in Canada and on far-flung fur trading adventures and trips to Europe. We maintained regular contact, especially since she and Autumn had grown close. She took on the role of aunt to my children and she would cross our paths many times in the future.

Autumn, Sunny, Little Blue Dogs, and I went back to our cabin in the woods, new puppies in tow, keeping contact with our friends and relatives. We functioned as a sort of half white and half Indian family. Our transition to the new reality was far easier than most. We raised more children, had many dogs, and had for a time, an idyllic life with all the love that my parents had showered on my siblings and me back in Virginia. Before long, we spent a winter back east, visiting my sisters and their families in Baltimore and the new capital, Philadelphia. But of course, we came back to our home and our extended Indian family that spring.

Even though the Indian wars of 1790-95, often called "President Washington's War," "Little Turtle's War," or "the Northwest Indian War," had now drawn to a close, the time would come when some of the Indian people would rise again under a fierce new leader and ally themselves with the British, once again bringing war and destruction to the frontier.

In many ways, the ensuing years eventually produced all the challenges and adventures that the first part of my life had.

There is so much I have not yet told. I would guess that I've only told about half of my story. Perhaps, if Kiche Manetoa grants me life long enough, I will yet tell the rest.

Jariah Randolph Jamison, in the year of our Lord, 1848

Chapter One

1. Manitous were spirits of considerable power to the woodland tribes of native Americans.
2. Northwest Trade Guns were popular in the Great Lakes region from the late 1750s to about 1830. The guns' smooth bores allowed them to be used as muskets or as shotguns. They earned their name because they were an important and sought-after trade item.
3. A stone weight is much disputed, but in general, one stone is equivalent to about 12-14 lbs.
4. Kekionga was the main Miami village near what would become Fort Wayne.
5. A rod is a unit of measurement approximately equal to 16. 5 feet.
6. Painter was a regional derivative of panther. It was essentially a North American cat called in various places: cougar, catamount, mountain lion, puma, etc.

Chapter Two

1. Braddock's command was ambushed, and severely defeated by combined forces of French and Indians on the Monongahela River, in the summer of 1755. Braddock was killed and Washington, who was a staff aid, is credited with orchestrating the retreat that probably saved many lives, and staved off complete disaster.
2. In 1754, in his first command (before Braddock's defeat) at the age of 21, Washington built a fort near present day Pittsburgh (Fort Necessity). Washington was forced to accept a humiliating surrender after losing several men. He was allowed to return to Virginia with his remaining men. This episode nearly ended his military career.
3. The standard issue smooth-bore musket of the British Army for many years. It was a highly durable and reliable weapon though it had limited range.

Chapter Four

1. The site of Fort Washington was at what later became Cincinnati.
2. Josiah Harmar had started the Revolutionary War as a Captain and risen through the ranks. He was chosen as courier to relay the Congressionally ratified Treaty of Paris to Commissioner Ben Franklin in 1783. He spent seven years as the senior most officer (brevet General) in the U. S. Army.

Chapter Five

1. Chilblains occur in predisposed individuals, and can manifest as blisters, redness, itching, etc. Exposure to cold can create capillary damage causing this malady. Keeping the extremities warm is the best prevention and treatment.

Chapter Six

1. A ravelin is normally a triangular outer-work designed to add further defensive capability to a fortress. The shape has the effect of dividing attackers, and allowing fire-power to be directed at the attackers with devastating effect.

Chapter Seven

1. Their parents having died, Cheesekau had finished rais-ing Panther Across the Sky, or Tecumseh. The little brother idolized his older sibling. After their villages in Ohio were attacked many times by Americans, including by George Rogers Clark, the brothers, along with a dozen or so other Shawnee warriors, went to Tennessee in 1789, to live and fight with Dragging Canoe of the Chickamauga Cherokee band. The brothers' parents had

lived in the south (present day Alabama) prior to Tecumseh's birth, and the brothers had some kinship, and
friendship ties to southern tribes, as may have
Cheesekau's wife. This may account for the later, impas-
sioned attempts of Tecumseh, to recruit southern tribes
to his cause, during the War of 1812. If Tecumseh appeared at Ft. Washington in the summer of 1790, he was
either acting on his own, or at Cheesekau's request, in
order to see what was happening north of the Ohio. He
would have realized that major battles were coming to
the area. His return to Tennessee could have lasted only a
short time because it is known that late in 1790, he returned north, but too late to participate in fighting
against General Harmar. By the summer of 1791, he was
serving as one of the principal scouts of the allied Indian
nations. Cheesekau never came north again, and died in
1792, as a result of wounds incurred at the Battle of
Bledsoe's Station, near Nashville.

Chapter Eight

1. As indicated earlier, the Indian appellation of God-like
   spirits.
2. This spot is identified today, by a roadside sign, on Indiana Highway 9 south of Columbia City, Indiana. It lies
   now as part of a farm.

Chapter Nine

1. Kenapakomoko was located on the western Eel River,
   just north of what was later to become Logansport, Indiana.
2. Chippewas were also known in other regions as Ojib-
   weys. Their main villages were in what would become
   Canada and what would become Michigan.

Chapter Ten

1. An Abenaki greeting similar to *hello*.
2. The Abenaki were an eastern people inhabiting the St. Lawrence River Valley in Canada, parts of Maine and at one time, as far south as Massachusetts. During the French and Indian War they had been allies of the French, and one of their main villages had been destroyed by Major Robert Rogers and his famous rangers, in retaliation for some ruthless raids on colonial communities.
3. The Iroquois were actually a confederation of six tribes, the Mohawk, Seneca, Onandaga, Oneida, Cuyuga, and more recently the Tuscarora. During the Great War for Independence from England, the Iroquois were officially neutral, though most of the group had leanings toward the British. Only the Oneida joined the American cause.

Chapter Eleven

1. A tree whose fruit appears something like a misshapen pear and whose rich yellow insides have been described as a cross between and pear and a banana in taste and texture.
2. The St. Joseph River to the west was in the area that was later to become South Bend, Indiana and Niles, Michigan. The River is quite large and flows into Lake Michigan. The buffalo herd there was one of two large herds in Indiana, the other being in the Ouiatenon area which later became Lafayette, Indiana. Once upon a time, the river had been called the River of the Miamis as the Miami people had lived in the area before moving to the Kekionga area. They were replaced by the Potowatomie.

Chapter Twelve

1. The St. Joeseph River, had dipped south and then, at this point, gone north toward Lake Michigan. This place gave

name, years later, to the city that was to grow up nearby, South Bend, Indiana.
2. In less than five years more, the herd was virtually gone.
3. The current tribe known to inhabit this area, that had, less than a hundred years earlier, been inhabited by the Miami people. In fact, early French explorer, LaSalle, had called the St. Joeseph River the *River of the Miamis*.

Chapter Thirteen

1. This area is present-day, Fort Recovery, Ohio, very close to the Indiana-Ohio boundary.
2. The Kentucky Militia.
3. French name for the Wabash River.
4. Disabling the cannons so as to render them temporarily useless to the enemy until they could be repaired.
5. The First Regiment, the best trained and most experienced fighters in the entire United States Army were not at the battle. They had been ordered by St. Clair to go back south, in search of deserters and of an expected supply column. What would have happened had these 300 professional soldiers been present is only speculation. Certainly, the Indians would have had a tougher fight on their hands. St. Clair later expressed the opinion that had the First Regiment been present at the battle, they too would have been overwhelmed. The entire U. S. Army would have been wiped out.
6. From the Journal of Major Ebeneezer Denny, An Officer in the Revolution and Indian Wars. Denny first published this during his lifetime, but subsequent to his death in 1822, there were other editions. Perhaps the most famous was commissioned by act of Congress in 1859, and printed by the Philadelphia Historical Society of Pennsylvania.
7. "The History of Fort Recovery, Ohio", from the "History of Mercer County, Ohio", by Hon. S. S. Scranton, published by Biographical Publishing Company, Chicago, Illinois, 1907.

8. Lt. General Richard Butler, a veteran of the British Army and the French and Indian War, as well as the American Army in the Revolution. He had served under Daniel Morgan. He remains the highest-ranking American officer ever killed in combat. He had been on Washington's staff at Yorktown. The Marquis de Lafayette had once said of the Butler family, "When I need something done right, I order the Butlers to do it." It is said that Washington himself offered a toast to the Butlers after Yorktown, so distinguished was their service to the American cause. Younger brothers, Thomas and Edwin, were also present at St. Clair's Defeat. Thomas was badly wounded, but was saved when Richard told Edwin to leave him (Richard) and to save Thomas. In 1803, Edwin died serving in Tennessee and his two sons (he also had two daughters) were raised by family friends, Rachel and Andrew Jackson. Thomas died in New Orleans around 1805, of yellow fever. Despite being a high-ranking officer, he had been court-martialed for failure to cut his hair, which he kept in a long braid to symbolize his service in the Revolution. His oldest daughters also became wards of Rachel and Andrew Jackson.

9. Henry Knox had unknowingly hired unscrupulous suppliers who had cheated the army, in contracted supplies of all manner, causing deadly consequences as in the case of gunpowder.

Chapter Fourteen

1. In the Northwest Territory, they were known as Wyandots. No less a one than Samuel de Champlain first signed a treaty with them and accompanied them on a victory over the Iroquois.

2. Lake Michigan, sometimes during this era called *Lac des Illinois* or *Lac St. Joseph*.

Chapter Sixteen

1. Fort Nelson was located at present-day Louisville, Kentucky.

Chapter Seventeen

1. Nothing public was ever done about Wilkinson being a Spanish agent. All was quiet and perhaps the government was simply monitoring the situation as Wilkinson seemed to discharge his military duties with loyalty. In 1796 Spanish couriers were captured on their way to give money to Wilkinson for his services to Spain. When Wayne found out he was moving toward a court martial of Wilkinson. However, he died suddenly, on a trip, allegedly of a ruptured stomach ulcer and complications from gout. Some historians have speculated that he was poisoned by Wilkinson who had gone to college to become a doctor before entering the Revolution, and would have likely had at least some rudimentary knowledge of various poisons. Washington named Wilkinson to succeed Wayne as the United States' high-ranking military commander. Wilkinson was later engaged in Aaron Burr's treasonous plot but turned informer, giving up Burr, and narrowly avoiding prosecution. He later became Minister to Mexico.

2. Author's Note: In 1810, James Wilkinson married Celestine Laveau Trudeau, niece of the former Spanish Lt. Governor of Louisiana (1792-1799), Don Zenon Trudeau. Presumably, Don Zenon would have been a point of relay for Wilkinson's spy payments that came from New Orleans. Don Zenon was stationed in St. Louis. The father of Celestine Trudeau was known as Don Carlos Trudeau when he was the Spanish Surveyor General of Louisiana. Later, when Louisiana became American territory, he anglicized his name to Charles Trudeau. For a brief time in 1812, he was Mayor of New Orleans.

Chapter Eighteen

1. The fifth cannon was not found until the 1830s when two young brothers found it while fishing in a nearby stream.

Chapter Twenty

1. Kiche Manitoa is the word for "God" in the Miami language.
2. The mushroom was probably psilocybin, a hallucinogenic substance found in many varieties of mushrooms and also used for thousands of years by indigenous peoples for religious practice.

Chapter Twenty-Two

1. These two young officers were to make their fame when President Jefferson appointed them to lead the Corps of Discovery to explore the Louisiana Purchase. Clark was the brother of Revolutionary War hero, George Rogers Clark, and Lewis was destined to become the Governor of the Louisiana Territory, succeeding of all people, James Wilkinson.

Chapter Twenty-Three

1. One of the many tall-tales surrounding the life of Davey Crockett.

Chapter Twenty-Four

1. Pacanne located his village near what would, in years to come, become Peru, Indiana.

CPSIA information can be obtained
at www.ICGtesting.com
Printed in the USA
BVHW031024240720
584409BV00005B/368

9 781506 908854